Latrice,
though our time together in Woo was short, I'm glad to have met you and look forward to hanging out with you in coming years!

Blown Covers

A novel

By
R.D. Thomas

Blown Covers

A Novel

By

R.D. Thomas

Boderlands Publications

Los Angeles

Blown Covers is a work of fiction. Names, characters, places and incidents are the products of the author's imagination or are used fictitiously. Any resemblance to actual events, locales, or persons, living or dead, is entirely coincidental.

2015 Borderlands Publications Paperback Edition

Copyright © 2015 by
Ryan David Thomas
Cover credit: Capooter Designs.

Book design by
Book Design Team (Around86 at Fiverr)

Library of Congress Catologing-in-Publication Data
Thomas, Ryan David
Blown Covers: a novel/Ryan David Thomas
p.cm.
ISBN-13: 978-1-505-8120-53

Printed by Amazon.com

For
Kristen, Megan, and Rachael

Acknowledgements

It is said that friends are the family you chose. I can easily say I would not be in this stage in my life without them. Thank you to Megan Wilson and Sabine Köstlmaier for believing in my work, motivating and helping me to restart on ideas I had all but given up on. Thank you to Justin Sevakis, Rubén Rodríguez- Cubiella, Sage Nenyue and Jazz Acuña for providing me constructive criticism and support, both morally and spiritually.

Lastly, I must also thank my three younger sisters and my Oma. You are my world and even though we are separated by distance and geopolitical realties, you will continue to inspire me to push through life's most difficult and unexpected realities.

Never trust a translation.
John P. Gabrielle

R.D. Thomas

Prologue

I remember the day of my birth. That might seem strange to some people, but I remember it. It was around the 1950s. Or maybe it was the 1960s? The year I'm a bit fuzzy on - parts of it get jumbled at times. But the event itself? That I remember very well.

Come to think of it, I don't think I've ever really told anyone about myself before. Though to be fair, no one's really asked. And to be honest, my life is quite boring, anyway. I prefer people-watching. Because people who live within this immense city are always changing - trying-failing-succeeding-struggling-standing-on-their-own-two-feet change. Sure, it's slow, but my job allows me to sit back and watch the human equivalent of the Grand Canyon erode into a masterpiece every day, so I'm happy.

My first conscious memory is when they put up the studs in my brick structure. They were made of some Douglas firs from Washington State, I'm told, but all that's meaningless to me. All I know is the beautiful Buena Avenue. Nothing made me prouder than when the construction workers put the finishing touches on me. I got a fresh coat of paint and some brand new locks. I was officially one of them: a Chicagoan.

Now, if there's one thing you need to know about us Chicagoans, it's that we are as proud as we are stubborn. For example, you out-of-towners may call it the 'Willis Tower,' but to us, it will always be the Sears Tower. I mean, imagine some stranger forcing you to call apples oranges. Find some other tower to rename. We like ours just fine.

That's not to say we don't appreciate diversity. If you come to us, we'll find you a home. From the *Gulab Jamun* of Devon to the *Kalbi* of Kimball, to the largest Polish population outside of Warsaw, we have

it all here. The more the merrier! And even if this is just a stepping-stone in your life, you can always find your reflection in the Bean on a warm summer's day.

Sometimes, a blank canvas can do some good to help us decide who we really are. Maybe that was what Freud truly meant with about the subconscious. It's something that no amount of Rorschach tests can ever fully reveal: an escape from rather than a delving into reality. Rather than trying to define the black ink splotched on a page by someone else, a blank canvas is a moment of clarity where you can make sense of your experiences on your terms with a full range of colors.

At any rate, the landlord came in last week to finalize a deal for my new tenants. A guy in a suit walked in to inspect my rooms and agreed to lease them for three interns. A week ago, some basic furniture was moved in: a couch here, a T.V. there, some beds without sheets. The kitchen was also stocked with basic cooking utensils.

The three tenants had their necessities. But I'm mostly interested in finding out what kind of people they each are and who they will become. I overheard the landlord gossiping about them: a Spaniard, a German, and an American. But what do I really know about those nationalities anyway? I've never traveled. I might have met a lot of people, but I've never met a Spaniard nor a German. What the hell would I know if I had? In my long life, I've found people love to lie, even to themselves. Especially to themselves. In a couple of months, they'll find the blank canvas that is my body. And me, I love artwork.

A key goes into the door and begins to turn and silence takes over

Part One

❖ ❖ ❖

Collisions

One

Highway to Hell

August, 2012

"Chainsaw, for sure."

"You crazy, man? Shotgun to the head. BOOM!"

"Please, what if you run out of electricity or bullets? A bad-ass *katana* is the best way to go."

David just sat there, laughing. All of his friends looked around, confused.

"What's so funny, smartass?"

"As if you pussies could actually wield any of those weapons in a zombie apocalypse."

"Shut up, you fucker!" yelled one of his friends, before tackling him.

***

That was the bucket of water that abruptly woke David Fisher from his dream in the back seat of his parents' car. Today he moved into an apartment downtown for his internship - *his* apartment. His parents, Corbin and Becki, were only driving him there to see him off, or so they kept insisting as his younger sister Laura sat next to him making faces. But David knew they were taking their last chance

Part One: Collisions

to be nosy and overbearing. After all, this wasn't high school any more: this was the real world.

At least that's what his parents had told him. Or rather, nagged at him, over and over again:

"You have to be professional now."

"You have to behave yourself."

"Why do you have to take a gap year before college?"

David banished the thoughts from his memory. He could hardly care less what his parents thought. He was finally free. *Free from homework, free to...*

"What's your beef with gay people?"

"Hey Obama, let Mama marry Mama."

David had barely had the time to contemplate what the *'real world'* meant when angry protestors stopped the car. The GPS had mistakenly taken them by a Chick-fil-A riot, and there was no getting past the protesters now – crowds of people making out in the street, clad in rainbows and 'No Mor Chikin' shirts, like a bad version of a pride parade he had seen on Fox News once. His parents just smiled and kept slowly but surely edging through the crowd, until some of the protesters approached their car.

"Hey, may we pass?" said Corbin cheerfully, rolling down the window. It was a hot day, and the jolting heat from the August sun quickly overwhelmed the air conditioning. Mixed with the oppressive humidity, even the weather was angry in Chicago.

"No! We're here, we're queer, get used to it!" a more rotund, black protester responded angrily. He was sweating through his tank-top.

"Sir, all I want to do is pass," Corbin said.

"With that N.O.M. bumper sticker? Today?" a skinny, Goth chick yelled back.

"No, you're making a statement, you homophobe!" the black protester responded.

"I love all of God's children!" Corbin said.

"Just not the ones having butt-sex," joked a colorfully clad Latino man.

"Love the sinner, hate the sin," Corbin recited.

"You ignorant scum..." began the Goth.

"...Would you rather the policeman over there handle this?" Corbin interrupted.

"What? And put me in jail? With other men?" laughed the black protester.

"Sir, back away from the automobile," the officer said from off in the distance as he walked towards the car.

"Or what?" the black protester said. "I know my constitutional rights!"

"Sir, don't make me..." The officer's voice trailed off as they drove away.

Though David's eyes wandered for a moment, it was soon over. They turned onto a bigger street and the protesters all disappeared behind the big white building on the corner.

"Geez," Becki laughed. "That was pretty ridiculous."

"You can say that again," Corbin said.

"Such discrimination," Becki said in disbelief.

"Yet if any man suffer as a Christian, let him not be ashamed; but let him glorify God on his behalf," Corbin recited. "1 Peter 4:16."

"Kids, I'm going to pray so that you can stay strong, and also to pray for those who trespass against us," Becki said.

David and Laura both groaned.

Part One: Collisions

"Is this going to be like when you prayed over us after Indiana Jones?" Laura asked.

"Listen to your mother, kids," Corbin said.

"Dear Lord, I pray that you bless David and Laura in everything they do, and..." Becki began, as they closed their eyes in reverence.

The reclaimed silence gave David more time to think. He had deferred his first year at Harvard because he had wanted a break from the sheer amount of time school required. If you weren't in class, you were studying for an AP exam in Calculus, or working in the honors society, or playing football, or doing community service at a soup kitchen, or Habitat for Humanity, or really doing anything else but sleep, all to compete against thousands of kids around the nation for admissions and scholarships. David was in the rat race, day in and day out. He had already gotten into college, a great one, even, and now he needed a break.

And yet, David had never wanted to go back to high school more than in that moment, as much as he hated to admit it. There was something about a hot day towards the end of summer that triggered back-to-school nostalgia, a fresh year filled with endless possibilities. Familiar sites like the football field and the halls between classes clouded his mind, but they were all empty now like a ghost town. Even his bros screwing around after class, shoving him into lockers when he, the quarterback, took all the credit for the win - they all began to disappear, their fading silhouettes reminding him of the good times he was leaving behind. Piecing together lost conversations, he completely forgot about everything else.

"And please protect David this year in everything he does, to your glory and honor, Amen," Becki said.

"Amen," David, Corbin, and Laura repeated in sync.

"Oh my, what a beautiful building, David!" Becki said. "You sure I can't take it off your hands?"

"Ma!" David groaned.

They parked and got out of the car to stretch from the long drive. As his dad went to pop the trunk, he looked up at his new home. The large apartment complex towered over him, overwhelming him. The beige columns were cross-sectioned by bark-brown balconies, with windows in between and the occasional air-conditioning unit jutting out. Although David had visited the Chi-town plenty of times, as he only lived a couple of hours away in Wheaton, back then he could come and go between the two as he pleased. But now that he was living here, David was no longer in Kansas. A tornado seemed to have transplanted him to some, huge foreign place where the windows glinted an emerald hue and needless to say, Dorothy needed some friends.

Unwilling to show his trepidation, David concentrated on unloading his most prized possessions: Mass Effect, Halo and a couple of other favorite video games, a football, a picture of his football bros and him - taken less than sober, unbeknownst to his parents.

That's all he really needed. David didn't like complications. Every time he tried dealing with complex things, like girls, it got messy. Everything else, he chose not to stress about, because it wasn't worth the hassle. So naturally he grumbled when he found how much extra junk his mother had packed for him, which he could see quite clearly through the translucent storage boxes she had put it all in.

"Mom, I don't need this many sheets and towels!" David exclaimed.

"It's going to be a long year! What if you ruin some your first time doing laundry?" Becki worried.

"I mean, booger brains is bound to fuck it up," Laura chimed in.

"Laura!" Becki said, aghast.

"Says the troll." David said.

"David!" Becki exclaimed. "Nothing unwholesome! I just said that five minutes ago!"

"More like thirty..." Laura mumbled.

"Laura!" Becki yelled.

"Swear jar, Laura," Corbin said.

"And you're grounded this evening, missy," Becki said.

"But I was going to go to the mall with Lucy!" Laura squawked.

"Honey, isn't that a bit harsh?" Corbin asked.

"Well, we can take about it later," said Becki sweetly.

As his parents scolded Laura, David sat there, longing to get away from the bickering. He was done with all the complicated rules and sneaking around. He just wanted to be straight with people about who he was. No more censorship. He could use his words to say what he meant, vulgar or not, just like he already did with his friends.

David's mom continued to quote some Bible verse at the two siblings - who were now sticking their tongues at each other - demanding that they be civil, but her movement towards the boxes in the trunk showed that she was nearing the end of her rant. His dad followed, silently agreeing with his wife, as they brought the boxes to the front door. A forty-something doorman in a wrinkled black uniform sat at an old, yellow-tinged desk, possibly from an age when smoking was allowed in the lobby. The doorman's wearied, irritated look said "if you have a question, ask someone else, goddammit - I'm on break," but David's dad went up to him without hesitation.

"Which floors are the Caliber Publishing interns at?" Corbin asked.

"ID?" the doorman said. His voice was joltingly dull in juxtaposition to Mr. Fisher's cheery Midwestern tone.

David proudly handed over his Illinois state I.D. The doorman looked at it and looked over his notes with a disinterested gaze.

"Ok, here ya go," the doorman said, giving them the key, which said '6C' in large black letters. "Go past the gym to the elevator. Take it to floor six. Can't miss it."

"Thank you very much, sir!" Becki said.

After pressing the button to get to the sixth floor, they waited for what seemed like an eternity for the elevator to start going up. He could almost swim through the awkwardness in the air. It was like a slow ascent to meet your maker, all of your flaws becoming immediately evident: they were sweaty, disheveled, and had nothing to show for your time in this mortal realm except a few measly boxes. Or perhaps that was just the lack of air-conditioning.

Suddenly, the eternal, delirious elevator ride ended in the blink of an eye as the door opened, as if 20 years had passed by in an instant. David was well on his way to becoming an adult. He was now about to be on an equal footing with his parents, a prospect that was both frightening and exciting.

Ignoring the tension in the air - also known as humidity - they looked down the hall in search of apartment 6C, as was written on the key. Corbin and Becki had bemoaned that morning that it was too early, saying he would be the only one there. After all, work didn't start till Monday, and it was only the third - a Friday. And while David knew his parents were probably right, he had still insisted he needed that time to settle in before he got all busy with work, which was partially true. But mostly, he was as anxious as a five-year-old kid on Christmas morning, ready to open his gifts; a new apartment, a new city, new experiences.

As they walked, David noticed that the hallway had been redone recently, as it was drastically different from the downstairs lobby. He couldn't tell why, but somehow the brand-new carpet and the fresh coat of white paint appeared to cover the past. Maybe not cover, but it brought a surprising feeling that anything could happen.

Part One: Collisions

When they spotted a door with a gold-lettered '6C' on it, Corbin awkwardly fumbled with the keys until he found the one that was labeled "front door."

"Who wants to open it?" Corbin asked.

Although truthfully David was excited to have a place he could call his own, his own key and all, he played it cool and just shrugged. Laura grabbed the key.

"I want to!" Laura said.

"No, I'm his mother. I want to see my son's place!" Becki insisted.

"Well, I have the keys!" Laura bragged.

"Laura Elisabeth Fisher!" Becki said.

The spat didn't last long. It's not often that a high-schooler wins an argument with an adult. Wisdom may not necessarily follow age, David realized, but a time-honored tradition of respecting thy elders hardly changes because of one teenager's temper tantrum.

But before Becki even got the chance to insert the key, the door opened from the inside. A young, tan guy with flashy highlighter-red, blue and green clothes appeared at the threshold. His eyes were jet black, as was his hair, which was slicked back in a chic model look. The guy gave them each a once-over with his eyes before saying a word, somewhere between sizing them up and checking them out.

"Hello, can I help you?" the tan guy said, with an unnatural amount of phlegm emphasized on the H's, and with the Y in "you" suddenly becoming a J.

"Hi, my name is..." David began.

"His name is David and he will be living here. Nice to meet you," interrupted Becki with a killer smile, holding out a hand ever so politely. "What's your name, dear?"

"Hey, Lena! The American's here!" the guy yelled back into the apartment, without taking notice of Becki's outstretched hand. "Oh, I'm sorry. My name is Cristiano Moreno-Torres."

David noticed how Cristiano's tongue glided over the R's much more naturally when saying his own name, which distracted David enough for him to miss Cristiano kissing his mother. Becki, taken by surprise, backed away.

"My! Aren't you cheeky!" Becki exclaimed, blushing like a southern belle. "I'm flattered, but I'm married. This is my husband."

"No, *señora*. That is how we say hi in Spain," Cristiano explained, hastily.

"Oh, how cute! It's just like those French people do in the movies!" Becki said.

"Well, the French do it differently. Here, let me show it to you," Cristiano said, playfully.

"Oh my," Becki exclaimed, taken aback. "I feel so cultured now!"

As Cristiano started to explain the concept of Spanish greetings and Becki became excited by this life-altering concept, a girl David assumed to be Lena came to the door. She was substantially taller than Cristiano, who was not short; he was more of average height. She had a bob-cut right out of a fashion magazine. Her dirty blond hair and blue eyes also were softer and less intimidating than the Spaniard's, despite her height.

"Knock it off, *Don Giovanni*," Lena said.

"But I was just..." Cristiano started.

"Save it," said Lena, cutting him off.

"Hi! I'm David's mother," said Becki, "and..."

"Hi, I'm Lena," Lena said with an accent that was almost but not quite British.

"Nice to meet you!" Becki said. "Where..."

Part One: Collisions

"David's room is here on the right," Lena said abruptly. "Let me know if there's anything I can do to help."

"I think we should be fine," Corbin said.

"Thank you so very much for the offer, though!" Becki said, nudging Corbin.

Becki and Cristiano continued to make small talk while the others moved David in. As David went by with each load, he noticed that Cristiano had inched closer each time. His mother and father were completely oblivious. David laughed to himself and ignored it, playing a game with himself instead as he picked up each box, imagining what was in it based on weight alone - *was this the PS3 or the Xbox 360?*

"Why must one believe in God? I'm an atheist and I'm doing just fine," interjected Lena.

"But life is so much better with God's love! Here, dear. Jesus said..." replied Becki.

"I couldn't care less what some delusional man said two thousand years ago in a desert," Lena replied curtly, cutting off Becki. "If he actually even existed. The texts all appear a hundred years after Christ's supposed death. Islam began a couple hundred years after. And god knows we don't know who the creator of Buddhism was - I mean, Buddha just means the *'Enlightened One.'* That's not even a real..."

"But, honey, we all need..." Becki began, undeterred.

"Don't you dare *'honey'* or *'dear'* me again!" Lena responded.

It was as if a zombie apocalypse had been unleashed within the apartment. The undead could hardly be stopped, whether by firearms or logic, or even a nuclear holocaust. Corbin, embarrassed, tried to break it up, but Becki continued anyway, deaf to the pleas of the living. And it could've gone on until molecular deterioration, had Lena and Becki had the stamina to match their anger.

"Well, that looks like that's it," Corbin said.

"Thank Christ," David said in his head, so his mom wouldn't hear him taking the Lord's name in vain. "See you guys!" he said out loud, quickly showing his family to the door.

"But David, don't I get a hug!" Becki said.

"Yes, mom," David said.

His dad gave him a handshake, respectfully staring him in the eyes.

"Best of luck, son," Corbin said.

"Don't look at me!" Laura said, sticking out her tongue.

As they all walked to the elevator, David closed the door with a sigh of relief. Rather than a heartfelt, teary-eyed parting, it seemed more like a disassociation. Although embarrassment had played its part, the sound of the elevator door cutting off his mother's tirade was pure freedom.

David didn't have people automatically looking up to him anymore, just for being the football captain or the guy who got into Harvard. Something had always seemed artificial in this awe-induced popularity and the responsibility that came with it. With no one knowing his past, his life and responsibilities were a direct consequence of the work he put into them.

The door now closed, David turned around to get to know his roommates better and hopefully smooth over the religion debacle. It started out friendly enough, with the basic where-are-you-froms and life stories. It wasn't anything substantial or deep, but rather superficial details to help ease along the process of working, and more importantly, living together.

· It certainly pissed off Lena, who glared and grimaced through a conversation that was obviously beneath her, but finding out little details like favorite foods, music, or even downright oddities like a favorite brand of toothpaste helped David humanize people. He

certainly was not looking for the one to walk down the aisle or to help him hide a body – each represented their own type of crazy, and was a potential reason to notify local authorities.

The roommate run-down merely existed to de-awkwardify the zone in which you're living, so that if you bring friends over, or God forbid, see the other naked, you still have a mutual respect in your own area of the apartment. However, the roommate run-down went a little too far when Cristiano and Lena started describing Madrid and Berlin.

"And in Berlin, we even have a gay mayor!" Lena said with a suppressed pride. "And you Americans can't even deal with a black President."

"His skin color doesn't really have anything to do..." David responded.

"Oh please. Romney wouldn't be even close in the polls, otherwise!" Lena replied. "He's a joke!"

"Obama's got bad policies. He's bankrupting our country!" David said.

"What? You mean the bankruptcy caused by wars to colonize oil-rich countries started by Bush? *Ach, du Schande,*" Lena huffed under her breath.

"Have you guys seen *The Avengers* yet?" Cristiano asked, breaking up the argument.

"Ah, yeah, man. That movie was so legit!" David exclaimed.

"You both are so immature," Lena said, rolling her eyes. She left for her room.

"Man, all it needed was that ginger to get it on with the archer," said Cristiano.

"What? Scarlett Johansson?" David asked.

"Sure. I would love to see her naked," Cristiano replied.

"Yeah... she is hot," David said. "But that's what the Internet's for, right?"

"Why are you Americans so afraid of a pair of tits on screen, though?" Cristiano asked.

"I...what?" David asked.

"Everyone in that movie is killing, but a tit is too much?" Cristiano laughed.

"It's about morality, or something like that," David responded.

"Right. Killing is moral, but sex is unnatural," Cristiano said between giggles. He was laughing so hard he had to hold his sides.

David had never really thought of it that way. He had certainly heard a sermon or two about the evils of violence on T.V., but never in relation to the lack of sex. His arguments, which had been top-notch for his high school debate class, were flustered and confused.

"But sex is something private," David said. "Between a married man and woman."

"What? Did your mommy just teach you about sex yesterday?" Cristiano laughed. "Besides, killing people with guns is illegal. Last time I checked, sex isn't, man. Unless Obama ruined that too!"

David didn't have an answer. It was something that had never really happened to him before. He could cheat the American system by saying exactly what he knew the teachers wanted to hear. But as he searched for an answer, he realized he had over-thought Cristiano's actually quite superficial motives. It wasn't as if David hadn't had sex with his girlfriends, but he only liked talking about that shit with his close bros. Regardless, he decided against continuing the argument - after all, he was going to live with these people for the next year.

"Yeah, I guess so, man," David said, laughing it off.

Part One: Collisions

"We just had this comedy come out, *Tensión Sexual No Resuelta*," Cristiano said. "Translated, it's called Unresolved Sexual Tension. It's hilarious."

"How is sex hilarious?" David teased.

"Well, there are all these love triangles, and sex puns," Cristiano said. "I guess you had to be there."

"I guess so," David said, laughing awkwardly.

"The main character is this hot blond chick. And at first she thinks sex and love are the same," Cristiano said. "But then she writes a book about sex. And all these people start having sex with who they want. But they don't know what they want."

"Sounds like a trip, man," David said. "But can we talk more about it a bit later? I'm a little tired right now. Just wanna settle in."

"Yeah, no problem, man," Cristiano said.

David clasped Cristiano's hand and put his other arm around his shoulders.

"Man, what is this?" Cristiano laughed.

"It's how we dudes say hi and goodbye in the U.S.," David said with a shocked look. "You guys don't do this in Spain?"

"No, I have no clue," Cristiano laughed.

"See, you put your opposite hand in a handshake, and bring the other arm around for the bro hug," David said.

"Haha, nice," Cristiano said. "See ya around, man."

David just needed to clear his head a bit. It was already five and he was incredibly hungry, after an event-packed day like that. David pulled out one of the food boxes his mom had made for him and had a couple of bites of a homemade granola bar to make his stomach stop calling his name. When he was satisfied, or at least satiated, David took out his football and collapsed on his bed, tossing the ball at the ceiling. There was something therapeutic about throwing the

ball at the blank white ceiling, even if - maybe even because - he occasionally smudged it.

Zwei

❖ ❖ ❖

Der Krieg der Welten

September, 2012

Die Augen der Fahrgäste in ihrer Umgebung blickten ausdruckslos. Sie war einfach nur in den Zug eingestiegen, mehr nicht – nur unterwegs zur Arbeit. Lena hätte es nicht anders haben wollen. Und außerdem war ihr die koffeingeschwängerte Kälte von The L[1] während des morgendlichen Berufsverkehrs wohlbekannt. Eine Qualität, der sie vertraute. Sie musste nicht mit Unbekannten über das Wetter plaudern oder die Zeit mit anderen Nutzlosigkeiten verplempern, mit Menschen, die sie sowieso nicht so sehr mochte. Dieser sogenannte Small Talk, den die Amerikaner so liebten, erschien ihr besonders dumm.

„Warum muss ich mit jedem befreundet sein?", fragte Lena sich. „Wir spielen nicht in einer Folge von ‚Verbotene Liebe'."

Auch wenn sie diese Serie liebte, war ein Drama natürlich immer lustiger anzuschauen als es selbst zu erleben – besonders wegen der schönen Menschen und der großen Gefühle.

Plötzlich stieg Dirk Moritz ein, der Schauspieler Daniel aus der Seifenoper ‚Verbotene Liebe', und setzte sich Lena Kluge genau gegenüber.

Two

❖ ❖ ❖

War of the Worlds

September, 2012

The passengers looked around her, every one expressionless. She had simply gotten on the train and that was that - she was on her way to work. Lena wouldn't have had it any other way. Besides, the caffeinated silence of the L during the morning rush hour was very familiar to Lena, a quality she trusted. She didn't have to speak to random strangers about the weather or waste her time on other useless facts with people that she didn't really like in the first place. This so-called 'small talk' that Americans loved so much was extremely dumb to her.

"Why do I need to be friends with everyone?" she asked herself. "We're not an episode of *Verbotene Liebe*."

Even though she loved the series, drama was always much more fun to *watch* than to *experience* - especially with eye candy and larger-than-life moments.

Suddenly, Dirk Moritz, the actor who played Daniel on the soap opera, boarded the train and sat directly across from Lena Kluge.

"What's a hot, up-and-coming doctor like you doing so far from

„Was macht so ein heißer, aufstrebender Arzt wie Sie so weit weg von Düsseldorf?", fragte Lena.

„Das könnte ich genauso gut eine Berlinerin fragen", konterte Daniel. „Aber woher wissen Sie, wer ich bin?"

„Ihr Ruf eilt Ihnen voraus. Woher wissen Sie, dass ich aus Berlin komme?", entgegnete Lena.

„Ich dachte, ich hätte den Anklang einer Berliner Schnauze vernommen", erwiderte Daniel.

Sie lächelten sich an und waren glücklich, sich getroffen zu haben. Es war, als hätte sich ihr Leben einfach nur durch dieses Treffen vollständig geändert.

„Sie haben meine Frage nicht beantwortet", sagte Lena.

„Sie meine auch nicht", erwiderte Daniel.

„Vielleicht könnten wir das nach der Arbeit bei ein paar Drinks ausdiskutieren?", fragte Lena.

„Würde mir gefallen", entgegnete Daniel.

Gerade als sie ihre Telefonnummern austauschen wollten, öffneten sich die Zugtüren. Die plötzliche Menschenmenge änderte die Situation vollkommen. Sowohl Daniel als auch der Schauspieler, der ihn dargestellt hatte, verschwanden. Die Leute gingen an Lena vorbei und sie saß einfach nur da und beobachtete sie wie durch eine Kamera.

„Die Typen um mich herum sind nicht von Autoren erdacht, um Lebensläufen eine Wende zu geben. Sie existieren einfach und nicht mehr. Nur Passanten, die niemals wiedergesehen werden", erinnerte sich Lena.

Inmitten dieses ganzen Getümmels und Gedränges schweiften ihre Gedanken für einen kurzen Moment zurück nach Berlin. *The L* verwandelte sich auf magische Weise in die Berliner S-Bahn, die sie zur Humboldt-Uni beförderte, während sie gerade am Tiergarten vorbeifuhren. Sie hätte schwören können, für einen kurzen Moment die Siegessäule gesehen zu haben. Der goldene Siegesengel starrte

Part One: Collisions

Düsseldorf?" asked Lena.

"I could ask the same of a Berliner," Daniel responded. "But how do you know who I am?"

"Your reputation precedes you. How'd you know I was from Berlin?" Lena responded.

"I thought I detected a slight *Berliner Schnauze*[1]," Daniel replied.

They smiled at each other, simply happy to have met each other. It was as if, by simply crossing paths, they had changed each other's lives completely.

"You never answered my question," Lena said.

"You didn't answer mine either," Daniel said.

"Well, perhaps we could discuss it over drinks after work?" Lena asked.

"I'd like that," Daniel replied.

As they were about to exchange numbers, the subway doors opened. A sudden rush of people changed the entire scene. Both Daniel and the actor that played him disappeared. Lena sat there as the people passed by, observing them like a camera.

"The characters around me are not exactly created by an author to evoke some kind of life-altering moment. They merely exist; nothing more. Just passers-by never to be seen again," Lena reminded herself.

In between all of the hustle and bustle, she disappeared back to Berlin for a moment. The L magically transformed into the *S-Bahn* and brought her to the Humboldt, just as the train passed by Tiergarten. She swore she saw the Siegesäule for half a moment, with the golden angel of victory staring down at her, as the leaves started to change color, and she just sat there, without an identity.

auf sie herab, während sich die Blätter färbten, und sie saß einfach nur da, ohne Identität. Es war nicht wichtig, woher sie kam oder wohin sie ging. Lena wurde von der Geräuschkulisse der Stadt verschluckt. So musste sie sich über die Unterschiede zwischen Berlin und Chicago keine Gedanken machen. Es waren einzig und allein einfach nur Städte.

Sie musste nicht darüber nachdenken, wer sie war und was sie vermisste. Für einen kurzen Moment war es eine Erleichterung, nicht mehr an ihre zu erledigenden Aufgaben denken zu müssen. Eine selbstbewusste, ehrgeizige, junge Frau wie Lena kämpfte immer für Ziele, die ihr wichtig waren, wie zum Beispiel für den Umweltschutz.

In Deutschland war die Arbeit für eine bessere Umwelt jedoch nicht unbedingt ein „Kampf". Man musste kein Mitglied der Grünen sein, um zu wissen, dass eine grünere Welt allen half. In den USA war das genaue Gegenteil der Fall. Recycling oder Sonnenenergie wurden hier nur mit einem Dollarzeichen ernst genommen. Diese Einstellung war ihr sehr fremd.

Außerdem hatte jeder einen solchen Stolz auf alles, was als „amerikanisch" bezeichnet wurde, egal, worum es wirklich ging. Dieser blinde Nationalismus machte Lena Angst, denn das kannte sie nur aus Geschichtsbüchern. Sie war noch immer erstaunt über die Unbekannte, die vor kurzem ohne Grund angefangen hatte, mit ihr in der Kneipe zu sprechen.

***

„Was vermisst du am meisten aus der Heimat?", fragte die Amerikanerin mit einem großen Lächeln.

Lena hatte sie gerade fünf Minuten vorher kennengelernt, aber das Mädchen benahm sich wie eine gute jahrelange Freundin. Lena war sich nicht sicher, ob alle Amerikaner so nett waren oder ob sie die Polizei rufen sollte, also ließ sie es drauf ankommen.

„Das Brot", sagte Lena. „Brezeln und Schwarzbrot mit Butter.

Part One: Collisions

Where she came from or where she was going wasn't important; Lena had disappeared in the background noise of the city. That way, she didn't have to think about Berlin and Chicago being so different. It was a city, first and foremost.

She didn't have to contemplate who she was, nor what she missed. It was a temporary relief from the list of tasks she needed to complete. A self-aware, ambitious young woman, Lena was always fighting for the causes she thought important, like defending the environment.

In Germany, working for a better planet was never so much of a 'fight' for environmental causes. You didn't have to be a member of *die Grünen*[1] to know that protecting the environment was in everyone's best interest. It was quite the opposite here in the U.S., where recycling, solar power, and the like were only taken seriously if they had a dollar sign on them. That was something very new to her.

Besides that, everyone had to be proud of that which was declared 'American,' no matter what it *really* was about. This blind nationalism scared Lena, who had previously only experienced it through history books. She was still taken aback by the stranger who had randomly started talking to her at the bar the other day.

***

"What do you miss most about home?" the American girl asked, with a big smile.

Lena had just met her five minutes ago, but the girl acted like they had been friends for years. Lena wasn't sure whether all Americans were this friendly or if she should call the police, so she played it by ear.

"The bread," Lena said. "*Brezeln* and *Schwarzbrot* with butter. *Brötchen* for breakfast with fresh cuts of meat and cheese."

Brötchen für das Frühstück mit frischen Teilchen und Käse."

„OMG, du machst mich jetzt wirklich hungrig", lachte die Amerikanerin und ließ fast ihr Bierglas fallen. „Ich hätte gerade so gerne die von Auntie Anne."

„Was sind die?" fragte Lena.

„Diese süßen Brezeln – ich fühle mich, als ob meine Oberschenkel 10 Pfund zulegen, nur wenn ich an die denke!", sagte die Amerikanerin.

„Bäh, ich werde mich nie an amerikanisches Brot gewöhnen", hatte Lena zu dem amerikanischen Mädchen gesagt, das sie in einer Bar kennengelernt hatte.

„Was? Wirklich? Warum?", hatte die Amerikanerin geantwortet.

„Es ist viel zu weich und süß", hatte Lena gesagt.

„Aber genau so muss es sein!", entgegnete das Mädchen.

„Man merkt, wie stark es verarbeitet ist. Das ist kein Brot. Brot muss frisch sein." Lena blieb hartnäckig.

„Du lieber Himmel, sind alle Europäer so eingebildet?", hatte die Amerikanerin gescherzt.

***

Lena ließ sich die Szene ein paarmal durch den Kopf gehen. Sie hatte nur gemeint, dass sie gutes von Hand hergestelltes Brot aus einer Bäckerei vermisste, weil es überall nur massenproduziertes billiges Brot von Walmart gab. Außerdem, warum wäre sie wohl für ein Jahr in den USA, wäre sie so antiamerikanisch eingestellt, wie diese Amerikanerin es den Europäern unterstellte?

„CLARK AND DIVISION...is next. Doors open on the left at...CLARK AND DIVISION", sagte eine monotone Tonbandstimme, die vor und nach dem Namen der Station eine lange Pause machte.

Die Türen öffneten sich mit so großer Wucht, dass es die alten Bänke des Zuges schüttelte. Ein Schwall kalter Luft wurde so in

"OMG, you're making my inner fat-child so hungry right now." The American girl laughed with her, nearly dropping her beer glass. "I could really go for some Auntie Anne's right now."

"What's that?" Lena asked.

"These sweet pretzels - I feel like my thighs gained ten pounds just thinking about it!" the American said.

"Ugh, I will never get used to American bread!" Lena said.

"Wait, really? Why?" the American replied.

"It's way too soft and sweet," Lena had responded.

"But that's the best way!" the American said.

"You can taste how processed it is! That's not bread! Bread should be fresh," Lena insisted.

"Geez, are all Europeans this stuck up?" the American joked.

***

Lena kept replaying the scene in her head. All Lena had meant was that she missed good hand-made bread from a bakery instead of this mass-produced Wal-Mart brand. After all, why would she be in the US for a year if she was as anti-American as this American girl believed Europeans to be?

"CLARK AND DIVISION...is next. Doors open on the left at... CLARK AND DIVISION," said a monotone, prerecorded voice which had a great pause before and after the name of the station.

The doors jolted open with a great bang, shaking the old frame of the train and the plastic seats on which Lena sat, bringing in a refreshingly cool breeze on the hot, muggy Midwestern morning. The train stood still once again for a couple of uncomfortable seconds, while busy passengers walked in and out with important paper briefings, on their way to their boring, unimportant offices.

einen heißen, schwülen Herbstmorgen des mittleren Westens hineingetragen. Der Zug hielt erneut einige unangenehme Sekunden lang, während Fahrgäste eilig ein- und ausstiegen. Sie waren mit ihren Unterlagen auf dem Weg zu ihren Besprechungen in unwichtigen und wahrscheinlich langweiligen Büros.

Ein ungepflegter Mann mit wettergegerbter Haut stolperte langsam auf den Sitzplatz neben Lena zu. Mit seinen zerrissenen Jeans und dem verblichenen grünen Hemd wirkte er inmitten der Männer in ihren Anzügen wie ein Fremdkörper. Es war deutlich zu sehen, dass er weder ein hoffnungsloser Allerweltsteenager ohne Modegeschmack noch ein lebendiges Kunstobjekt eines erfolglosen Künstlers war, der ein Zeichen gegen die Armut setzen wollte. Seine zerrissene Kleidung und sein schmales Gesicht mit dem struppigen Bart waren viel zu ekelhaft und schäbig, als dass dies hätte beabsichtigt sein können.

Mal ganz davon abgesehen, dass von dem Moment an, als er das Abteil betrat, ein übler Geruch durch den Zug waberte. Ganz wie ein Abfallhaufen, den man noch zwei Straßen weiter riechen konnte. Er starrte Lena an. Sie fühlte sich so unbehaglich, dass sie unbewusst sofort einen innerlichen Schutzwall aufbaute. Als der Geruch und das Unbehagen so unerträglich wurden, dass sie beschloss, den Platz zu wechseln, begann der unheimliche Mann zusammenhanglos zu faseln.

„Die Bomben", schrie der Mann in den Raum hinein, „SIE KRIEGEN DICH!"

Die Leute im Abteil ignorierten ihn. Einige starrten auf ihre Füße, immer bemüht, dem Verrückten nicht in die Augen zu schauen, so, als wäre sein Zustand ansteckend.

„Die Männer in Washington. Denen ist alles egal", sagte er und begann zu weinen. „Denen ist alles egal."

Ein Mann hatte Mitleid mit den Tränen und blickte auf. Als der verwahrloste Penner merkte, dass man ihn anschaute, verwandelten sich seine Tränen in Zorn.

Part One: Collisions

Amongst the men in suits, a scruffy man with weather-beaten skin, ripped jeans and a sun-bleached green shirt stood out like a sore thumb. He slowly stumbled over to the seat beside Lena. It was obvious that he was neither your run-of-the-mill, hopelessly fashion-less American teenager, or a living avant-garde art exhibition from some struggling artist making a statement about the poor. His ripped clothes and thin face, with an unkempt beard, were way too gruesome and weathered to be intentional.

Not to mention, the man had such a stench that it invaded the train from the moment he entered, like a dumpster you can smell from two blocks away. He stared directly at Lena, giving her an uncanny feeling which caused her to unconsciously scooch over a bit. After the smell and the awkwardness became so much that she decided to switch seats, the uncanny man began to babble incoherently.

"Them bombs," the man yelled at no one in particular. "THEY'RE COMING FOR YA!"

Everyone in the car ignored him. Some of them looked at their feet, afraid to look the lunatic in the eye, as if his condition were contagious.

"Those men in Washington. They don't care." The man began weeping. "They don't care."

The tears made another man look up out of pity. Suddenly, the unkempt man realized he was being watched and went from tears to anger.

"Why are ya looking at me like that, pussy!" the unkempt man yelled, walking towards his would-be sympathizer. "You wanna use me too, like some cheap whore for Uncle Sam?"

The passer-by looked back at the floor, and the crazy guy started to calm down.

"Was glotzt du mich so an, Alter?!", schrie er und bewegte sich auf seinen Möchtegern-Mitfühlenden zu. "Willst du mich auch ausnutzen, so wie eine billige Hure für Vater Staat?"

Der Passant blickte zurück auf den Boden und der Verrückte beruhigte sich.

"So ist's gut. Feigling", murmelte der Penner und setzte sich hin.

Nach endlosem irrem Gebrabbel kamen sie an der Haltestelle Harrison an. Zumindest in einem hatte der verwahrloste Verrückte recht: Es würde heute Krieg geben. Zwar ohne Bombenhagel, aber nicht alle Kriege wurden auf dem Schlachtfeld geführt. Lena kämpfte sich durch die Soldaten in grauen Anzügen, als sie den Zug verließ. Sie hatte das Gefühl, jetzt sofort zur Arbeit gehen zu müssen und nicht eine einzige Minute später – obwohl sie in Wirklichkeit sogar zehn Minuten zu früh dran war. Stattdessen konzentrierte sie sich auf ein Zitat von Albert Einstein: "Für unsere Arbeit sind zwei Dinge wichtig: Nicht endende Beharrlichkeit und Bereitschaft."

Sie war wahrlich keine Physikerin. Aber obwohl sie sich wegen ihres Universitätsabschlusses in Germanistik meist von Grodek oder Faust inspirieren ließ, fiel ihr dieses Zitat ein; und sie empfand es als besonders motivierend. Schließlich lebten auf dieser Welt sieben Milliarden Menschen und alle kämpften nur um das eine: im eigenen Leben eine Hauptrolle zu spielen. Krieg ist das Hauptfach, egal wie und wo.

Auf dem Weg ins Büro ging Lena jeden Morgen am Einkaufszentrum an der Grand Avenue vorbei. Normalerweise war es einfacher Orientierungspunkt für sie, aber heute fiel ihr ein, dass sie neue Schuhe brauchte. Sie holte ihren Terminplaner heraus und notierte: "neue Schuhe". Weil sie als Praktikantin den ganzen Tag herumlaufen musste, waren all ihre Schuhe ziemlich abgetragen.

Sicher hatte sie noch andere Schuhe, aber sie waren alle so langweilig geworden. Außerdem hatte sie genug Geld, um sich von

"That's right. Coward," the unkempt man mumbled, sitting down once again.

After an eternity of psychotic babbling, she arrived at the Harrison station. At the very least, the unkempt lunatic was right about one thing: there would be a war today. Albeit, free of bombs, but then again, not all wars are waged on the battlefield. Lena fought through the various soldiers in grey suits as she disembarked. She was certain she needed to get to work right now and not a minute later - even if in reality she was around ten minutes ahead of schedule. She focused instead on a quote from Albert Einstein: "Two things are necessary to our work: unending perseverance and readiness."

She was surely no physicist. While her college major in German literature more often led her to find inspiration in *Grodek*[1] or *Faust*, this was the quote that came to mind that day, and she found it to be particularly motivational. After all, it was a harsh world of seven billion people, all fighting to be the protagonist in their own story. War has no major.

On her way to work, Lena walked past the shopping center on Grand Avenue, as she did every morning. Normally, it was a simple landmark, but today, it reminded her that she wanted to buy some new shoes. She pulled out her organizer and wrote down 'new shoes.' After all, her shoes were wearing kind of thin because of all the walking she did as an intern, so she could certainly justify the expense to herself.

Of course, she had other shoes, but they all had become so boring. Besides, she had enough money from her small income as an intern to buy more than just food and coffee now and again. And new shoes were certainly at the top of the list. A new pair just made her feel so fresh, sexy, and ready to take on the world, whether they were for work, going out, or casual wear.

As she turned right onto Michigan Avenue, Lena turned her

ihrer Praktikantenvergütung hin und wieder mal etwas außer der Reihe kaufen zu können statt nur Lebensmittel und Kaffee. Und neue Schuhe standen auf ihrer Liste mit Sicherheit ganz oben. Sie gaben ihr das Gefühl, lebendig und sexy zu sein, bereit, die Welt zu erobern, egal ob es welche für den Job, zum Ausgehen oder für den Alltag waren.

Als sie nach rechts in die Michigan Avenue einbog, dachte Lena an das, was heute zu erledigen war. Sie holte ihren Terminplaner noch einmal heraus, um einen Blick auf ihre Checkliste für den Morgen zu werfen.

„Abgleich für Lisa?", dachte sie. „Ja, klar. Logisch, das habe ich doch schon gestern gemacht, bevor ich am späten Abend gegangen bin. Ich bin ein Idiot."

Lena strich den Punkt durch.

„Angebotsbriefe und Buchentwürfe?" Sie las es sich laut vor und kaute an ihrem Stift, während sie versuchte, sich zu erinnern. „Die Angebotsbriefe müssen geprüft werden, aber ich muss abklären, ob Cristiano seinen Teil erledigt hat, damit ich nicht blöd dastehe."

Sie strich auch diesen Punkt durch und betrat eine Starbucks-Filiale, um sich ihren täglichen Kaffee Latte zu holen. Beim Versuch dieses Multitaskings rempelte sie beinahe einen verärgerten Chicagoer an.

„Tschuldigung", sagte sie in einem täuschend echten amerikanischen Slang.

Der Mann starrte sie nur an, sagte aber nichts und wankte davon wie ein zorniger Koffeinjunkie.

Sie hielt ihren Kaffee zum Mitnehmen in der Hand und starrte angestrengt auf den Plastikdeckel, während sie zum Zebrastreifen hastete, ganz so, als ließe sich damit ein Überschwappen verhindern. „*Cuidado Caliente – Careful Hot – Attention Chaud*" stand auf dem Deckel. Dabei war die Wärme Warnung genug, was bei einem Fehltritt passieren könnte. Das InterContinental Hotel mit

Part One: Collisions

thoughts to what she had to do. She brought out her organizer once again to look at her morning checklist.

"Collating for Lisa?" she thought. "Yeah, of course. Duh, I did that before leaving last night. I'm such an idiot."

Lena crossed out that bullet point.

"Query letters and book drafts?" she read to herself, biting on the end of her pen as she tried to remember. "Check on the query letters, but I need to make sure Cristiano has actually done his fucking half of the job so I don't look bad."

She began crossing off that bullet point, as she entered Starbucks for her daily latte, nearly knocking into a pissed-off Chicagoan.

"I'm so sorry," she said, feigning a perfect American accent.

The man just glared back at her, not saying a word, and staggered away like an angry caffeine zombie.

After getting her coffee to go, she quickly scurried to the cross walk, glaring at the lid as if that would prevent its contents from spilling, as she quickly scurried to the cross walk. "*Cuidado Caliente - Careful Hot - Attention Chaud,*" the lid reminded her, as if the warmth she felt even through the cardboard sleeve of the cup weren't reminder enough of what one misstep could cause.

Out of the corner of her eye, Lena saw the InterContinental Hotel come into view with the crisp red, white, and blue of the US flag, the bland yellow, white, and black of the Cook County flag, and the pale white and blue stripes and brilliant red stars of the Chicago flag.

Lena mentally added some international grandeur by switching out the red stars of the Chicago flag for the yellow sun of the Argentinian flag. While the rest of the crowd began to cross the street the minute the traffic stopped, she imagined herself as an

dem frischen Rot, Weiß und Blau der US-Fahne, dem faden Gelb, Weiß und Schwarz der Fahne des Cook County und den blassen blau-weißen Streifen mit den prächtigen roten Sternen der Flagge Chicagos erschien in Lenas Blickfeld.

Lena begann zu träumen. Sie stellte sich einen pompöseren Auftritt vor und ersetzte in Gedanken die roten Sterne der Flagge von Chicago mit der gelben Sonne Argentiniens. Während die Autos anhielten und der Rest der Menschenmenge um sie herum die Straße überquerte, war sie einen Moment lang eine wichtige deutsche Politikerin oder Geschäftsfrau, die zwischen Buenos Aires und Shanghai für ein paar Tage in der Stadt einen Zwischenstopp einlegte. Doch als das Ampelmännchen aufleuchtete, erwachte Lena aus ihrem Traum. Schließlich hatte sie auch noch Sachen zu erledigen.

Sie betrat das Foyer, begrüßte den Hotelportier, betrachtete ihr Spiegelbild im Aufzug und entschied sich dafür, ihr Make-up aufzufrischen. Der Lidschatten ihres linken Auges passte nicht zum rechten und sie wollte im Büro nicht als Schlampe abgestempelt werden. Überhaupt, wenn sie ihre Körperpflege nicht ernst nahm, wer sollte sie dann im Berufsleben für voll nehmen?

Kurz vor dem 10. Stock war sie fertig. Dann wartete sie im Praktikantenzimmer auf ihren Chef. Sie saß ein paar Minuten herum und wusste nichts mit sich anzufangen. Sie überlegte, den Tisch aufzuräumen – aber der war schon wie aus dem Ei gepellt –, als ein blonder Muskelprotz in Discounterklamotten zur Tür hereinkam. Wenigstens sah er darin besser aus als in seinen üblichen schlabbrigen Basketballhosen und dem Hemd, das zwei Nummern zu groß war.

„Hey, David. Hast du heute unseren Faulenzer schon gesehen?", fragte Lena.

„Bist heute mal wieder unter die Klugscheißer gegangen, was?", lachte er ihr ins Gesicht. „Damit der Kerl pünktlich hier ist, muss er von einem verdammten Supermodel am Schwanz

important German political figure or businesswoman, in the city for a couple days in between Buenos Aires and Shanghai. Lena instead broke out of her trance the minute that the crosswalk lights changed - she had goals to chase.

She entered the lobby, greeted the concierge, and upon checking her reflection in the elevator, decided to touch up her makeup. The eyeshadow on her left eye seemed slightly uncoordinated with that on her right, and she didn't want to be laughed out of the office for being a slob. After all, if she couldn't take care of her personal hygiene, who would take her seriously in a professional setting?

She finished just before reaching the tenth floor and waited for her boss in the interns' room. She sat there for a few minutes and, unsure what to do while she waited, reorganized the table - despite the fact that it already looked spick and span - till a blond muscle-head with some cheap off-brand formal attire walked in. At least it was better than his normal clothes, which consisted of baggy basketball shorts and a shirt that was two sizes too big.

"Hey, David. You see the lazy one on your way in?" asked Lena.

"What? Already being a smart-ass today, are we?" replied David, laughing. "That guy needs a fucking supermodel dragging him around by his dick to actually get him here on time."

"Hey, come on!" said the olive-skinned man, that appeared in the blink of an eye, like a thief. He was only a couple of centimeters taller than David, but much better dressed, even if his bright red pants from Ralph Lauren, black shirt from Desigual, and golden sunglasses from D&G were a bit too flashy for her taste. "Relax guys. I've got a good grip on the situation. Everything is under control."

"Oh, for sure, Cristiano. Which genitals you've got a grip on...

hergezogen werden."

„Hey, was soll das?!", sagte ein olivgrüner Typ, der ganz plötzlich wie ein Dieb dastand. Er war nur ein paar Zentimeter größer als David, aber viel besser angezogen. Auch wenn seine knallroten Hosen von Ralph Lauren, das schwarze Hemd von Desigual und die goldene Sonnenbrille von D&G für ihren Geschmack ein klein wenig zu auffallend waren. „Nur die Ruhe, ey. Ich hab alles im Griff. Alles im grünen Bereich."

„Ja klar, Cristiano. Aber was du da konkret im Griff hast, das ist eine komplett andere Geschichte. Hast du's gestern 'nem Mädel mit dem Mund besorgt oder 'nem Typen einen geblasen, Don Giovanni?", fragte Lena.

Lena bemerkte, dass der normalerweise laute David zum Thema schwieg, statt sich einzuschalten. Sie hatte im vergangenen Monat eine Weile gebraucht, um es zu merken, weil es fast unmerklich geschah, aber sie war fast sicher, dass die Bisexualität von Cristiano das einzige war, was den religiösen Extremisten aus der Fassung brachte. Eine fehlende Bemerkung hier, kein Daumen hoch da – es war allzu auffällig. Oder vielleicht bildete sie sich das auch nur ein.

„Oh, nur weil ich Action habe und du nicht, meinst du, du musst hier einen auf Eifersucht machen, oder?", entgegnete Cristiano ebenso herablassend.

„Gedisst!", sagte David. „Wie groß waren ihre Möpse?"

„Seine Brustmuskeln waren ganz ordentlich", antwortete Cristiano, „aber mir gefiel sein Sixpack noch besser."

„Oh", meinte David.

„Was. Bist du jetzt so prüde wie deine Eltern, oder was?", sagte Lena. „Das wäre mir neu."

„Nee", entgegnete David schüchtern. „Ich kann's mir nur nicht vorstellen, weißt du?"

„Hey, Alter. Alles klar", sagte Cristiano und gab seinem besten

well, that's another question entirely. So did you eat pussy or suck cock yesterday, Don Giovanni?" Lena asked.

Lena noticed that the normally boisterous David was very quiet on the subject instead of chiming in. It had taken her a long time over the past month to realize it, because it was so subtle, but she was almost certain that Cristiano's bisexuality was the one thing that threw the religious extremist off his game. A missing statement here, or a missing high five there - it was too convenient. Or maybe it was just all in her head.

"Aw, just because I'm getting hot ass and you're starving doesn't mean you have to get all jealous," Cristiano replied, with some condescension.

"Boom, roasted!" David said. "How big were her boobs, dude?"

"His pecs were pretty legit," Cristiano responded. "But I liked his six pack better."

"Oh," said David.

"What, you've become as prudish as your parents now?" Lena said. "That's a new one."

"N'aw," David said, shyly. "I just can't relate, ya know?"

"Hey, man. It's all good," Cristiano said, trying to back his best friend. "Not everyone can keep up with me."

"Not even rabbits," Lena joked.

"Hey, don't hate the player. Hate the game!" Cristiano replied, using the American idiom David had just taught him. He walked over to David and patted him on the back as he continued. "Speaking of which, when are you bringing home some hot chick, my man?"

"N'aw, man. I'm waiting till marriage," David replied.

Freund Rückendeckung. „Nicht jeder kann's mit mir aufnehmen."

„Nicht mal 'n Karnickel", witzelte Lena.

„Hey, schieb's nicht auf den Spieler, sondern auf das Spiel!", antwortete Cristiano. Das war eine amerikanische Redewendung, die David ihm gerade beigebracht hatte. Er klopfte ihm auf die Schulter und fuhr fort: „Weil wir gerade dabei sind, wann bringst du dir denn mal 'ne heiße Braut mit nach Hause, mein Lieber?"

„Nee. Ich warte damit bis nach der Hochzeit", antwortete David.

„Moment mal, all das Gerede und dann bist du am Ende wirklich genauso prüde wie deine Eltern?", sagte Lena und verbiss sich ein Lachen.

„Wo steht in der Bibel, dass man die Aussicht nicht genießen darf", flachste David.

„Jungs", unterbrach Lisa die beiden und hielt ein paar Listen hoch. „So fesselnd diese Unterhaltung auch ist, können wir uns bitte jetzt wieder an die Arbeit machen? Irgendwann in diesem Jahrhundert will ich mich mal mit diesen Autoren in Verbindung setzen."

„Ja, ok", brummelten die anderen und klangen dabei wie Fünfjährige, denen man ihre Süßigkeiten abgenommen hatte. Jeder nahm seine Aufgabe und ging an die Arbeit.

Lena fand die Datei für die erste Aufgabe auf der Liste im freigegebenen Laufwerk. Sie erstellte hundert Kopien der 10-Seiten-Pakete und heftete sie mit der gleichen kontrollierten Inbrunst zusammen, die ein religiöser Fanatiker empfinden musste.

„Lena, komm runter", sagte sie sich. „Tief atmen. Lass deine Wut nicht an den Papieren aus."

Aber dann erinnerte sie sich an die Szene vom vergangenen Tag mit Cristiano in der Küche und es war vollkommen nutzlos. Lena hatte stundenlang mit ihm diskutiert und er hatte einfach nur gelacht. Lena kochte vor Wut, als die Situation immer wieder vor

Part One: Collisions

"Wait, all this talk and you really are as much of as a prude as your parents?" Lena said, nearly laughing.

"Where did the Bible say anything about not enjoying the view?" David joked.

"Hey, guys," Lisa, their boss, interrupted, holding up a pair of lists. "As riveting as this conversation is, could we please get some work done now? I'd like to get back to some of these authors within this century."

"Yeah, sure," they all mumbled back in some fashion, like five-year-olds caught stealing sweets. They each took their appropriate assignment and settled into their routine.

Lena found the file for the first item on the list in the office shared drive. She printed off a hundred copies of the ten-page packet and stapled them together with the controlled fervor of a religious zealot.

"Lena, calm down," she said to herself. "Deep breath. Take it all out on the papers." But then her brain dug up a scene with Cristiano in the kitchen from the other day and it was just useless. Lena had argued with Cristiano for hours and he simply laughed in response. Lena simmered in anger as she replayed the scene over and over in her head.

***

"Why would you even date "evil women" anymore if they were so bad?" Lena asked. "After all, you're bi. Just date men. Admit it, we're not that bad."

"Women are a necessary evil. Men are a temporary replacement when picky chicks don't leave their plumbing to the professionals," Cristiano joked, winking at David.

"Plus, a night between two real bros, without all of that *pluma* shit," Cristiano said, with an effeminate wave of the hand on the

ihrem geistigen Auge ablief.

***

„Warum gehst du mit den ‚dummen Weibern' immer noch aus, wenn du sie doch so furchtbar findest?", hatte Lena gefragt. „Schließlich bist du bi. Sonst geh halt nur mit Männern aus. Gib's zu, so schlimm sind wir nicht."

„Frauen sind ein notwendiges Übel. Männer sind nur ein Provisorium, wenn wählerische Weiber ihre Möse nicht den Profis überlassen", scherzte Cristiano und zwinkerte David zu.

„Außerdem ist eine Nacht zwischen zwei echten Kerlen, also ohne den Tuntenscheiß" – Cristiano machte eine tuntige Handbewegung bei dem Wort –, „eine nette Abwechslung von dem ganzen Frauengedöns. Ach Gottchen, mein Schuh hat 'nen Kratzer!"

„Oh Scheiße! Brauchst du 'ne Salbe für den Tiefschlag?", fragte David Lena, als sich die beiden Männer abklatschten. Lena hatte geschrien und war frustriert aus der Küche geflohen.

***

Und sie musste mit den beiden Arschlöchern jeden Tag zusammenarbeiten. Lisa gab ihnen alle einfachen Aufgaben, aber diese beiden Idioten machten ihr die Sache schwer. Weil sie von nichts eine Ahnung hatten, musste sie die Arbeit oft noch einmal machen, damit die Arbeiten des Amerikaners und des Spaniers korrekt abgeliefert werden konnten. Alles musste seine Richtigkeit haben. Wie hatte ihr Vater immer gesagt? „Sauberkeit kommt gleich nach der Gottesfurcht."

Die Kopien mussten alle mit einer Büroklammer zusammengesteckt und in einem Ordner abgelegt sein, damit sie keine Knicke bekamen oder verloren gingen. Lena wollte vermeiden, dass man sie wegen der Inkompetenz der anderen Praktikanten angriff oder am Ende feuerte.

„Egal, irgendwann wird es sich auszahlen", redete sie sich ein und sortierte die Unterlagen für die Besprechung mit einem

Part One: Collisions

word *pluma*. "It's a nice break from all the bullshit of you women. Like, oh my god, I scratched my shoe!"

"Oh, shit! Do you need some aloe for that burn?" David asked Lena. The men exchanged a high five. Lena screamed in frustration and ran out of the kitchen.

***

And she had to work with these assholes every day. Lisa gave them all simple tasks, but these two idiots made even those difficult. Since the others didn't know anything, she often had to redo the work to make sure the American and the Spaniard had done it right. Everything had to be in its proper place. As her father always said, "Cleanliness is next to godliness."

The copies had all had to be bound with a paperclip and put in a folder, so that they didn't get crinkled or lost. And Lena would not be accused and later inevitably fired for the incompetence of the other interns.

"Regardless, it'll all be worth it one day," she reassured herself as she finished collating the papers for the meeting with an important client after the lunch break. After all, the first page had the accompanying prospectus, which her boss, Lisa, had given her to format.

"You see?" Lena said to herself as she finished up. "Hard work pays off."

She went across the hall to lay the packets on Lisa's desk, but suddenly, she saw her sworn enemy, Cristiano. He was always talking in Spanish in the break room with his other American friend, Javier, who was of Mexican descent. How Javier managed to be employed full-time was a miracle in and of itself. He was lazier than the other two - always on a break, late, or staying at home.

As for the location of the third musketeer, David, she couldn't

wichtigen Kunden nach der Mittagspause.

Und tatsächlich fand sich auf der ersten Seite ein Prospekt, den ihr ihre Chefin Lisa zum Formatieren gegeben hatte.

„Siehst du", sagte sie zu sich selbst, als sie ihre Arbeit abschloss. „Harte Arbeit zahlt sich aus."

Sie ging über den Flur, um den Stapel auf Lisas Schreibtisch zu legen. Plötzlich sah sie ihren Erzfeind Cristiano. Er redete im Pausenraum immer spanisch mit Javier, dem Amerikaner mit mexikanischem Migrationshintergrund. Wie es Javier schaffte, nicht entlassen zu werden, war ihr ein ewiges Rätsel. Er war noch fauler als die beiden anderen – entweder war er in der Pause oder er kam zu spät oder blieb gleich ganz zu Hause.

Sie hatte keine Ahnung, wo sich im Augenblick David, der dritte der Musketiere, aufhielt. Hin und wieder arbeitete er tatsächlich. Aber die meiste Zeit, wenn Lena dabei war, tat er nur so, als würde er arbeiten, ging dann rüber zu den beiden anderen, sagte „Wer die Arbeit kennt und sich nicht drückt, der ist verrückt" und ließ sich feiern.

Das süffisante Grinsen der beiden jungen Männer ärgerte sie. Es kam ihr so vor, als würden Javier und Cristiano über „die eingebildete Deutsche, mit der wir arbeiten müssen", tratschen, anstatt zu arbeiten. Eigentlich war ihr klar, dass das ihrerseits schon an Paranoia oder sowas in der Art grenzte. Aber es war viel einfacher, sie zu hassen. Und wenn sie es mit ihren Fähigkeiten letzten Endes zu einer Führungsposition gebracht hatte, dann konnte sie solche Versager einfach feuern.

Ganz egal, die Uhr schlug zwölf – sie hatte ihre Mittagspause verdient und konnte diesem Blödsinn wenigstens zeitweilig den Rücken kehren. Lena wollte sich mit ihrer guten alten Freundin Marie Steiner aus ihrer Wiener Zeit auf der Terrasse eines Cafés treffen.

Lena hatte Marie vor ein paar Wochen in Chicago wiedergesehen. Sie hatten festgestellt, dass sie in der gleichen

Part One: Collisions

say. Now and again he actually did his work. But he mostly faked being a hard-working employee when Lisa was around, then went straight over to the other two to say "Fake it till ya make it, bro!" with a following celebratory high five.

The smug smile of those two young men angered her, as if Javier and Cristiano were gossiping about that "stuck-up German they work with" instead of doing their work. She knew deep inside that it was merely a case of paranoia, or something like that. However, it was far easier to hate them. And when her hard work finally brought her to a managerial position, then she could simply fire such incompetents.

Either way, the clock had struck 12:00 - she had earned her lunch break and she could finally leave this nonsense, albeit only momentarily. Lena left the building and went down the street to meet a Viennese friend of hers, Marie von Steiner, out on the patio of a café.

Lena had met Marie in Chicago a few weeks ago, and when the found out they worked close to each other, they decided to meet up at least every Wednesday. It was a good way to relax. They had even made an agreement to forget about work or politics for an entire half hour to assure that.

"So? How's your love life?" asked Marie.

"What? I'm a free woman. Am I not allowed to be happily single?" responded Lena.

"Hey! I don't mean nothing by that, hun! It's just a little small talk. Don't be so saucy!" said Marie, laughing. "What's gotten into you?"

"Nothing. Just forget it," Lena answered.

"Oh, really? Sounds a little like homesickness to me," said Marie. "Oh, I know! We can go to Kuhn's or Olga's this weekend

Gegend arbeiteten, und seitdem trafen sie sich mindestens jeden Mittwoch. Es war eine gute Gelegenheit, ein wenig abzuschalten. Sie hatten deshalb sogar ausgemacht, eine ganze halbe Stunde lang weder über die Arbeit noch über Politik zu reden.

„Na, was macht die Liebe?", fragte Marie.

„Was meinst du damit? Ich bin eine sorgenfreie Frau. Darf ich kein glücklicher Single sein?", antwortete Lena.

„Hey! So war das doch nicht gemeint, Mädel. Das ist doch einfach nur so dahingesagt. Sei doch nicht so schnippisch!", lachte Marie. „Was ist denn in dich gefahren?"

„Nichts. Vergiss es", antwortete Lena.

„Ehrlich? Das klingt für mich nach Heimweh", sagte Marie. „Ah, ich weiß. Wir können am Wochenende bei Kuhn oder Olga deutsch essen gehen. Keine Widerrede!"

„Ach nein. Es sind nur mal wieder diese Idioten in meinem Job", sagte Lena.

„Noch ein Grund mehr, am Wochenende abzuhängen", antwortete Marie. „Aber mal im Ernst. Widerrede ist zwecklos."

„Ich bin ok, ehrlich. Ich werde ein bisschen von Schirach lesen und dann geht's mir wieder gut", sagte Lena.

„Quatsch. Juristische Schriftstücke und ein muffiges Apartment?", empörte sich Marie. „Ich will nichts mehr davon hören. Außerdem habe ich gehört, dass in Boystown eine neue, süße Boutique aufgemacht hat. Nennen wir es Frustshoppen."

„Du weißt, dass ich mir das nicht leisten kann", sagte Lena, obwohl das nicht ganz stimmte.

„Darum wirst du das Bezahlen mir überlassen", meinte Marie.

„Nein, das kommt nicht in Frage", sagte Lena in einem letzten Versuch, sie aufzuhalten.

„Nun gerade", beharrte Marie. „Ich verdiene genug und du bist nur eine arme Praktikantin. Außerdem würde es mir auch guttun. Keine Widerrede."

for some German food. It's decided!"

"Oh, please, no. It's just those idiots at work again," said Lena.

"All the more reason to have a fun weekend," replied Marie. "Seriously, I won't take no for an answer."

"I'm fine, seriously. I'll just read some Von Schirach and I'll be fine," Lena said.

"Nonsense. A bunch of depressing legal briefs and a stuffy apartment?" Marie scoffed. "I won't hear of it. Besides, there's a cute new boutique in Boystown I heard about. We'll call it retail therapy."

"You know I can't afford that," Lena said, not quite lying.

"That's why I'm paying," Marie said.

"No, I couldn't," Lena said.

"You can and will," Marie insisted. "I make enough, you're a poor intern, and besides, I could really use this too. I won't take no for an answer."

"…Fine," Lena finally conceded.

"Hooray! I'll see ya at 11:00 on the dot, sweetie. Ciao!" Marie answered as Lena secretly smiled.

The break and the new plans made Lena happy and gave her a little more energy, even though she would still be plagued with four more hours of busywork. Despite it all, she forgot everything for a moment that had bothered her before. With newfound vigor, she walked briskly back to her work space and there was nothing in the world that…*WHAT!?!*

On her desk lay a note with the word "FEMI-NAZI" in large letters. She was so flustered that she knocked over some pens and binders reaching for the note and heard someone chuckling in the

„Na gut, ok", gab Lena schließlich klein bei.

„Hurra! Wir treffen uns um Punkt elf, meine Liebe. Ciao!", antwortete Marie, und Lena musste heimlich lächeln.

Die Pause und die neuen Pläne machten Lena glücklich und sie fühlte sich energiegeladen, obwohl sie noch vier weitere Stunden Mühsal vor sich hatte. Für einen kurzen Moment vergaß sie alles, was ihr vorher Kummer bereitet hatte. Mit neuem Elan kehrte sie an ihren Arbeitsplatz zurück. Es gab nichts, was sie nicht ... WAS!?!

Auf ihrem Schreibtisch lag ein Zettel mit der Aufschrift „FEMINAZI" in Großbuchstaben. Sie war so überrascht und geschockt, dass sie ein paar Stifte und Ordner umwarf. Aus dem Nachbarzimmer drang Gekicher an ihr Ohr.

Den Rest des Tages versuchte Lena eine professionelle Haltung an den Tag zu legen, aber sie wollte den drei Musketieren jetzt noch viel mehr in die Eier treten.

„Es ist es wert, es ist es wert, es ist es wert. Verdammt", wiederholte sie gebetsmühlenartig. Die Zeit war noch nie so langsam vergangen und als es endlich fünf Uhr schlug, fand sie es fast schade, Atheistin zu sein. Sie hätte gerne an eine höhere Macht gedacht. Und fast daran geglaubt.

Als sie zu Hause ankam, setzte sie ihren iPod Shuffle auf, weil sie einfach nur abschalten wollte. Der Song ‚Girls' von Marina and the Diamonds plärrte in ihren Ohren.

„Ich werde mich niemals verbiegen lassen, Cristiano und David", sagte Lena, während Marina von perfekten Mädels sang, die nie alt wurden.

Lena begann den Songtext mit großer Wut mitzuschmettern. Und wenn man genau hingeschaut hätte, dann hätte man gesehen, wie eine flüssige Substanz an Lenas rechter Wange herunterlief. Aber das hätte man natürlich überinterpretiert.

room next door.

Lena tried to stay professional for the rest of the day, but she wanted more than anything to kick the Three Musketeers right in the balls.

"It's worth it, it's worth, it's worth it, goddammit," she repeated continuously, flustered. The time had never gone by more slowly. When the clock finally struck five, she almost wished she wasn't an atheist so she could thank a higher power. Almost.

When she got home, she turned on her iPod Shuffle to tune everything else out. Marina and the Diamonds' "Girls" whined in her ears.

"I am not going to bend over and take it, Cristiano and David!" Lena said, as Marina sang about perfect girls who never grow old.

Lena began belting out the lyrics in a righteous rage. And if you looked closely enough, you might have sworn you saw a glistening substance running down Lena's right cheek. But of course, you would be over-thinking things.

Tres

❖ ❖ ❖

¡Vete a un convento!

Octubre, 2012

—¡Y una mierda! —gritó un hombre guapo y encantador en broma por Skype. Su piel suave y sus ojos oscuros seguramente habían atraído a cientos de mujeres con los años. De no ser por las canas, cualquiera podría pensar que era uno de los amigos de Cristiano.

—No, ahora en serio —respondió Cristiano entre risas—. De verdad, ¡no creo que vaya a acostumbrarme nunca a esta jodida costumbre de cenar a las seis!

—¿O sea que cenamos a la vez? —contestó Manuel con una seriedad que tan solo duró un segundo, riendo mientras escupía las próximas palabras—. ¿A seis horas de diferencia horaria?

—Espera, ¿ya es medianoche allí? ¡Venga ya! —dijo Cristiano—. No me jodas, hombre.

—¿Por qué clase de padre me tomas? Saluda a tu madre y que aproveche. Y que te aproveche *la noche* también —dijo Manuel—. ¡Oye! ¿Te paso el bastón, abuelito?

—¡Cállate, papá! —dijo Cristiano con una sonrisa en la cara mientras se movía en la pantalla.

—¿Eh? —dijo una voz ahogada en el fondo antes de que Cristiano viera una mano desencarnada darle a Manuel una

Three

❖ ❖ ❖

¡Vete a un convento!

October, 2012

"No fucking way!" screamed the charmingly, handsome man jokingly on Skype. He had smooth skin and dark eyes that had undoubtedly attracted hundreds of women over the years. One could almost mistake him for one of Cristiano's friends, were it not for the white hairs. "Seriously?"

"Seriously!" responded Cristiano, laughing. "To be honest, I don't think I'll ever get used to eating at six in the fucking afternoon!"

"So we're eating at the same time?" Manuel answered, a little more seriously. But that only lasted a short moment, laughing as he choked out his next words: "From six hours away?"

"Wait, it's already midnight over there?" said Cristiano. "Don't you fuck with me, man."

"What kind of father do you take me for? Say hi to your mom and enjoy your meal. Well, and enjoy the *night* as well," Manuel said. "Hey, let me give you my cane, gramps!"

"Shut your face, dad!" Cristiano said with a grin on his face as he motioned at the screen.

"Huh?" said a voice in the background, almost drowned out by

colleja—. No me dijiste que mi hijo estaba en Skype, ¡desgraciado!

—¡Hola, mamá! ¿Qué tal? —intentó decir Cristiano soltando una carcajada en lugar de palabras.

En una esquina de la pantalla apareció media cara.

—Cielo, la cámara está allí —dijo Manuel, señalando a la parte superior de la pantalla.

—Ya, ya lo sabía —dijo Juana, para después darle a Manuel en el dedo y recolocar la pantalla para que se le viera. Juana era una mujer baja, de pelo rubio corto y con bastantes arrugas. La expresión de "no-toleraré-gilipolleces-de-nadie" que tenía en ese momento realzaba particularmente cada pliegue de su piel, cada uno de los cuales, en sus propias palabras, había sido causado por sus dos hijos Cristiano y Manuel. De pronto, se le iluminó el rostro en cuanto reconoció a Cristiano en la pantalla.

—¡Hola, cariño! Por favor, prométeme que te cuidarás, ¿de acuerdo? Me muero de miedo de pensar las travesuras que harás por la noche, ¿sabes? —explicó Juana con la seriedad que solamente puede tener una madre.

—Pero bueno, cielo. Yo hice lo mismo a su edad y sobreviví —respondió Manuel.

—¡Oh, claro, dale ánimos! —dijo Juana llena de sarcasmo—. Ya ves, Cristiano, sigue vivo. Pero ¿a qué coste? Ahora tiene encefalograma plano. ¿Quieres acabar como este chiflado?

—¡Oye! —protestó Manuel—. ¿Qué dices?

—Lo que oyes, tonto —insistió Juana.

—No pasa nada, Cristiano, siempre y cuando aparezcas en el curro el lunes —dijo Manuel—. Y llévate a alguna chica al huerto. A mí no me queda más que esta maruja.

—¿Maruja? Te voy a matar, coño —dijo Juana.

—¿Coño? ¿Ves lo que tengo que aguantar, Cristiano? —bromeó

the laughter. A disembodied hand whacked Manuel on the back of the head. "You didn't tell me my own son was on Skype, you bastard!"

"Hey, mom. How are you?" Cristiano tried to say, instead letting out a cackle in place of words.

A face appeared in the corner of the screen, half cut off.

"Honey, the camera's there," Manuel said, pointing towards the top of the screen.

"I knew that," said Juana, hitting Manuel's finger. She readjusted the screen to include her. Juana was a short, well-wrinkled woman with short blonde hair. Her current I-will-not-take-anyone's-shit expression emphasized each crease, which Juana would likely explain to you were the fault of her two sons - Cristiano and Manuel. Suddenly her face brightened as she recognized Cristiano's face in the screen.

"Hi, sweetie. Please promise you'll take care of yourself, all right? Your midnight shenanigans scare me to death, you know," explained Juana, with the seriousness that only a mother can have.

"Oh, come on, honey. I did the same thing at his age and I survived!" responded Manuel.

"Oh, of course. Encourage him," said Juana, her words dripping with sarcasm. "Ya see, Cristiano? He survived, but at what cost? Now he's brain-dead! You want to end up like this lunatic?"

"Hey," Manuel protested. "What are you saying?"

"You heard me, idiot," insisted Juana.

"Just make sure you show up to work on Monday and you'll be fine, Cristiano." said Manuel. "And snag yourself a cutie for me. I'm stuck with this old hag, ya know."

"Hag? I'll kill you, coño[1]," Juana said.

"Coño? See what I put up with, Cristiano?" Manuel joked.

Manuel—. ¡Nunca te cases con una mujer, hijo! ¡Te arruinarán la vida!

—Deberías tomarte esto más en serio o será la última vez que ves el coño de esta 'maruja' —dijo Juana—. Las chicas son mucho más brutas que en nuestra época y se hacen más brutas cada año. Te piden bebidas, las sigues a un bar desconocido en el quinto pino y, de repente, se desvanecen como si fueran fantasmas.

Después de cinco minutos de pelea entre Manuel y Juana, así como un montón de medias verdades/descaradas mentiras por parte de Cristiano, Juana se quedó contenta con el interrogatorio. O al menos eso creían, cuando...

—Si realmente quisieras convencerme de que estás bien, me llamarías más —se lamentó Juana—. Llevas tres meses allí y es la primera vez que oigo de ti.

—La segunda, mamá —respondió Cristiano.

—Excusas, excusas —dijo Juana—. ¿Acaso quieres matar a tu pobre madre?

—No, pero... —intentó explicar Cristiano.

—¡Excusas! —respondió Juana.

—Ya está bien, dale un respiro al chico, cielo —dijo Manuel—. Seguro que ha estado muy ocupado con el trabajo.

—¡Demasiado ocupado como para llamar a su madre! —respondió Juana para luego dirigir su rabia a Cristiano—. ¡Te crié para ser mejor que todo esto!

—Pero cariño... —interrumpió Manuel.

—A mí no me digas cariño —exclamó Juana—. Te juro que a veces me dan ganas de...

—Mamá, te entiendo. Te llamaré más, ¿vale? —le cortó Cristiano.

—¿Me lo prometes? —preguntó Juana.

"Never marry a woman! They will ruin your life!"

"You should take this more seriously or you'll never get any coño from this 'hag' again," said Juana. "Girls are so much more brutal than in our day and they get more so ever year! They'll ask you for drinks, and once you follow them to an unknown bar in the middle of nowhere, suddenly - POOF - they've disappeared into thin air like a couple of ghosts."

After five minutes of fighting between Manuel and Juana and a bunch of half-truths/full-blown lies from Cristiano, Juana became satisfied by her interrogation. Or at least, they thought they had…

"If you really wanted to convince me that you're safe, you'd call more," Juana lamented. "You've been there nearly three months and this is the first I've heard of you!"

"Second, mamá," Cristiano responded.

"Excuses, excuses," Juana said. "You want to kill your poor mother?"

"No, but…" Cristiano tried to explain.

"Excuses!" Juana replied.

"Now give the boy a break, honey," Manuel said, "I'm sure he's been busy with work."

"Too busy to call his mother?!" Juana replied to Manuel, and then redirecting her rage back at Cristiano. "I raised you better than that!"

"But *cariño*…" Manuel butted in.

"Don't *cariño* me," Juana exclaimed. "Sometimes I could just…"

"Ma, I get it. I'll call more, ok?" Cristiano cut in.

"You promise?" Juana asked.

"I swear," Cristiano said.

—Te lo juro —contestó Cristiano.

—Bien —dijo Juana dando por finalizado el interrogatorio ahora que se había salido con la suya—. ¡Ay! Ojalá pudiera enviarte jamón serrano...

—La verdad es que lo tenemos aquí en EE.UU. —dijo Cristiano—. Incluso tiene la etiqueta de *"Elaborado en España"*.

—¿Y croquetas? —preguntó Juana—. No me digas que allí también las hacen, porque seguro que como yo no, y lo sabes.

—¡Ay! Sí que las echo de menos —dijo Cristiano con tal añoranza que se le hizo la boca agua.

—Pues claro —dijo Juana orgullosa—. No tardes demasiado y vuelve a casa para que te haga mis croquetas de jamón y queso roquefort.

—¡Buen plan, mamá! —respondió Cristiano dándole la razón a su madre.

Todo parecía haber vuelto a su cauce hasta que Cristiano se despidió de ellos con un "Japi Jalogüin" y Juana se puso como loca por no saber que hoy era el día de *esa* fiesta. Juana explotó en otra intensa discusión más sobre las payasadas de "American Pie", pero gracias a Dios, Manuel colgó para seguir su discusión con Juana por su cuenta. Cristiano sonrió pensando en la conversación.

Su madre le quería, él ya lo sabía. Pero a veces lo trataba como si fuera uno de sus estudiantes en el instituto de secundaria donde daba clase y Cristiano ya estaba harto de las lecciones. No necesitaba permiso para vivir como quería.

Prefería mucho más charlar con su padre. Aunque quería a su madre, como se supone que cada niño quiere a sus padres, Manuel no era simplemente su padre, también era su mejor amigo. No le atosigaba por cada detalle de su vida. Sí, le daba a Cristiano consejos de vez en cuando, como los que daba a sus pacientes sobre la importancia de usar hilo dental cada noche, pero su padre nunca

Part One: Collisions

"Good," Juana said, immediately ending the interrogation now that she had gotten her way. "Ay, if only I could send you some *jamón serrano*."

"Well, they actually have that in the US," Cristiano said. "Even has *Elaborado en España* right on the package."

"How about *croquetas*?" Juana asked. "And don't tell me they make those too, because no one makes them like me and you know it."

"Oh, I do miss your *croquetas*," Cristiano said wistfully, almost drooling.

"Of course," Juana said, proudly. "So hurry on home, so I can give you the ones with ham and roquefort."

"Sounds good, *mamá*," Cristiano responded in pacifying agreement.

Everything seemed settled until Cristiano said goodbye with a *'Japi Jálogüin*[1]*'* and Juana became frantic, not knowing that today was *that* holiday. Juana exploded in another intensive argument about the shenanigans of *American Pie*, but thank god, Manuel hung up to continue the discussion with Juana on his own. Cristiano laughed, imagining the conversation.

His mother loved him, that much Cristiano knew. But sometimes she treated him like one of her high school students, and Cristiano was tired of the lectures. He did not need permission to live it how he wanted to.

He much preferred chatting with his dad. While he loved his mother just as he supposed every child loved their parents, Manuel wasn't just his father - he was also his best friend. He didn't bother Cristiano about every detail of his life. Sure, he gave Cristiano the occasional suggestion, just like he told his patients to floss every night, but Manuel didn't bust his balls if Cristiano got a cavity.

Regardless, that call reminded Cristiano how much he really

le rompió las pelotas si Cristiano tenía alguna caries.

En cualquier caso, la llamada le recordó a Cristiano cuánto estaba echando de menos España mientras caminaba a la cocina. Llevó su ordenador con adaptador americano y empezó a poner canciones en *Itunes* y a preparar arroz a la cubana. Pero, mientras cocinaba en su espacioso apartamento situado varios pisos sobre el paisaje urbano de Chicago, su mente ya estaba en Madrid.

Está claro que el barrio de Guindalera, lleno de gente estirada y criticona, nunca había sido su lugar favorito. Sin embargo, de alguna manera, pasear por aquellos rincones y calles familiares de sus recuerdos le daba una nostalgia inexplicable por un tipo de vida que nunca nadie en Chicago podría entender. Y, quizá, la propiedad de estos recuerdos, algo que era únicamente suyo, le hacía extrañar un lugar sobre el que había tenido, como poco, sentimientos ambivalentes.

Aún podía recordar a sus amigos en el momento justo enviándoles mensajes por SMS:

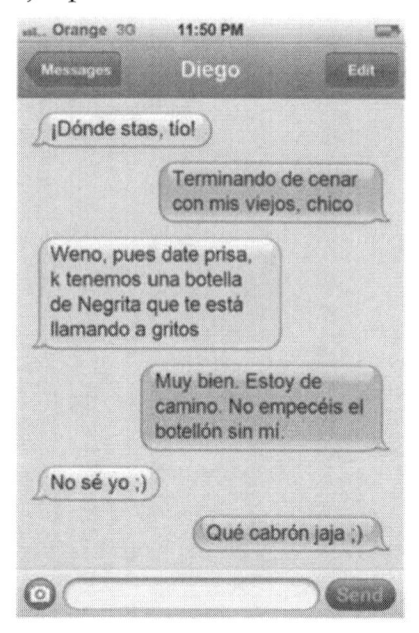

```
Orange 3G          11:50 PM
Messages           Diego           Edit

¡Dónde stas, tío!

              Terminando de cenar
              con mis viejos, chico

Weno, pues date prisa,
k tenemos una botella
de Negrita que te está
llamando a gritos

              Muy bien. Estoy de
              camino. No empecéis el
              botellón sin mí.

No sé yo ;)

              Qué cabrón jaja ;)

                              Send
```

had missed everything in Spain as he walked to the kitchen. He brought his computer with the American adapter with him, and began playing some songs on iTunes as he cooked *arroz a la cubana*. But as he cooked in a spacious apartment several floors above the cityscape of Chicago, his mind was in Madrid.

Of course the Guindalera district had never been his favorite place, filled with stuck-up and slightly judge-y residents. But somehow, walking the familiar streets and hangouts of his memories gave him an unexplainable nostalgia for a place and a way of life that no one he knew in Chicago would ever truly understand. And perhaps it was the ownership of these memories, something that was uniquely his, that made him miss a place about which he had previously felt, at best, ambivalence.

He could even remember his friends sending him a text right then on WhatsApp:

```
Orange 3G    11:50 PM
Messages     Diego            Edit

Where ya at, man!

                Finishing dinner w/ the
                rents, dude.

Well, hurry up. B/c
we've got a bottle of
Negrita with your name
on it

                Alright. On my way.
                Don't start the botellón
                without me.

No promises ;)

                Dick haha ;)
```

Cristiano se terminó las patatas bravas y se ofreció a limpiar el plato. Aunque sabía que su madre haría como si no hubiera escuchado su proposición, al menos él se mostró dispuesto. Al fin y al cabo, Juana era su madre, y Cristiano quería ayudar.

—No, ¡qué va, hijo! —dijo Juana llevando el plato a la cocina—. No lo limpiarás bien del todo. Vete a recoger tu cuarto o sacaré la artillería pesada de un momento a otro.

—¡Vale, vale! —dijo Cristiano de camino a la habitación para prepararse para una noche de fiesta.

—Cristiano, no te tomes las amenazas de tu madre a la ligera —dijo Manuel con rostro impasible—. Prometió convertirme en un buen hombre, y mira qué puto muermo soy ahora.

Juana le dio una colleja que hizo que los tres se quedasen parados intentando no desternillarse de risa. Entonces Manuel y Juana se miraron y en el comedor perdieron el control. Acabaron contagiando sus carcajadas a Cristiano, mientras intentaban recomponerse al verle regresar a la habitación.

—Me voy, que he quedado con Diego y Carlos —dijo Cristiano dirigiéndose a la puerta—. Prometo no hacer mucho ruido al volver a casa.

—Bien —dijo Manuel entre bromas—. Algunos necesitamos dormir bien para pagar por lo manta que eres.

—¡Eh, perdona! —dijo Juana horrorizada—. NO vas a salir con esas pintas.

—¿Cómo? —dijo Cristiano.

—¿No has visto que estamos a 13 grados? No merece la pena pillar un resfriado por lucir músculos para las chavalas —exclamó Juana—. ¡Ponte una chaqueta, por Dios!

—Pero si... —comenzó Cristiano.

Juana le fulminó con la mirada que hizo que dejase su frase a

Part One: Collisions

Cristiano finished off his *patatas bravas,* and offered to clean his dish. While he knew that his mother wouldn't hear of it, he at least liked to offer. Juana was his mother, after all, and he wanted to at least try to help out.

"No, of course not, *hijo,*" Juana said, taking the dish away to the kitchen. "You won't clean it right. Just clean your room, or else I'm going in there with heavy machinery."

"Ok, ok," Cristiano said, on the way to his room to freshen up for a night out.

"Cristiano, don't take your mother's threats idly," Manuel said with a straight face "She promised to make a proper man out of me, and look at me now! Boring as fuck."

Juana slapped him over the head. The three of them all stopped what they were doing trying to hold in their laughter. Then Manuel and Juana looked at each other in the eyes and lost it in the dining room. The laughter spread like a ripple effect to Cristiano, and they all tried to recompose themselves as Cristiano came back in the room.

"Well, I'm off to meet Diego and Carlos," Cristiano said as he headed towards the door. "I promise to be quieter when I come home this time."

"Good," Manuel said, half-joking. "Some of us need a good night's sleep to pay for your lazy ass."

"Excuse me," said Juana sharply. "You are NOT going out in that."

"What?" Cristiano said.

"It's 60 degrees outside! Showing off your muscles for some girl is not worth catching a cold," Juana exclaimed. "Put on a jacket, for God's sake."

"But ma..." Cristiano started.

medio terminar y que Manuel sonriera, como espectador de este cómico intercambio de impresiones.

—De acuerdo□—dijo Cristiano ante la derrota.

—Así es mi chico —dijo Juana—. Ten cuidado y no hagas nada que yo no haría.

—¿Pero te crees que puede hacer milagros? —dijo Manuel.

Juana se volvió para sermonearle mientras Cristiano salía. Cogió la línea cuatro en Diego de León y, a pesar de tener bono de estudiante, saltó el torno. El trayecto fue bastante coñazo, porque le había tocado sentarse en uno de los pocos trenes viejos que aún quedaban en la línea del Metro. La verdad es que podría haber esperado a otro más nuevo, pero a medianoche habría tenido que esperar demasiado tiempo. Fue entonces cuando recordó cuando todos eran así, unos ocho años atrás.

Cristiano trató de recordar dónde estaba allá por 2004, pero aquel vagón destartalado no hacía más que enturbiar los recuerdos de su pubertad. Unos jóvenes de catorce años. Había un chico, una chica. Los tres entrando por el invernadero de Atocha a las siete de la mañana. No, las 7:30. No podía recordar el porqué de levantarse tan pronto ese día, pero allí estaban, poco a poco bajando a los andenes. Y pocos minutos después, una explosión a lo lejos, pero que se sintió muy cerca. Alguien le agarró la mano. ¿Fue el chico? ¿Fue la chica? ¿Fueron los dos a la vez? Sintió miedo, pero a la vez se sintió seguro, y no podía recordar de quién era la mano que había acallado sus temores mientras perdía el conocimiento por la impresión dentro de aquella abarrotada estación. *Bum, bum*.

—Próxima estación...Argüelles —dijo una voz enlatada que alternaba entre una voz grave y masculina y una voz femenina y alegre—. Correspondencia con líneas... tres y seis.

Cristiano se bajó del tren y salió de la pequeña estación en dirección a la Calle Princesa. Pasó por delante de tiendas cerradas, del Corte Inglés, de uno de los muchos cines de la ciudad, y de

Part One: Collisions

Juana just gave Cristiano a silent stare that stopped him in mid-sentence. Manuel grinned silently, enjoying the exchange.

"Fine," Cristiano said in defeat.

"That's my boy," Juana said. "Now stay safe and don't do anything I wouldn't."

"What is he, a miracle worker?" Manuel said.

Juana turned around to lecture him as Cristiano made his way out the door. He grabbed line four at Diego de León, jumping over the turnstile, even though he had a student pass. His ride over was rather annoying, as he had grabbed one of the few old trains that was still left. He remembered when they were all like that, almost ten years ago. He could have waited for a newer one, but at midnight, it would have been too long of a wait.

Cristiano tried to remember where he had been in 2004, but the rickety old train only jumbled up his memories of puberty. A couple of fourteen year olds. There was a guy, a girl. The Atocha gardens at seven in the morning. No, at 7:30. He couldn't remember why he had gotten up so early that morning, but there they were, heading down to the bus station. And then, a couple minutes later, an explosion from far away that felt all too close. Someone had grabbed his hand. Was it the guy? Was it the girl? Was it both? He felt fear, but he also felt safety, and he couldn't remember which hand had silenced his fears as he faded in between the tall palm trees of the crowded bus station. *Boom, Boom*

"*Próxima estación...Argüelles,*" a prerecorded voice said, alternating between a deep manly voice and a cheery womanly voice. "*Correspondencia con líneas...tres y seis.*"

Cristiano got off the train and made his way out of the small station to *la Calle Princesa*. He walked past the closed shops, the Corte Inglés, a random theater, and a bunch of bars. Slowly he made his way to the Templo de Debod, where his friends had already broken out the tall, thin, clear, recyclable cups.

unos cuantos bares. Poco a poco llegó al Templo de Debod, donde sus amigos ya habían sacado todos los vasos de tubo de plástico reciclable.

—¿No os había dicho que me esperarais, cabrones? —dijo Cristiano.

—¿Hasta cuándo? ¿Hasta la seis de la mañana? —dijo Diego.

—¿O hasta que nos salgan canas? —añadió Carlos.

—¡Qué os den! —dijo Cristiano en broma, empujando a Carlos mientras cogía la botella de Negrita de Diego y se lo bebía a palo seco.

—Tío, tienes un problema —dijo Diego.

—¿Qué pasa? ¿Ahora tengo que estar sobrio con lo borrachos que estáis? —dijo Cristiano riéndose—. ¡Venga, no me jodáis!

—Sigue siendo culpa tuya, maricón —dijo Diego en broma.

Todos se partieron de risa por un rato y, finalmente, Diego acabó agarrando la botella de alcohol para rellenar su vaso. Carlos echó un buen trago de su copa y retomaron la conversación sobre tías y fútbol. Sin embargo, al poco de comenzar a hablar de las buenas tetas de Penelope Cruz, empezaron una discusión sobre el Madrid y el Barça en la que Carlos y Diego intentaban defender a su equipo.

—El Barça no vale una mierda —dijo Diego—. Tenemos a uno de los mejores futbolistas del mundo.

—¡El Barça tiene un equipo bien formado!— dijo Carlos—. Tenemos a Messi, Xavi, Puyol. ¿Y vosotros qué tenéis? ¿A la maricona de Cristiano Ronaldo?

—Venga, si tú nos envidias —dijo Diego.

—Ya podéis tener cuidado con Javier —dijo Cristiano.

—¿El del Athletic? ¿Por qué? Sólo es de Bilbao —dijo Diego.

—Sí, pero es bueno en ataque y defensa y es una fiera en el

Part One: Collisions

"Didn't I tell you fuckers to wait for me?" Cristiano said.

"Till when? Six AM?" Diego said.

"Or till we're all old and dead?" Carlos chimed in. He mimed walking with a cane.

"Fuck you, bastards," Cristiano joked, shoving Carlos. He grabbed the *Negrita* from Diego and took a swig of the black rum straight from the bottle.

"*Tío*, you have a problem," Diego said.

"What, because now I gotta catch up to you guys?" Cristiano laughed. "Now whose fault is that?"

"Still you, *maricón*," Carlos joked.

They all laughed for a while and Diego stole back the alcohol to add some more to his own glass. Carlos took a big swig from his own cup and they started talking about *fútbol* and chicks. But mid-conversation about the great rack on Penelope Cruz, they started to get in an argument about Madrid and *Barça,* and Carlos and Diego started arguing who was better.

"*Barça* is a piece of shit," Diego said. "We've got one of the best players in the world."

"*Barça* has a well rounded team!" Carlos said. "We have Messi, Xavi, Puyol, and you have what? That cocky bitch Ronaldo?"

"Please, you're just jealous," Diego said

"But you all better watch out for Javier," Cristiano said.

"Why? He's just from Bilbao," Diego said.

"Yeah, but he's a great attacker, defender, and incredibly aggressive," Carlos said.

"Aggressive? In bed as well, I hope," Cristiano said with a wink.

campo —dijo Carlos.

—¿Una fiera? Espero que en la cama también —dijo Cristiano con un guiño.

—¡Pero bueno, tío! —dijeron Carlos y Diego mientras le empujaban.

Entonces Diego levantó la vista a las ruinas egipcias iluminadas, corrió hasta la fuente donde estaban y les hizo un corte de mangas. Carlos y Cristiano le echaron una mirada y después corrieron tras él, intentando empujarle al agua. Al no poder, decidieron hacer lo mismo. Ninguno sabía la razón, ni por qué se peleaban, pero se sentían bien en su estado de embriaguez.

—¡Joder!, si son casi las dos ya —dijo Carlos.

—Ya podemos ir tirando al *Tupperware* —dijo Diego después de pegarle otro trago a la bebida.

De camino hacia allí, los chicos dejaron los vasos, la botella de ron y la bolsa del chino en la acera haciendo compañía a aquel cementerio de cristales rotos y plásticos que se adueñaba de Madrid después de medianoche y que, por arte de magia, desaparecía al día siguiente por la mañana.

Después de andar entre esas calles llenas de basura, pillaron el último metro por los pelos y, al llegar a Tribunal, hicieron cola para entrar a un pub decorado con graffitis e imágenes tan familiares como ridículas de diferentes colores rojos y rosas fluorescentes, y la palabra *ROCK* escrita en mayúsculas de color verde por encima. A los diez minutos de hacer cola y después de que el segurata les echase una mirada escéptica, lograron cruzar el umbral. Al entrar, pasaron la multitud pintada en la pared con escenas de personas bebiendo, bailando y jugando al billar. La imagen parecía reflejar el bar como un espejo cubista en la memoria de Cristiano. Si bien anteriormente no le había prestado demasiada atención después de haber estado allí cientos de veces, en ese momento todo le parecía de lo más surrealista.

Part One: Collisions

"Dude!" Carlos and Diego said, playfully shoving him.

Diego then looked up at the lighted Egyptian ruins, ran up to the pool they were in and gave it the middle finger. Carlos and Cristiano both gave each other a look and then ran after, trying to shove Diego in. After failing, they both decided to do the same. None of them was really sure why, nor what they were defying, but it felt right in their drunken stupor. Suddenly Carlos looked at his watch.

"Oh fuck, it's almost two," he said.

"Shit. We'd better make our way to *Tupperware*," Diego said after another swig.

As Diego, Carlos, and Cristiano headed out, they all dropped their cups, the bottle of rum, and the bag from the *Chino*[1] on the sidewalk to join the graveyard of broken glass and deformed plastic that appeared in Madrid after midnight, and magically disappeared before noon the next day.

After wading through the trash on the streets, just barely catching the last subway of the night, and arriving in Tribunal, they stood in line at a club decorated with graffiti and ridiculous-yet-familiar images in various shades of red and florescent pink, with the word ROCK written in large green letters at the top. After waiting ten minutes or so in line, and after the bouncer gave them a skeptical once-over, they entered the threshold. They passed the crowd painted on the wall with scenes of people drinking, dancing and playing pool on their way to the second floor. The image seemed to reflect the bar like a Cubist mirror in Cristiano's memory. It hadn't fazed him before, as he had passed it a million times, but in his memories, it seemed so surreal.

Cristiano and his friends climbed the stairs with a buzzed swagger, as if they were VIPs. And with that, the nightly competition between Cristiano, Diego, and Carlos began: find the hottest, most prudish girl in the bar and win her over before the

Cristiano y sus amigos subieron las escaleras con un contoneo entonado, como si fueran VIP. Y así empezó la competición entre Carlos, Cristiano y Diego para encontrar a la tía más buena, la que más se hiciera la estrecha, y conquistarla antes que los otros.

Era un juego en el que Cristiano nunca perdía, él era un experto. Había aprendido a decirle a cada una lo que quería oír. No es que contara mentiras exactamente, sino que exageraba sus historias sobre sus acciones caritativas y sus fracasos amorosos, en este mundo obsesionado con el sexo, con tal convicción que resultaban de lo más creíbles. ¡*Vaya cachondeo!*

Él no tenía la culpa de que todas esas chicas fueran tan tontas como para tragarse sus cuentos. Eran adultas, mayores de edad, no niñas inocentes que acababan de aprender que "papá pone una semillita en mamá'. Si todavía no entendían el concepto de un rollo de una noche a estas alturas, que no hubieran estado en un bar. O por lo menos, eso es lo que se dijo a sí mismo.

Además, el juego era una adicción para Cristiano. Él sexo era una ventaja, seguro. Sin embargo, a Cristiano lo que mas le gustaba era la descarga de adrenalina de poder encandilar a cualquiera y salir corriendo en cuanto se cansase; dependían completamente de él y sus anhelos.

Claro, a veces lo que había en el bar le aburría, o eran feas o era demasiado fácil seducir. Pero le daba igual. Todavía podría ir a una discoteca con sus amigos, bailar hasta olvidar todo lo demás en un estupor hedonista, desayunar, y regresar a casa sobre las ocho. Y si ya estuviera muriéndose de hambre, siempre podría ir a Chueca, en vez de bailar con sus amigos, para pillar cacho con un hombre en el *Delirio*. Siempre y cuando el chico se largase antes de que se despertaran sus padres. Ellos no tenían por qué saber de los tejemanejes de su hijo, mejor sería que vivieran en la ignorancia.

Cristiano dejó de soñar despierto cuando el arroz empezó a quemarse. Rápidamente apagó el fuego y apartó el cazo para salvar lo que pudo, mientras intentaba desvanecer el humo abriendo la

other two.

It was a game Cristiano never lost - he was an expert. He had learned how to tell each one what she wanted to hear. It wasn't so much that he told them lies—rather, they heard his passionate exaggerations about his generosity to the poor and his failed attempts at finding love in this world obsessed with sex. *What a joke!*

It wasn't his fault that the chicks he met were idiots that believed every word of it. They were adults - consenting adults - not innocent kids who had just learned the concept of what "daddies do when they love mommies very much." If they still didn't understand the concept of a one-night stand, they shouldn't have been at a bar. Or at least, that was what he told himself.

Besides, the game was addictive to Cristiano. The sex was a perk, for sure. But more than anything, Cristiano loved the adrenaline rush of being able to make anyone fall for him and to leave on his terms when he lost interest. They were completely dependent on him and his desires.

Of course, sometimes everyone in the bar would bore him, either because they were ugly or too easy to seduce. But it didn't matter to him. He still could just go to a club with his friends to dance until he forgot everything else in a hedonistic stupor, get breakfast, and head home around eight AM. And if he were absolutely starving of a sexual hunger, he could always go to Chueca instead and find some man-meat at Delirio. Well, so long as the dude left his house before his parents woke up. His parents didn't need to know about his temporary male trysts - what they didn't know couldn't hurt them.

Cristiano woke up from his daydream when the rice began to burn. He quickly turned off the stove and took the pot off to try to salvage as much as he could. He opened a window to dissipate the smoke before it wafted up to the fire alarm. When the smoke

ventana antes de que llegara al detector. Cuando se disipó la humareda, vio el arroz, el cual le pareció bastante pasable para comer. No necesitaba un plato de alta cocina, sino algo que meterse en la barriga antes del pedo de esa noche. De repente, la canción *Danza Kuduro* en *Itunes* cambió a *Bohemian Rhapsody* y, recordando las letras, se puso a cantarlas en su cabeza, desdibujando las líneas entre la vida real y la fantasía por un momento único.

Fue a la nevera a coger un pincho de tortilla de patata que sobró el día anterior. Cristiano llevó su plato torcido a la mesa mientras David entraba para tomar leche.

—Tío, ¿qué comes? —dijo David justo antes de ponerse a beber del cartón.

—Un poco de arroz y tortilla —dijo Cristiano antes de cortar el huevo que estaba encima, y la dorada yema desapareciera entre los recovecos del arroz teñido de naranja.

—¿Tortilla? Tío, no tienes ni idea —dijo David riéndose con malicia, al ir a echarle un ojo al plato de Cristiano—. Las tortillas se hacen con harina para burritos.

—¿Eres mexicano ahora? ¡Andale, güey! —bromeó Cristiano dándole un codazo a David—. Todo el mundo sabe que los españoles hacen tortilla con huevo y patatas.

—¡Que te follen, tío! —dijo David con una sonrisa y flexionando sus músculos a lo Hulk Hogan—. Ya estamos en América.

—¡A ti primero! —respondió Cristiano mientras David volvía a su cuarto.

—Así lo haré —respondió David, haciendo un gesto como si se hiciera una paja, un inmaduro insulto americano para Cristiano—. Me voy —dijo David con saludo militar mientras giraba a su cuarto y volvía a beber leche del cartón.

Cristiano le ignoró y empezó a simular que tocaba la guitarra, acompañando a Brian May, regresando así a su karaoke

Part One: Collisions

cleared, he saw the rice was tolerable enough to eat. It wasn't like he needed a gourmet dish anyway - just enough to coat his stomach before drinking tonight.

Suddenly, the song *Danza Kuduro* on iTunes changed to Bohemian Rhapsody. Remembering the words, he broke out into song in his head, blurring the lines of real life and fantasy for a singular moment.

He went to the fridge to take out a piece of leftover *tortilla española* from yesterday. Cristiano brought his lopsided plate to the table, as David came in to get the milk.

"Dude, what are you eating?" David said, directly before he started to chug the milk.

"A *tortilla* and some rice, dude," Cristiano replied. He cut the egg on top and watched the golden yolk disappear between the crevices of the orange-tinged rice.

"*Tortilla?* Dude, I don't think you understand," David laughed, smugly, as he went to examine Cristiano's plate. "That's made with flour for *burritos.*"

"What are you, Mexican? *Andale, güey,*" Cristiano joked, playfully shoving David. "Everyone knows Spanish people make *tortilla* from egg and potatoes."

"Fuck you, man," David said with a grin, adding jokingly flexing like Hulk Hogan. "This is America."

"Fuck you too," Cristiano responded. While David returned to his room.

"Will do," David replied, making a masturbatory motion as an immature insult to Cristiano. "David out." David saluted, turned towards his room, and chugged some more of the milk as he left.

Cristiano ignored him and started to play air guitar, accompanying Brian May as he returned to his karaoke improv. He

improvisado. Quería olvidarse de sus responsabilidades y dejarse llevar por la música como Freddy Mercury. No estaba infeliz, sino frustrado. No por fuera, claro. Se sentía un poco solo, pero no era tan malo y seguramente lo podría soportar.

Cristiano resolvía estos problemas compartiendo partes de sí mismo con cada uno de sus amigos. Por ejemplo, David entendía los problemas de Cristiano con las mujeres dependientes. Javier, un colega chicano, sabía lo que era sentirse frustrado al no poder expresar algunos sentimientos intraducibles, como cuando se tomó un puente improvisado fingiendo estar enfermo el viernes antes del finde americano del Día del Trabajo. Y con Lena, aunque odiaba admitirlo y no se lo diría nunca en voz alta a la listilla alemana, podía discutir las costumbres europeas que los dos echaban de menos. Y es que hablar de sexo entre susurros, como si fuera un pecado, se convirtió en algo aburrido muy rápido.

Cristiano acabó el pincho de tortilla, dejando los restos de arroz y ajo quemado a un lado. Regresó a la cocina y dejó los platos sucios en el fregadero. No pasaría nada. Los fregaría durante la resaca del próxima día. O si tuviera mucha suerte, la alemana tendría un ataque de nervios y ella misma los lavaría. Bueno, Cristiano tenía la opinión de que si ella tenía tantas manías que ni siquiera podía esperar un día, bien merecido lo tendría.

Tras sacar los ingredientes necesarios de los armarios, empezó a mezclar la sangría para la fiesta de Halloween que iban a montar Cristiano y sus amigos. Cortó el limón y lo añadió al cuenco de líquido rojo que tenía ante él. Había convencido a los demás de que sería la mejor elección, explicando que la palabra *'sangría'* viene del término *'sangre'*, y no hay nada como beber sangre para Halloween.

Sus motivos no eran lógicos si no más bien egoístas, en parte porque la sangría sabía a zumo y les subiría a todos rapidísimo. Pero a decir verdad, era más una cuestión de que Cristiano estaba harto de cerveza de mierda. Y el americano, David, no ponía pegas - era su colega. Pero la alemana vivía discutiendo simplemente por

wanted to forget his responsibilities and disappear in Freddy Mercury's music. It's not that he was unhappy, but rather frustrated. Not outwardly, of course. He almost felt alone, but it wasn't that bad. Surely he could handle it.

Cristiano solved this by sharing parts of himself with each of his friends. For example, David understood Cristiano's problems with clingy bitches. Javier, his *Chicano* colleague, knew his frustrations at times with wanting to say phrases that were not translatable, like that time he took an impromptu *Puente*[1] by faking sick the Friday before the American Labor Day weekend. And Lena, although he hated to admit it and never would say it aloud to that smart-ass German, could discuss European customs that they both missed. Because discussing sex in a hushed tone as if it were a sin got really boring really quickly.

Cristiano finished off his piece of *tortilla* and set the leftover burnt rice and garlic aside. He went back to the kitchen and left his dirty dishes in the sink. No big deal. He would wash them during his hangover the next day. Or, if he was really lucky, the German girl would have a nervous breakdown and clean them herself. In Cristiano's opinion, if she was so OCD that she couldn't let it go for one day, she deserved it.

Taking the necessary ingredients from the cupboards, he began to mix the *Sangria* for the Halloween party that Cristiano and his roommates were throwing that evening. He cut a lemon and added it to the large bowl of red liquid in front of him. He had convinced the others that it would be the best choice, explaining that the word 'Sangria' comes from the term 'sangre,' and there was nothing like drinking blood for Halloween.

His real reasons were a lot less logical and a lot more selfish. Part of it was that *Sangria* tasted like juice and would get everyone drunk super quickly. But to tell the truth, Cristiano was also really tired of shit beer. The American, David, didn't question his motives - they were bros. But the German girl was skeptical. She was

discutir. La aguafiestas de turno que siempre tenía que hacer preguntas.

—¿Qué pasaría si se cayera la bebida al suelo? Es nuestra casa, y yo no quiero servir vino tinto a personas que no conozco que puedan manchar la alfombra. Y además... Bla bla bla, esto y lo otro.

—¡Qué mojigata! —pensó Cristiano, mientras acababa de trocear los melocotones y las naranjas echándolos en la mezcla con un montón de azúcar.

Entonces abrió la bolsa de azúcar y empezó a echarla directamente en el cuenco. Mientras la disolvía lentamente, la miraba flotar por arriba poco antes de ser invadida por el vino. Al hundirse en el fondo, no pudo evitar gritar "¡azúcar!", como si fuera un Café cubano. La probó y decidió que podría salirse con la suya echando unos cuantos chupitos a escondidas de orujo a la sangría. La probó de nuevo.

—¡Mmm! Dulce de manera peligrosa —pensó Cristiano—. Me quedan unas horas hasta que podamos empezar esta sexy locura.

Mientras tanto, puso su bol de sangre en la nevera y fue a ducharse, afeitarse, y ponerse el disfraz de Drácula. Al fin y al cabo, le era difícil mantenerse en su papel de príncipe azul, pero valdría la pena esperar.

***

—¡Chicos, bajad el volumen! —gruñó David por encima del bullicio y la música de fondo al entrar por la puerta con una sudadera de fútbol—. Los vecinos dicen que llamarán a la policía como sigamos así.

Todos resoplaron.

—¿En serio? —dijo Cristiano entre dientes—. No son ni las diez.

—Se ve que hay gente que duerme por las noches —apostilló Lena sin perder el ritmo—. Y, sobre todo, un miércoles.

—Y hay gente que folla —dijo Cristiano a Lena desde el grupo

Part One: Collisions

always the buzz-kill; she had to question everything!

"What if the drink fell? This is our place and I don't want to serve red wine to people I don't know that could stain the carpet. And besides, blah blah blah, this and that..."

"What a tight-ass!" Cristiano thought, as he finished cutting up the peaches and oranges and threw them in the mix.

He then opened a bag of sugar and started pouring it directly into the bowl. As it slowly dissolved, he watched it float on top for a little while before it was swallowed by the wine. As it sank to the bottom of the tart mixture, he couldn't help but yell *'azúcar!'* as if it were a Café Cubano. He tasted it and decided he could get away with sneaking a clandestine swig of brandy or two. He tasted the *sangría* again.

"Mmm. Dangerously sweet," Cristiano thought. "Just a couple hours and we can get this hot mess started." Meanwhile, he put his blood in the fridge and went to take a shower, shave, and change into his Dracula costume. Playing the role of the knight in shining armor was hard work, but it would be well worth it.

***

"Hey guys, keep it down," David grunted over the chatter and background music as he returned from the door in his football jersey. "The neighbors say they're calling the cops next time."

There was a simultaneous groaning.

"Seriously?" Cristiano mumbled under his breath in disbelief. "It's not even ten."

"Well, some people sleep at night," Lena said, not missing a beat. "Especially on a Wednesday."

"And some people get laid," Cristiano said to Lena from the middle of David's group of high school bros. Lena sighed as Cristiano got a round of high fives.

de los colegas del instituto de David. Lena suspiró hastiada mientras Cristiano estaba ocupado chocando los cinco con todo el grupo.

Por su puesto que bajaron unos minutos el volumen, pero entonces ya fuera por el alcohol o quizá por una historia tan interesante e importante como para revelarla susurrando, volvieron a hablar al mismo nivel. Eso es la magia de una fiesta, al fin y al cabo - colegas y personas que acabas de conocer, con quienes ayer podrías aburrirte, ahora se transforman en criaturas fantásticas, caballeros andantes y bellas damiselas como en un cuento de hadas. Por una noche, todos entienden la locura de Alonso Quijano, incluso la razón de la sinrazón.

Cristiano, por otro lado, estaba frustrado. Le encantaban las buenas fiestas, pero esta era un desastre. Quizá no era la palabra adecuada, ya que en esta situación, un desastre podría haber dado algo de vida a este muermo de quedada. En teoría parecía el plan perfecto: cócteles, gente de todo el mundo y canciones sacadas de la lista de "Los 40 Principales"; sin embargo, en la práctica, era un infierno.

Las amigas de Lena habían llegado primero, a las 20:30 en punto. Se saludaron entre ellas con unos "Hallos" y "Grüß Gotts", besando a cada uno, ligeramente, como duques y duquesas en un baile de máscaras, cuidándose de no revelar las identidades de los demás, como si las llevasen para convertir sus personalidades aburridas en algo, *aunque fuera una cosa,* en interesante.

—¡Qué horterada!— pensaba con una sonrisa que enmascaraba sus verdaderos sentimientos—. Llevan un disfraz de carnaval para Halloween.

—Encantada de conocerte —dijo la chica alta y delgada que llevaba un vestido amarillo mostaza que resultaba demasiado formal.

—No te hagas la tonta, Sissi —dijo la morena algo más bajita y

Part One: Collisions

Of course they kept it down for a couple of minutes, but then whether it was because of the alcohol, or maybe because of a story too interesting and important to reveal whispering, they returned to speaking at the same level. That's the magic of a party, after all - colleagues and people you've just met, who yesterday would have bored you, transform themselves into fantastical creatures, knights and damsels of yore like a fairytale. For a night, they all understood the insanity of Alonso Quijano, including the reason of unreason.

Cristiano, on the other hand, was frustrated. He loved a good party, but this one was a disaster-or perhaps that was the wrong word. An actual disaster might have spiced up this dull get-together. Sure, on paper this would look like a fun party - cocktails, people from all over the world, and top-40 music tracks. But the devil was in the details.

Lena's friends had been the first to arrive, at 8:30 on the dot. They greeted each other with their *"Hallos"* and *"Grüß Gotts,"* kissing each other softly on the cheek like dukes and duchesses at a *mascarade*, taking care not to reveal their identities. It was as if they wore masks to change their boring personalities into something, *anything,* that was interesting.

"How tacky," he thought, with a smile that hid his true sentiments. "Arriving on time to a party. And wearing carnival outfits for Halloween."

"Pleased to make your acquaintance," said the tall, skinny brunette in a mustard-yellow dress, far too politely.

"Don't be so coy, Sissi," said the slightly plumper, shorter brunette with wearing a blonde wig right next to her in a large frilly white dress as the group broke into laughter.

"And don't lose your head, Antoinette," Sissi responded, and the group roared.

"And who are you supposed to be?" Cristiano asked the hot bottle blonde in the backless green dress.

rellenita que llevaba una peluca rubia y un vestido muy recargado y arrugado de color blanco.

—Y no pierdas la cabeza, Antoinette —respondió Sissi, y las chicas se volvieron locas.

—Y ¿quién se supone que eres tú? —preguntó Cristiano a la rubia guapa de revista que llevaba un vestido verde con la espalda al aire.

—Alguien que no te interesa, guarro —le cortó Lena, que llevaba un vestido verde con volantes.

—¡Aguafiestas! —respondió Cristiano.

—¡Subnormal! —dijo Lena.

—¿Dónde está la bebida? —preguntó Sissi, tratando de cambiar de tema de una manera bastante obvia.

Lena y Cristiano las llevaron de mala gana hasta la cocina, donde estaba esperando David, y donde las presentaciones volvieron a empezar.

—Y yo soy el Rey Fritz —dijo el esbelto y delgado chico que llevaba un 'trench' azul que le favorecía, ante la atónita mirada de Cristiano y David.

—Sí, claro, muy bien tío —dijo David.

—Un placer, su majestad —dijo Cristiano.

Lena suspiró y volvió a intentar cambiar de tema.

—Dejando a este Voltaire de lado, ¿habéis oído hablar del Mecanismo Europeo de Estabilidad que se acaba de firmar? —preguntó Lena.

—Sí, ya era hora —dijo Marie Antoinette.

—No, ¿qué es? —preguntó la rubia de verde.

Y así Lena comenzó su sermón: que si la economía alemana salvó a Grecia, que si hay que proteger los bienes... Lo justo y

Part One: Collisions

"None of your business, horndog," Lena cut in. She was dressed in a frilly red dress.

"Spoilsport," Cristiano replied.

"Asshole," Lena said.

"So where are the drinks?" Sissi asked, obviously trying to change the subject.

Lena and Cristiano begrudgingly brought them into the kitchen, where David was seated, and the introduction process began anew.

"And I'm King Fritz," said the tall, thin, well-groomed guy in a blue trench coat that complimented his figure, to a confused Cristiano and David.

"Yeah, cool, man," David said.

"Nice to meet you, your majesty," Cristiano said.

Lena just sighed and tried to change the subject.

"Voltaire over here aside, did you guys hear about the European Stability Mechanism they just signed?" Lena asked.

"Yeah, about time," Marie Antoinette said.

"No, what is it?" asked the blonde girl in the green dress.

And so Lena went on her spiel about the German economy, saving Greece this and protecting assets that. It was enough to drive Cristiano away. Economics at a party was enough, but he was sure this whole economic crisis was that idiot Merkel's fault anyway. So Cristiano and David, who was also incredibly confused, sat over on the couch with their glasses and talked about Metallica.

After around fifteen minutes had passed, there was another knock on the door. David's phone buzzed, and he looked at it and stood up in surprise.

necesario para espantar a Cristiano. Hablar de economía en una fiesta ya era demasiado, aunque Cristiano estaba convencido de que toda esta crisis era culpa de la imbécil de Merkel. Evitando estos debates, Cristiano y un David que parecía muy confundido, se sentaron en el sofá con sus copas a hablar de *Metallica*.

Casi un cuarto de hora después, volvieron a llamar a la puerta, y David vio un mensaje en su móvil que hizo que se levantase sorprendido.

—¡Mierda! —dijo David entre risas.

—¡Déjame pasar, cabrón!— dijo una voz estridente.

—¡Perdóname, Jenny! —dijo David abriendo la puerta a una chica de ojos verdes, rubia y con coletas que llevaba un disfraz de dos piezas de enfermera tres tallas más pequeño.

Lena, Marie Antoinette, Sissi y la chica de verde trataron de disimular su asombro. El rey Fritz se esforzaba al máximo por apartar la vista, pero Cristiano le pilló mirando el atuendo tipo bikini de Jenny.

—¡Hace un frío que pela! —dijo Jenny.

—Tú lo que necesitas es alcohol, loca —sonrió David.

—¡Pues claro! —dijo Jenny con una mirada asesina.

—Si me permites —dijo Cristiano.

—Parece que aquí hay al menos un caballero —dijo Jenny.

—¡Serás guarra!—dijo David de broma.

—Cristiano Moreno-Torres —dijo él.

—Jenny Lief —dijo ella.

Cristiano siguió ligando con ella mientras las alemanas continuaban inmersas en su debate político. De vez en cuando David intentaba captar a Jenny con preguntas casuales sobre su ciudad, pero Cristiano era el que tenía las riendas de la conversación.

Part One: Collisions

"Oh shit," David said, laughing.

"Asshole, let me in!" a shrill voice said.

"Sorry, Jenny," David said as he opened the door. The girl standing there wore a two-piece nurse's outfit that was three sizes too small. She had a blonde ponytail and childlike green eyes.

Lena, Marie Antoinette, Sissi, and the green-dressed girl all tried to hide their disbelief. King Fritz was trying his best to look away, but Cristiano saw how he kept glancing back to Jenny's nearly bikini costume.

"It is freezing out there," Jenny said.

"You just need some liquor, crazy," David laughed.

"Duh," Jenny said with a glare.

"Please, allow me," Cristiano said.

"Wow, at least someone here's a gentleman," Jenny said.

"Bitch," David joked back.

"Cristiano Moreno-Torres," he said.

"Jenny Lief," she replied.

Cristiano continued to flirt with her as the Germans continued their conversations about politics. David occasionally tried to catch up with Jenny with the odd question about home, but Cristiano led the conversation.

"So, do ju have a boyfriend?" Cristiano asked, feigning a thick Spanish accent. But just before she could answer, there was another knock at the door.

"Yo, dude. Let us in," two gruff, disembodied voices said.

"Hold your tits," David replied.

Two large guys with big guts, big arms, and buzzed heads came in. One was dressed as a man riding a mustang, with the head of

—¿Tienes novio? —preguntó Cristiano fingiendo un acento español muy forzado. Pero justo antes de que contestara, volvieron a llamar a la puerta.

—Tíos, ¡dejadnos pasar! —gritaron dos voces ásperas.

—Parad el carro —respondió David.

Entraron dos hombres rapados fuertes con buenas barrigas y brazos bien grandes. Uno de ellos iba vestido como un conductor de un Mustang, y de su entrepierna sobresalía la cabeza del conocido caballo como si de una polla enorme se tratase. El otro llevaba una camiseta que decía "WOLF PACK" con un coyote que aullaba.

—¡Ya está aquí el alma de la fiesta! —dijo el Mustang, chocando los cinco con David mientras Jenny se reía.

Cristiano les miró incrédulo a la vez que el grupo de Lena echó un ojo y retomó su conversación.

—Tío, la tengo como un caballo. ¿Lo pillas? —dijo el Mustang.

—El Sr. Davidson quiere decir que cree que la tiene grande —dijo Jenny.

—¿Qué lo creo? Ya te gustaría a ti probarla —dijo Brandon.

—¿Yo? ¡Ni muerta! —dijo Jenny empujándole en broma.

—Y él es Justin Van Gorden —dijo David.

—Querrás decir que soy Zach Galifanakis —dijo Justin mientras sus amigos le chocaban los cinco por su disfraz sencillo del actor americano con barba.

—Pues, este tipo de aquí —dijo David, señalando a Brandon— era mi receptor. Justin era mi *open end*—.

Cristiano reprimió la risilla por los nombres en inglés, que le sonaron más a posiciones sexuales que posiciones deportivas.

—Y este es mi "amigacho", Cristiano —dijo David.

the illustrious steed emerging from his crotch as if it were a giant dick. The other wore a shirt that said 'WOLF PACK' with a howling coyote on it.

"The party has arrived!" the Mustang said. David high-fived both of them as Jenny laughed.

Cristiano stared blankly at them, as Lena's group gave a quick glance and then went back to their conversation.

"Dude, hung as a horse. Get it?" the Mustang said.

"It means Davidson here thinks he has a big dick," Jenny said.

"Think? You just jealous you haven't got with this," Brandon said.

"Ugh, as if." Jenny pushed him playfully.

"And this is Justin Van Gorden," David said.

"You mean I'm Zach Galifianakis!" Justin said. The dudes gave him a round of high fives for his simple costume of the bearded American actor.

"So this guy here," David said, pointing to Brandon, "was my wide receiver. Justin was my open end."

Cristiano stifled a snicker at the names, which sounded more like sexual positions than sports positions to him.

"And guys, this is my homeboy, Cristiano," David said.

"What up, brah?" they both said, extending their hands for a fist bump.

"I gotta get something from my closet," David said, "Can you help my bros, Cristiano?"

Cristiano brought them to the *Sangría*, which they poured into those Yankee-style red cups from the Hollywood films, before congregating in the living room between the T.V. and the sofa. A couple of minutes later, another knock sounded on the door, and

—¿Qué pasa, tío? —dijeron ambos extendiendo las manos para chocar los puños.

—Voy al armario a por una cosa —dijo David—. ¿Puedes ocuparte de ellos?

Cristiano les llevó hasta donde estaba la sangría, que echaron en los típicos vasos yanquis de plástico rojo de esos que aparecen en las películas de Hollywood, y se reunieron en el salón entre la tele y el sofá y junto a la ventana. Poco después volvieron a llamar a la puerta, y Cristiano abrió a un *Superman* de pelo castaño desaliñado y vello facial descontrolado y a un diablo de pelo castaño que llevaba dos cuernos pequeños.

—¡Ey, Da Brewski! —dijo Brandon mientras Cristiano volvía a la sala.

—Tío, ¡cuánto tiempo! —dijo David.

—Ya ves, tío —dijo él.

—¿Qué tal la empresa de transportes de tu padre? —preguntó David.

—No le va mal —respondió—. Pero, ¡qué ganas tengo de pillarme un buen pedo!

—Sí. ¿Dónde está la bebida? —preguntó la chica escasamente vestida agarrada de su brazo.

—Cristiano, este es Tony Dabrowski y su novia Wendy Recht —dijo David—. Y el alcohol está en la cocina.

—¡Vale! ¡Vamos a moñarnoooos! —gritó Wendy.

Mientras iban y se llenaban los vasos, David y Cristiano volvieron con Brandon y Justin, que estaban hablando de gilipolleces.

—¡Oye! ¿Te acuerdas de cuando en el último año llenamos la escuela de papel higiénico?

—¿Y te acuerdas tú de que casi nos pillan por tu culpa,

Part One: Collisions

Cristiano opened the door to Superman with long mussy brown hair and out-of-control facial hair, and a sexy, brown-haired devil with two small red horns.

"Hey, Da Brewski," Brandon said, as Cristiano walked back into the room.

"Dude, it has been forever!" David said.

"Yeah, man," he said.

"How is your dad's transport company?" David asked.

"Ain't bad," he replied. "But I am so ready to get fucked up!"

"Yeah, where is the alcohol?" the scantily clad devil on his arm asked.

"Cristiano, Troy Dabrowski and his girlfriend, Wendy Recht," David said. "And the alcohol is in the kitchen."

"Alright, time to get schwasted!" Wendy yelled.

As they went and got their drinks, David and Cristiano turned back to Brandon and Justin, who were just talking about stupid shit.

"Hey, remember when we TP'd the school our senior year?" Brandon said.

"And you almost got us caught, you loser?" David said.

"Fatass," Justin added.

"Fuck off!" Brandon replied.

Cristiano just stood there awkwardly. He couldn't exactly insert himself in a conversation about memories he never took part in, nor that he understood. He thought he could go back to the Germans, but the dull ones stood there between the couch and kitchen talking about boring issues that would have put him to sleep. At least the stories of past mischief were interesting. But then the footballers finally started speaking Cristiano's language:

cabronazo? —dijo David.

—¡Hijo de puta! —añadió Justin.

—¡Vete a la mierda! —contestó Brandon.

Cristiano se quedó parado y sintiéndose extraño, porque realmente no podía integrarse en una conversación sobre recuerdos de los cuales no había formado parte y que ni siquiera entendía. Se le ocurrió volver con las alemanas, pero los sosos estaban entre el sofá y la cocina hablando de temas aburridos que le daban sueño. Al menos las historias de travesuras pasadas eran algo interesantes. Pero claro, poco tardaron los futbolistas en discutir la forma de hablar de Cristiano:

—¿Salma Hayek? ¡Está como un queso! Le daría hasta reventar! —dijo un chico bastante grosero y gordo, ahuecando las manos como si estuviera tocando unas tetas imaginarias.

Se llamaba Brandon... ¿Cual era su apellido? Empezaba con D...Davies...Davidson... No importa. Más que los nombres, lo que más asombró a Cristiano fue que todos estos chicos pasaban más tiempo imaginándose polvos con famosas que aprovechando a las chicas de su ciudad.

Quizás era porque no cuidaban sus cuerpos. Él notó que serían muy guapos si se afeitaran y se dieran un buen baño. Su aspecto le recordaba a los "canis" de España que llevaban pantalones anchos y que se creían de lo más guay, pero en realidad no podían ser más chungos que si los hubieran comprado a un marroquí en el Retiro.

Al menos distaban algo de la imagen estereotipada de los americanos que tenía en su cabeza. Siempre había pensado que eran puritanos por la censura en las películas. España se había liberado de ese tipo de dictadura con la muerte de Franco. Así que los Estados Unidos iba a la zaga en derechos humanos y continuaba el miedo al sexo y a la sexualidad mientras que España tenía sus películas del "destape" — el nombre que Cristiano y sus amigos gritaron en alto en la clase de historia cuando estaban estudiando la

"Salma Hayek? She's so hot. I'd fuck her brains out!" said a rather crude and large guy, cupping an imaginary pair of tits.

His name was Brandon...what was his last name again? It started with a D... Davies? Davidson? Whatever. More than the names, Cristiano was impressed by the fact that everyone talked more about imaginary sex with famous stars than enjoying the girls in their own city.

Maybe it was because they didn't take care of themselves. They would have been somewhat handsome if they had shaved and showered, he thought. They reminded him of the *Canis* in Spain, wearing baggy pants that they thought were cool, but in reality couldn't be more sketchy even if they had bought them from a Moroccan in Retiro.

At the very least, they were different than the stereotypical Americans he had always imagined. He had always thought that Americans were Puritans based on the censorship in their films. Spain had been liberated from that kind of dictatorship with the death of Franco, right? That's why the United States lagged behind in human rights and continued their fear of sex and sexuality while Spain had its "titty film" - or at least, that was the name Cristiano and his friends had yelled in history class when they studied *la movida madrileña.*

He was starting to doubt everything that he had learned culturally about the U.S.A., until they started to talk about American football.

"Dude, did you see the Pats last weekend?" Justin asked.

"Fuck Tom Brady," Brandon said.

"That long pass to Gronkowski was pretty sweet though," David said.

"Yeah, but then that fumble on the next play just ruined it," Justin said.

movida madrileña.

Ahora dudaba de todo de lo que aprendió culturalmente de EE.UU., al menos hasta que empezaron a hablar de fútbol americano.

—¡Tío! ¿Viste a los Pats el finde pasado? —preguntó Justin.

—¡Puto Tom Brady! —dijo Brandon.

—De todas formas, eso con Gronkowski fue la hostia —dijo David.

—Sí, pero al caerse después la cagó en la siguiente jugada —dijo Justin.

El fútbol americano le aburría a más no poder. Cristiano no tenía tiempo para estos debates. ¿Cómo podrían llamar a algo 'fútbol', o incluso 'deporte', cuando sólo se sucedían jugadas de diez segundos cada vez y se promovía, de esta manera, la obesidad.

—No —pensaba Cristiano—. Un deporte consta de 45 *MINUTOS* de correr y regatear, no unas putas focas dándose patadas.

—A ver, sabía usar las manos, pero besaba fatal —escuchó Cristiano decir a Marie Antoinette.

—Por fin —pensó, dirigiéndose a la reunioncilla alemana.

—¡Claro! Eso fastidia un poco las cosas —dijo Lena.

—¡Fue lo peor! —dijo Marie Antoinette☐—. Todo lo demás puede enseñarse, pero ¿aprender a besar?

—Aún peor... —dijo Lena mientras Cristiano se acercaba— es que un rollo de una noche se enamore locamente de ti.

—En serio —añadió Marie Antoinette—. ¡Me hizo eso exactamente! Y era él quien me dijo que quería hacerlo 'sin complicaciones, nena'.

—¿Alguna vez te ha pasado eso? —dijo Cristiano a la chica con la espalda al aire, mientras Lena ponía los ojos en blanco.

Part One: Collisions

American football bored him to tears. Cristiano was done with this conversation. How could they call something 'football,' or even a sport, when it only happened one ten-second play at a time, and thereby promoted obesity.

"No," Cristiano thought. "A sport is 45 *MINUTES* of running and fancy footwork, not a couple of fucking fat-asses running into each other."

"I mean, he was good with his hands, but he was such a bad kisser," Cristiano heard faintly from Marie Antoinette.

"Finally," he thought, heading back over to the small German enclave.

"Yeah, that kind of ruins it," Lena said.

"The worst," Marie Antoinette said. "Anything else you can teach, but a bad kisser? Damaged goods."

"Worse," Lena said, as Cristiano approached. "A one-night stand that becomes madly in love."

"Seriously," Marie Antoinette added. "He totally did that! And he was the one who told me 'nothing serious, babe.'"

"You ever had that happen?" Cristiano asked the backless-dress girl as Lena rolled her eyes.

"Not really," she said.

"Do you want another drink," he asked.

"Sure," she replied.

"I'm not one for one-night stands," Sissi said. "But some men you have to cut off."

"Your ex was such an asshole," Marie Antoinette said, as Cristiano came back with the backless-dress girl's refill. As they continued to talk about relationships, and he continued his side conversation with the backless-dress girl, Cristiano grew bored. He

—La verdad es que no —dijo ella.

—¿Quieres otra copa? —preguntó Cristiano.

—¡Claro! —dijo ella.

—A mí los rollos de una noche no me van —dijo Sissi—. Pero a algunos hombres hay que pararles los pies.

—Tu ex era un gilipollas —dijo Marie Antoinette mientras Cristiano volvía con la copa de la chica del vestido con la espalda al aire. Conforme continuaba la conversación sobre las relaciones, y Cristiano su charla paralela con la chica, éste empezó a aburrirse. Sabía que tan sólo debía recurrir a su seductor encanto español para hacerlas desconectar de la monotonía de sus vidas, lo cual no supondría un desafío. Cristiano quería, no, *deseaba*, no, *necesitaba* que se hicieran de rogar. Por esa razón, fue a por más sangría, a recolocarse su traje y seguir al acecho.

Cristiano dio una vuelta por la sala de conversación en conversación, hablando con Lena y David para ocultar sus flirteos ocasionales. No es que quisiera ligar con nadie en la sala - o eran feos o aburridos. Pero como un drogadicto, necesitaba su dosis. Cristiano ya había pasado por el diablo, la enfermera, y el *Superman* que halagaba a Troy para distraerle mientras su novia y su mejor amigo charlaban, cuando sobre las diez volvieron a llamar a la puerta. David fue a la puerta y Javier entró.

—¡Tío, qué alegría verte! —dijo David dándole un abrazo con un solo brazo.

—Ey, ¿dónde anda Cristiano? —preguntó cuando Cristiano le saludó—. ¡Oye güey!

—¿Cómo te va? —dijo Cristiano cuando Javier se acercaba.

—Un largo viaje por la línea roja —respondió Javier—. ¿Quienes son las gringas?

—Jenny, Troy y Wendy —dijo Cristiano. Después de saludarse educadamente, las chicas volvieron a su conversación sobre Taylor

Part One: Collisions

knew that he merely needed to break out his Spanish charm to distract one of them from their repetitive life, which would easily seduce them, but that wouldn't be challenging at all. Cristiano wanted, no, *desired*, no, *needed* a good fight! For that reason, Cristiano went to get a little more *Sangría* and to readjust his costume, lying in wait.

Cristiano wandered through the living room, conversation to conversation, talking with Lena and David to hide his occasional flirting. It's not that he wanted to hook up with anyone in the room - they were either ugly or they were boring. But, like a drug addict, he needed his fix. Cristiano had made his way over to the devil, nurse, and Superman, stroking Troy's ego to see if he could distract him while his girlfriend and her best friend blabbered on, when there was a knock on the door around ten. David went to the door, and Javier walked in.

"Dude, good to see ya!" David said, giving him a one armed hug.

"Yo, where Cristiano at?" Javier asked, as Cristiano waved at him. *"Oye, güey."*

"How ya doin?" Cristiano said when Javier came over.

"Long ride on the Red Line, man," Javier replied. *"¿Quienes son las gringas?"*

"This is Jenny, Troy, and Wendy," Cristiano said. After they politely said hi, the girls went back to their conversation about Taylor Swift.

"I just relate so much to *I knew you were trouble*," Jenny said. "Ya know?"

"Omg, totally. Guys are all just such sleazebags. All they want is sex and then they leave ya," Wendy responded.

"Totally!" Jenny said.

Swift.

—Me identifico mucho con *I knew you were trouble* —dijo Jenny—. ¿Sabéis?

—Claro, tía. Los hombres son todos unos imbéciles. Prometen hasta que la meten y después de metido nada de lo prometido.

—Ya ves, tía —dijo Jenny.

—Pobre... —dijo Troy.

—Sabes que a ti no te incluyo, cielo —dijo Wendy.

—Chicas —dijo Troy a Cristiano—. Ni con ellas ni sin ellas. ¿Tengo razón o no?

—¡Claro! —dijo Cristiano haciéndole picar el anzuelo dándole en el pecho—. Los amigos antes que las guarrillas ¿no?

—Eso mismo, ¿sabes? —respondió Troy.

—¡Qué malos sois! —dijo Wendy, dándole pequeños puños a Troy.

—En fin, hombres. ¿No os encantaría tener a los chicos que aparecen en *Gilmore Girls*? —dijo Jenny—. Dean es mi favorito.

—¿Qué carajo es Las chicas Gilmore? —le preguntó a Javier el chicagüense nativo en español.

—Es una serie romántica que les encanta a las chicas, güey —respondió Javier.

—¿Y los hombres? —preguntó Cristiano.

—Ni siquiera la ven. Menos los maricones —bromeó Javier.

En ese momento, tocó otra vez alguien a la puerta de modo autoritario y con gran estruendo.

—Policía de Chicago. Abran la puerta, por favor —dijo una voz. David le abrió a un policía bajo y de mediana edad que parecía bastante serio y cuya placa decía 'T. Williams'.

—¿Qué ocurre, señor? —preguntó David en su voz más

Part One: Collisions

"Ouch, hun," Troy said.

"Oh, you know I mean everyone but you, hun," Wendy said.

"Girls," Troy said to Cristiano. "Can't live with 'em, can't live without 'em. Am I right?"

"Yeah," Cristiano said, giving him some more bait. He jabbed Troy in the chest as he said "Bros before hoes, right?"

"Dude, ya feel me?" Troy replied.

"Meanies," Wendy said, play-hitting Troy.

"Ugh, men. Don't you wish we could have the men of Gilmore Girls?" Jenny said. "Dean is my favorite."

"*¿Qué carajo es Las chicas Gilmore Girls?*" Cristiano asked Javier, the native Chicagoan.

"*Es una serie romantica que les encanta a las chicas, güey,*" Javier replied.

"*¿Y los hombres?*" Cristiano asked.

"*Ni siquiera la ven. Menos los maricones,*" Javier joked.

In that moment, someone else knocked at the door, loudly and with authority.

"Chicago PD. Open up," said a voice. David opened the door to a short, middle-aged police officer with a serious look on his face, and the small metal pin that said 'T. Williams.'

"Sir, what seems to be the problem?" David asked in his best professional voice, trying to appear sober.

"We received a noise complaint from the neighbors," Officer T. Williams said. "Look guys, I was young once. I understand. But you need to move it to a club. If I have to come back, it'll be a $500 fine, and an I.D. check. Ok?"

"Yes, officer," David replied.

profesional, intentando parecer sobrio.

—Hemos recibido quejas de los vecinos por el nivel de ruido —dijo el agente Williams—. A ver, chicos, yo también fui joven y lo entiendo, pero a estas horas tenéis que ir a la discoteca o algo. Como tenga que volver, os pondré una multa de 500 dólares y tendré que mirar carnés, ¿entendido?

—Sí, señor —respondió David.

—Pasadlo bien, chicos — dijo el agente T. Williams—. Y no hagáis locuras.

—Chicos, mi primo acaba de decirme que vayamos a *Big City Tap* —dijo Brandon.

—¡Claro! Vamos allí casi siempre —dijo David.

—¿En serio? — preguntó Brandon.

—Sí, está muy cerca —dijo David—. ¡Y es muy barato!

—Bueno, de acuerdo —dijo Justin.

De camino a la estación del 'L', vieron al agente Williams en la calle hablando a un chico negro, alrededor de su misma edad, sin disfraz. De repente, el agente exigió al joven que pusiera las manos en el muro mientras el agente le cacheaba. La escena le golpeó de lleno a Cristiano por un momento - el agente no era para nada la misma persona que antes. Pero Cristiano lo olvidó rápidamente cuando un Justin borracho se chocó contra él.

—Tío, me alegro que no sea yo —río Justin.

—¿Verdad? Porque yo tengo un DNI falso para beber —dijo Troy—. Mi padre me mataría si lo supiera.

Después de salir en la estación Belmont, Cristiano entró por la puerta del bar con los paneles en madera y las conocidas lámparas de araña, mientras charlaba con Javier. Se acercó a la barra, que tenía unas televisiones sobre los camareros emitiendo partidos en ESPN, y con música pop que retumbaba al fondo.

Part One: Collisions

"Have a good evening, kids," Officer T. Williams said. "And be safe."

"Hey, my cousin at Northeastern texted me to go to that Big City Tap," Brandon said once the officer had left. Nobody could think of anything better. After all, Cristiano, Lena, and David went there often given how close it was, as well as how cheap the drinks were.

"Yeah, we go there all the time," David said.

"Really?" Brandon asked.

"Yeah, it's super close," David said. "And cheap!"

"Well, it's settled then!" Justin said.

On their way to the L station, they saw Officer Williams on the street, speaking with a black guy around their age without a costume. Suddenly the officer demanded with a yell that the guy to put his hands on the wall as the officer frisked him. Cristiano was struck by this scene for a moment - the officer hardly seemed like the same person they had just met. But Cristiano quickly forgot about it when a drunk Justin bumped into him.

"Dude, so glad that isn't me," Justin laughed.

"Right? Because I have a fake I.D.," Troy said. "My dad would kill me if he found out."

After they got off at Belmont Station, Cristiano walked through the door of the bar with its wooden paneling, and familiar chandeliers while chatting with Javier. Cristiano went over to the bar, with its flat-screen T.V.s showing games on ESPN above the waiters and pop music booming in the background.

As always, he ordered a PBR with lemon - the cheapest beer - and the bartender gave him a confused look yet again. He knew that the lemon wasn't a very common request. In return, Cristiano acted like he didn't know one had to pay a tip in the U.S.A. The

Como siempre, él pidió una PBR con limón —la cerveza más barata— y el camarero le devolvió una mirada de extrañeza ya que el limón no era una solicitud común. Como respuesta, Cristiano hizo como si no supiera que hay que pagar propina en EE.UU. El camarero volvió a mirarle enfadado mientras Cristiano se reía y entonces, después de provocarle y entretenerse bastante, le dio por fin una propina de un dólar. No era culpa suya que le faltara sentido de humor ni que su salario fuera una mierda.

Los que fueron desde casa al bar se reunieron en una pequeña mesa redonda —la última que quedaba a esas horas. Unos se sentaron y los demás hablaron de pie. Por lo menos, el alcohol les había relajado y mezclado así que los grupos eran menos distinguidos. Se dice que la muerte es el gran nivelador, pero si quieres equilibrar unas personas antes del inframundo, no hay nada como el alcohol. De esa forma, incluso la conversación más aburrida o tonta puede transformarse en una historia épica como si *Torrente* fuera *la Divina Comedia*.

De acuerdo con el principio de 'vivir el momento,' Cristiano vio a unas chicas guapas por la pista de baile que rechazaban a todos los que intentaban bailar con ellas y de repente estaba allí, atraído como un polo sur magnético que ha localizado su polo norte. A Cristiano le estaba permitido bailar con ellas durante media hora, posiblemente porque era mucho más guapo que los personajes asquerosos que llenaban el bar o porque era mucho más suave. Fuera lo que fuera, ellas al final acababan yéndose y no conseguía ni un solo móvil, lo que le desilusionaba tras la tediosa velada.

Después de unos chupitos más de *Jäger* para olvidarlas, salió del bar para dar unas caladas afuera. Se apoyó contra la pared, doblando la rodilla y poniendo su pie en ella cuando David apareció. Cristiano estaba como una cuba y casi no entendía a David cuando éste le ofreció ayudarle a llegar a casa.

—Tío, ya es tarrrrrde. Está tó cerraaaaao —dijo David arrastrando las palabras y tambaleándose de un lado a otro—. Y

bartender gave him an angry look while Cristiano laughed. After provoking the bartender and entertaining himself enough, he finally gave him a tip. It wasn't his fault that the bartender lacked a sense of humor, nor that his salary was shit.

Those who had made it from the house to the bar regrouped at a small round table, the only one that was left at that point. Some of them sat and the rest talked while standing. At the very least, the alcohol had relaxed and mixed them, such that the groups were less distinguished. They say that death is the great equalizer, but if you want to even the playing field between people before the underworld, there's nothing like hard liquor. That way, even the most boring or stupid of conversations can be transformed into an epic history, as if the movie series *Torrente* were the Divine Comedy.

In keeping with the principle of 'living in the moment,' Cristiano saw a couple of hotties on the dance floor that were rejecting everyone who tried to dance with them, and suddenly he was there, attracted like a magnet. Cristiano was allowed to dance with them for a half an hour, possibly because he was much more handsome than the normal scum that filled the bar, or because he had much more game. They left without him, though, and he didn't have a single number, which left him disillusioned after the boring night thus far.

After a few more shots of *Jäger* to forget the girls, he left the bar to take a smoke outside. He leaned back on the wall, bending his knee and putting his foot up, when David appeared. Cristiano was drunk as fuck and almost didn't understand David when David told Cristiano that he could help Cristiano walk home.

"Dude, it'sss late. The barsss closing," David slurred as he stumbled over. "And youuuu're drunk."

"You didn't know, Dabid? We Spaniardsssss, weeeee're…we're vampires." Cristiano responded, slurring his words a little and

essstáaas borraacho.

—¿No sabíasss, Dabid? Nosotros los españolessss, sommmos… somos vampiros —respondió Cristiano de la misma forma y poniendo énfasis en su disfraz de Drácula—. ¡Nos encantaaaa la noche! Eres tú, quien… debe tener cuidado con nosotros.

—¿Y si no lo hago yo? *Are joo going to suck mah blood?* —se atrevió David en un acento rumano fingido, muy serio, poniéndose de pie e inflando su pecho envalentonándose frente a Cristiano, como si fuera capaz de defenderse contra cualquier intento de chupar su sangre. Pero unos segundos después, su cara seria rompió en carcajadas. Dio tumbos y empezó a caerse. Cristiano, casi cayéndose al suelo, agarró el cuerpo de David empujándolo contra la pared. Quizás fuera el alcohol o su necesidad de conquistar, pero Cristiano le besó en la boca, cogiéndole la nuca con ternura con su mano. David no hizo nada, paralizado. Pero en el mismo momento que Cristiano pensó que David le correspondería, sus amigos futbolistas salieron y gritaron.

—¡Maricones!

—¡Idos a un hotel, pervertidos!

—Espera, ¿es David?

—Tío, ¡qué cojones…!

—¿Eres… eres… maricón?

Y en ese momento, David expresó un sentimiento que Cristiano no había visto nunca en su cara, normalmente inexpresiva, el miedo. Puro terror.

Part One: Collisions

playing up his Dracula costume. "We lovvvve the night! You're the one whooo...should be worried."

"And if I'm not? Are joo going to suck mah blood?" David attempted a completely fake Romanian accent, dead serious, standing up tall and inflating his chest in front of Cristiano, as if he were capable of defending himself against any attempt to suck his blood. But a couple of seconds later, his serious face broke into laughter. He swayed drunkenly and began to fall. Cristiano caught ahold of him, almost falling to the ground himself. David's body pinned him against the wall.

Perhaps it was the alcohol or his need to conquer something tonight that did it. Cristiano kissed him on the mouth, tenderly taking David's neck with his hand. David was paralyzed. But at the very moment that Cristiano thought David would return the kiss, his football friends came out of the bar and started yelling.

"Faggots!"

"Get a room, you perverts!"

"Wait, is that David?"

"Dude, what the fuck…"

"You're… You're… You're a fag?"

And in that moment, David wore an expression that Cristiano had never before seen on his normally inexpressive face - fear. Pure terror.

Part Two

❖ ❖ ❖

Pieces

Vier

❖ ❖ ❖

Die Begnadigung eines Truthahns

November, 2012

Bumm! *Pause* Bumm! *Pause* Bumm! Eine Kugel schlug Lena direkt in die Schläfe und das Blut lief ihr in den Kopf wie bei einem Monsun. Noch nie in ihrem Leben hatte sie solche Schmerzen erlitten. Es war schon lange her, seit sie das letzte Mal um vier Uhr morgens aufgestanden war. Sie konnte die ganze Nacht aufbleiben, und es machte ihr auch nichts aus, um sechs oder sieben Uhr morgens unter der Woche aufzustehen, aber vier Uhr war viel zu früh, um aufzuwachen, besonders an ihrem freien Tag. Außerdem war es draußen arschkalt! Sie drückte die Schlummertaste, kuschelte sich in das schöne weiche Kissen und rollte sich unter ihren warmen Decken zusammen.

Sie wollte sich an den Traum erinnern, aus dem sie brutal gerissen worden war. Wenigstens noch für zehn Minuten. Der mit den Gummibären. Sie war wieder zehn Jahre alt und spielte mit farbigen Haribos auf einem Spielplatz. Die roten, gelben und orangenen rutschten alle zusammen eine Rutsche hinunter. Aber unten trafen sie auf ein Stück Baklava und alle erstarrten. Das Baklava wollte mit Lena reden, aber seine fremdartige braune Farbe und die faltigen Blätter jagten den Gummibärchen solche Angst ein, dass alle davonrannten und sie alleine ließen. Sie wollte nicht alleine bei einem Fremden bleiben, also rannte sie den Haribos

Four

❖ ❖ ❖

The Pardon of a Turkey

November, 2012

Boom! *Pause* Boom! *Pause* Boom!

A bullet hit Lena straight in the temple and blood rushed to her head like a monsoon. She hadn't felt so much pain in her entire life. It had been a long time since she had woken up at four in the morning. Lena could stay up the entire night, and she wouldn't have had a problem waking up at six or seven during the week, but four AM was much too early to get up, especially on her day off. Besides, it was bloody cold outside! She hit the snooze button, cuddled her nice, soft pillow, and curled up into a ball under her warm sheets.

Lena tried to get back into the dream just for ten more minutes. The one with the gummy bears. She was ten years old again, playing with a group of colorful Haribos on a playground. Red, yellow, and orange, they jumped down the slide together. But at the bottom, a piece of baklava stopped them all dead in their tracks. The baklava tried to talk with Lena, but his unfamiliar brown color and wrinkled leaflets scared the gummy bears so much that they all ran away and left her. Not wanting to be left alone with a stranger, she ran after the Haribos, but no matter where she went, the baklava followed her. She ran from Charlottenburg on die Straße

hinterher, aber wohin sie auch rannte, das Baklava folgte ihr. Sie rannte von Charlottenburg zur Straße des 17. Juni und versuchte sich mit den Haribos im englischen Garten hinter dem Schloss Bellevue zu verstecken, aber das Baklava fand sie. Lena rannte zurück zu ihrer Schule und hoffte, in der Menge untertauchen zu können, aber das Baklava war bereits da. Also rannte sie zum Haus ihres Freundes aus der Schulzeit, schloss die Tür und knutschte mit ihm herum, so als könnte sein Körper sie schützen. Aber sie konnte das Baklava immer noch spüren. Plötzlich klingelte ihr Handy.

„Süße, bist du für deinen ersten *Black Friday* bereit?", fragte eine schwungvolle österreichische Stimme.

„Wer oder was ist das?", murmelte Lena in das Kissen.

„Sag mir nicht, dass du den größten Schnäppchenverkauf des Jahres vergessen hast! Komm schon!"

Lena schaute kurz auf das Display ihres Handys, um die Anruferkennung zu sehen. „Natürlich nicht, Marie. Aber müssen wir wirklich um ..." Sie schaute auf die Uhr. „Scheiße, Fünf Uhr ist es schon?"

„Ja, wir sind alle in der Lobby und warten nur auf dich! Man sagt, Morgenstund hat Gold im Mund. Und wenn ich Gold sage, meine ich natürlich Prada und Louis Vuitton! Also, beweg mal deinen Hintern!", scherzte Marie.

Lena hängte ein, sprang blitzschnell aus dem Bett, zog die bereits gestern hingelegten Klamotten an und rannte ins Badezimmer, um sich zu schminken. Sie fühlte sich eklig ohne eine Dusche, aber damit musste sie auskommen, da sie selbst dran schuld war. Sie hatte ihren Freundinnen versprochen, sich mit ihnen um fünf Uhr morgens in ihrer Lobby zu treffen, weil diese am zentralsten von allen gelegen war, und anscheinend gab es die besten Schnäppchen früh am Morgen nach Thanksgiving.

Lena griff zum letzten Mal zu ihrem Lippenstift, holte ihren beigefarbenen Geldbeutel und verließ schließlich die Wohnung. Während der Fahrt mit dem Aufzug hatte Lena ein schlechtes

Part Two: Pieces

des 17. Juni, trying to hide in the English gardens behind Bellevue Palace with her Haribo friends - but the baklava found her. Lena ran back to her high school, hoping to get lost in the crowd - but the baklava was already there. So she went to her high school boyfriend's house, closing the door, making out with him as if his body could shield her. But she could still feel the baklava. Suddenly her cell phone rang.

"Sweetie, are you ready for your first Black Friday?" an enthusiastic Austrian voice asked.

"Who, wait, what?" mumbled Lena into her pillow.

"Don't tell me you've forgotten the biggest sale of the year? Come on!"

Lena looked at the caller ID on her phone. "Of course not, Marie. But does it really have to be at..." She looked at her clock. "Shit, is it already five?"

"Yeah, we're all in the lobby waiting on you! They say the early bird gets the worm. And when I say worm, I certainly mean Prada and Louis Vuitton! So, move your butt!" Marie joked.

Lena hung up and jumped out of bed with lightning speed. She put on the outfit she had laid out yesterday and ran to the bathroom to put on some makeup. She felt so disgusting without a shower, but she would have to make do, seeing as she only had herself to blame. She had promised her friends that she would meet them at five o'clock in the lobby, because she was the most centrally located of them, and apparently the best deals were early in the morning after Thanksgiving.

Lena put the final touches on her lipstick, grabbed her beige wallet, and finally left the apartment. During the elevator ride down, Lena felt deeply ashamed, which was only accentuated by how disheveled she felt. She must have accidentally turned off her

Gewissen, was ihr Gefühl, unpünktlich zu sein, nur verstärkte. Sie musste den Wecker dummerweise ausgeschaltet haben, anstatt auf „schlummern" zu drücken. Sie war jetzt 21 Jahre alt und bisher noch nie zu spät gekommen. Und wenn sie einmal zu spät kam, dann gab es sicher ein zweites Mal und vielleicht sogar ein drittes Mal und dann würden ihre Kollegen und Freunde denken, dass sie faul wäre. Dann konnte Lena das Ganze vergessen. Keine Beförderung, kein Erfolg, keine Zukunft. *Bist du komplett verrückt, Lena?*

Als Lena die Lobby erreichte, sah sie eine Gruppe von Frauen, die sich zwischen den gläsernen Schiebetüren und der Tür zum Fitnessraum versammelt hatten. Marie stand ganz vorne. Sie trug ein dünnes, schwarzes Kleid mit einem grünen Gürtel und ragte mit ihren hochhackigen Sandaletten leicht über die anderen hinaus. Sie war immer so elegant angezogen, als wäre sie jederzeit bereit für einen Fotoshooting.

„Sind wir so weit, Mädels?", fragte Marie.

„Soweit ich es zu dieser Uhrzeit sein kann", antwortete Sophie. „Lasst uns gehen."

„Ich weiß nicht", sagte Brigitta. „Ich könnte erst mal eine Tasse Kaffee vertragen."

„Du hättest dir einen vom Starbucks um die Ecke besorgen können, während wir gewartet haben", antwortete Sophie verärgert.

„Sorry, verbrannter Espresso mit Zucker ist kein Kaffee", sagte Brigitta. „Das ist ein Verbrechen."

„Dann hättest du dir selber einen machen sollen", gab Sophie zurück. „Du wirst vor acht Uhr morgens nirgends einen vernünftigen Kaffee bekommen."

Sophie, die rechts von Marie stand, hatte einen Pagenschnitt und ein sanftes, leicht rundes Gesicht. Sie trug dem Wetter angemessenere Kleidung als Marie, nämlich einen halsfernen hellgrauen Pulli, bequeme dunkelblaue Jeans und hübsche

Part Two: Pieces

alarm instead of pressing snooze. At the age of 21, she had never arrived late to anything. If she had been late once, there'd certainly be a second time and maybe even a third time and then her colleagues and friends would think she was lazy. Then she could just forget the whole thing. No promotion, no success, no future. *Are you crazy, Lena?*

When she got to the lobby, she saw a group of women congregated between the clear sliding door and the doors of the see-through gym. Marie was in front, wearing a skinny black dress with a green belt and stood slightly higher than the others with her high-heeled sandals. She always dressed so elegantly, as if she was ready for a photoshoot.

"Well, are we ready, ladies?" Marie asked.

"As much as I'm ever gonna be at this hour," Sophie answered. "Let's go."

"I don't know," Brigitta said. "I could use a cup of coffee first."

"You should have gotten some from that Starbucks around the corner while we were waiting," Sophie responded, cross.

"I'm sorry, burned espresso with sugar is not coffee," Brigitta said. "It's a crime."

"Then you should've made it yourself," Sophie snapped. "No self-respecting coffee place will be open until at least eight."

Sophie was the slightly shorter brunette with a bob-cut and a slightly rounder, softer face on Marie's right. She was wearing more weather-appropriate clothing than Marie: a light gray cowl-neck sweater, comfortable dark blue Levis, and some cute black Ariane boots. Sophie was a bit too happy-go-lucky for Lena; she was a freelance dancer and actress who went from job to job and wasn't responsible to anyone but herself. It all appeared too easy. She normally wouldn't have been friends with someone like Sophie, but

schwarze Ariane-Stiefel. Sophie war eine freischaffende Tänzerin und Schauspielerin, die von Job zu Job hüpfte und nur für sich selbst verantwortlich sein wollte. Lena fand sie ein wenig zu leichtlebig. Es schien alles einfach viel zu einfach zu sein. Normalerweise wäre sie mit jemandem wie Sophie nicht befreundet, aber sie landeten oft auf den gleichen Partys und es war nett, wenn man hin und wieder mal mit jemandem Hochdeutsch reden konnte. Zumindest war Sophie intelligent und konnte eine Konversation führen.

Über Brigitta war sie sich andererseits noch unschlüssig. Lena hatte sie bei Marie zum Abendessen getroffen. Damals sagte Brigitta nur einige Worte über das Wetter und aß weiter ihre *Bruschetta*. Sie war auch zu der lustigen Halloweenparty gekommen, hatte dort aber auch wenig gesagt. Egal ob dumm oder schüchtern, Lena hatte keine Lust, sie außerhalb der gelegentlichen Gruppenzusammenkünfte zu treffen. Brigitta hatte langes, lockiges blondes Haar und stechende Augen so grün wie Jade. Im Moment stand sie weiter hinten. Sie trug ein rosa gemustertes kurzes Jäckchen, einen hellbraunen Mantel und eine khakifarbene Cordhose.

„Mädels, Mädels. Wir sind heute früh alle noch nicht in Form", sagte Marie mit dem Versuch, zu vermitteln. „Wir können Kaffee im Laufe des Shoppingtrips bekommen, wenn wir die ersten Geschäfte hinter uns gebracht haben."

„Es tut mir leid, dass ich so spät dran bin", sagte Lena, als sie zum L gingen.

„Kein Problem, mein Schatz", versicherte Marie.

„Wir hatten die Wahl zwischen der Location hier und dem Bahnsteig der U-Bahn", erklärte Sophie. „Und in der Lobby ist es zweifellos wärmer."

„Ja, aber ...", sagte Lena.

„Entspann dich", verlangte Sophie und fügte in einem dramatischen Tonfall hinzu: „Irren ist menschlich, vergeben

they often ended up at the same parties and it was nice to talk to someone in standard German once in a while. And at the very least Sophie was intelligent and could hold a conversation.

On the other hand, with Brigitta, she was never quite sure. Lena had met her at a dinner party at Marie's. At the time, Brigitta only said a couple of words about the weather and continued to eat her bruschetta. She had come to the surprisingly fun Halloween party as well, but she hadn't said much of anything there either. Stupid or shy, Lena didn't care to meet with her outside of the occasional group outings they had. Brigitta, who had long, wavy blonde hair and piercing jade-green eyes, now stood in the background. She was wearing a rose-patterned camisole, a light brown jacket and khaki corduroys.

"Ladies, ladies. We're all a bit unhinged this morning, " Marie said, trying to mediate. "We can get some at the Loop after we've gone to a few shops."

"I'm so sorry for being so late," Lena said as they walked to the L.

"No worries, *Schatz*," Marie said.

"It was either here, or on the subway platform," Sophie said. "And the lobby is definitely warmer."

"Yes, but..." Lena said.

"Lighten up," Sophie insisted. With dramatic pomp, she continued: "To err is human; to forgive, divine."

While the others easily forgot about it, it continued to eat Lena up inside. She continued to beat herself up silently, until they got to the train. It almost would've been easier if they had told her off, but now she had to do it to herself so she didn't get lazy.

The subsequent train ride to the Mag Mile downtown was very

göttlich."

Für die anderen war es keine große Sache, aber es machte Lena immer noch zu schaffen. Sie machte sich auf dem ganzen Weg zur U-Bahn Vorwürfe. Es wäre besser gewesen, wenn die anderen mit ihr geschimpft hätten. So musste sie es selber tun, denn sie wollte nicht als faul gelten.

Während der darauf folgenden Zugfahrt zum *„Mag Mile"* in die Stadtmitte waren alle sehr schweigsam. Nach dem Adrenalinkick in der Lobby erinnerten sich ihre Körper jetzt daran, wie viel Uhr es war. Die Stille wurde zum Puffer zwischen Tag und Nacht, dem Wachen und Schlafen und sie gab Lena genügend Zeit, die vergangenen paar Tage zu überdenken. Sie hatte über Thanksgiving viel Freizeit gehabt, da die WG während dieser Zeit leer war. David war nach Hause zu seiner Familie gegangen, um Ruhe und Erholung zu finden, und Cristiano nach L.A., um ‚Spaß' zu haben.

Sie hatte das Apartment für sich allein, was eine willkommene Abwechslung war, besonders wegen der Vorfälle der letzten Zeit. Vor ein paar Wochen war zwischen David und Cristiano ein kalter Krieg ausgebrochen, so als ob sich das Wohnzimmer wie durch Zauberei in eine Berliner Mauer verwandelt hätte. Monatelang waren diese beiden eine unzertrennliche, geeinte Kraft gewesen, und über Nacht hatte jemand diese Mauer zwischen ihnen errichtet und in Ost und West getrennt. Lena hatte manchmal versucht, im Wohnzimmer zu lesen oder fernzusehen, aber dieses Niemandsland war so still. Sie hatte das Gefühl, als würde die Stasi sie jeden Augenblick erschießen oder verhaften, also blieb sie in ihrem Zimmer.

Sie hätte natürlich Herrn Gorbatschow bitten können, die Mauer niederzureißen mit der Frage, was denn verdammt noch mal los sei. Aber es betraf sie eigentlich nicht und deshalb machte sie sich keine großen Gedanken. Um ehrlich zu sein, hatte es auch Vorteile, denn da die beiden sie in Ruhe ließen, konnte sie bei der Arbeit jetzt viel produktiver sein. Und zu Hause genoss sie zur

taciturn. After the adrenaline kick in the lobby, their bodies remembered the time. The silence became a space in between day and night, awake and asleep. Lena used the time to reflect on the past couple of days. She had had plenty of free time over Thanksgiving vacation, living in the apartment alone. David went home for some rest and relaxation with his family and Cristiano went to L.A. for some 'fun.'

Having the apartment all to herself was a welcome change for her, especially recently. The last couple of weeks had been like a cold war between Cristiano and David, as if the living room had magically transformed itself into the Berlin Wall. For months, these two had been inseparable, a united force, and overnight someone had erected this wall between them, dividing them into East and West. Lena had occasionally tried reading there or watching T.V. in the living room, but this no-man's-land was so silent, it made her feel like the Stasi would shoot or arrest her at any moment. So she eventually kept to her room.

While she could have asked Mr. Gorbachev to tear down this wall by asking what the hell had happened, it didn't really concern her, so she didn't worry about it too much. In fact, without them pulling pranks on her, she had been more productive than ever at work. And at home, she had peace and quiet for once. Eerie though the silence was, she wasn't miffed by the outcome.

Her roommates' issues aside, normally she would have used an opportunity like Thanksgiving as an excuse to travel - to see the skyscrapers of New York, the politics of the American capital, or the shopping of Los Angeles - but Marie had invited her to Black Friday shopping back in September, and she couldn't just break her word on a whim. Besides, she thoroughly enjoyed having the time for the little things again - practicing yoga, reading a novel, autobiography, or play, or taking the train to an art exhibit at the M.C.A. without all of that stress.

Abwechslung den Frieden und die Stille. Obwohl die Stille unheimlich war, hatte sie nichts gegen die Folgen einzuwenden.

Mal von den Problemen mit ihren Mitbewohnern abgesehen, hätte sie eine Gelegenheit wie Thanksgiving normalerweise als Ausrede genutzt, um zu reisen (die Hochhäuser von New York, die Gebäude der amerikanischen Hauptstadt oder sie wäre zum Einkaufen nach Los Angeles geflogen), aber Marie hatte sie schon im September zum *Black Friday Shopping* eingeladen und sie konnte ihr Versprechen nicht aus einer Laune heraus brechen. Außerdem genoss sie es sehr, endlich mal wieder Zeit für die kleinen Dinge zu haben, so zum Beispiel für Yoga, um ein Buch, eine Biographie oder ein Theaterstück zu lesen oder stressfrei mit dem Zug zu einer Kunstausstellung im M.C.A. zu fahren.

Auch hatte sie nun genügend Zeit, zu einem Feinkostladen zu gehen, um traditionelles Thanksgiving-Essen zu kaufen und so eine *authentische* amerikanische Erfahrung zu machen. Obwohl die Füllung ihr zu matschig vorkam und der Truthahn sehr trocken war, war der Kürbiskuchen mit Zimtzucker aber sehr lecker gewesen. Für ihren Geschmack wurde in amerikanischem Essen Qualität zu oft durch Zucker ersetzt, aber dieser Kuchen war weder zu süß noch zu sauer – er war genau richtig. Als sie sich zurückerinnerte, wie sie am vergangenen Abend diesen Thanksgiving-Nachtisch gegessen hatte, fühlte sie sich wie in einem idyllischen, friedvollen Norman-Rockwell-Gemälde. Der traumgleiche Zustand im Zug erlaubte ihr, ihre Gedanken zu verlangsamen und jeden köstlichen, zuckrig-zimtigen Bissen nachzuerleben.

Als die Gruppe an der Grand-Red Station ausstieg und die Michigan Avenue hinausging, wurde sie jäh aus ihrem Tagtraum eines kitschigen amerikanischen Essens mit der Familie gerissen. Die Stille am gestrigen Feiertag, der die gesamte Stadt zeitweise in eine Geisterstadt verwandelt hatte, hatte sich über Nacht in einen Kampf verwandelt, bei dem nur der Stärkere überleben konnte. Riesige Menschenmassen kämpften sich durch gigantische

Part Two: Pieces

It also gave Lena the time to go out to a deli in order to buy traditional Thanksgiving food, so she could enjoy the *authentic* American experience. While the stuffing was too squishy for her and the turkey was extremely dry, the pumpkin pie was delicious, with a sugary cinnamon flavor. She felt that most American food tended to substitute sugar for quality, but this was neither too sweet nor too tart - it was just right. Lena sat there and imagined herself in an idyllic, peaceful, Norman Rockwell painting, as she remembered eating Thanksgiving dessert the previous evening, slowing down her memory in her dreamlike state on the train and allowing her to savor every delicious, sugary, cinnamon-tasting little bite.

She was suddenly ripped out of the daydream of a kitschy American family dinner when the group disembarked at Grand-Red station and they made their way to Michigan Avenue. The quiet holidays of yesterday, which had temporarily rendered the entire city a ghost town, had transformed overnight into a Darwinian survival of the fittest. Enormous crowds fought through gigantic lines just to enter the stores. One had to have patience, strength and cunning to maneuver through the masses. When Lena finally got in the store, she was figuratively thrown off the tracks. She had had the foolish hope that once she got in the store, it would be business as usual - she could quietly browse and leisurely try on clothing. But the crowds had regressed to base impulses, taking clothes she was looking at straight from her hand, as if she were the weakest of the herd. And the lines to the fitting room were at least a half-hour wait, if not longer.

In the end, Lena had to bump everyone out of the way in order to see the clothing racks. She learned that she had to be quick, or else the good clothes would already have disappeared and with them, her chances. So she started a system. Do I like this dress? Put it on my shoulder and I'll decide the details later - stopping is weakness. After a little while, she had collected ten articles and

Schlangen, nur um in Geschäfte hineinzukommen. Man musste Geduld, Kraft und Können aufbringen, um sich durch diese Massen hindurchzubewegen. Als es Lena schließlich in einen Laden geschafft hatte, wurde sie buchstäblich aus der Bahn geworfen. Sie hatte dummerweise gehofft, dass alles wieder normal sei, wenn sie erst einmal drin war, dass sie in Ruhe aussuchen und anprobieren konnte. Aber die Massen handelten aus niederen Beweggründen und rissen ihr die Kleidung aus der Hand, gerade so, als wäre sie das schwächste Tier in der Herde. Vor den Umkleidekabinen musste man mindestens eine halbe Stunde warten, wenn nicht länger.

Am Ende lernte Lena, wie man drängelte, damit man an die Kleiderständer herankam. Sie lernte auch, dass sie schnell sein musste, denn sonst waren die guten Klamotten rasch weg und damit auch ihre Chancen, etwas zu ergattern. Sie entwickelte deshalb ein System. Gefällt mir dieses Kleid? Häng es dir über die Schulter und entscheide später – wenn man aufhört, zeigt man Schwäche. Nach kurzer Zeit hatte Lena zehn Artikel gesammelt und sah sie durch. Sie fragte sich, welche ihr so gut gefielen, dass sie es wert waren, ihren Geldbeutel zu strapazieren, und welche zu teuer waren.

Nach vier oder fünf Stunden fand Lena das perfekte weiße, trägerlose *Givenchy* Kleid aus der letzten Saison für nur $90 – ein unschlagbares und unglaubliches Schnäppchen. Ein Kleid aus der aktuellen Saison würde zwischen einigen hundert und einigen tausend Dollar kosten. Zufrieden legte sie es für 30 Sekunden auf einen Stuhl, um ihren Lippenstift wieder aufzutragen, weil die Schminke während all des Ellbogenstoßens verschmiert worden war und sie nicht wie eine Schlampe an der Kasse stehen wollte. Aber plötzlich tauchte eine Frau aus dem Nichts auf und versuchte es direkt vor ihren Augen zu klauen! Lena riss das Kleid schnell an sich und schaute der anderen Frau direkt in die Augen, als wollte sie ihr Revier markieren. Dann ging sie zur Kasse mit ihrer Beute und wartete ungeduldig in der Schlange, während das Mädchen

Part Two: Pieces

sorted through them, asking herself which ones she actually liked enough to stretch her finances and which were too expensive.

After about four or five hours, Lena found the perfect white, strapless *Givenchy* dress from last season for only $90 - an unbeatable and unbelievable deal. A dress like that in-season would have been anywhere from a couple hundred to a couple thousand dollars. Satisfied, she laid it on a chair for 30 seconds to reapply her lipstick, because her makeup had been smudged during all the elbowing and she didn't want to look like a slob at the check-out. But suddenly, a woman out of nowhere tried to steal it right in front of her eyes. Lena snatched it quickly and looked directly in the other woman's eyes, marking her territory. She then went over to the register with her haul, and waited impatiently in the long line, as the disheveled girl at the front of the line yelled at the cashier.

"WHAT THE FUCK DO YOU MEAN!!!" the girl screeched.

"This coupon is only valid for purchases of $250 or more," the cashier said.

"I don't believe you! Where is your manager!" yelled the girl.

"Ma'am, please," the cashier said.

Lena was so bored it made her angry. She looked around to calm herself, and suddenly the cashier's gaze met hers. And for that brief moment, all she felt was pain and despair. She heard a little pudgy girl, talking to her desperate mother.

***

"Where's daddy, mommy?"

"At work, honey."

"He's always at work."

vorne den Kassierer anschrie.

„ZUM TEUFEL, WAS MEINST DU DAMIT??!!", empörte sich das Mädchen.

„Dieser Gutschein gilt nur für Einkäufe von $250 oder mehr", erwiderte der Kassierer.

„Ich glaub dir nicht! Wo ist dein Manager?", fragte das ungepflegte Mädchen.

„Gnädige Frau, bitte ...", sagte der Kassierer.

Lena war so gelangweilt, dass es sie verärgerte. Sie schaute umher, um sich zu entspannen, und plötzlich begegnete ihr Blick dem des Kassierers. Und in diesem kleinen Moment fühlte sie nur Schmerz und Verzweiflung. Sie hörte ein dickliches Mädchen, das mit ihrer hoffnungslosen Mutter sprach.

***

„Wo ist der Papa, Mama?"

„Auf der Arbeit, Süße."

„Er ist immer auf der Arbeit."

„Ich weiß, Süße. Aber er macht es für dich."

„Ja, ja. Was gibt es zum Abendessen?"

„McDonalds."

„Schon wieder? Das ist das dritte Mal in dieser Woche."

„Ich weiß, aber Oma kann nicht mehr kochen, während ich zur Arbeit gehe. Zumindest hat das Happy Meal ein Spielzeug drin!"

„Yay!"

***

Dann wurde Lena vom Typ hinter ihr angestupst.

„Du bist dran!", sagte er ungeduldig.

Lena schüttelte den Tagtraum ab und vermutete, es hatte mit dem Schlafentzug zu tun. Sie lief mit ihren Freundinnen zum

"I know, dear. But he's doing it for you."

"I guess. What's for dinner?"

"McDonald's."

"Again? That's the third time this week."

"I know, but Grandma can't cook anymore while I go to work. At least the Happy Meal has got a toy in it!"

"Yay!"

***

Then Lena was pushed by the guy in back of her.

"It's your turn!" the man said impatiently.

Lena shook off the daydream, chalking it up to sleep deprivation. She walked with her friends to the next store, and easily lost herself again in the 80% off section.

At 11 AM, the girls had had it. Either because of a lack of money or a lack of energy, they were done shopping. Proud of their conquests, which they would show off for months to come, they wandered around aimlessly, like the cool-down after a marathon. Eventually, they made their way to the Chicago *Christkindlmarkt* on Washington Street.

The wafting smells of cinnamon and *Lebkuchen* reminded her of home, and made Lena hungrier than she had ever been before. She went in and bought a couple of *Stollen* and then they loitered around the surprisingly authentic German Christmas market. The rest of the food there was too expensive - seven to ten dollars for a *Wurst*? And it was still too early to have *Glühwein*, as much as they wanted to drink it. They all looked longingly at the gigantic pot as the red wine slowly gave off steam.

nächsten Laden, und verlief sich einfach wieder in der Abteilung mit den 80 %-Rabatt-Aktionen.

Um 11 Uhr hatten die Mädels genug. Egal ob aus Geld- oder Energiemangel, aber keiner hatte mehr Lust auf Shopping. Sie waren auf ihre Errungenschaften stolz und würden in den folgenden Monaten damit angeben. Sie schlenderten ziellos durch die Straßen, als würden sie sich nach einem Marathon abkühlen, und landeten schließlich auf dem Chicagoer Christkindlmarkt in der Washington Straße. Der Duft von Zimt und Lebkuchen erinnerte Lena an zu Hause und machte sie so hungrig wie noch nie zuvor. Sie gingen hinein und kauften ein paar Stollenstücke und dann lungerten sie auf dem erstaunlich authentischen deutschen Weihnachtsmarkt herum. Das Essen dort war aber viel zu teuer. $7 – 10 für eine Wurst? Für Glühwein war es auch noch zu früh, auch wenn sie ihn gerne probieren wollten. Alle guckten sehnsüchtig den riesengroßen Topf mit dampfendem Rotwein an.

„Vielleicht kommen wir später zurück, um ein paar Gläser zu kaufen, wenn wir was im Magen haben", sagte Sophie hoffnungsvoll und blickte auf die einladende, heiße Flüssigkeit.

„In Ordnung", antwortete Marie. Sie versuchte, ihre Hände warm zu reiben, während sie ihre Einkaufstaschen trug.

Als die Gruppe überlegte, wo sie zum Mittagessen hingehen könnten, schweifte Lena mit ihren Gedanken ab und genoss den Anblick einer Weihnachtspyramide, die sich im Kreis drehte. Der kleine Jesus lag entspannt in der Mitte. Eigentlich hatte er überhaupt keinen Gesichtsausdruck, sondern nur zwei Punkte als Augen auf einer weißen Kugel als Kopf. Je länger Lena die Kugel anstarrte, desto seltsamer sah es aus, so als ob jemand sein Gesicht geklaut hätte. Lena kam es komisch vor, dass sie niemals zuvor bemerkt hatte, wie leichenblass die ganze Szene der Geburt Christi dargestellt war.

Auf einmal unterbrach eine fröhliche rothaarige Verkäuferin mit Sommersprossen, vor Kälte rosigen Wangen und einer

"Maybe we'll come back later to have a couple of glasses when we have something in our stomachs," Sophie said, as she looked at the hot, welcoming liquid.

"Agreed," answered Marie. She tried to warm her hands by rubbing them together, as she held her shopping bag.

In the meantime, the group tried to think where they could go to for lunch as Lena zoned out. She stared instead at a *Weihnachtspyramide* that was spinning around. The little baby Jesus lay relaxed in the middle. He actually didn't have any facial expression - just two points of eyes on a white ball for a head. The more Lena looked at the ball, the more uncomfortable she became. It was as if someone had stolen his face. In fact, it was funny to Lena that she had never noticed how deathly pale the entire Palestinian scene of the birth of Christ was portrayed.

All at once, a cheery, freckled, redheaded saleswoman with rosy cheeks from the cold and a homely figure, wearing a name tag with "Hello, My name is…Doris" on it, interrupted her thoughts.

"Hey, honey! The three-story one there only costs $75," said Doris, as if she had known Lena for years.

Lena shook her head, realizing her mistake, and tried to back away to her friends.

"Come on! It's hand-made in the snow-covered German mountains! A real steal! Besides, it's the perfect gift for moms! She'll love you for it," Doris said.

"No, thanks," Lena responded. "I'm from Germany."

"*Oh, tut Leid,*" Doris said in German with a big smile. She had a huge American accent. "*Shonen Tag nach.*"

Lena left the booth and caught up with the others before they realized that she was already gone. Brigitta, who had been silent up

reizlosen Figur ihre Gedanken. Sie trug ein Namensschild, auf dem „Hallo, Ich heiße ... Doris" stand.

„Hallo, *Honey*! Die Dreistöckige da kostet nur $75", sagte Doris, als ob sie Lena seit Jahren kannte.

Lena bemerkte ihren Fehler und schüttelte den Kopf. Sie wollte so schnell wie möglich zurück zu ihrer Gruppe gehen.

„Komm schon! Sie wurde in den schneebedeckten deutschen Bergen von Hand gefertigt! Ein echtes Schnäppchen! Außerdem ist es ein perfektes Geschenk für die Mutti! Sie wird dich dafür lieben", sagte Doris.

„Nein, danke", erwiderte Lena. „Ich komme aus Deutschland."

„Oh, tut mir leid", sagte Doris auf Deutsch mit einem dicken amerikanischen Akzent und setzte ein Lächeln auf. „Shonen Tag nach."

Lena verließ den Stand und holte die anderen ein, bevor diese bemerkten, dass sie weg gewesen war. Brigitta, die bis dahin geschwiegen hatte, schlug schließlich einen Dönerladen in der Nähe vor, den *I Dream of Falafel*. Auf den konnten sich endlich alle einigen. Mit ihrem iPhone fand Marie zudem auf Yelp heraus, dass *I Dream of Falafel* eine 4-Sterne-Bewertung hatte. Außerdem waren sie sehr hungrig und viel zu müde und erfroren, um draußen stehen zu bleiben und noch länger zu debattieren.

Als sie den Laden erreichten, stellten sie fest, dass es besser gewesen wäre, weiter weg von dem Trubel des ‚*Black Friday*' zu essen, denn es gab eine Riesenschlange bis hinaus auf die Straße. Sie wollten zwar nicht warten, blieben dann aber doch, weil es genauso lang dauern würde, ein neues Restaurant zu finden, mit dem sie alle einverstanden sein würden.

„Diese Amerikaner mit deutschen Familiennamen sind die schlimmsten!", entschied Marie.

„Mannomann! Das verwirrt mich immer wieder!" erwähnte Sophie. „Mein Chef heißt ‚Michael Braun', aber ratet mal, wie er es ausspricht!"

to that point, finally suggested *döner kebab,* something they could all agree upon. After Marie whipped out her iPhone and found *I Dream of Falafel* nearby on *Yelp* with a four star rating, it was settled. Everyone was too hungry, tired, and frozen to stay outside and argue over it any longer.

When they got to the shop, they realized that it would've been better to go farther away from the Black Friday traffic, because there was a gigantic line out the door. Although they didn't want to wait, they decided it would take just as long to find a new restaurant that they could all agree on, so they stayed.

"These Americans with German last names are the worst!" Marie decided.

"Oh man! Those always confuse me!" Sophie said. "My boss's name is 'Michael Braun,' but guess how he pronounces it?"

"How?" laughed Brigitta.

"Meik-all Bran," Sophie responded, rolling her eyes.

"Wait, what?" Lena said, surprised.

"Seriously! I wouldn't lie to you guys!" Sophie promised.

"That's just pathetic," Lena said. "No foreign languages and they can't even pronounce their last name? Do these Americans study *Jackass* at school or something?"

"I find it adorable," Marie said. "I went on this *OkCupid* date, and the girl told me she went to *Adidas* to pick up new gym shoes. When she said '*Adi-de-s*,' I just wanted to pinch her cheeks."

"Wait, you went out with a girl?" Sophie said, looking slightly uncomfortable. "I didn't know you had become a lesbian."

"*Schatz*, I've always been flexible," Marie said with the elegance that only she could.

„Wie?", lachte Brigitta.

„Meik-all Bran", erwiderte Sophie und verdrehte die Augen.

„Wie bitte?", sagte Lena erstaunt.

„Ehrlich! Ich würde euch nie belügen!", beteuerte Sophie.

„Das ist so armselig", sagte Lena. „Keine Fremdsprachen und sie können noch nicht mal ihren eigenen Nachnamen richtig aussprechen? Was lernen die Amerikaner in der Schule? Wie man ein Blödmann wird?"

„Ich finde es liebenswert", sagte Marie. „Einmal war ich auf einem OkCupid Date und das Mädchen erzählte mir, dass sie bei Adidas ihre neuen Sportschuhe abgeholt hat. Als sie ‚Adi-de-s' sagte, wollte ich ihr am liebsten in die Wange kneifen."

„Moment mal, du bist mit einem Mädchen ausgegangen?", sagte Sophie und sah unbehaglich aus. „Ich wusste nicht, dass du eine Lesbe bist."

„Schatz, ich war schon immer anpassungsfähig", sagte Marie mit einer Anmut, die nur sie so rüberbringen konnte.

„Schön für dich", sagte Sophie peinlich berührt mit einem gezwungenen Lächeln und wechselte sofort das Thema. „Was haltet ihr von dem Ausdruck ‚Teen Angst' auf Englisch? Ist das nicht lustig?"

„Moment, so wie in ängstliche Teenager?", fragte Lena. „Oder eher in Richtung krankhafte Angst?"

„Nein, in diesem Fall bedeutet es ein Gefühl der Furcht bei Heranwachsenden", sagte Marie fröhlich.

„So wie bei all den pathetischen Gothic Kids, die nur schwarz angezogen rumlaufen", fügte Sophie hinzu.

„Wow, wissen die nicht, was Angst wirklich bedeutet?", fragte Lena. Und während sie in der Reihe weiter vorrückten, brachen alle in Gelächter aus. „Ok, dumme Frage."

Jeder starrte die seltsamen Menschen an, die in einer fremden Sprache lachten, und es fühlte sich gut an, mal wieder ein Teil von

Part Two: Pieces

"Well, good for you," Sophie awkwardly said with a slightly forced smile, and promptly changing the subject. "What do you guys think of the phrase 'Teen angst' in English? Isn't it funny?"

"Wait, as in scared teenagers?" Lena asked. "Or a phobia of teenagers?"

"No, here it means feelings of dread or anxiety felt by adolescents," Marie said cheerfully.

"Like all those overdramatic Goth kids who wear black," Sophie added.

"Wow, do they not know what *angst* really means?" Lena said. They all broke into laughter as they stepped forward in line. "Wait, dumb question."

As everyone else stared at the weird people laughing in a foreign language, it felt good to be part of something again. Lena often felt so out of place at the apartment, but here they knew her inside and out. They had the same experiences as her - a collective German consciousness that allowed them to talk frankly, and a sense of community and belonging.

"Hey, are we eating here or are we getting it in a *Sackerl?*" Marie asked.

"A *Sackerl?*" Brigitta asked, confused by the unfamiliar word.

"Sorry, I meant bag," Marie said. "Sometimes my Viennese dialect comes out."

"No worries. My mom talks in *Schwäbisch* sometimes," Sophie said. "I wish I knew how to, but I guess it skipped a generation."

"I think it sounds pretty," Brigitta said. "Don't you guys have a special word for 'apricot'?"

"*Marille*," Marie said, the L's rolling off her tongue.

etwas zu sein. Lena fühlte sich in ihrer Wohnung so oft fehl am Platz, aber hier kannte sie sich aus. Alle teilten ihre Erlebnisse – ein kollektives deutsches Bewusstsein, das es ihnen erlaubte, frei heraus und mit einem Gefühl der Verbundenheit und Zugehörigkeit miteinander zu reden.

„Essen wir hier oder lassen wir uns ein Sackerl geben?"

„Ein Sackerl?", wunderte sich Brigitte, denn das Wort kannte sie nicht.

„Sorry, ich meinte Tüte", sagte Marie. Manchmal geht mein Wiener Dialekt mit mir durch."

„Keine Sorge. Manchmal redet meine Mutter mit mir schwäbisch", sagte Sophie. „Ich wünschte, ich könnte das auch, aber ich habe, glaube ich, eine Generation übersprungen."

„Es klingt hübsch", sagte Brigitte. „Habt ihr nicht ein eigenes Wort für Aprikose?"

„Marille", sagte Marie so, als wäre ihr das Rollen des ‚L' in Fleisch und Blut übergegangen.

Sie redeten jetzt über Dialekte, aber ihr Gespräch wurde von dem Typen hinter ihnen unterbrochen:

„Hey, passt auf. Ihr seid dran! Verdammte Kinder."

Sie blickten ihn abfällig an, drehten sich dann wieder um und Lena stellte fest, dass der Laden funktionierte, als ob er ein Fließband wäre. Die erste Servicekraft fragte, was man als Beilage wollte – Reis, Salat, Humus, Baba Ghanoush und/oder Rotkohl in einer Pita oder einfach auf dem Teller. Dann wählte man sein Hauptgericht bei der zweiten – Falafel, Hähnchen, Lamm oder Steak. Es gab so viele Auswahlmöglichkeiten und es ging so schnell vorbei, dass Lena sich kaum entscheiden konnte, was für eine Sauce sie wollte.

„Chili-Sauce", sagte sie aus Gewohnheit.

„Das haben wir nicht", sagte der Kellner. „Unsere schärfste ist *Spicy Tomato*."

Part Two: Pieces

As they started to discuss dialects, their conversation was cut off by the guy behind them:

"Hey, pay attention. You're next! Goddamn kids."

After giving the guy a snide look, they turned back around. Lena realized that the store functioned like an assembly line. The first waiter asked what you wanted for a base: rice, salad, hummus, and/or red cabbage. Then you got to choose your protein with the second one: *falafel*, chicken, lamb or steak. There were so many choices and it went by so fast that Lena hardly knew what kind of sauce she wanted.

"Chili sauce," she said, out of habit.

"We don't have that," the waiter said. "Our spiciest one is Spicy Tomato."

"Sounds good," Lena said. "And where do I pay?"

"Over there," he said, lazily pointing somewhere to the right, as he hurriedly helped the next customer.

As she went to the checkout, the man behind the counter gave her a once-over. It was creepy, sure, but assholes were hardly unexpected in a big city, so she just shrugged it off. In a couple of minutes, she would be siting at a table and finally have a chance to rest her tired feet.

Not even a Kamikaze fighter could stop have stopped Lena from completing her mission. She got out her money, without thinking twice, and held it out to the cashier, thinking only about a comfortable chair. Strangely enough, he didn't say anything and just continued to ogle her.

"Excuse me?" Lena spit at him.

"Bakar misiniz?" he said. He played with the words like a

„Klingt gut", sagte Lena. „Und wo bezahle ich?"

„Dort drüben", sagte er, zeigte irgendwo nach rechts und bediente schon den nächsten Kunden.

Als sie zur Kasse ging, musterte sie den Mann, der dahinterstand. Krass war das, sicher, aber Arschlöcher gab es in großen Städten immer und deshalb ließ sie es nicht an sich herankommen. In einigen Minuten würde sie an einem Tisch sitzen und ihre müden Füße hätten endlich die Chance, sich auszuruhen.

Nicht einmal ein Kamikazeflieger hätte Lena jetzt stoppen können. Ohne zu zögern holte sie das Geld heraus und hielt es dem Kassierer entgegen. Sie dachte nur noch an einen bequemen Stuhl, aber komischerweise sagte er nichts und gaffte Lena einfach weiter an.

„Entschuldigung?", sagte Lena mit Nachdruck.

„Bakar misiniz?", sagte er und spielte dann wie ein professioneller Schürzenjäger mit den Worten. *„Bekam misiniz?"*

„Sus git, Epik", erwiderte Lena in fließendem Türkisch.

„Wow! Ich wusste nicht, dass du Türkisch kannst!" sagte Marie. „Das war echt geil!"

„Nein, das war nichts", sagte Lena und lief rot an.

„Doch! Das war echt klasse! Fast, als ob du Türkin wärst!", sagte die ansonsten zurückhaltende Brigitta ziemlich laut. Die anderen drehten sich erstaunt zu ihr um.

Das war Lena viel zu viel. Sie zahlte mit einem Zehndollarschein und ließ ihn das Wechselgeld behalten, steckte den Döner in ihre Einkaufstasche und lief davon. Ihre Freundinnen mussten etwas dazu gesagt haben, denn Lena spürte hinter sich ein leichtes Chaos, aber sie wollte es nicht hören. In ihrem Kopf hörte sie das hysterische Lachen eines acht Jahre alten Jungen vom Spielplatz. Die Stimme in ihrem Kopf wiederholte sich andauernd, wurde immer lauter und kam immer näher. Sie rannte immer schneller die Monroe Street entlang in Richtung der nächsten „L"-

professional womanizer. *"Bekam misiniz?"*

"Sus git, Epik," Lena answered in fluent Turkish.

"Wow! I didn't know you could speak Turkish!" Marie said. "That's really cool!"

"No, it was nothing," Lena said, turning red with shame.

"No, that was sweet! Almost as if you were Turkish!" said the normally quiet Brigitta, quite loudly. The others turned in surprise.

That was too much for Lena. She payed with a ten dollar bill and told him to keep the change as she put the *döner* in her shopping bag and ran away. Her friends must have said something, because Lena noticed a slight chaos behind her, but she didn't want to hear it. She heard the maniacal laughter of a young boy from years ago on a playground. The voice played over and over in her head, getting louder and closer, making her run faster and faster down Monroe in the direction of the nearest L-train station, fueled solely by a sudden adrenaline rush.

"I'm not a *Kanak*," Lena mumbled through her tears and panting as she turned off her now-ringing phone. "I'm not."

Lena got in the station just as she heard the train for the north-going Red Line approaching the platform. She ran down the steps like an Olympic train-catcher. She was afraid that her friends would find her if she missed the train. Lena had no clue what Marie or even Sophie would say if they caught up, but she didn't want to find out. And even though some small part in the back of her mind whispered that she was probably overreacting, but she blocked it out and concentrated on putting one foot in front of the other. It was easier that way - no politics, no history, no emotions. Just the finger-like myosin filaments grasping and pulling each actin filament, contracting the muscles of her legs and moving her one step closer to forgetting the world around her. So she ignored the

Station. Lena war erschöpft und wurde nur durch den plötzlichen Adrenalinrausch aufrecht gehalten.

„Ich bin kein Kanake", murmelte Lena keuchend unter Tränen und schaltete ihr klingelndes Handy aus. „Das bin ich nicht."

Lena betrat die Station genau in dem Moment, als der Zug der nördlichen Rotlinie einfuhr. Sie rannte die Treppe so schnell hinunter, als wäre es eine olympische Disziplin. Sie hatte Angst, dass ihre Freundinnen sie vielleicht finden würden, wenn sie diesen Zug verpasste. Lena hatte keine Ahnung, was Marie oder Sophie sagen würden, wenn sie sie eingeholt hätten, aber sie wollte es auch nicht wissen. Und obwohl Lena irgendwie wusste, dass sie vielleicht überreagiert hatte, ließ sie den Gedanken nicht zu und konzentrierte sich darauf, einen Fuß vor den anderen zu setzen. So war es viel einfacher – keine Politik, keine Geschichte, keine Gefühle. Nur die Muskelstränge, die ihre Beine bewegten und sie die Welt um sich herum vergessen ließen. Sie ignorierte die Fremden, die sie anstarrten, und rannte noch schneller. Sie erreichte den Zug gerade noch so und die Türen schlossen sich hinter ihrer Einkaufstasche.

Atemlos, ideenlos und am Ende ihrer Flucht angekommen, starrte Lena ihr Spiegelbild im Fenster an. Sie versuchte wieder zu Atem zu kommen und sich zu beruhigen. Ihr Spiegelbild hob sich sehr deutlich vom pechschwarzen Hintergrund des Tunnels ab. Sie konnte ihre feuchten blauen Augen in ihrem bleichen Gesicht erkennen. Sie wurden zu tiefen Wasserlöchern, die bis zu ihrer innersten Seele hinabreichten, wo die Vielfalt und Widersprüche ihrer Persönlichkeit und ihrer Herkunft friedlich zusammenlebten. Aber das Eintauchen in die unbekannten Tiefen einer chaotischen Welt jagte ihr Furcht ein. Das oberflächliche Antlitz, das Lena vor wenigen Stunden noch so vertraut war, wurde ihr fremd und feindlich. Lena wollte in diesem Moment einfach nur ihre Augen schließen und in einer anderen Welt Schutz suchen, in einer, die einfacher und sauberer war.

Der Zug fuhr aus dem Untergrund heraus auf eine

strangers staring at her and ran even faster, just barely getting on the train before the doors closed on her shopping bag.

Out of breath, out of ideas, and with nowhere left to run, Lena stared at her reflection in the window as she tried to catch her breath and regroup. She saw herself very clearly against the pitch-black background of the tunnel, wherein she could see her damp blue eyes in her pale white face. They became two deep pools of water that reached down to the innermost part of her soul, where the complexities and contradictions of her personality and background coexisted peacefully. But diving into the unknown depths of a welter world scared her. Her skin-deep visage, which had been so familiar to Lena a few hours earlier, became foreign and adversarial. Lena wanted in that moment nothing more than to close her eyes and protect herself in another world, one that was simpler and cleaner-cut.

Suddenly the train came out from underground to an elevated railway section. As the downtown buildings ran by around her, her reflection became less clear, as if the pace of the big city had hidden it. She wiped away her tears and tried to forget everything that she saw in her reflection.

Lena made a list of everything that she still had to do today, or at the very least should do. She would certainly eat the *döner* first - that was a no-brainer - then perhaps do her laundry. What else? She could perhaps stay ahead of the game and take care of some of her work assignments for next week. That'd work. If she had enough time, then maybe it would also be possible to clean her room over again and reorganize it.

"No, maybe I should clean the kitchen first," Lena thought to herself, as she got off at the Sheridan station.

On her walk home, Lena contemplated how she would accomplish each task on her list. Everything else would be

Hochbahnstrecke. Als die großen Gebäude der Stadtmitte an ihr vorüberzogen, wurde ihr Spiegelbild unschärfer, ganz so, als ob es durch das Tempo der großen Stadt versteckt wurde. Sie wischte sich die Tränen ab und versuchte alles zu vergessen, was sie in ihrem Spiegelbild sah.

Lena machte eine Liste von all dem, was sie heute noch tun musste oder zumindest tun sollte. Den Döner würde sie natürlich zuerst essen, logisch, dann vielleicht die Wäsche machen. Was sonst? Sie konnte vielleicht der Konkurrenz vorauseilen und ein bisschen für die nächste Woche vorarbeiten. Das wäre toll. Wenn sie genug Zeit hätte, dann wäre es auch möglich, das Zimmer wieder mal abzustauben und umzustellen.

„Nee, vielleicht sollte ich zuerst die Küche sauber machen", dachte Lena, als sie an der Haltestelle Sheridan ausstieg.

Auf dem Weg nach Hause dachte Lena daran, wie sie jede Tätigkeit auf ihrer Liste ausführen würde. Alles Übrige könnte sie ausblenden und überhaupt nicht mehr daran denken. Sie hatte ein Ziel und würde es erreichen, ganz gleich, was passierte. Sie hatte alles im Griff.

Lena riss die Tür auf und warf sie wieder zu. Sie freute sich auf die Einsamkeit des leeren Apartments. Aber als sie in Richtung Wohnzimmer ging, erschien es ihr, als würde sie David sehen. Sie blinzelte mit den Augen und schaute genauer hin. Es war keine Illusion. David saß auf dem Sofa im Wohnzimmer und hielt seinen Kopf mit den Händen. Mit einer Mischung aus Frustration, Ärger, Traurigkeit und Resignation starrte er an die Decke. Bei Lenas forschem Eintreten setzte er sich aufrecht hin und wirkte verlegen und leicht in Panik. David starrte Lena wortlos mit todernsten Gesicht an. *Warum war er so früh nach Hause gekommen?*

Lena vergewisserte sich, dass sie nicht genauso aussah und setzte ein glückliches Gesicht auf, während sie schnell und heimlich die Reste ihrer Tränen abwischte. Aber am Ende verschmierte sie ihr am Morgen schnell zusammengeschustertes Makeup nur noch

forgotten, no longer even crossing her mind. She had a goal and she would reach it, no matter what happened. She had everything under control.

Lena ripped open the door and slammed it closed again, ready for the solace and safety of an empty apartment. But as she headed into the living room, she thought she saw David there. She blinked her eyes and did a double take. It wasn't an illusion. David was sitting on the sofa in the living room with his hand on his head out of an apparent mix between frustration, anger, sadness, and resignation as he looked at the ceiling. He abruptly sat up after Lena's harsh entrance, embarrassed and slightly panicked. David looked at Lena with an attempt at a deadly serious face, without saying a word. *Why had he come back home so early?*

Lena made sure that she didn't look the same, putting on a happy face while she quickly and secretly brushed off any remnants of her tears, but in the end just further smudged her hastily applied make-up from that morning. They stood their ground in an awkward silence for a few moments, not knowing how two puffy-eyed work colleagues should greet each other. Each of them hoped that the lack of recognition would maintain the illusion that everything was fine, willingly choosing ignorance that both of their faces were betraying them.

"Hey, asswipe," Lena said halfheartedly as she headed to the couch.

"Whatever, bitch," David replied with equal enthusiasm.

They sat next to each other in silence for a few more minutes in a trance-like state, neither of them willing to make the first move or possessing the energy to do so. The sunlight was shining outside on that brisk fall day, and a gorgeous layer of leaves was falling lazily around Chicago in various hues of deep reds, light yellows, and brilliant oranges. Through the window, the sun shone on calm,

mehr. So standen sie sich eine Weile steif gegenüber und wussten nicht, wie sich zwei Berufskollegen mit feuchten Augen begrüßen sollten. Sie hofften beide, dass sie die Illusion aufrechterhalten konnten, dass alles in Ordnung war, wenn sie es sich nicht eingestanden. Wobei ihnen klar war, dass ihre Gesichter eine andere Sprache sprachen.

„Hallo Arschgesicht", sagte Lena halbherzig und ging zum Sofa.

„Gleichfalls, Schlampe", erwiderte David mit der gleichen Begeisterung.

Sie saßen nebeneinander und schwiegen ein paar Minuten lang, als wären sie in Trance. Keiner hatte die Energie, den ersten Schritt zu machen. An diesem frischen Herbsttag schien draußen die Sonne. Durchs Fenster konnte man sehen, wie wunderschöne Blätter langsam auf große rote, hellgelbe und orange Haufen rund um Chicago fielen. Das Sonnenlicht ergoss sich auf den ruhigen und majestätischen Michigansee.

Lena begann über die Tiefe des anscheinend unveränderten Sees nachzudenken. Man konnte es von oben nicht sehen, aber unter der Oberfläche befand sich ein ganzer Mikrokosmos mit komplexen Hierarchien und Nahrungsketten. Da gab es tausende große, kräftige, schlanke, silberne Lachse, kleine Barsche mit schwarzen Streifen auf blassgrünen Schuppen und schwarze Zebramuscheln, die ihr weiches Inneres zum Schutz vor Raubtieren in einer starken Schale versteckten. Trotzdem waren sich die Chicagoer dieser fremden, vielfältigen Welt genau vor ihrer Nase so gut wie gar nicht bewusst, außer wenn sie ihnen auf ihren Tellern bei *Catch Thirty Five* serviert wurde. Und selbst dann ging es nur um Ernährung und Unterhaltung.

„Lena", unterbrach David plötzlich ihren Gedankenstrom. Er hatte seine Hände im Schoß und starrte auf den Boden.

„Ja", sagte Lena und starrte immer noch aus dem Fenster.

„Alles klar?", fragte David.

majestic, unending Lake Michigan.

Lena began to think about the depths of the seemingly unchanged lake. You can't see it from the surface, but underneath lay a whole microcosm, with its own complex hierarchies and food chains. Thousands of big, powerful, pure silver, elongated salmon, wiry perch with black stripes on their pale green scales, and pitch-black zebra mussels. They hid their soft insides in a strong shell to protect themselves from predators, but in large numbers, they could take down entire ecosystems. Yet Chicagoans were mostly unconscious of this foreign, complex world right under their noses, except when they were served as seafood on their plates at Catch Thirty-Five. And even then, it was only about sustenance and entertainment.

"Lena," David said, interrupting her train of thought. He was sitting forward with his hands in his lap, staring at the ground.

"Yeah?" Lena said, still staring out the window.

"You all right?" David asked.

"Of course. Always," Lena replied, turning around. "You?"

"I think… it's possible… I mean, I could be… I am… g… I don't know." David said, beating around the bush, not able to actually finish whatever word he was trying to say. There was a long pause. "I think I might be attracted to men."

Another long pause.

"Well, I'm Turkish," Lena said, surprised at herself as the words passed over her lips.

"Wait, I thought you were German," David said, completely confused.

"I am. It's complicated," Lena said, very seriously. Then she

„Natürlich. Immer", erwiderte Lena und drehte sich um. „Und du?"

„Ich glaube ... es kann sein ... ich meine, es wäre möglich ... ich bin ... sch ... weiß ich nicht." sagte David und redete um den heißen Brei herum. Er konnte keinen Satz zu Ende bringen. Noch eine große Pause. „Ich glaube, ich stehe vielleicht auf Männer."

Noch eine große Pause.

„Na ja, ich bin Türkin", sagte Lena und war überrascht, als ihr die Silben über die Lippen kamen.

„Warte mal, ich dachte, du bist Deutsche", sagte David ganz verwirrt.

„Bin ich. Es ist kompliziert", entgegnete Lena ernst. Dann brach sie die Stille mit einem Lächeln und stieß David leicht mit ihrer Schulter an. „Und ich hab dich für einen schwulenfeindlichen Muschilecker gehalten."

„Verpiss dich", lachte David und stieß sie spielerisch zurück.

Lena holte ihren Döner heraus, der jetzt mehr wie ein Dürüm aussah, und bot David ein Stück an. David nahm es und sie stießen noch einmal miteinander an, als sie ihn aßen.

„Idiotin."

„Trottel."

laughed and gave David a light bump on the shoulder. "And I thought you were a homophobic pussy eater."

"Fuck you," David laughed, giving her a playful shove.

Lena took out her *döner*, which at this point looked more like a *dürüm*, and handed David a piece. David took it and they bumped each other once more, as they ate it.

"Idiot."

"Moron."

Five

❖ ❖ ❖

Out, Damned Spot!

December, 2012

David punched a wall on his way out of work. He was frustrated with everything these days. One moment, he was in the office, doing his assignments at the last minute, as per usual. The next minute, the printer had a paper jam, and the normally stoic, anything-goes David transformed into a sinister Mr. Hyde.

"What in the...?" David said as the words 'Paper Jam' appeared on the printer screen. He walked over to the side of the machine, opened it, and slowly removed the sheet. Some of the toner had gotten on his fingers in the process, and he grabbed a couple sheets of scrap paper so he didn't accidentally smudge it on his work clothes.

"Why won't this ink come off? It's not that fucking..." David muttered, eventually giving up. He threw his hands up in the air in resignation. "Whatever."

David took a deep breath and stepped back to the front of the printer. He pressed the start button again, but an error message popped up again, asking him to empty the tray. He went back to look at the side compartment, but there was nothing there. David tried to close it and just leave it up to IT, but now the side door wouldn't close. He tried again. Nothing. Then he tried forcing it. It didn't budge.

"God fucking dammit, just print, you goddamn abortion of a street corner whore!" David screamed, repeatedly hitting the side door against the printer.

"David, what on earth are you doing?" said Lisa. One could almost confuse her stern face for a cool and collected one, were it not for the slight creases around her eyes, her pursed lips, and ever so slightly agitated voice.

"Lisa, I..." David started.

"No, David. I don't want to hear it," Lisa said. "This is completely unprofessional and will not be tolerated."

"I'm sorry," David responded.

"I ought to fire you," Lisa said calmly. "Damage to company property and you're only an intern."

"It won't happen again, ma'am," David said, mustering up a tough, cocky look on his face, but unable to hide the fear in his eyes.

"It better not," Lisa said, with a piercing stare, towering over the guy twice her size. "I must be getting soft. Take the day off. Get your head straight, tighten whatever screws you need to, and then come back when you can work like an adult."

"Thanks for the offer, but I'll be fine," David said. "It was just a lapse in judgment. I can handle it."

"Did I ask you?" Lisa said. "You take the day off, or I call security now to escort you out permanently. Your choice."

"Yes, ma'am," David said, avoiding eye contact.

"Jesus, millennials," Lisa scoff under her breath.

Walking down the stairs, the slight embarrassment David had felt in front of Lisa turned to anger. He imagined this must have been how Billy Cundiff felt after missing that crucial field goal.

Part Two: Pieces

"Stupid, **Stupid, STUPID!**" David repeated, louder and louder until, in a moment of blind rage, he punched the wall.

"Fuck," he whispered under his breath as the adrenaline wore off. He let himself chuckle for half a moment, despite the trickles of blood through the broken skin of his knuckles. "Looks so much cooler on TV."

As he exited the doors of the building onto Michigan Avenue, David felt a strange pang in his consciousness. He had been trained all his life to push through the pain for that perfect white-picket fence, a wife, 2.5 kids, and a dog named Spike or Rufus. With that pang, that crystal-clear image began to blur, and the dog began to howl. The image was now overlaid with another, like two translucent projector slides - the image of Norman Bates in front of a hotel.

"Stop overthinking things, David," he thought to himself. He shook off the image and brought his dazed eyes up from his feet.

He thought back to the last time he had had the day off: Senior Skip Day, just half a year earlier. His friends had created a *Ferris Buehler's Day Off* - like list of the things they could do in Chicago.

***

Like most plans, the list eventually fell by the wayside, and they ended up just fucking around in the city for the day, doing whatever came into their heads. Upon seeing a first steakhouse downtown, they decided to go up to the short, skinny waitress in front. She had a black dress shirt, dress pants, calm black eyes, and a slicked-back black hair with so much gel that it glistened.

"We have an important meeting at this fine establishment," Troy said in his best pretentious businessman voice. Justin let out a snort behind him.

"Dude, shut the fuck up," Brandon whispered to his friend through his own stifled laughter while nudging him.

"Mhm," the waitress responded, rolling her eyes. And who, may I ask, are you?"

"Lee Williams," Troy said with a straight face, as the others snorted behind him.

"Well, I am sorry, I can't seat you right now, Mr. Williams," the waitress said. "We're a bit busy with actual customers."

"Do you know who I am?" Troy said. "I demand to speak with your manager!"

"I'm sure you would, sir," the waitress said. Her patience was clearly wearing thin. "But some of us have to make rent."

"How rude!" Troy joked. "Where would you have us go!?"

"Maybe somewhere more age-appropriate," the waitress said. "I hear Chuck E. Cheese's has openings."

"What's going on?" said another waiter, as he approached them. His silver name tag with the words Ricky G., G.M. on printed in a fine century gothic script.

"We have a meeting that will change the world of business!" David boomed. "And this woman won't seat us."

"I'm so sorry," Ricky said, giving the waitress a glare. "I would be more than happy to help you find a table."

"Well, we're no longer interested," David said.

"We will give you 10 percent off for your trouble and comp dessert. Would that help?" Ricky said.

"No, thank you, sir," Troy yelled. "We've had quite enough. Good day to you!"

As they walked off, they heard yelling in the background.

"...but they were stupid kids!" the nameless waitress said.

"I don't care! This is the last straw, Julia! They were paying customers." Ricky said.

Part Two: Pieces

"Oh shit," Brandon said, as they all let out a howl.

"But I have a daughter, Ricky. Please, don't..." The voice trailed off in the back of his memory.

***

Somehow, everything had been different back then. Simpler. David could take on the world back then, and now he was just so helpless. *Was he just missing his friends? Was he just being a pussy? What could he do to fix it?* He wasn't even sure anymore.

David had been texting Troy, Brandon, and Justin since he moved to Chicago, but he hadn't really talked to any of them since Halloween. It had been easy enough to convince them the next day, after the drunken haze had lifted, that the kiss wasn't his idea. *So why did talking with his friends still seem so awkward?*

"Goddamn Spaniard," David said. He kicked halfheartedly at an empty water bottle on the street. "Fucking up my life just for shits and giggles."

He wanted so hard to believe that. The days of watching Zombieland and fucking shit up on Call of Duty with his friends were a distant memory. It was as if the kiss had lifted a shroud to reveal an ominous wall between Chicago and Wheaton that had been growing for months. His friends were completely content to spend their time without him, either with their girlfriends or working at their parents' local businesses in Wheaton. They'd go to places like the North Side Sports Bar & Grill with fake IDs, getting drunk on cheap beers and eating burgers and soggy nachos, occasionally fumbling through an attempt at getting down a girl's skirt on the weekends.

And then there was Troy, who David had seen on Facebook was now engaged to Wendy. Back in high school, Troy would have told him about it personally before he even got down on one knee - and now, it was nothing but a reminder of what was and what could have been. And to make matters worse, he was nowhere close to

reaching that milestone - no girlfriend, no real job, he wasn't even in college yet - as the wedding and pregnancy announcements from various high school friends and acquaintances flooded his Facebook feed.

David wanted so badly to cross back over to that simpler lifestyle and forget about everything else. He would send his guy friends a blog post from Barstool Sports, and sometimes he would receive a quick, disinterested "Hey, how are you?" back on the Facebook messenger. But every time David tried to scale the wall to get back, he fell hard like Humpty Dumpty and broke into a million pieces.

Back then, rather than mope in a pity party for one about it, David decided to take action. About a month ago, David had gotten permission from Lisa to take an entire week off for Thanksgiving. After work on the Friday before Thanksgiving, he had gotten a bag of dirty laundry together for his mother to clean, and jumped on the L to the end of the line. David ran over it again and again in his mind as he moped down the cold, wet, Chicago street.

***

"David!" Becki yelled out, waving at the station with overwhelming delight.

"Ma, stop it," David said, hiding his smile. "You're embarrassing me!"

"You're embarrassing yourself," his mother said. She reached up and flipped around his backwards baseball cap. "Haven't they taught you to wear a hat properly yet in that fancy internship of yours?"

"I can wear it how I like," David said, switching it back around to a glare from his mother. She then softened up as she took another look at him.

"Aw, you look so grown up!" she said as she hugged him tight.

"It's only been a couple of months, mom," David said as he gave her a big bear hug back.

"Half a year," she said, scolding him. "That's a lifetime."

David smiled for a moment as he threw his big duffel bag in the back of his mom's SUV. She proceeded to talk to him about all the town gossip as he zoned out on the ride home.

"Oh, and pray for Mrs. Dixon," Becki said, sweetly.

"My kindergarten Sunday School teacher?" David asked, puzzled. "Why?"

"You didn't hear? Well, she got caught..." Becki said as David zoned out.

David was exhausted to the point that had he closed his eyes, he would have fallen asleep right there and then. But he fought to keep them open despite himself. When they got to the house, he got a respectful, one-armed man-hug from dad.

"Welcome home, son," Corbin said.

"Thanks, dad," David replied, respectfully. "Where's the snot-nosed brat?"

"Oh, brother. Don't you call your sister that, young man," his mother said.

"David?" David heard from afar.

"Laura?" David said.

"You're home!" Laura screeched. She ran into the room with a smile on her face and gave him a big hug.

"Yeah, been a while," David laughed, until Laura punched him.

"Don't you ever stay away that long again!" Laura said.

"Laura!" Becki said. "Behave."

"Wait, am I getting this right?" David said, smugly. "You missed me? She likes me. She really really likes me."

"Do not!" Laura said resentfully.

David left his bags at the bottom of the stairs and continued to taunt her the entire night as they all went to the kitchen for some home-grilled burgers, a side of home-fried sweet potato fries, and milkshakes fresh from the blender. That evening was as perfect as he had remembered it.

Yet on Sunday morning, he awoke to more than just frizzy bed-head and a case of bad breath. From the minute his family parked their cars in the lot between the church and the lake, it was as if these two bodies cut the congregation off from the rest of the world, and the building itself came alive and morphed into a city on a hill. They walked to their pews in the large (and rather plain) brown-and-white congregation hall, the walls reaching as high as the heavens themselves as Jesus looked down at them from his holy position on the cross in front.

"David, is that you?" said a slightly overweight woman in a colorful Hawaiian dress.

"Mrs. Dixon!" David said. "Long time no see!"

"Sure has! How is Chicago?" Mrs. Dixon asked. "You've been going to church there every Sunday, right?"

"I may have missed a couple," David lied.

"David, be careful!" Mrs. Dixon said. "You know the devil loves to tempt us!"

"Yes, Mrs. Dixon," David said. He noticed Mr. Dixon wasn't with her at the service for the first time since he could remember.

"I'll be praying for you, David," Mrs. Dixon said.

"Well, thanks," David said, trailing off. Out of the corner of his eye, he saw Justin and Brandon, who were just walking in. "I appreciate it."

"Any time, dear," Mrs. Dixon said.

"Well, it was good seeing you," David said with fake cheer.

"Likewise! Have a good service!" Mrs. Dixon chimed back.

Part Two: Pieces

David approached Justin and Brandon, but as he got closer, he realized their Sunday best was wrinkled, as if it hadn't been washed in months.

"Dudes, what's up?" David said.

"Tired. Talk later?" Justin yawned. He shook his head as they walked away. Brandon was just holding his head as if a crew of construction workers had set up a jackhammer in the center aisle. David smelled a whiff of too much mouthwash and Axe hairspray as they passed by. No one paid it much mind though. David attempted to forget about it all by singing the words on the screen from "Here We Are to Worship," but worship was the last thing on his mind. The gigantic walls of the church loomed above him, transforming into the tower of Babylon, falling down, and swallowing him whole. Silence fell as the crowd turned around, all two thousand of them pointing at him with an angry glare. But just before they could chase him down, the music faded, the pastor approached the pulpit, and all was forgiven.

"Jesus told the man that it is easier for a camel to go through the eye of a needle than a rich man to go to heaven. But what does that mean?" the pastor preached.

David always found the verse fairly strange, but he had never questioned it before. *Why a camel? Why a needle?*

Maybe it was like that time Lena had translated her thoughts from German literally. They had had a good laugh when she said that she felt like she could "pull out trees today," at least after she had looked up a more fitting translation on her phone and explained to David that was how Germans said „I feel like a million bucks."

David decided to pull out his iPhone and check it himself. *There probably wouldn't be anything, but what was the harm in checking what the pastor was saying?* He searched for 'Camel and needle bible' in Google and clicked on the first blue link, titled *'kamêlos* vs. *kamilos.'* But before the article could fully load, his dad yanked the phone out of his hands.

"Hey!" David whispered.

"You'll get it back after the service," Corbin whispered back, as Laura stuck out her tongue at him.

"So what does this verse mean?" the pastor asked the congregation. "It's a reminder of the ten percent tithe we should give to the Lord, as part of our covenant to him."

And with that, the choir began to sing "How great is our God" as two people walked down each aisle with round wooden tithe plates, each person in the pews monotonously handing out a check as the pastor spoke of the eternal life that would soon be theirs. David looked around as everyone opened their wallets while dressed in their Sunday best: Hollister, Abercrombie and Fitch and Lacoste.

David then looked at the Jesus on the wall with a pure white cloth strategically draped over his well sculpted body, but became entranced instead by the one on the cover of his Bible, which was far more destitute, dressed only in rags and blood. It was painful to look at, but somehow he was couldn't help staring at the one thing in the service that wasn't perfect. The Bible's cover reminded David of the older hobo with weathered skin and a long, unkempt beard he passed every day on his way home from work. The hobo was always holding up a piece of cardboard with the words 'Let's be honest - it's for booze.' As David tried to think about why he had made that connection, an ad from Focus on the Family played on the projectors and distracted him.

David spent the rest of his time in Wheaton trying to remember his high school experience in a positive light and dismiss that uneasy day at church like an out-of-body experience, or a nightmarish episode of the X-Files. So naturally, he went to the place where he had his best memories: the football field.

And what was the football field without his bros? David texted them all to see if he could have one last hurrah with them:

Part Two: Pieces

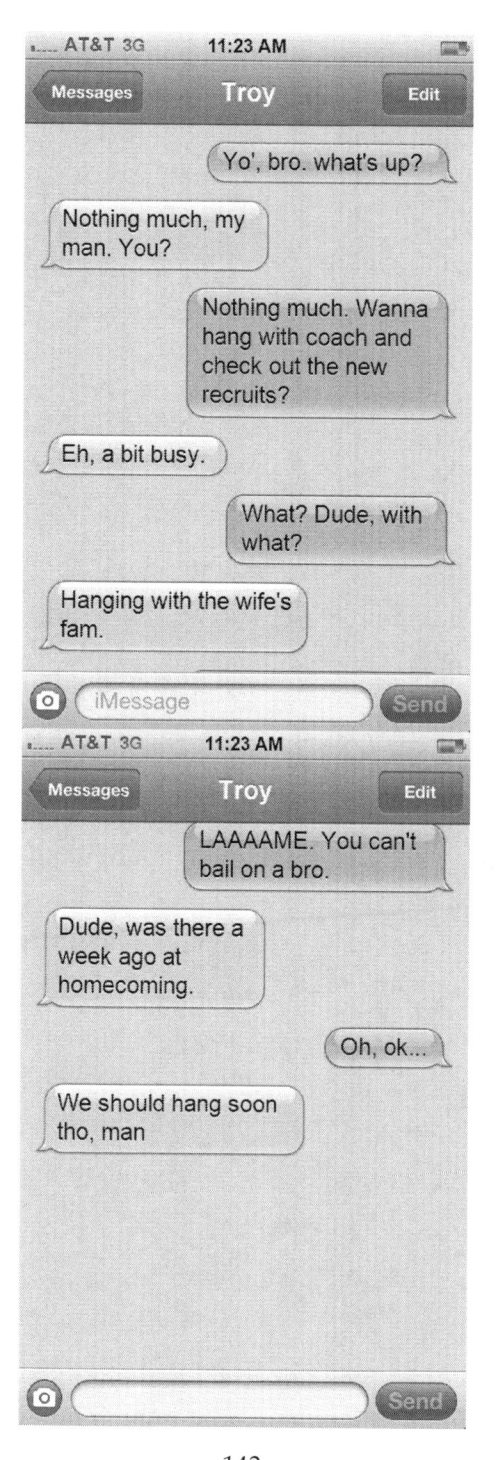

Troy

> Yo', bro. what's up?

Nothing much, my man. You?

> Nothing much. Wanna hang with coach and check out the new recruits?

Eh, a bit busy.

> What? Dude, with what?

Hanging with the wife's fam.

Troy

> LAAAAME. You can't bail on a bro.

Dude, was there a week ago at homecoming.

> Oh, ok...

We should hang soon tho, man

143

David hardly wanted to go to practice on his own - he didn't want people to think he was a creepy loner. But he'd rather go anywhere than stay stuck inside his own head, so he slowly psyched himself up for it and forced himself off the couch.

When David got back to his high school, the guys were in the middle of a scrimmage, so he jumped out of his car in the back parking lot and headed toward the field. Seeing the huge stainless steel stadium surrounding that majestic, familiar lawn filled him with an enormous sense of pride, remembering that time they had won State, or his surprise blitz against Wheaton North, their rival. He crossed the large, clay-colored track between the bleachers and the field and found his coach, as per usual, yelling and gesticulating with his clipboard.

"David? Is that you?" his coach said. "What are you doing here?"

"Back home for Thanksgiving," David said.

"Hey, Joe, don't let him just fuck you up the ass! BLOCK HIM!" the coach yelled. He turned back to David. "Sorry, I'm a little busy."

"It's all good," David said. "Figured. Hope I'm not interrupting..."

"N'aw, not at all. Glad to see ya, sport. You're free to stay for as long as you'd like," Coach said. "Maybe show these guys a few things. DAN! STOP THROWING LIKE A PANSY!"

"Not sure how long I can stay," David said. *Had coach always talked like that? Was his coach smoking him out? Did even Coach know about the kiss with Cristiano?*

"Haha, oh, I see. Got an old maid already?" Coach said smugly, with a smile. "Good for you, son."

"Haha, got me, Coach," David lied. *Was that just the way Coach had always talked? No, it couldn't be. It had only been half a year.*

"You guys are pathetic! Take five!" Coach said.

Part Two: Pieces

"But my muscles are on strike," a soft voice joked. A couple of others snickered underneath the darkness of their helmets.

"You see that?" Coach said, and he slowly rubbed his thumb and index finger together. "World's smallest violin playing the world's saddest song. 50 burpees for that, gentlemen."

The entire team groaned as Coach turned around.

"Always good seeing one of my best quarterbacks, son," Coach said. "Happy Thanksgiving."

"Thanks, coach. That means a lot, coming from you," David said, uneasily. "I should probably head home for dinner though. Don't want to piss off my mother."

"Ok, David," Coach winked. "Hope to see ya again soon, son."

"For sure! Some other time!" David said.

"Hey, what up, Dave?" an unfamiliar voice said from among the darkness of the helmets as they began their post-burpee break.

It was probably from one of the linebackers out in the distance heading for water, but he just ignored it and continued straight to his car. Being on the sidelines was surprisingly overwhelming. His coach's yelling used to pump him up, and in the middle of the action, that voice transformed every game into what he imagined the Super Bowl to be like. But now Coach's voice reminded him of a crying baby, as if the Detroit Lions and Cleveland Browns had produced an awkward football love child, reminding him of how much of an amateur he truly was.

Trying desperately to find something that was exciting as he remembered it, David drove to the Danada Square mall. He sat in his car in the parking lot, and looked at all the shops, wistfully remembering the fun times he'd had at all of them, like the time he went with his ex-girlfriend for their first date at Houlihan's.

The store strip mall had stood there virtually unchanged for the past eight years, as if it were a time capsule. David shifted

the car into gear, and suddenly had the urge to leave. He worried that if he stood there for any longer, he would soon become part of this living museum exhibit. Like Bill Murray in *Groundhog Day*, he would be cursed to live the same day over and over again with the knowledge of exactly what would happen. While he could try to change it, the constant repetition would slowly drive him insane, as everyone else remained in blissful ignorance.

David spent the rest of the time at his parents' nice, pristine home on Evergreen Street, the lawn perfectly mowed and the garden carefully weeded and pruned. His dad had waged a war with the neighbors to make sure of that - a war that David was pretty sure the neighbors had no clue about.

David looked out the window at the frost that now covered the well-maintained lawn on that Thanksgiving morning, wearing his comfortable winter PJs while enjoying a sweet glass of cocoa and toast. He was glad to be safe inside his house, with the warmth of the fireplace burning away the rest of his worries.

At least there he could relax and enjoy the short time with his family, getting fat on turkey and cranberry sauce later on and falling asleep during whatever predictable family debate happened afterwards in the living room. David ignored most of it, as he was more interested in the football game, but his uncle had gotten louder with each beer he'd had from the after-dinner six-pack.

"You know what I truly can't stand? Obama giving all these handouts to his lazy black friends with my hard-earned taxes!" Becki said.

"Finally, we agree on something!" Uncle Albert said. He was a larger man in a polo and khakis with a couple of white whiskers where his hair should have been. "He's turning the US into a moocher state!"

"Exactly! Why don't they just work hard for their money like everyone else!" Becki said.

Part Two: Pieces

"Says the housewife," Uncle Albert joked.

"You know what I mean!" Becki said, laughing.

"Worse is those faggots getting married!" Uncle Albert said. David began to listen in a little more intently, as thoughts raced through his head. *Did they know? About the kiss, not him being gay. He was a quarterback, not some fag. How could they?* "Sorry, 'homosexuals' - political correctness gone mad, I say. I heard they can get married in ten states now!"

"I'm sure it's just those liberals on the coasts," Becki said, spitting out the word *liberal*.

"No, even Iowa has made it legal now!" Uncle Albert said with disgust.

"No way! I don't believe you!" Becki said in shock.

"Heard it right on Focus on the Family," Uncle Albert said. "Even adopting kids!"

"Wow, all those drugs and premarital sex," Corbin piped in. "It's no wonder this nation's become such a den of sin."

His mom and Uncle Albert nodded.

"What do you think, son," Uncle Albert said. "You seem pretty interested."

"What?" David said, shaking his head. "Sorry, just zoned out there."

"You big doofus," Laura said.

"Boogerhead," David said. He got up, grabbed her around the neck, and gave her a noogie.

"Stop it, stop it! MOM!" Laura yelled.

"Be nice to your sister," Becki said disinterestedly, returning to her conversation with Uncle Albert.

David let out a sigh of relief. However, as the debate raged on, David became increasingly restless. He began tapping his foot and shifting around in his seat until his nerves were tense enough that he had to leave the room, much like the murderer in the Tell Tale Heart. He felt the blood pounding in his ears like a bass drum and could hardly hear anything else anymore.

"Oh, shit!" David said.

"Watch your language, son," Corbin said.

"Crap, sorry," David said.

"What's wrong?" Uncle Albert asked.

"I forgot I need to go in tomorrow," David said.

"Oh come now, David. It's Black Friday tomorrow," Becki said.

"Boom Boom, Boom Boom," David heard as blood rushed to his head.

"Not in our London office," David said, anxious to get out before he heard the sound of that beating heart between the floorboards again.

"Well, ask for another day off!" Becki asked.

"I took them all off for the past week," David said, shrugging.

Boom Boom, Boom Boom.

"Well, I'm gonna give your boss a stern talking to, ruining my holiday," Becki joked.

"Haha, good one, mom," David said awkwardly, as he headed to his room to pack.

BOOM BOOM, BOOM BOOM.

The next morning, his mother drove him to the nearest L station around eight a.m. with his bag.

"Love you, David," Becki said, giving him a huge hug.

"Love ya too, ma," David said halfheartedly.

David watched his mom get back into her black SUV and slowly drive away from the station. He waved goodbye to her, but only saw his reflection in the windows and the dead trees lining the street behind her. He let out a sigh of relief and walked over to the green benches.

As he waited, David imagined wild stories about the place. He looked up at the silo attached to the large brick building, the town's name plastered on the gateway in a beautiful black script, as if it were a Midwestern castle. He tried to imagine knights and quests to save princesses, so that he could forget about the wind blowing through him. But when he looked up to the left and saw a sign that said "Carlson - Glass and Mirror" in red, blue and white, it was hard to continue daydreaming.

Just underneath that overwhelming sign, he saw a Caribou Coffee. He looked at his phone to check the time and wondered if he had enough time to get a drink to warm and wake him up. But just then the train blew into the station. It would have to wait until he got into the city.

David picked up his bags and carried them to the open doors. It seemed to him that their weight had mysteriously doubled in the past week, and he struggled to pull them through the doors. At least the warmth of the train allowed him to get comfortable. Plus, the carriage was completely empty. Sitting there, watching the barren landscape of late fall pass him by in complete silence, he got an urge he hadn't had in years - not since he was twelve. David held it in, but the further the train went, the stronger it grew.

BOOM BOOM, BOOM BOOM, BOOM BOOM, BOOM BOOM.

"Why, why me?" David asked himself as water began to well around his eyes.

The sensation became overwhelming and he finally broke down in tears like a baby on the empty train. It was an uncontrollable

waterworks and he couldn't stop it no matter how hard he tried. All he had wanted was to be home. *But where was home?* After the dirt and grime of living in Chicago, Wheaton hardly recognized him. And Chicago still looked at him with disdain, saying "You'll never make it here."

Halfway to the city, the doors opened and several commuters entered his car. David suddenly became embarrassed that he had let himself go so much. He held his bag close to him and wiped away his tears, putting on a disinterested face, as if to prove how much of a real grown-up he was. And yet, people still stared at him.

"Do I have spinach in my teeth?" David wondered.

BOOM BOOM, BOOM BOOM, BOOM BOOM, BOOM BOOM.

David composed himself after returning to the apartment, but his eyes were still red and puffy.

"Boys don't cry. Boys don't cry. Boys don't cry," David repeated to himself.

And yet, try as hard as he might, after he found out no one else was there, they began rolling again. He fell down on the couch and just gave in to them at that point, crying until he ran out of tears. David almost wished they would keep going so he wouldn't have to think about why he was crying in the first place.

David just sat there for hours, his bag of laundry freshly done by his mother still sitting right next to the couch, refusing to admit to himself the only possible answer, the one he had run from all his life. He wasn't even sure he could say it aloud. And then Lena came in and offered him a gyro.

***

A car honked and brought David back to the streets of Chicago on that brisk December afternoon.

"Watch it, asshole!" the stranger yelled from his car.

Part Two: Pieces

David looked up from his feet, which he had been mindlessly dragging across the sidewalk like thirty-pound weights as he reminisced, and gained his bearings. Snowflakes were falling and melting on the pavement. He looked past the snowflakes and saw a big castle-like structure in front of him.

"Ok, that's the Water Tower, so I'm still on Michigan," David muttered.

David walked across the street to the mall and stared longingly at a Christmas tree in the window. It was decorated with white lights, tinsel that glinted silver, red and green bulbs, and a bright, hopeful white angel at the top. The angel, decorated in fine lace with a small halo, blinded him for a moment. He remembered his dad picking him up as a five-year-old to put the angel on the tree.

***

"Why do we put the angel on the tree, daddy?" David asked.

"It's our guardian angel. It protects us from all the bad guys," his dad said.

"Even the boogeyman?" David asked.

"Yes, even the boogeyman," his dad laughed. "Just look at their bright light, and they'll always guide you out of the darkness."

"I like angels," David said.

***

David closed his eyes in front of the window. He felt a pair of strong arms, covered in lace, reach around from behind him, giving him a big hug. David stood there and took it in, eventually putting his arms on top of those arms and giving in to the warm, safe embrace, until he realized no one was actually there and shook it off. The plan had been to head home and take his rage out on a Madden game, but what could it hurt to look around the mall first?

"Chestnuts roasting on an open fire," hummed a crackling older voice in the background. As he entered the mall, he remembered simpler times - eggnog secretly spiked with a little extra Christmas cheer, home-baked goods, the unspoken promise that family members would temporarily declare a truce until December 26.

Ever since the beginning of December, Chicago had definitely come to life. Christmas trees popped up like winter flowers, with each company and building owner fighting to show how much more Christmas cheer they had than the next one. The familiarity of it was comforting and made the unwieldy city more homely. It was as if at any moment, little nutcrackers and sugarplum fairies would pop out of the walls and start dancing to Tchaikovsky.

"Wait, really? Fairies? That's the best you could come up with? Come on, David, something less gay," David thought to himself. "Maybe candy canes? Yeah, that's better. Candy canes."

David bought a Bears hat at Lids on the first floor as a Christmas gift to himself. He wandered up the escalator to see what else was upstairs, promising himself he would only window-shop. But the freshly made holiday sweets at the Godiva store looked so good. Just a couple of snowflake-shaped malt chocolates couldn't hurt his budget. And after tasting the gooey caramel center, he finally started to relax, as if that chocolatey goodness had the magical ability to wash away all of his shortcomings in the outside world.

David walked down the hall to Marbles, and saw a balance board at front of the store. He was instantly tempted to jump on it. A cute bearded guy in a Marbles shirt with small black earring plugs came up to him.

"You know you want to," the salesman said.

"But I shouldn't," David said.

"Don't over-think it," the salesman said, smiling. David knew that the guy was only making a sale, but he liked having the cute salesman talk to him, so against his better judgment, he tried it.

Part Two: Pieces

"Wha... woooo," David said as he fell on his ass, the salesman laughing with him.

"Maybe not for you, man," the salesman said, as David turned red.

By the time he got to the Lego store, David was as happy and carefree as a kid at a playground. He saw a gingerbread house that the store had put up for Christmas that looked almost delicious enough to eat. David's stomach growled, and he realized that it was dinnertime. He looked at the Legos and considered going in, not wanting to leave and return to the storm outside, but his stomach rumbled again so he decided to go home.

"I'm... g... g... ga... gay." David practiced saying it aloud a couple of times on the subway ride home, whispering and looking over his shoulder each time. His tongue tripped over the simple yet foreign phrase, as if he had just gotten his braces removed.

"That wasn't so bad," he thought proudly to himself. "I can do this."

David opened the door, eager to heat up a pizza or maybe even splurge at the Thai delivery place down the street and play some video games for the night. But instead, he found himself face to face with his parents, sitting on the couch and talking politely but distantly with Cristiano.

"Hey mother and father. What are you doing here so early?" David asked.

"Since when are we 'mother' and 'father'?" Becki asked, dismayed. "It's like we don't even know you anymore!"

"Oh, sorry. I just..." David tried to answer.

"Just what?" said Corbin, deadly serious, as if someone in the family had cancer.

"Troy told us about Halloween," Becki said.

David's face went white as he processed what was going on. His heart raced. He was not prepared for this. He needed more time. Just enough time to figure out things for himself.

"I'm sorry. I had alcohol with a fake I.D.," David bluffed. "It won't happen again, sir."

"Don't play coy," Corbin said. "You know exactly what I mean, son."

His mother began to cry without stopping.

"There's therapy for this kind of stuff, David. We can fix you" declared Corbin, matter-of-factly. "Just come with us."

"I think you should go," responded David with the little strength he had, a stern look on his face.

"Great. We have a center picked out already and…"

"I said YOU should go!" David yelled at the top of his lungs.

Corbin and Becki Fisher headed towards the door, his dad comforting his mom in his arms.

"I am so disappointed in you, son," Corbin said, standing in the doorway as he lectured. "You had the potential to be a city on a hill, but you let the devil lead you…"

"I said GO!"

David watched the two of them leave. His dad calmly closed the door behind them.

After ten seconds of staring at the closed door with unbroken resolve, David realized he was shaking. It suddenly became uncontrollable and he fell to the ground in tears.

Lena appeared from around the corner a few seconds later. Without knowing what to do, she sat next to David and rubbed his back. He just let his head fall into her lap and closed his eyes, crying. At that moment, David didn't care if it made him a wuss or a fag - he was just a human in pain, doing whatever he could to survive.

Part Two: Pieces

And then David felt another person embracing him. Part of David wanted to throw Cristiano off. Part of him wanted to punch him in the face. But David didn't. He had no more strength to. Because in that singular moment, he had no more fucks to give.

Seis

❖ ❖ ❖

Coming Undone

Enero, 2013

—¡¡¡¡¡FELIZ AÑO NUEVO!!!!! —postearon los amigos de Cristiano en su muro de *Facebook* y *Tuenti*. Podía escuchar sus voces cantarinas en su cabeza. Fotos de uvas, buenos propósitos de año nuevo, y estados divertidos invadían sus últimas noticias pero, de alguna manera, todos estos mensajes le sonaban a Cristiano mucho más optimistas que las personas que las habían posteado. Ni siquiera quiso echar un vistazo al *Twitter*.

A Cristiano le parecían muy graciosas las redes sociales. Claro, las tenía porque le ayudaban a mantenerse en contacto con sus amigos de siempre, los cuales se encontraban dispersos por el mundo. Pero, ¿y los demás? Cristiano no necesitaba mantener el contacto con su ex-novia de hace diez años, pero tampoco quería borrarla, porque entonces podría pensar que era un mezquino. ¿Y su mejor amigo de primaria? No habían hablado desde hacía muchos años, y a veces, sus mensajes constantes del 'salvador de la economía española', Mariano Rajoy, o sus mensajes alabando al Rey Juan Carlos le sentaban mal. Pero cada vez que consideraba quitarle de su lista de amigos, al final decidía no hacerlo.

Por otra parte, entre los mejores amigos de Cristiano, notaba

Six

❖ ❖ ❖

Coming Undone

January, 2013

"Happy New Year!!!!!" Cristiano's friends posted on his Facebook wall and Tuenti. He could hear their happy, singsong voices in his head. Photos of grapes, well-meaning resolutions, and fun-filled statuses overran his news feed, but somehow these posts all sounded more happy-go-lucky to Cristiano than the people who had posted them. He didn't even want to take a look at Twitter.

Social networks were a riot to Cristiano. Sure, he kept them because they helped to keep in contact with his close friends who had scattered around the world. But what about the rest? Cristiano hardly needed to keep in contact with his ex-girlfriend from ten years ago, but he also didn't want to de-friend her, because then she might think he was petty or overdramatic. And his best friend from primary school? They hadn't really talked in years, and the constant posts about the 'savior of the Spanish economy,' Mariano Rajoy, or some post praising Juan Carlos were annoying. And yet, every time Cristiano considered taking him off his friends list, he decided against it at the last minute.

Even for Cristiano's close friends, their personalities were amplified by social media. Facebook Messenger, WhatsApp,

cómo sus personalidades se magnificaban en las redes sociales. En los tablones y mensajes de *Facebook, Whatsapp, Skype*, todos le habían revelado algo nuevo, como las complicadas capas de un caleidoscopio, mostrando un rico tapiz que se hacía más transparente con cada cuenta de cristal coloreado. Cristiano se desplazó por las biografías de sus amigos para ver las vidas que vivían: fotos de la playa en Valencia —donde su amigo no se quedó más que una hora antes de pelearse con su tío— o fotos de ese finde de caminata por las inmaculadas colinas de Bilbao —que realmente era un sitio lluvioso y ventoso— o fotos de esa cojonuda fiesta en Ibiza —donde parte de sus amigos estaban drogados— e incluso fotos de la nueva relación de su amiga con un francés —de quien se quejaba constantemente porque era demasiado aburrido.

Internet transformó a personas normales en personalidades imponentes como si fueran estrellas de Hollywood. Todas las interacciones cautelosas entre esas famosas imágenes públicas le recordaban a una canción que su estudiante francés de intercambio le había enseñado, pero no lograba recordar el nombre. El ritmo de *Stromae* empezó a sonar en su mente mientras le costaba recordar toda la letra y su significado.

—¿Qué era *l'oiseau*? Un ave, ¿verdad? Pero ¿qué coño tiene esto que ver con los *hashtags* y *followers* de *Twitter*? —pensó Cristiano.

Al final Cristiano se dio por vencido, se lo tomó a risa y cerró la sesión, tras lo cual comprobó la hora.

—¡Mierda! ¿¡¿Ya son las diez de la noche?!?— se dijo Cristiano estupefacto por el tiempo que había perdido cotilleando en perfiles de *Facebook* de amigos, familia, enamorados, rollos de una noche, leyendo artículos de humor, 'memes' y 'gifs' animados en su biografía entre otras fantasías—. Tengo que empezar a hacer botellón ahora si quiero llegar a las discos antes de medianoche y divertirme. Si no, también puedo quedarme en casa. Ahora, ¿dónde está mi botella?

El alcohol en EE.UU. era tan caro que no se podía permitir

Skype - they all revealed something new, like complicated layers of a kaleidoscope, revealing a rich tapestry that became more clear with each bead of colored glass. Cristiano scrolled through his friends' timelines, seeing them together with the lives they lived. Pictures on the beach in Valencia, where his friend had been for no more than an hour before having an argument with his uncle, or pictures of a weekend hiking in the pristine hills of Bilbao, which had been mostly rainy and windy. Pictures of that sick party in Ibiza, where a group of his friends had ended up getting drugged. Pictures of the French guy his friend was dating, who s/he constantly complained about as being too boring.

The Internet changed normal people into larger-than-life personalities, as if they were Hollywood stars. All the guarded interactions between these famous personas reminded Cristiano of a song his French *Intercambio*[1] had showed him, but he couldn't remember what it was called for the life of him. Stromae's beat started playing in his head as he struggled to remember all the lyrics and what they meant.

"What does *l'oiseau* mean again? It's bird, right? But what the hell does that have to do with hashtags and Twitter followers?" Cristiano thought.

Eventually he gave up, laughed it off and signed off. He looked at the clock.

"Shit! It's already ten at night?!?" Cristiano thought to himself. He was shocked at how much time he had spent dicking around Facebook, stalking friends, family, crushes, flings, and reading funny articles, memes, and animated gifs on his timeline, among other daydreaming. "I have to start pre-gaming now if I want to get to the clubs before midnight and enjoy myself - otherwise I might as well just stay in. Now, where's my bottle?"

The alcohol in the U.S. was too expensive to allow for anything more than a sip in the bars. There was a so-called 'sin tax' for

beber nada más que un trago en los bares. Había algo llamado 'impuesto del pecado' por el alcohol —algo que sólo podía pasar en EE.UU.— que doblaba los precios. Eso lo había aprendido Cristiano por experiencia cuando su cuenta corriente llegó a estar casi vacía hacía unos meses, aunque todo lo que había estado comprando eran botellas de cerveza de 0.4 litros. A cinco putos dólares cada cerveza, el dinero se esfumaba rápidamente. Así que el whisky cola se convirtió en su bebida preferida. Una de las únicas bebidas alcohólicas que podía hacer bien EE.UU. y —lo más importante— era mucho más barata que todas las demás bebidas, solo ocho dólares una botella entera de Jack Daniels.

Cristiano se fue a la cocina a buscar su whisky, y vio a David y Lena sentados en el sofá. La televisión estaba encendida en el canal de la CNN, en el que aparecían Anderson Cooper y Kathy Griffin en Times Square, hablando sobre la tormenta *Sandy*, que había destruido varias zonas de Nueva York unas semanas antes. Cristiano siguió escuchando la tele a medias mientras buscaba en la nevera, donde normalmente ponía el Jack. *¿Quizá en la alacena?* Nada. Intentó recordar si ya se lo había acabado cuando vio el whisky justo enfrente de él en la mesa.

—¡Qué tonto soy! —se dijo Cristiano—. Lo debí de haber dejado fuera al tomarme un vaso en la cena.

Con el whisky en una mano, cogió con la otra, como pudo, un vaso y la botella de Cola. Pero mientras se servía una copa, Cristiano oyó el saludo de David llenando la sala.

—¡Ey, Cristiano! Por cierto, ¿no te importará que te robe un poco de Jack, no?

—Da igual, Dave.

—*Cool, bro.*

La amistad entre los dos había estado mejorando lentamente desde el fiasco de las Navidades, pero todavía tenía que andar con pies de plomo. Cristiano no pudo menos que acabar con los ojos

alcohol - something that only the U.S. would think of - that doubled the price. Cristiano had learned that lesson when his checking account nearly went dry a couple of months ago, even though all he had been buying were 0.4 liter bottles of beer. But at five fucking dollars apiece, they really added up quickly. That was how whiskey-cola had become his preferred drink. It was one of the only alcoholic drinks that the US could make well and - most importantly - it was much cheaper than everything else, at only eight dollars for an entire bottle of Jack Daniels.

Cristiano made his way to the kitchen to find his whiskey, and saw David and Lena seated on the couch. The television was tuned to CNN with Anderson Cooper and Kathy Griffin in Times Square, talking casually about the storm Sandy, which had destroyed parts of New York a couple weeks earlier. Cristiano continued half-listening to the T.V. as he searched through the fridge where he normally put the Jack. *Maybe it was in the cabinet? Nothing.* He tried remembering if he had already finished it when he saw the whiskey right in front of him on the table.

"Duh, I'm such an idiot!" Cristiano thought to himself. "I must've left it out when I got a glass at dinner."

With the whiskey in hand, he grabbed his glass and some Coke. As he was making himself a drink, Cristiano heard a yell from David in the living room.

"Hey, Cristiano. Hope you don't mind that I stole some of your Jack, man."

"It's all good, Dave."

"Cool, bro."

Their friendship had been slowly getting better since the Christmas fiasco, but it was still a delicate balancing act. Cristiano couldn't help but let his eyes glaze over as he watched the T.V., thinking about the past couple of months.

vidriosos mientras veía la tele, pensando en lo que había sucedido en el último par de meses.

***

Los padres de David irrumpieron en el apartamento con una pasión fervorosa, pero infundada.

—¿Sabes quién podría haber hecho eso? —le preguntó Becki atemorizada.

—Becki, ¡cálmate! —respondió Corbin, tranquilizando a su esposa antes de que Cristiano pudiera meter baza.

—Pero es un buen chico, te lo juro —suplicó Becki, como si Cristiano lo pudiera arreglar.

Cristiano estaba completamente confundido por lo que pasaba. De repente, David abrió la puerta.

—Madre, padre ¿Qué hacéis aquí tan temprano? —dijo David torpemente.

—¿Desde cuándo somos 'madre' y 'padre'? — preguntó Becki con un sentido de santurronería.

—¡Ay! Lo siento, sólo... —intentó contestar David.

—¿Sólo... qué? —escupió Corbin.

—Troy nos contó lo de Halloween —dijo Becki desilusionada.

Cristiano se retiró cuando empezaron a gritar entre ellos, no quería formar parte de eso. De todas formas David había sido un gilipollas en los últimos meses. Cristiano se acordó de esa mañana en la que por accidente se encontró con él tras el fiasco, al mismo tiempo que desconectaba de los gritos a su espalda.

—¡Mira por dónde andas, mamón! —dijo David mientras le hacía retroceder.

—¡Relájate, tío! Sólo fue un error —respondió Cristiano

***

David's parents barged into the apartment in a zealous, albeit uninformed fervor.

"Do you know who could've done this?" Becki asked him, terrified.

"Becki, calm down," Corbin responded, reassuring his wife before Cristiano could get a word in. "I'm sure he would've helped if he could have."

"But he's a good boy, I swear," Becki pleaded, as if Cristiano could fix it.

Cristiano was completely confused by what was going on. Suddenly David opened the door.

"Hey mother and father. What are you doing here so early?" David said, awkwardly.

"Since when are we 'mother' and 'father'?" Becki asked, with an air of self-righteousness. "It's like we don't even know you anymore!"

"Oh sorry, I just..." David tried to answer.

"Just what?" Corbin spat out.

"Troy told us about Halloween," Becki said, disappointedly.

Cristiano backed away when they started yelling at each other - he wanted no part in this. And besides, David had been an asshole for the past couple of months, anyway. Cristiano remembered accidentally bumping into David at work that morning before the fiasco, as Cristiano tuned out the yelling behind him.

"Watch where you're going, asshole," David said as he pushed back.

manteniéndose en calma.

—¿Relajarme? ¿Con un maricón como tú? —respondió David asqueado.

—No soy maricón. Sólo soy un chico que a veces se divierte con chicos —se rio Cristiano.

—Pues, llámalo como quieras. Todo es el mismo pecado asqueroso —dijo David, evitando su mirada.

—Bueno, no recuerdo que te quejaras —bromeó Cristiano metiendo el dedo en la llaga.

—Mira, por favor, déjame hacer mi trabajo —dijo David exasperado y enfadado como si de un perro amenazado y acorralado se tratase—. Dentro de unos meses todo esto acabará y podrás volver a tus cosas…europeas —le replicó torpemente, siguiendo entre dientes—. Y yo por fin a las mías.

Aquella mañana había sido de coña. Mientras que David tuvo que marcharse del trabajo después del arrebato de ira con su jefe Lisa, Cristiano estaba distraído por la reacción de David sobre el beso que supuestamente no había significado nada. Después de todo, lo había olvidado hacía una eternidad antes de que David lo desenterrara. Cristiano estaba borracho y sólo quería liarse con alguien. Pensaba que David estaba en la misma onda, pero por la manera en la que reaccionó, Cristiano había decidido hacer como Poncio Pilato: se lavaría las manos, y David, los platos.

David le recordó a Cristiano cómo adulaba a sus novias en los viejos tiempos —un niño enamorado hasta las trancas de chicas a quienes no les importaba ni una mierda. Las relaciones y el sexo eran complicadas en esos días, pero todo era cuestión de una única cosa: cuanto más te importara, menor era el poder que tendrías. ¿Pesimista? Quizá. Pero era un principio que había funcionado para Cristiano hasta ahora.

Part Two: Pieces

"Relax, man. It was just an accident," Cristiano responded, keeping his cool.

"Relax? Around a fag like you?" David responded in disgust.

"I'm no fag. I'm just a guy who sometimes has fun with other guys," Cristiano laughed.

"Well, whatever you want to call it. It's all the same disgusting sin," David said, avoiding eye contact.

"Well, I don't recall you complaining," Cristiano joked, egging him on.

"Look, please just let me get my job done," David said in anger and exasperation, like a cornered dog. "In a couple of months, this will be over, and you can get back to your European... stuff," he said awkwardly, continuing under his breath: "And I can finally get back to my life."

That morning, it had been funny. Even when David had to leave work early because of his outbursts with Lisa, Cristiano was amused by how much David had been overreacting about a kiss that supposedly meant nothing to him. After all, Cristiano had long forgotten about it before David dredged it up again. Cristiano had been drunk as shit and just wanted a simple hookup. He thought David was on the same page, but with the way David reacted, Cristiano was determined to wash his hands of it.

David reminded Cristiano of how he used to fawn over his girlfriends back in the day - a dumb little kid, head over heels for chicks who couldn't care less. Relationships and sex were complicated things these days, but they all came down to one thing - the more you cared, the less power you had. Pessimistic? Maybe. But it was a principle that had worked for Cristiano thus far.

And yet, even though Cristiano had moved on from David,

Aunque Cristiano ya había dejado de pensar en David así, escuchar a sus padres gritar y discutir con él le hizo sentir una punzada de culpa. Cristiano dio por hecho su interés en los chicos, no se lo había dicho nunca a sus padres. Más porque habría sido una molestia, su madre explotaría sobre 'el peligro del SIDA', y su padre le preguntaría cosas incómodas sobre el sexo gay. Pero no como esto. Cristiano pensaba que luchas como esa, sobre la sexualidad, sólo pasaban en la tele.

De repente, los gritos pararon y a Cristiano le vino de vuelta a la mente el fiasco de las Navidades con el portazo. Y entonces surgió el llanto. Un llanto de miseria completa. Cristiano y Lena se atrevieron a salir, Lena le echó una mirada sucia y acusatoria a Cristiano, como si dijera "¿te alegras ahora, gili?" mientras iba a consolar a su amigo.

Inseguro sobre cómo consolar incluso a sus amigos más íntimos de España en un día bueno, Cristiano no tenía ni idea de cómo consolar a su colega, ex-mejor-amigo, y follamigo fallido, pero Cristiano se acercó lentamente y dio a David una palmadita insegura en la espalda como una manera de disculparse silenciosamente. David se veía claramente perturbado al principio, pero después de unos segundos se calmó y aceptó la disculpa pasivamente. En ese momento, inapropiado como fue, Cristiano por fin entendió el modismo americano de 'no cagar donde duermes'.

Si a Cristiano, David, y Lena les hubiera pasado lo que querían, probablemente habría acabado esta tregua precaria entre los tres — un final desgarrado de la temporada de una serie sentimental de Hollywood que no sería elegida para seguir después del receso de invierno. Pero los planes son divertidos así, a la vida no le gusta cooperar, aunque te prepares tanto como Lena, sea para bien o para mal.

Para David era obvio, ir a su casa no era una opción, y el precio de un vuelo en el último minuto costaría más que su escaso sueldo.

Part Two: Pieces

hearing David's parents yell and argue with David made Cristiano feel a pang of guilt for once. Cristiano had always taken his interest in guys for granted - he had never even told his parents. Mostly because telling them would have been an inconvenience - his mom would have likely gone off about the 'danger of AIDS,' and his dad might have asked something awkward about sex. But not like this. Cristiano thought that fights like this about sexuality only happened on T.V.

Suddenly, the yelling stopped and Cristiano was brought back to the Christmas fiasco as the apartment door slammed. And then he heard someone crying. It was a sound of complete misery. Cristiano and Lena both ventured out. The German gave Cristiano a dirty, accusatory look, as if to say "Happy now, you ass-wipe?", as she went to comfort her friend.

Unsure how to comfort even his closest friends from Spain on a good day, Cristiano hadn't the slightest clue how to comfort your colleague, former best friend, and failed fuck-buddy, but he carefully inched over and gave David a small, unsure pat on the back as his way of silently apologizing. David was visibly shaken at first, but after a few seconds calmed down and passively accepted the apology. It was in that moment, inappropriate as it was, that Cristiano finally understood the American idiom 'Don't shit where you sleep.'

Had Cristiano, David, and Lena had their own way, it probably would have ended as that uneasy truce between the three of them - a heart-wrenching season finale for some sappy Hollywood show that wouldn't get picked up after the winter break. But plans are funny like that; life doesn't tend to cooperate, even if you prepare as much as Lena, for better or for worse.

David was obvious - going home wasn't an option any longer, and the prices for last-minute flights would have been above his meager salary. Not that David even had the energy to leave

Ni siquiera tenía la energía para salir de Chicago, aunque la nueva amistad con Lena le dio un nuevo sentido a la pasión por los viajes.

En cuanto a Cristiano, la aerolínea se puso en huelga y Cristiano estaba tirado en O'Hare. Después de esperar en el aeropuerto un día entero un vuelo alternativo, Cristiano por fin dio por vencidos sus sueños de celebrar las Navidades con sus amigos y familia, consiguió el reembolso del billete y cogió el largo viaje a casa con el 'L'.

—¡Cómo te atreves! —le gritó Juana por *Skype*.

—Mamá, Iberia se ha puesto en huelga de nuevo —dijo Cristiano—. No había nada que pudiera hacer.

—¡Excusas! —gritó Juana.

—¿Qué debía hacer, cielo? —dijo Manuel metiendo baza desde el fondo—. ¿Decirles que su madre española les atosigaría con sus preocupaciones?

—¡Cómo te atreves! —dijo Juana, dándole una colleja mientras Cristiano se aguantaba una carcajada—. Por lo menos me das tu dirección, cariño.

—¿Por qué? ¿Para qué le puedas enviar una brigada de asesinos?— preguntó Manuel con sarcasmo.

—Para que le pueda enviar regalos de Navidad, ¡tonto! —espetó Juana.

—No permiten pasar jamón serrano por la aduana, cielo —dijo Manuel.

—Eso lo sé —dijo Juana, ya ignorándole.

Una semana después, Cristiano recibió un paquete gigante de Cola Cao, mazapanes, y una extraña caja de churros con chocolate instantáneo. Cristiano tenía demasiada comida para comérsela él solo, así que llamó a la puerta de David.

—¿Sip? —contestó un David grogui, sin afeitar, y semidesnudo

Chicago, even if Lena's new friendship had given him a newfound wanderlust.

As for Cristiano, the airline went on strike and Cristiano was left stranded in O'Hare. After an entire day of waiting in the airport for an alternate flight, Cristiano finally gave up on his dreams of celebrating Christmas, New Year's Eve, and *el Día de los Reyes* in Spain with his family and friends, cashed his ticket, and took the long L ride back.

"How could you!" Juana yelled at him on Skype.

"*Mamá*, Iberia was on strike again," Cristiano said. "There was nothing I could do."

"Excuses!" Juana yelled back.

"What was he supposed to do, dear?" Manuel chimed in from in back. "Tell them his Spanish mother would worry their heads off?"

"How dare you!" Juana said, slapping him. Cristiano stifled a laugh. "At least give me your address, sweetie."

"Why, so you can send a hit squad?" Manuel asked sarcastically.

"So I can send him his Christmas gifts, idiot!" Juana snapped back.

"They don't allow *jamón* through customs, dear," Manuel said.

"I know that much," Juana said, ignoring him.

A week later, Cristiano got a gigantic package of *Cola Cao*, marzipan, and a strange box of instant *Churros con Chocolate*. Cristiano had way too much to eat on his own, so he knocked on David's door and asked if he wanted some.

A groggy, unshaven, half-naked David answered the door in a pair of boxers with flaming chili peppers and the words 'Red Hot'

en un par de bóxers diseñados con unos ardientes chiles cayendo y las palabras 'Red Hot'.

—¡Tío! Acabo de recibir una caja de comida de mi madre —dijo Cristiano, mientras le pasaba una caja con 'Producido en Toledo' escrito por arriba—. ¿Quieres algo?

—¡No! —dijo David, restregándose los ojos y repondiendo con un bostezo—. Acabo de despertarme, tío.

—¿Cómo? ¡Casi son las 17:00! —rio Cristiano.

—¡Ay, mierda! —dijo David pensando en ello otra vez—. Quizá un poco.

Demasiado impacientes por probar la comida que le habían entregado y demasiado perezosos como para prepararse algo ellos mismos, terminaron en la sala con una cena relativamente callada de dulces y azúcar. David encendió la tele y empezaron a ver el especial de Charlie Brown, probablemente como ruido de fondo, pero ambos ya habían olvidado el espacio vacío sentado entre ellos en el sofá. El hueco se había convertido en un ser tácito durante los últimos meses, y ninguno tenía agallas para discutir, como si pedirle que se fuera pudiera acabar en un holocausto nuclear entre David y Cristiano. Sin embargo, sentarse y compartir una comida incómoda era distinto y se le hizo más difícil de ignorar. Finalmente, Cristiano, envalentonado, dijo lo que pensaba.

—Por cierto, tío —dijo Cristiano.

—Dime —dijo David.

—Halloween, el beso, tus padres… —dijo Cristiano, mientras su voz iba apagándose.

—¡Ah! ¿Eso? —dijo David, fingiendo mal que no le importaba—. Se me olvidó completamente. No pasa nada, hombre.

—Sabes, Papá Noel, y Feliz Navidad, y muérdago, y regalos para las chicas guapas —empezó el personaje de Lucy, gritando desde la tele mientras intentaba besar al pianista Schoerder, quien

Part Two: Pieces

printed across them. "Yeah?" he said.

"Dude, I just got a care package from my mom," Cristiano said, handing over a box with *Producido en Toledo* written on top. "Want some?"

"N'aw," David said, rubbing his eyes and yawning. "Just got up, man."

"What? It's almost 5 PM!" Cristiano laughed.

"Oh shit," David said, rethinking. "Maybe just one."

Too impatient for take-out and too lazy to make anything themselves, they ended up in the living room with a relatively silent dinner of sweets and sugar. David turned on the T.V., and they started watching the Charlie Brown Christmas special, probably as white noise, but both of them had already forgotten the empty space sitting between them on the couch. The space had developed into an unspoken being over the past months that neither of them had had the guts to tell off, as if asking him to leave would have ended in Cristiano and David's nuclear holocaust. But sitting down and sharing a meal with the awkwardness was different and made him harder to ignore. Eventually, the emboldened Cristiano spoke up.

"By the way, I'm sorry, man," Cristiano said.

"About what?" David asked.

"Halloween, the kiss, your parents..." Cristiano trailed off.

"Dude, that?" David said, poorly feigning that it didn't matter to him. "I had forgotten all about that. No big deal, man."

"You know, Santa Claus, and ho-ho-ho, and mistletoe, and presents to pretty girls," Lucy started belting from the T.V. She tried to kiss the pianist, Schroeder, who denied her by playing an angry, childish version of Jingle Bells in lieu of a response.

la rechazó tocando una versión enfadada e infantil de *Jingle Bells* en vez de dar una respuesta.

—¡ESO ES! —gritó Lucy después, asustando a Schroeder hasta hacerle caer.

David y Cristiano no pudieron evitar reírse. No era tan gracioso pero aun así casi se mueren de la risa. Y con esa risotada la situación incómoda no tuvo más remedio que salir.

Mientras tanto, Lena se había ido a Key West durante sus vacaciones para quedar con unas amigas alemanas, los planes con los que se había estado obsesionando, al menos, durante el mes anterior. Lena se pasaba todo el tiempo en la sala para estar cerca del WiFi y cotillear en *Skype* por unas horas, un *GENAU* ocasional para mostrar su acuerdo volando desde la pantalla tan rápida y alegremente como unos chicos incontrolables después de haber tomado demasiado azúcar.

—*Aber wirklich?*

—*GENAU!*

—*Ich dachte er mächte das nie*

—*GENAU!*

—¿Qué cojones dices?

—Si quería que lo supieras, lo diría en inglés.

Sin embargo, unas semanas antes, sus amigas empezaron a dar excusas. Algunas se quejaban de dinero, y otras tenían emergencias familiares misteriosas. Cada vez que ocurría, Lena despotricaba por todo el apartamento, frustrada de que esas supuestas amigas le fueran a abandonar en el último momento. Al fin y al cabo, solamente su amiga Natalie había reservado los billetes, pero Lena estaba decidida a quedarse con lo mejor de todo esto. Y aunque regresó pronto, estaba determinada a mostrar que lo pasó bien.

—Y aquí está el ceviche del restaurante cubano por sólo siete dólares a las afueras de Miami —dijo Lena.

Part Two: Pieces

"THAT'S IT!" Lucy yelled back, startling Schroeder and causing him to fall.

David and Cristiano couldn't help laughing together. It wasn't even that funny, and yet, they almost fell to the floor themselves in their amusement. And in that laughter, the awkwardness had no choice but to leave.

Meanwhile, Lena had gone to Key West for the holidays to meet up with some German friends, which she had obsessed about for the past month. Lena would get into the living room to be near the wi-fi and would gossip on Skype for hours, an occasional *GENAU* in agreement flying from the screen, as quickly and as happily as a couple of kids hyped up on sugar.

"*Aber wirklich?*"

"*GENAU!*"

"*Ich dachte er mächte das nie.*"

"*GENAU!*"

"What the hell are you saying?"

"If I wanted you to know, I'd say it in English."

A few weeks before though, her friends had started making excuses. Some complained of money, and others had mysterious family emergencies arise. Lena had ranted around the apartment each time, frustrated that these supposed friends of her left her stranded at the last minute. In the end only her friend Natalie actually booked tickets, but Lena was determined to make the best of it. And even when she came home early, she was determined to show off.

"And here's the ceviche from the Cuban restaurant for just seven dollars on our way out of Miami," Lena said.

"The what?" Cristiano asked.

—¿El qué? —preguntó Cristiano.

—Ceviche —respondió.

—¿Estás segura que eso es algún tipo de comida? —bromeó Cristiano.

—¡SÍ! ¡No me jodas! —gritó Lena.

—Porque me parece más un crimen de guerra —rió Cristiano.

—¿Ya has terminado? —respondió Lena.

—Ke$ha acaba de llamar. Quiere que le devuelvas su vagina rebozada en purpurina —respondió Cristiano, poniendo una sonrisa en la cara de Lena—. Ahora sí, ya he acabado.

Como era de esperar, Natalie se puso muy enferma después de comer marisco un poco sospechoso. Tras unos días vomitando y, finalmente, pagando una pequeña fortuna en un viaje a un hospital americano, Natalie decidió volar a casa un poco antes. En vez de quedarse sola en el hotel, Lena decidió recortar sus gastos y regresar a Chicago después de que su amiga se fuera, llegando así a casa justo antes de Nochebuena.

Compañeros de mala suerte, se consolaron con el hecho de que no fueran los únicos con contratiempos. Pero a pesar de lo tedioso que era estar en el piso durante las Navidades, les hizo acercarse entre ellos de alguna manera.

—Tío, no hay nada que hacer —se quejó Cristiano.

—¿Quieres jugar al FIFA otra vez? —preguntó David.

—Ayer nos pasamos todo el día jugando a la Play 3 —dijo Cristiano.

—¿Unas cartas? —preguntó Cristiano.

—No, Cristiano, que haces trampas —dijo David.

—¡Qué no! —gritó Cristiano, lanzando un cojín al aire en dirección a David —. Solamente porque no sabes ganar...

Part Two: Pieces

"Ceviche," she replied.

"Are you sure that is some kind of food?" Cristiano joked.

"YES! Stop making fun of me," Lena yelled back.

"Because it looks more like a war crime," Cristiano laughed back.

"Are you quite done yet?" Lena replied.

"Ke$ha called - she wants her bedazzled vagina back," Cristiano replied, putting a smile on Lena's face. "There, now I'm done."

Unsurprisingly, Natalie had gotten extremely sick after some suspect shellfish. After spending a couple of days throwing up, and eventually spending a small fortune on a trip to an American hospital, Natalie had decided to fly home early. Rather than stay alone at the hotel, Lena decided to cut her losses and change her tickets, getting back just before Christmas Eve.

Companions in bad luck, they took solace in the fact that they weren't the only ones with setbacks. But as mundane as being at the apartment on Christmas was, somehow that time brought them all closer together.

"Dude, there's nothing to do," Cristiano complained.

"You wanna play me in FIFA again?" David asked.

"We played PS3 all yesterday," Cristiano said.

"Cards?" Lena asked.

"No. Cristiano cheats," David said.

"Do not!" Cristiano yelled, lofting a throw pillow at David. "Just because you don't know how to win..."

"You snuck extra cards, you ass!" Lena stopped him as they all laughed.

—Trajiste cartas extra a escondidas, mamón —le paró Lena mientras reían.

—Eres *ruthless*, tío —dijo David sobre sus trucos.

—¡Ya tengo a Ruth! —insistió Cristiano mientras volvía a tirarle una almohada a la cara.

—¡Oye! ¿Puedes prestarme uno de tus libros? —preguntó David a Lena.

—¿El nuevo de Rachel Maddow? —preguntó, mientras Cristiano encendía la consola para jugar solo al "Call of Duty".

—No, no me gusta la política —dijo David.

—¡Todo es política! —sostuvo Lena.

—¡Sí, claro! Ya sabes lo que digo. No me gustan los comentarios políticos —respondió David.

—¡Bien! —respondió Lena mientras rumiaba sobre las opciones—. ¿Qué tal si acabo el de Maddow y empiezo el del nuevo autor que encontré y que me muero por leer?

—¿David Sedaris? —preguntaron a la vez.

Aunque los tres comenzaban a estar muy unidos ahora, David y Lena habían sido inseparables hasta ese momento. Cristiano no lo entendía. David y Lena eran polos opuestos gran parte del tiempo, pero ahora tenían una relación tan cercana que incluso un día alguien les tomó por una pareja de camino a Big City Tap.

—Parece que todo empezó por Acción de Gracias... —pensó Cristiano, pero entonces decidió no analizarlo mucho. De todos modos, no era asunto suyo. De hecho, sería mejor así. Cristiano prefería ser un fantasma que un amigo, pasando de un grupo de amigos a otro.

***

Cristiano saltó de su mirada distraída y de repente regresó a la sala donde celebraba la Nochevieja justo a tiempo para darse

Part Two: Pieces

"You're ruthless, man!" David yelled.

"I have Ruth!" Cristiano insisted, as a pillow hit him in the face.

"Hey, can I borrow one of your books?" David asked Lena.

"The new one from Rachel Maddow?" she asked, as Cristiano turned on the console to play by Call of Duty by himself.

"No, I don't like politics," David said.

"Everything is politics!" Lena argued.

"Ok, fine. You know what I mean. I don't like political commentary," David responded.

"Fine," Lena responded as she mulled it over. "How about I finish the Maddow one, and you can start the one from that new author I found that I'm really excited about?"

"David Sedaris?" they both asked at the same time.

Even though all three of them were getting much closer, David and Lena had been inseparable as of late. Cristiano didn't understand it - David and Lena were polar opposites most of the time, and yet they were so close now that someone had mistaken them for a couple on their way to Big City Tap the other day.

"It all seemed to start around Thanksgiving..." Cristiano thought, but he decided not to over-think it. Whatever it was was their business. In fact, it would be better this way. Cristiano preferred to be a ghost of a friend anyway, floating from one group of friends to the next.

***

Cristiano broke out of his mindless gaze, and suddenly he was back in his living room on New Year's Eve, just in time to realize what was going on in front of him. The redhead, Kathy what's-her-name, bent down in front of the white-haired guy and looked like she was about to suck his dick on live T.V.

cuenta de lo que estaba pasando frente a él: la pelirroja, Kathy "fulana mengana", se agachó ante el hombre canoso y parecía que le estaba comiendo la polla allí mismo.

—¡Adiós, estado puritano! —dijo Cristiano, echando un piropo.

—¿Qué dices? —respondió Lena, indignada, mientras Anderson Cooper hacía a Kathy retroceder, inquieto.

—¡Ay! ¿No se la va a chupar al viejo? —preguntó Cristiano decepcionado.

—¡Qué va! El principal objetivo de Kathy Griffin es hacer sentir incómodo a Anderson —espetó Lena—. Ella es una humorista y él es gay.

—Además, es diez años más joven que Kathy. Le salieron canas a los 20 años —murmuró David como si no quisiera que los otros le oyeran—. Por eso le llaman el zorro plateado.

—¡Anda, mira quién tiene novio ya! —dijeron Lena y Cristiano al unísono.

—¡Venga ya! ¡Qué os den! —negó David intentando ocultar su vergüenza—. ¡Zorras!

Se siguieron metiendo con David, frotándole la cabeza con los nudillos y golpeándole de coña en el costado.

—¡Cabrón! Estoy seguro de que Anderson te la comería aquí en vivo y en directo —le dio a entender a Cristiano, guiñando un ojo mientras David se sonrojaba.

—No, yo... —comenzó David.

—Anderson tendría suerte de tenerle —dijo Lena—. Pero no somos exhibicionistas.

—Habla por ti, aguafiestas —dijo Cristiano—. Bueno... ¿Y tú? ¿A quién te follarías?

—¿Cómo? Yo... —respondió David.

—El cretino aquí pregunta que por qué estrella estás pillado —

"Goodbye, Puritan state!" Cristiano said with a cat-call.

"What are you saying?" Lena responded, indignant, as Anderson Cooper awkwardly pushed Kathy away.

"Aw, she's not going to suck off the old guy?" Cristiano asked, disappointed.

"No way! Kathy Griffin's goal is to make Anderson uncomfortable," Lena snapped. "She's a comedian and Anderson is gay."

"Besides, he's ten years younger than Kathy. He just turned grey when he was 20," mumbled David, as if he didn't want the others to hear. "That's why they call him the Silver Fox."

"Oh, look who's got a got a boyfriend!" Lena and Cristiano said in unison with a cooing sound.

"No way! Fuck you guys!" David denied, trying to hide his embarrassment. "Assholes."

They continued to mess with David, giving him noogies and hitting him gently in the ribs.

"Dude, I'm sure Anderson would've given *you* an on-air blowjob," Cristiano hinted, winking as David blushed.

"No, I..." David started.

"Anderson would be so lucky," Lena said. "But we're not exhibitionists."

"Speak for yourself, party-pooper," Cristiano said. "So who would you fuck?"

"What! I..." David responded.

"The cretin is asking who your star crush is," Lena said.

"Guys, this is all new to me. I'd rather not..." David said.

dijo Lena.

—Chicos, todo esto es nuevo para mí. No quiero... —dijo David.

—¡Anda, venga! —dijo Cristiano—. ¿Channing Tatum?

—Estoy segura de que prefiere a Ryan Gosling —dijo Lena.

—¡Basta ya! —dijo David.

Después de meterse con David hasta que los "basta-yas" se hicieron bastante indignados, cambiaron de conversación a algo menos polémico. Pero tras relajarse y de que Lena y David empezaran a ver el show de la Nochevieja, Cristiano comenzó a aburrirse.

—¡Bueno, me voy chicos! —dijo Cristiano de repente.

—¿No puedes esperar hasta medianoche? —dijo Lena.

—Deberíais venir conmigo —dijo Cristiano—. Podemos beber el champán en cualquier sitio.

—Íbamos a ver la caída de la bola de Times Square —dijo David.

—Como los fuegos artificiales de la Puerta de Brandenburgo en Berlín —insistió Lena.

—¡Qué aburrido! —dijo Cristiano—. ¿Os vais a quedar en casa toda la noche?

—Quizás salgamos después —dijo Lena de manera poco convincente.

—Como queráis —dijo Cristiano—. ¡Os veo mañana!

—¡Adiós! —dijeron Lena y David cansados.

A Cristiano le dio igual. Más farra para él. Y seguro que la necesitaba. Desde su viaje a Los Angeles, había pasado por un periodo de sequía. Habrán sido las *Valley Girls* de allí. Eran todas unas pijas. Cristiano se fue de copas por Hollywood Boulevard e

"Oh, come on," Cristiano said. "Channing Tatum?"

"I'm sure he's more of a Ryan Gosling fan," Lena said.

"Enough, guys!" David said.

After humiliating David until the "enough's" became sufficiently indignant, they changed the conversation to something less polemic. But after they relaxed and Lena and David began to watch the New Year's Eve show again, Cristiano got bored.

"Ok, I'm on my way out, guys," Cristiano said, suddenly.

"You can't stay till midnight?" Lena asked.

"You guys should come," Cristiano said. "We can have champagne at midnight anywhere."

"We were going to watch the ball drop," David said.

"Like the fireworks at the Brandenburg Gate in Berlin," Lena insisted.

"How boring," Cristiano said. "You guys are going to stay in all evening?"

"We may go out after," Lena said, unconvincingly.

"Whatever," Cristiano said. "See you tomorrow!"

"Bye," Lena and David said, sounding exhausted.

It was all the same to Cristiano. More partying for him. And he definitely needed it. Ever since his trip to Los Angeles, he had been having a dry spell. It had to be those valley girls out there. They were stuck-up, every last one. Cristiano went bar-hopping down Hollywood Boulevard, from a dive bar on Yucca Street to the $22 cocktails of the Powder Room, and even that crazy club called Avalon, using every trick and ploy that he knew. And even still he would often return to the hotel, alone. His funk had followed him all the way back to Chicago, and he couldn't shake it, no matter

hizo uso de todos los trucos y estrategias que conocía, desde el antro de la calle Yucca hasta los cócteles de 22 dólares del Powder Room e incluso la loca discoteca "Avalon". Pero aun así, solía regresar solo al hotel. Esta racha de mala suerte le había seguido hasta Chicago y no podía deshacerse de ella…

—En la vida, hay que beber y comer —pensó Cristiano.

Intentó recordar lo que haría si todavía estuviera en Madrid.

Chueca. Se iría a *Chueca*. Si no lograba beber del coño de una pija, iría a por algún rabo. Y si echaba un polvo por fin, volvería seguramente a dominar la noche.

Empezó andando por la Avenida Buena y giró a la derecha en la Avenida Clarendon hacia la zona gay. Aunque llevaba un abrigo y una chaqueta debajo, Cristiano aún sentía cómo el frío le rozaba la piel. Y aún así, los cero grados de esa noche le hacían sentirse tranquilo. ¡Sí! ¡*Tranquilo*! No podía creerlo.

—Bueno, es la ciudad del viento —le dirían todos los americanos, aunque todos los chicaguenses nativos siempre le corregirían diciendo que en realidad la expresión no tiene nada que ver con el tiempo.

A Cristiano le había encantado esta definición de Chicago, como si el viento sobre el lago Michigan pudiera soplar sobre la ciudad para aliviar el opresivo calor veraniego, animando de nuevo a todos los ciudadanos a *aprovechar* la vida. Y esa sensación hacía, por supuesto, disfrutar también a Cristiano. Pero se había dado cuenta de que el viento también podía ser un arma de doble filo que podía oprimir tanto como los húmedos veranos de Chicago. Se dice "todo en su medida" y no hay nada como el tiempo, una gran fuerza inmutable, para enseñar eso.

Normalmente Cristiano podía coger un autobús y evitar la lección de la Madre Naturaleza, pero el *CTA* había cerrado la ruta 145. En metro eran sólo dos paradas por lo que esta opción no merecía la pena. Pensó en *Du hast* de Rammstein y empezó a

Part Two: Pieces

how hard he tried.

"In life, you have to eat and drink," Cristiano thought.

He tried to remember how he would have done it if he were still in Madrid.

Chueca. He would go to *Chueca*. If he couldn't drink from the twat of some stuck-up bitch, he could eat some dick. And after he finally got some, surely he would go back to ruling the night.

He began walking down Buena Avenue and turned right on Clarendon towards the gays. Even though he was wearing an overcoat and a jacket underneath, Cristiano could still feel the cold touching him. And supposedly, since it was in the 30s, it was a mild night. *Mild!* He couldn't believe it.

"Well, it is the Windy City," the Americans always told him, even though all native Chicagoans would correct them directly afterwards, claiming that the saying had nothing to do with the weather.

And yet, Cristiano loved that description of Chicago. Over the summer, it was as if the wind from over Lake Michigan had blown into the city to alleviate the oppressive heat, reanimating all of the citizens so that they could enjoy life. And Cristiano had enjoyed it, for sure. But recently he had found the wind to be a double-edged sword; it could also oppress him just as much as the muggy Chicago summers did. They say "everything in moderation", and there's nothing like time, the great immutable force, to teach that.

Normally, Cristiano could catch a bus and avoid Mother Nature's lesson, but the CTA had closed line 145. And besides, the metro was only two stops; it wouldn't be worth the money. He thought of *Du hast* by Rammstein and he started singing it softly as he was walking, trying to forget the cold. He hummed the words that he didn't know, which was most of the song.

"What a pain in the ass!" he swore through his teeth, lifting his

cantarla en voz baja mientras caminaba, intentando olvidar el frío. Tarareaba las palabras que no conocía de la canción (que era la mayor parte de ella).

—¡Qué coñazo! —maldijo entre dientes, elevando la mirada que tenía clavada en la acera.

Fijó sus ojos en la calle de abajo y vio finalmente el principio de las banderas arcoíris donde la calle de North Broadway se bifurcaba. Cristiano se animó, sabiendo que en un momento llegaría a un bar o a una disco y podría calentar sus extremidades congeladas con la calefacción del lugar y el alcohol.

Cristiano vio a la derecha un restaurante llamado El Mariachi Tequila Bar & Grill, cerrado, sin ninguna luz en el edificio. Había tantos restaurantes mexicanos en Estados Unidos como kebabs en España. Una sonrisa brotó de sus labios al pensarlo, pero rápidamente desapareció porque le dolían sus labios secos.

Cristiano lamentaba que el restaurante estuviera cerrado mientras pasaba delante de sus ventanas cubiertas de flores coloridas y una publicidad de tequila Patrón, que se convertiría en una terraza maravillosa en verano. Deseaba una cena tardía en un patio como ese durante una tibia noche veraniega, tal y como haría en su país. Al menos, a Cristiano le hubiera encantado tomarse unos chupitos de tequila que había visto en la ventana para simular con el alcohol que se encontraba en una cálida playa en lugar de sentirse como un soldado invadiendo Rusia. No sabía cómo aguantaría hasta la primavera, pero él no se acostumbraría nunca a ese tiempo, eso seguro.

La parte del tequila le recordó a Javier, que estaba en Pilsen, celebrando la Nochevieja con su familia. Cada año llevaba a sus tíos varios tipos de tequila añejo y, mientras se emborrachaban, iban todos poniéndose al día sobre sus parientes lejanos. Y, por supuesto, había mucho arroz y tamales caseros. Las madres se pasaban todo el día cocinando para un festín tan grande que duraría los siguiente tres días. ¡Qué envidia tenía! No había tenido

eyes from the pavement.

He looked down the street and finally saw the beginning of the rainbow flags where North Broadway forked off. It encouraged Cristiano, knowing that in a moment, he would arrive in a warm bar or club. Between the heating and the alcohol, he could warm up his uncomfortably frozen extremities.

Cristiano saw a random restaurant on the right called El Mariachi Tequila Bar & Grill. It was closed, without a light on in the place. There were just as many Mexican restaurants in the U.S. as there were kebab shops in Spain. He smiled at his own joke, but the smile rapidly disappeared as it hurt his dry lips.

Cristiano lamented the restaurant being closed as he passed its folding windows, which were covered in colorful flowers and an advertisement for Patrón. It looked like you could open them to make the vestibule a patio in the summer. He longed for a late meal out on the patio during a warm summer night, just like back home. At the very least, Cristiano would have loved to take a couple of shots of the tequila he saw in the window to give him an extra alcohol blanket, as if he were on the beach instead of a soldier invading Russia in the winter. He didn't know how he was going to last until spring, but he would surely never get used to this weather.

The tequila part reminded him of Javier. Javier was in Pilsen, celebrating New Year's Eve with his family. Every year, his uncles brought different types of *tequila añejo,* and everyone caught up with distant relatives as they got drunk. And of course, there was a lot of rice and home-made *tamales* that the mothers had spent the whole day making. It was such a big feast that it would last for the next three days. He was so jealous! He hadn't had an experience like that since he lived in Spain, though his uncle had done most of the cooking, as he was a *Chef de Cuisine* in Barcelona. Right then, his mother would probably be giving his uncle a dirty look while he

una experiencia así desde que vivía en España, aunque su tío cocinaba la mayor parte del tiempo, porque era Chef de Cocina en Barcelona. Ahora mismo, su madre probablemente le estaría lanzando una mirada asesina a su tío mientras insistía en que ella descansara.

***

—¿Descansar? ¿Por qué debería descansar? —preguntó Juana desde el salón—. ¿Me estás llamando vieja?

—¿Por qué complicarse la vida, hermanita? —dijo el tío Antonio cortando el cordero.

—Porque eres mi hermanito —dijo Juana—. ¡Y debería estar cocinando para ti! ¡Tú eres el invitado!

—Bueno, supongo que soy más simpático que tú —dijo Antonio—. Ahora, ¡déjame cocinar en silencio, por favor!

—¿Simpático? ¡Y una mierda! —respondió Juana—. Crecimos juntos, ¿te acuerdas?

—Sí, intento olvidarlo —dijo Antonio—. ¡Pero nunca me dejas!

—¡Bien! Te dejaré olvidarlo... —dijo Juana caminando tras el plato— si ahora me dejas cocinar el lechazo.

—No, no, ¡aparta! —dijo Antonio quitándole el plato de las manos—. ¡Lo vas a fastidiar!

—¡Lo siento! ¿No te gusta cómo lo preparo? —dijo Juana en shock.

—¡Pues no! Está soso, es aburrido y no me dice nada —admitió Antonio.

—¿Y tú dices que eres mi hermano? —gritó Juana mientras Manuel miraba desde el sofá en silencio.

***

Cristiano se preguntaba si su familia le estaría echando de menos. A él sinceramente le daba igual, pero a la vez, tenía

Part Two: Pieces

insisted that she rest.

***

"Rest? Why should I rest?" Juana asked from the living room. "Are you calling me old?"

"Why do you have to make this difficult, sis?" Uncle Antonio said, chopping the goat.

"Because you're my little brother," Juana said. "And I should be cooking for you! You're the guest!"

"Well, I guess I'm nicer than you," Antonio said. "Now let me cook in silence, please!"

"Nice, my ass," Juana replied. "We grew up together, remember?"

"Yes, I try to forget," Antonio said. "But you never let me!"

"Fine, I'll let you forget, poor thing," Juana said, walking towards the plate. "That is, if you just let me just cook this *cabra asado* now."

"No, no, get away from that!" Antonio said, snatching up the plate. "You'll ruin it!"

"I'm sorry, what's wrong with my cooking?!" Juana said, appalled.

"It's plain, boring, and uninspired," Antonio admitted.

"My own brother!" Juana yelled back, as Manuel watched from the couch in amused silence.

***

Cristiano wondered if they would miss him this year, as they yelled back and forth. He didn't really care, but at the same time, he was curious.

curiosidad.

Mientras pensaba en eso, pasó por unos restaurantes elegantes, unas tiendas locales con artículos hechos a mano, tiendas de especias e incienso relajante de la India, ropa de segunda mano, unos cafés, un gimnasio e incluso una iglesia, todo cerrado por ser día festivo. Todo era bastante aburrido y cotidiano, hasta que finalmente alcanzó un montón de gente caminando cerca de la calle *Belmont*, con luces brillantes y hombres bien vestidos con abrigos europeos y bufandas a juego. Por supuesto que había llegado.

Cristiano había ahorrado dinero en unos deliciosos mojitos del Minibar. Se los había servido un australiano guapísimo y musculoso, con unos hombros grandes y un pecho firme que casi explotaba su ceñida camiseta, que era unas tallas menor a la que le correspondería. Un misterioso gigante, ese era el tipo de chicos que le gustaba seducir a Cristiano. No era tan fácil como seducir a esos hombres desesperados que se follaban a cualquiera, así que era un reto, pero al menos era más fácil que seducir a chavalillas.

Desafortunadamente, había tanta gente en el bar que Cristiano tuvo que esperar 20 minutos para pedir. Mientras esperaba, flirteó con un guapo llamado John Smith, que estaba visitando a unos amigos de Chicago por Nochevieja desde un pueblo campesino en Indiana, el estado de al lado. Cristiano fingía que le preocupaban sus problemas financieros y familiares, los cuales no le permitían mudarse del "culo del mundo" y todo eso. Pensaba que ya habían hablado suficiente, así que Cristiano le dijo si podía invitarle a una copa. Pero al regresar con otro mojito, el histérico se había desvanecido.

Unos minutos después, encontró a otro guapo llamado Marlon Brando y empezó a hablar con él sobre sus propósitos de año nuevo. Marlon quería ir al gimnasio y comer más comida orgánica y menos carbohidratos para no parecer 'tan gordo', aunque Marlon no tenía ni un puto gramo de grasa corporal.

—¿Y tú? ¿Cuáles son tus propósitos? —preguntó Marlon a

Part Two: Pieces

He passed a couple of elegant restaurants, local shops with hand-made goods, shops with spices and relaxing incense from India, thrift shops, some cafés, a gym, and even a church - all closed for the holidays. It was all pretty boring and mundane, until he finally reached a crowd of people walking the streets close to Belmont, with brilliant lights and well-dressed men in European overcoats and winter scarves that complimented them. He had definitely arrived.

Cristiano had saved money for the delicious *mojitos* at Minibar. They were served by a handsome, muscled Australian, whose big arms and firm chest nearly burst through a tight shirt that was a couple of sizes too small. A mysterious giant - that was what Cristiano liked in the guys he seduced. Not as easy as your average guy who was desperate and would fuck anyone, so it was still a challenge, but still easier than seducing chicks.

Unfortunately, there were so many people in the bar that Cristiano had to wait 20 minutes to order. While he waited, he flirted with a hot guy named John Smith that was visiting some friends from Chicago for New Year's. He was from a small farm town in Indiana, the state next door. Cristiano pretended to care about his financial and family problems that didn't allow him to move from "the fucking middle of nowhere," and on and on. He thought he had sealed the deal, so he asked if he could grab the guy a drink. But when he got back with another *mojito*, the basket case had disappeared into thin air.

A couple minutes later he had found another hottie named Marlon Brando and began talking with him about his New Year's resolutions. Marlon wanted to go to the gym and eat more organic food and less carbs so that he 'wouldn't look as fat', even though Marlon didn't have a fucking gram on his body.

"And you? What are your New Year's resolutions?" Marlon asked Cristiano.

Cristiano.

Cristiano no tenía ni puta idea. ¿Salir más? ¿Beber más? ¿Pasarse las tonterías de los demás por el forro?

—Más o menos lo mismo —dijo Cristiano—. Me permites un momento, ¿por favor? Tengo que ir al servicio.

—No, no te lo permito —dijo Marlon de broma y Cristiano río con él—. Te esperaría una eternidad, mi mexicanito picante.

Cristiano se fue a mear, pensando en lo tonto que era Marlon. Sus propósitos para el nuevo año eran realmente superficiales. Seguramente, perdería su atractivo corporal en unos años y luego, ¿qué? Por no mencionar el hecho de que creía que era mexicano. Ni siquiera había adivinado el continente correcto. *Pero si como un mexicano picante me ves, jugaré a que lo soy, güey.* Cuando regresó, caliente como un mono, Marlon no había dejado ni rastro.

A estas alturas, ya estaba harto de todos estos juegos. Era la una de la madrugada y Cristiano decidió como última oportunidad ir al *Spin*, justo enfrente. Seguro que allí encontraría a alguien. Esa discoteca era un lugar increíblemente chungo, como ya sabía todo el mundo.

Pagó 25 dólares por la entrada especial de Nochevieja y al pedir una cerveza, se dio cuenta de que todos los camareros llevaban solo unos calzoncillos rojos. *"Perfecto"*. Se respiraba tanta sexualidad en el ambiente que seguro que todos estaban tan cachondos como él. Bajó las escaleras hacia la pista con bola de espejos que estaba bajo el nivel de la calle para ver lo que había.

Sin embargo, cuanto más lo intentaba Cristiano, más calabazas le daban. Y cuanto más le rechazaban, más enfadado se ponía. Era un círculo vicioso de malas decisiones hasta que el segurata le echó por perrear con un desconocido insistentemente. Se tambaleaba por la calle, con un hambre sexual insaciable, pero le duró un momento hasta que dio cuenta de que sus tripas también estaban rugiendo. Entonces se dejó caer en una tradicional cafetería americana de los

Part Two: Pieces

Cristiano didn't have a fucking clue. Party more? Drink more? Give less of a fuck about the stupidity of others?

"More or less the same," Cristiano said. "Can you excuse me for a moment? I have to use the bathroom."

"No, you're not excused," Marlon joked, and Cristiano laughed with him. "I would wait for you forever, my spicy little Mexican."

Cristiano went to take a piss, thinking about how stupid Marlon was. His New Year's Resolutions were so superficial. He definitely would lose that body in a couple of years, and then what? Not to mention thinking that Cristiano was Mexican. Not even from the right continent. *But if you see me as a spicy Mexican, then I can play the part, güey.* And yet when Cristiano got back, hornier than ever, Marlon hadn't even left a trace.

At this point, he was fed up with the games. It was one AM. Cristiano decided to go to Spin just across the street as a last-ditch effort. Surely, he would find someone there. That club was incredibly sleazy and everyone knew it.

He paid $25 as a special New Year's Eve entrance fee, and upon ordering a beer, he found that the waiters were dressed in tiny red undies. *Perfect.* In a club this sexual, everyone would surely be as horny as he was. He went downstairs to the stage and disco ball below street level to see what he could find.

However, the more Cristiano tried, the more he got rejected. And the more he got rejected, the drunker he became. It was a vicious circle of bad decisions that lasted until security threw him out for grinding on a reluctant stranger. He stumbled through the streets with his insatiable sexual hunger, but it took him a moment to realize that his stomach was also rumbling quite literally. So he stumbled into a traditional American 50s diner named Clark's for some drunchies. He pointed to the first plate on the menu that he saw. When it arrived, Cristiano scarfed down eggs, potatoes and bread, the form of which he was not sober enough to recall, and

años 50 llamada *Clarks*. Era un capricho de borracho. Señaló al primer plato que vio en el menú. Cuando llegó, Cristiano comió los huevos, las patatas y el pan de una forma que no estaba bastante sobrio a recordar y entonces eructó en alto.

Salió de *Clarks*, olvidando pagar y entonces continuó su paseo por la inmensa e indiferente noche.

—¡Qué te den, noche! —gritó Cristiano.

Silencio

—¡Soy lo mejor que recibirás nunca! —gritó Cristiano.

Silencio

—¡Te arrepentirás de haberme dejado, tú "sonvabitch" oscuro! —gritó Cristiano.

Silencio.

Durante su ebrio devenir de la conciencia, Cristiano fijó su mirada en una figura en la distancia con una chaqueta negra y un vestido rojo intenso. *No, también con rayas brillantes amarillas, como si Zeus hubiera lanzado unos rayos desde los cielos y ella los hubiera recogido para decorar su vestido.* A lo mejor era su desesperación o que todavía estaba borracho, pero mientras Cristiano se acercaba, la iba encontrando más bella que ninguna otra mujer que hubiese visto en su vida. Su pelo negro largo y suelto, una nariz pequeña, labios tan grandes que le incitaban a mordérselos, unas preciosas orejas finas y una piel morena impoluta.

—*Hhhow are joo*, guapa? —Cristiano le preguntó, anticipando un desmayo al oír su acento exagerado y la palabra *'guapa'*.

—Tu acento americano es horrible, perra —dijo la mujer en español, con una actitud brusca de hombre—. Y estaba esperando el autobús tranquilamente antes de que tú *and yo' drunk-ass* aparecieras.

—Lo siento. Es que no sé cómo comportarme alrededor de tanta belleza —respondió Cristiano.

then burped loudly.

He left Clark's, forgetting to pay, and then continued his walk through the immense, uncaring night.

"Fuck you, night!" Cristiano yelled.

Silence.

"I'm the best you'll ever get!" Cristiano yelled.

Silence.

"You'll be sorry, you fucking pitch-black sonuvabitch!" Cristiano slurred.

Silence.

During his drunken monologue, Cristiano saw a figure far off in the distance with a black jacket and a pure red dress. *No, it also had brilliant yellow stripes! It was as if Zeus had thrown lightning bolts from the sky and she had collected them to decorate her dress.* Maybe it was his desperation or that he was already drunk, but as he approached her, he found her to be the most beautiful woman that he had ever seen in his life - long, flowing black hair, a small nose, lips so big that he wanted to bite them, fine ears, and dark skin without a single defect.

"Hhhow are joo, *bella*?" Cristiano asked her, expecting her to swoon upon hearing his exaggerated accent and the word *'bella.'*

"Your American accent is horrible, *perra*," the woman said in Spanish, with the brusque attitude of a guy. "And I was waiting for the bus in peace until *you* and yo' drunk-ass showed up."

"I'm sorry. I just don't know how to act around such beauty," Cristiano responded.

"You mean, you can't hold your liquor," she answered.

"No way! I haven't had even had a drop," Cristiano said.

—Vamos, que no sabes beber —contestó ella.

—¡Qué va! No he bebido ni un puto trago —dijo Cristiano.

—¡Claro que no! —respondió ella con sarcasmo cambiando a inglés por un momento con voz muy seria, como si estuviera recitando algo—. Y si es una violación legítima, el cuerpo femenino se protege contra el embarazo.

—La violación no es una broma —dijo Cristiano seriamente—. Déjame protegerte, señorita… ¿Cómo te llamas?

—Carmen. Y creo que podré con ello —dijo ella—. La feminidad no significa debilidad, cabrón.

—Nunca —afirmó Cristiano casi olvidando la frontera entre actuar y ser.

—Y como soy una mujer libre... —dijo Carmen girando a Cristiano y acariciando su pecho para abajo— puedo tener relaciones con quien quiera, ¿verdad?

—Sí... —susurró Cristiano como si al hablar en voz alta rompiera la fantasía. Le entraban sudores fríos mientras la mano de Carmen se iba acercando a su paquete.

Se acercó un paso más a él, la mano tirando del cinturón y los labios a punto de besarle. Pero en vez de hacerle una paja en la mismísima calle, apartó su mano.

—Y como 'hombriego', soy capaz de irme cuando quiera —dijo Carmen poniendo la mano de Cristiano en su polla bajo el vestido.

En ese momento, el autobús llegó a la parada y ella le soltó, completamente hipnotizado. Cuando despertó del trance, se sintió roto. Como si ella hubiera abierto un espacio en su propio ser que siempre había tenido, pero que nunca había querido admitir que existía: dependencia.

Cristiano caminó a la estación del L, decidiendo coger el metro a casa. Había sido una noche larga y sólo quería salir de allí. Esperó unos veinte minutos, con sus piernas tumbadas en el frío banco de

Part Two: Pieces

"Of course not," she responded, sarcastically, changing to English for a moment in a very serious voice, as if she was reciting something: "And if it's a legitimate rape, the female body has ways to shut that whole thing down."

"Rape is no joking matter," Cristiano said, acting serious. "Let me protect you, *señorita*... what's your name?"

"Carmen. And I think I'll manage," Carmen said. "Femininity doesn't mean weakness, dickhead."

"Never," Cristiano expressed, almost forgetting the line between acting and being.

"And as a free woman," Carmen said, turning to Cristiano and caressing him down his chest, "I'm free to have sex with whoever, right?"

"Sí..." Cristiano whispered, as if speaking aloud would end the fantasy. He sweated in the cold as Carmen's hand approached his manhood.

She took one step closer to him. Her was hand pulling at his belt and her lips seemed about to kiss him. But instead of jacking him off right there in the street, she grabbed his hand.

"And as a manwhore, I'm capable of leaving whenever," Carmen said, putting his hand on the dick under her dress.

At that moment, the bus came to the stop and she left him. He was completely hypnotized. When he woke from the trance, he felt broken. It was as if she had opened a space in his very being that he had always had, but never wanted to admit existed: dependence.

Cristiano walked over to the L station, deciding to take the metro home. It had been a long night and he just wanted an easy way out. He waited for a good twenty minutes, sprawling his legs on the cold cement bench until a cold winter wind washed over him and woke him. He looked up, angry at himself, at the winter,

cemento hasta que un viento frío de invierno le golpeó y le despertó. Elevó la vista, enfadado consigo mismo, con el invierno, con Carmen, y entonces se dio cuenta de que el viento venía del tren y las puertas estaban a punto de cerrarse. Corrió hacia el vagón, atascándose en las puertas, y al librarse de ellas, tropezó hacia las sillas, dejando las puertas un poco entreabiertas hasta la siguiente parada.

Cristiano miró la ciudad pasar a través de las ventanas mientras maquinaba en él su odio. Entonces se rió por lo serio que se estaba tomando todo aquello. Pero cuando miró su reflejo en la ventana, desaliñado y lleno de sudor, casi no pudo reconocerse.

—¿Quién soy? —gritó Cristiano bañando en lágrimas.

Cuanto más intentaba cerrar y olvidar que existía esa caja vacía, esa dependencia adentro, peor era su sentimiento de soledad infinita. Tras pasar lo que le pareció una eternidad, llegó por fin a casa conteniendo sus lágrimas para que Lena y David no lo descubrieran. Se tiró en la cama y se acurrucó con su almohada, pero no había ni una puta cosa que pudiera arreglar esa fachada.

Part Two: Pieces

at Carmen, and then realized that the wind had come from the train and the doors were about to close. He ran to the train, got stuck in the doors, managed to free himself, and stumbled over to the chairs, leaving the doors slightly ajar as the train moved to the next station.

He watched the city pass him by through the windows as he just marinated in his hatred. Then he laughed at how serious he was being about this. But when he looked at his reflection, disheveled and full of frozen sweat, he hardly recognized it.

"Who am I?" Cristiano yelled in tears.

The more he tried to close the doors and forget the empty box inside him, forget that this dependency inside him existed, the worse his infinite feeling of loneliness. When he arrived home after what seemed like an eternity, he was holding back his tears so that Lena and David wouldn't catch him. He fell down in his bed and cuddled with the pillow, but not a fucking thing could fix this façade.

Part Three

❖ ❖ ❖

(De)construction

Sieben

❖ ❖ ❖

Der gute Mensch von Sezuan

Februar, 2013

Bumm! *Pause* Bumm! *Pause* Bumm! Schalte den Wecker aus. Steh so langsam auf wie möglich. Kämpfe mit David um die Dusche. Verlier die Rangelei mit David, weil er größer ist. *Verdammt.* Geh in die Küche. Mach dir ein Brötchen. Iss es und warte. Überleg, ob du dir einen Kaffee machst. *Oh, Moment. David ist schon raus. Egal.* Geh zurück unter die Dusche. Warmes Wasser. So entspannend. *Was steht heute an? Vielleicht sollte ich Wäsche waschen. Oh verflixt, hör auf zu träumen.* Spül das Haar aus. Geh aus der Dusche. Du fühlst dich frisch und sauber. *Oh, es ist so kalt!* Zieh dich an. Schmink dich. Gib David einen Klaps, wenn er fragt, warum du so langsam bist. Such deine Handtasche und geh mit David zur Arbeit.

Die Augen der Fahrgäste blieben ausdruckslos, als Lena David unbarmherzig nach seinem neuen Freund fragte. Oder besser gesagt junger Lover, denn das war wahrscheinlicher. David bestand immer darauf, sie „Freunde" zu nennen, obwohl er mit ihnen immer nur ein oder zwei Wochen zusammen war. Lena würde diesen Versagern nicht mal eine Woche geben, aber das hatte sie nicht zu entscheiden. Er benahm sich wie ein Zwölfjähriger. David versuchte einen Platz in seiner neu entdeckten Sexualität zu finden, an dem sich seine pubertären Vorstellungen und seine alten Werte trafen. Lena entschied, dass

Seven

❖ ❖ ❖

Der gute Mensch von Sezuan

February, 2013

Boom! *Pause* Boom! *Pause* Boom! Turn off the alarm clock. Get up as slowly as possible. Fight with David for the shower. Lose a tussle with David just because he's bigger. *Goddammit.* Go to the kitchen. Make a *Brötchen*. Eat it and wait. Consider making a cup of coffee. *Oh wait, David's already out. Nevermind.* Go back to the shower. Warm water, so relaxing. *What do I have to do today? Probably should do the laundry. Oh shoot, stop daydreaming!* Rinse hair. Get out. Feel fresh and clean. *Oh, it's so cold!* Get dressed. Put on makeup. Hit David playfully when he asks why I'm so slow. Find the handbag and go with David to work.

The eyes of the passengers looked expressionlessly around her as Lena relentlessly asked whether David had a new boyfriend. Or rather, a boy toy, as was more likely the case. David always insisted on calling them "boyfriends," even if he only ended up dating them for a week or two. Lena honestly wouldn't have given these train wrecks even that long, but that wasn't really her place to decide. Like a tween, David was trying to find a place for his newfound sexuality to meet where his equally pubescent beliefs and his old values crossed paths. Lena decided she had no right to judge or tell David how to think; after all, she had been there, albeit when she was actually going through puberty. David would have to figure out how to walk that line with his own two feet. But that didn't

sie kein Recht hatte, über ihn zu urteilen oder David zu sagen, wie er zu denken hatte – schließlich hatte sie das selbst mal erlebt. Auch wenn sie sich da noch in der Pubertät befunden hatte. David musste selbst herausfinden, was für ihn am besten war. Was natürlich nicht hieß, dass sie ihn nicht wenigstens aufziehen durfte.

„Wer ist das Opfer der Woche?", scherzte Lena.

„Was?", fragte David verwirrt und erschöpft, denn es war ein trister Montagmorgen.

„Mit wem wirst du diese Woche ausgehen?", fragte Lena. „Hast du einen neuen Freund?"

„Nein, können wir über etwas anderes sprechen?", antwortete David.

Lena bemerkte, dass er rot angelaufen war, als sie ihn nach dem Freund gefragt hatte, und setzte noch einen drauf.

„Oh, also hast du einen!", stellte Lena fest. „Wie war noch mal gleich der Kinderreim, mit dem du mich vor ein paar Monaten genervt hast? Du erinnerst dich, als ich dich und Cristiano wegen des One-Night-Stands in der Bar versetzt hatte? David und wer-auch-immer sitzen in einem Baum. K – Ü – S – S – E – N!"

„Halt die Klappe!", sagte David kaum hörbar. „Kannst du nicht sehen, dass uns die Leute im Zug anstarren?"

Es stimmte. Die Fahrgäste sahen jetzt verärgert aus, so als hätte ihnen jemand saure Milch in ihren Kaffee geschüttet. Aber Lena war es so was von egal, ob ein Mann mit einem erbärmlichen grauen Hut und Trenchcoat oder eine Frau in einem hässlichen Kleid mit Tigermuster angeekelt waren. Das, was sie mit David besprach, betraf nur sie beide allein. Die anderen Fahrgäste sollten vor ihrer eigenen Tür kehren und David musste nur mehr Rückgrat zeigen.

„Wie heißt er?", fragte Lena.

„Ich will nicht darüber sprechen", sagte David.

„Was? Versteht ihr euch nicht?", fragte Lena. „Oder ist er

Part Three: (De)construction

mean she couldn't tease him.

"So who is this week's victim?" Lena joked.

"What?" David asked, confused and groggy on the dreary Monday morning.

"Who are you dating this week?" Lena asked. "Do you have a new boyfriend?"

"No, can we talk about something else?" David responded.

Lena noticed that he turned as red as a rose when she asked him about the boyfriend and pushed further.

"Oh, so you do have one!" Lena said. "How does that nursery rhyme go-the one you taunted me with a couple of months ago? You know, when I ditched you and Cristiano for the one-night stand in the bar? David and someone, sitting in a tree. K-I-S-S-I-N-G!"

"Shut up!" David said, just above a whisper. "Don't you see the people looking at us here on the train?"

It was true. The passengers looked angry now, as if someone had put spoiled milk in their coffee. But Lena didn't give a shit if a man in a depressingly grey hat and trench coat, or a women with hideous taste in a tiger-striped dress with a neon-colored handbag were disgusted. What she discussed with David only concerned the both of them. The other passengers just needed to mind their own business, and David just needed to show some backbone.

"So what's his name?" Lena asked.

"I don't want to talk about it," David said.

"What, did you guys not hit it off?" Lena asked. "Or is he just bad in bed?"

"Lena!" David said, embarrassed. "Fine, I'll tell you. But not

schlecht im Bett?"

„Lena!", entrüstete sich David, peinlich berührt. „Also gut, ich werde es dir sagen. Aber nicht hier, ok?"

„Du meinst, nicht hier in der Öffentlichkeit", sagte Lena.

„Ich weiß nicht. Vermutlich", meinte David. „Es ist … komisch."

„Was? Schwulensex?", entgegnete Lena.

„Nein, ich …", fing David an.

„Denn ich bin mir sicher, dass du das letzte Nacht nicht gesagt hast", sagte Lena und zwinkerte.

„Lena!", sagte David und wurde rot.

„Oh, Oh, Oh", stöhnte sie im Spaß und erwartete beinahe, im Hintergrund Estelle Reiners „Ich will das haben, was sie hat" zu hören.

So ging es weiter. Lena nahm David auf den Arm und David war hin- und hergerissen zwischen sichtbarer Verlegenheit und unterdrücktem Gelächter. Das war eine andere Seite von David, die sie während der Winterpause kennengelernt und in der Vergangenheit oft ignoriert hatte, weil sie ihn ja verabscheut hatte.

Als sie die Haltestelle ‚Harrison' erreicht hatten, stiegen sie ruhig aus, aber ihre Unterhaltung ging weiter.

„Alles andere, nur das nicht", sagte David.

„Was zum Beispiel?", antwortete Lena.

„Such dir ein Thema aus!", rief David aus. „Es ist mir egal, was es ist! Nur nicht … das!"

„Ok, ok", sagte Lena. „Selbst ich verstehe den Wink mit dem Zaunpfahl. Wie wäre es mit Politik?"

„Nein", sagte David.

„Ja", antwortete Lena.

„NEIN", sagte David.

„JA!", sagte Lena.

here, ok?"

"You mean not in public," Lena said.

"I don't know. I guess?" David said. "It's just...weird."

"What? Gay sex?" Lena said.

"No, I..." David tried to say.

"Because I'm sure you weren't saying that last night," Lena said, winking.

"Lena!" David said, turning red again.

"Oh, Oh, Oh," she jokingly moaned, half-expecting to hear "I'll have what she's having" from Estelle Reiner in the background.

Their conversation went on, Lena teasing David again and David changing between visible embarrassment and occasional contained laughter. It was another side of David which she had gotten to know better since winter break, one she had often ignored him in the past because she was too busy loathing David.

When she reached the Harrison station, she got out smoothly, not stopping her chat with David for even a moment.

"Anything but this," David said.

"Like what?" Lena replied.

"Pick a topic!" David exclaimed. "I don't care what! Just not...this!"

"Fine, fine," Lena said. "A girl can take a hint. How about politics?"

"No," David said.

"Yes," Lena replied.

"NO," David said.

„Du weißt, wie du dann wirst", sagte David.

„Wie ‚werde' ich denn?", sagte Lena und malte mit den Fingern Gänsefüßchen um das Wort ‚werde'.

David stellte sich vor sie hin, verschränkte die Arme und starrte sie einfach nur an. Sein Gesichtsausdruck sagte etwas wie „Das meinst du jetzt nicht ernst" und „Verkauf mich nicht für dumm".

„David und noch jemand sitzen in einem B...", fing Lena an.

„NA GUT!", gab David klein bei. „Aber keine Endlosschleifen und fühl dich nicht persönlich angegriffen, wenn ich anderer Meinung bin, und wir hören damit auf, wenn wir im Büro angekommen sind."

„Einverstanden!", stimmte Lena zu.

Die Anzugträger drängelten sich zwischen sie, um ein- oder aussteigen zu können, aber der Krieg war überraschenderweise so banal geworden, dass Lena fast vergessen hatte, dass es ihn gab. Der Kampf ging weiter und Lena und David waren immer noch mittendrin. Aber diesmal dachte sie nicht daran, was sie heute alles vorhatte. Lena nahm es einfach so, wie es kam, und irgendwie wurde trotzdem alles gut.

Lena und David wurden langsamer, als sie unterwegs jemanden in einem Calvin-Klein-Anzug sahen. Er war ein Augenschmaus mit braunem Haar, stechend grünen Augen und einem kleinen Bärtchen. Normalerweise mochte Lena keine Dreitagebärte, aber irgendwie sah der Bart an diesem Typen sehr sexy aus. Nicht dass er ein Adonis war oder wie Marlon Brando aussah. Aber ein knuffiger Teddybär hatte auch seine Vorteile. Als das Sahnestückchen an ihnen vorbei war, stießen sie einen Seufzer aus und David blickte auf sein Handy, vermutlich, um nach seinen Facebook-Nachrichten zu sehen.

„Oh Scheiße", sagte David.

„Ich weiß", sagte Lena. „Mit dem würde ich auch was anfangen."

Part Three: (De)construction

"YES!" Lena said.

"You know how you get," David said.

"How do I 'get?'" Lena said, motioning quotes on the word 'get.'

David walked in front of her, crossed his arms, and just stared at her. 'Really?' said the look on his face. 'Don't play dumb with me.'

"David and someone sitting in a tr..." Lena began.

"FINE!" David gave in. "But no endless loops, no feeling personally victimized when I disagree, and we end when we get to the office."

"Deal," Lena agreed.

The suits pushed through to get on and off the trains, but surprisingly, the war had become so mundane that Lena had almost forgotten it even existed. The fighting went on, and Lena and David were still in the middle of it. But this time, Lena fought to the top without worrying about her plans for the day. Lena simply took it one thing at a time, and somehow it all still turned out all right.

Lena and David slowed down when they found some eye candy in a Calvin Klein suit on the way, with brown hair, piercing green eyes and a small beard. Lena didn't normally like the scruff, but somehow it looked very sexy on this guy. Not that this guy was an Adonis or had the charm or good looks of a Marlon Brando. But a cuddly teddy bear had its own advantages. After the eye candy passed by, they both sighed. David looked at his phone out of habit, probably to see if there were any Facebook messages.

"Oh shit," David said.

"I know," Lena said. "I'd have my way with him."

„Nein, nicht das", erwiderte David und zeigte ihr sein Handy. „DAS!"

„Oh Scheiße", rief Lena aus, als sie sah, wie spät es war.

Sie gingen jetzt schneller, denn sie wollten nicht zu spät zur Arbeit kommen. Obwohl sie beinahe einen Dauerlauf einlegten, redeten sie trotzdem weiter über Politik. Es war nicht unbedingt eine hitzige Diskussion, die sie nicht beenden konnten, weil keiner nachgeben wollte. Lena und David hatten sehr unterschiedliche Ansichten und genau das machte die Sache so spannend. So sehr, dass es ihnen schwerfiel aufzuhören, als sie ihren Arbeitsplatz erreicht hatten.

„Man wird Schusswaffen niemals ganz loswerden können, Lena", sagte David.

„Nein? Sind Amerikaner eine Art Barbaren?", fragte Lena scherzhaft.

„Nein, es ist nur ...", begann David. Er versuchte den richtigen Ausdruck zu finden, mit dem er den Satz beenden konnte. „... unsere Kultur."

„Waffen? Die waren auch in Deutschland mal Teil der Kultur", sagte Lena. „Das ist eine faule Ausrede."

„Das verstehst du nicht", beharrte David.

„Wieso nicht?", antwortete Lena.

„Amerika wurde während eines Krieges gegründet", antwortete David.

„Und Europa befand sich etwa nicht auch andauernd im Krieg?", fragte Lena.

„Das ist was anderes", sagte David. „Unsere Unabhängigkeit hing davon ab, ob man eine Waffe trug."

„Europa hat fast jedes Jahr Unabhängigkeitskriege geführt, und das bis zum Ende des Zweiten Weltkriegs", antwortete Lena.

„Das hätte man nicht ohne Waffen machen können", gab David zu bedenken.

Part Three: (De)construction

"No, not that," David said as he passed her his phone. "THIS!"

"Oh shit!" Lena exclaimed as she looked at the time.

They started down the street at a quick pace, not wanting to be late to work. As they nearly jogged, they continued their political discussion. That's not to say that it was a particularly heated discussion that they couldn't end because they didn't want to lose. Lena and David still had very different opinions, which is what made it so interesting - so much so that they often could hardly end them by the time they finally got to work.

"You'll never fully get rid of guns, Lena," David said.

"No? What, are Americans some sort of barbarians?" Lena said, jokingly.

"No, it's just..." David said, trying to find the appropriate word to finish the sentence. "Cultural."

"Guns? They used to be 'cultural' in Germany too," Lena said. "That's just a bad excuse."

"You wouldn't understand," David insisted.

"How so?" Lena replied.

"America was founded as a country at war," David responded.

"And Europe wasn't constantly at war?" Lena asked.

"This is different," David said. "Our independence depended on having the right to bear arms."

"Europe had wars over independence every other year up until the end of World War Two," Lena responded.

"They couldn't have done that without guns, though," David pointed out.

"Kosovo and Mexico did," Lena responded. "And Catalunya

„Der Kosovo und Mexiko schon", antwortete Lena. „Und Katalonien und Schottland sind gerade dabei."

David fehlten die Worte, während er seine Gedanken sortierte und sich eine passende Antwort überlegte. Normalerweise hätte Lena diesen Augenblick ausgenutzt, um seine Argumentation anzugreifen und in der Luft zu zerreißen. Stattdessen entschied sie sich dafür, Davids Ansichten diesmal eine Entwicklungsmöglichkeit zu geben – eine Möglichkeit, trotz ihrer Meinungsverschiedenheiten neben ihren eigenen Ansichten zu bestehen.

„Ich kann zumindest die soziokulturelle Gepflogenheit des Jagens als Freizeitbeschäftigung verstehen", fügte Lena hinzu.

„Wirklich?", fragte David überrascht.

„Aber es sollte viel strenger reguliert werden!", ergänzte Lena, denn sie wollte ihm nicht zu weit entgegenkommen.

„Reguliert? Was?", spottete David, aber er lachte dabei. „Big Brother, der entscheidet, was ich tun darf und was nicht? Das ist ein Schritt näher zur Diktatur!"

„Oh, wie dramatisch", antwortete Lena. „Glaubst du wirklich, dass Zivilisten automatische Gewehre brauchen?"

„Man sollte die Wahl ihnen überlassen!", entgegnete David.

„Was ist mit Sandy Hook?", wandte Lena ein. „Wenn sie kein Schnellgewehr gehabt hätten oder wenn die Überwachung strenger gewesen wäre, dann wären nicht so viele unschuldige Kinder gestorben."

„Das kannst du nicht wissen", sagte David. „Und außerdem hätte er sich genauso leicht ein Messer besorgen können."

„Genau das ist in deiner chinesischen Grundschule mal passiert", sagte Lena. „Also ja, ich weiß das. Alle 20 Kinder haben nach einem längeren Krankenhausaufenthalt überlebt."

„Zwischen China und den USA besteht ein Unterschied", beharrte David.

Part Three: (De)construction

and Scotland are in the process of doing just that now."

David was at a loss for words as he tried to regain his thoughts and think of an appropriate comeback. Normally Lena would have used this moment to jump on his argument and crush it. But instead, Lena decided to give David's opinion a fair chance to develop, a chance to co-exist despite her disagreement.

"I can at least understand the socio-cultural practice of recreational hunting though," Lena added.

"Really?" David asked in surprise.

"But it needs to be much more heavily regulated!" Lena added, not comfortable with giving too much.

"Regulated? What?" David scoffed, smiling. "Big Brother deciding what I can and cannot do? That's one step closer to a dictatorship!"

"Oh get off your dramatics," Lena replied. "You really think civilians need automatic guns?"

"I think it should be their choice!" David responded.

"What about Sandy Hook?" Lena said. "If he didn't have such a quick gun, or the screening was better, not as many innocent kids would have died."

"You have no way of knowing that," David said. "And even still, he could have gotten a knife just as easily."

"That actually happened at a Chinese elementary school," Lena said, "So yes, I do. It ends with all 20+ kids surviving after a lengthy visit to the hospital."

"China and the US are different though!" David insisted.

"Yeah, at least one of them is sane!" Lena joked.

„Ja, zumindest einer der beiden ist vernünftig!", scherzte Lena.

„Ich erlaube mir, anderer Meinung zu sein", sagte David lächelnd. „Sie haben dich trotzdem ins Land gelassen."

„Ah! Arschloch!", sagte Lena mit gespielter Entrüstung.

„Oh, diesen Arsch hättest du wohl gerne", sagte David, stellte sich vor sie hin und wackelte mit seinem.

„Ha! Träum weiter", sagte Lena und schubste ihn.

„Hey, das ist unfair!", sagte David und konnte sich gerade noch auf den Beinen halten.

So waren ihre lebhaften Diskussionen im letzten Monat abgelaufen. Sie waren selten einer Meinung, aber David riss dann einen dummen Witz oder Lena schwärmte von heißen Typen wie Ryan Gosling, und dann brachen beide in ansteckendes Gelächter aus und das beendete das Wortgefecht. Wie im Fluge waren sie auf der anderen Straßenseite vom InterContinental. Der monotone Fußmarsch von der Haltestelle bis zum Arbeitsplatz war vergessen. Sie warteten ungeduldig, dass die Ampel grün wurde, und Lena bemerkte erst jetzt wieder die merkwürdige Mischung aus langweiligen Geschäftsleuten und Touristen mit ihren glänzenden Augen, die heute Morgen früh aufgestanden waren und jetzt die Mag Mile bevölkerten. Als die Autofahrer anhielten, schnappte sie sich David, der ihr gehorsam folgte und stürmte waghalsig über die Straße. Die Ampel hatte noch nicht mal Zeit auf grün zu wechseln. Von dem kleinen Mann in der Ampel ließ sie sich doch nicht aufhalten.

„何だこれ?!?", rief ein Mann mittleren Alters geschockt, als er aus dem Hotel trat. Instinktiv beschützte er seine Sony-Kamera, als ihn Lena beinahe umrannte.

„Sorry!", entschuldigte sich Lena und rannte zum Gebäude nebenan. Völlig außer Atem erreichten Lena und David den Aufzug und wollten gerade die Tür schließen, als sich noch ein Mann hineinzwängte und den Knopf für den zweiten Stock drückte. David und Lena warfen sich verärgerte und ungeduldige

"I beg to differ," David said, smiling. "They still let you in."

"*Ach! Arschloch[1]!*" Lena said, faking offense.

"Oh, you only wish you could have this ass," David said, stepping ahead to wiggle his in front of her.

"Ha! Dream on," Lena said, pushing David.

"Hey, no fair!" David said, as he almost fell over.

And that was how their lively discussions had progressed over the past month. They rarely agreed, but luckily David would crack a bad joke or Lena would segue into the world of hot stars like Ryan Gosling, and that would cause them to break into a contagious laughter and end the heated debate. In no time at all, they were across the street from the InterContinental, having completely forgotten the monotonous walk from the station to work. As they waited impatiently for the light to change, Lena finally noticed the strange amalgamation of boring businessmen and bright-eyed tourists getting an early start on the Mag Mile. Suddenly noticing that the traffic in the street had stopped, she grabbed David and bolted across the street with reckless abandon before the light could even change, David trailing behind her like a rag doll - the little man in the street light held her no longer.

"何だこれ?!?" exclaimed a middle-aged man in shock as he exited the hotel. He instinctively covered his large Sony camera as Lena almost ran into him.

"Sorry!" Lena apologized as she ran on over to the building next door. Lena and David made it into the elevator, short of breath, and were about to close the door when a man squeezed through and pressed the button for the second floor. David and Lena shot each other a look in between annoyance and impatience that this guy didn't simply take the stairs. They checked their phones again - 2 minutes. After the douchebag slowly walked out, David quickly pushed the button a couple of more times, anxious

Blicke zu. Warum hatte dieser Typ nicht die Treppe benutzt? Ein erneuter Blick auf die Uhr zeigte: noch zwei Minuten! Als der Trottel den Aufzug wieder verlassen hatte, drückte David gleich ein paarmal auf den Knopf, um die Tür wieder zu schließen. Nach einer gefühlten Ewigkeit kamen sie auf ihrer Etage an und gingen so schnell wie möglich zum Büro, immer darauf bedacht, dass niemand bemerkte, wie sehr sie außer Atem waren.

Sie waren gerade im Büro angekommen, als Lisa hereinkam. Die Chefin schaute sich um und hielt einen Augenblick inne.

„Wo ist Cristiano?", fragte Lisa.

„Spät dran", antworteten David und Lena.

„Ja, klar …", seufzte Lisa. „ich dulde sehr viel, aber bei dieser schlechten Arbeitsmoral und dem Zuspätkommen bin ich mit meinem Latein am Ende. Sagt ihm, dass ich ihn sprechen will, wenn er kommt."

Lena und David nickten mit dem Kopf. Als Lisa die beiden zum Archiv begleitete, weil sie die Bücher neu ordnen sollten, war Lena sich nicht sicher, warum Cristiano noch nicht da war. Cristiano hatte in den letzten Wochen mehr gearbeitet als im gesamten Jahr zuvor und Lisa hatte noch nie ein Problem damit gehabt. Lena konnte sich die Veränderung nicht erklären. Letzte Woche war sie überrascht gewesen, als er jeden Tag pünktlich war und selbst darüber kein Wort verlor. Im Gegenteil, er erledigte seine Aufgaben schneller und es war offensichtlich, dass er sie zur Abwechslung mal richtig machte. Lena konnte sich aber nicht erklären, warum er das tat.

„Ich will das hier thematisch und alphabetisch geordnet haben. Schreibt eine kurze Zusammenfassung und heftet sie an den Anfang", sagte Lisa. „Bei Fragen könnt ihr euch an mich wenden."

Lena und David zogen weiße Manuskriptseiten heraus und überflogen sie. Lena musste die erste Seite ein paarmal lesen, bevor sie verstand, um was es ging, denn ihre Gedanken waren ganz woanders. Irgendwie vermisste sie den alten Cristiano, auch wenn

Part Three: (De)construction

for the door to close. After what seemed like an eternity, they got up to their floor and walked to the office as quickly as they could without being caught, trying to cover their lack of breath. They arrived in the office in the nick of time, just before Lisa walked in. Their boss looked around the office and paused for a second.

"Where is Cristiano?" Lisa asked.

"Late," David and Lena answered.

"Of course..." Lisa sighed. "I can stand a lot, but his poor work ethic and tardiness have me at my wits' end. Let him know I asked to see him when he gets in."

Lena and David nodded. As Lisa brought them to the company archive to rearrange the books on hold, Lena wondered about Cristiano's tardiness After all, Cristiano had worked harder in the past few weeks than the entire last year combined, and Lisa had never had a problem with him being late before. Lena didn't have any clue what had brought about this change. She had been surprised last week; he came on time every day without a single word about how early it was. Plus, he completed his assignments faster. It was obvious that he was actually applying himself to his work for a change, but Lena couldn't put her finger on why.

"I want these arranged thematically and alphabetically, after you write a quick synopsis to attach to the query letter on top," Lisa said. "Let me know if you have any questions!"

Lena and David started breaking out white copies of manuscripts and skimming through them. She had to read the first one twice before she could understand it - her mind was elsewhere. Lena somehow missed the old Cristiano, even though she hadn't seen him in months. She still protested his sexist opinions, yet thinking back on it, she realized that his words and actions showed a very different picture. Perhaps Cristiano talked a big game out of survival, putting on a tough guy attitude to be accepted. Lena's

sie ihn schon seit Monaten nicht mehr entdeckt hatte. Sie wehrte sich noch immer gegen seine sexistischen Ansichten, aber irgendwie ließen sie sie nicht los. Ihr war jetzt klar, dass seine Worte und Taten zwei Paar Schuhe waren. Vielleicht trug Cristiano deshalb so dick auf, weil er überleben wollte. Vielleicht mimte er den starken Typen, weil er akzeptiert werden wollte. Während sie vor sich hin arbeitete, schweiften Lenas Gedanken in die Vergangenheit.

***

Lena hatte in ihr Kissen geweint und dem Stress bei der Arbeit die Schuld dafür gegeben, dem Mann in der L, der ihren Hintern begrapscht hatte und auch dem kalten Wintertag. *Es war alles so wie immer, warum also weinte sie? Vielleicht weil alles an diesem Tag zusammengekommen war.*

„Es tut mir leid, ich komme später noch mal …", sagte Cristiano.

Lena drehte sich um, sah Cristiano im Türrahmen stehen und lief so rot an wie eine Tomate.

„Warum bist du in meinem Zimmer?", rief Lena und sprang aus dem Bett. Die erste Hälfte ihres Satzes rief sie noch im Schockzustand, die andere Hälfte aber bereits voller Ärger und Wut.

„Weil … du hast die Fernbedienung." Cristiano zeigte zur Seite.

„Oh", sagte Lena und blickte peinlich berührt zum Tisch. *Warum hatte sie sie mitgenommen? Dumm, dumm.* „Entschuldige."

Cristiano wirkte unbeholfen. So, als sei er sich nicht darüber im Klaren, ob er wieder gehen oder sie trösten sollte. Lena hoffte, dass er in sein übliches hochnäsiges Verhalten zurückfallen würde, wenn sie ihm die Fernbedienung schnell genug gab. So konnte sie ihre miese Laune wieder in aller Einsamkeit und unbeobachtet kultivieren.

„Hier", sagte Lena und warf sie ihm hinüber. „Alles klar?"

mind wandered as she continued organizing.

***

Lena had been crying into her pillow. She blamed it on the stress on work, the man on the L that had groped her ass, and the cold winter breeze. *It all seemed like a pretty normal day, so why was she crying? Maybe the combination of all of them on the same day?*

"I'm sorry, I'll come back later..." Cristiano said.

Lena turned around and saw Cristiano behind her in the doorway and turned as red as a strawberry.

"What, why are you in my room?" Lena said, jumping out of her bed.

"It's just...you have the TV controller." Cristiano pointed to her side.

"Oh," Lena said, embarrassed, looking at the coffee table. *Why had she brought it in with her so absentmindedly? Stupid. Stupid.* "Sorry."

Cristiano looked awkward, as if he didn't know whether to leave the room, or to try to comfort her. Lena had a feeling that if she gave him the TV controller quickly, he would revert to his more selfish tendencies. Then she could go back to sulking in privacy where no one could witness it.

"Here," Lena said, tossing it over. "Ya good?"

"What's wrong?" Cristiano asked as he caught the controller. He looked uncomfortable, but genuinely interested.

"Nothing. Don't worry about it," Lena said, just wanting to get out of this awkward situation in any way possible.

"Oh, ok," Cristiano said with an unsatisfied voice. Lena felt the butterflies of embarrassment in her stomach start to go away. The

„Stimmt was nicht?", fragte Cristiano und fing die Fernbedienung auf. Es war ihm sichtlich unbehaglich zumute, er klang aber irgendwie doch interessiert.

„Alles ok, keine Sorge", sagte Lena. Sie wollte so schnell wie möglich aus dieser eigenartigen Situation wieder heraus.

„Ok", sagte Cristiano ohne Überzeugung in der Stimme. In Lenas Magen beruhigten sich die Schmetterlinge langsam wieder. Das Adrenalin baute sich wieder ab und sie sank zurück in ihre Kissen. Aber gerade als sie dachte, dass sie ihn endlich los war, drehte er sich um und sagte: „Warst du heute früh deswegen so verärgert?"

„Was du nicht sagst, Sherlock", wollte sie eigentlich sagen, aber stattdessen sagte sie: „Nein, wir streiten uns doch dauernd."

„Aber nicht so wie heute", sagte Cristiano. „Was ist passiert?"

„Als ob dich das interessiert", sagte Lena verängstigt. „Lass mich in Ruhe."

„Ich gehe erst, wenn du es mir gesagt hast", sagte Cristiano.

„Darauf kannst du lange warten", sagte Lena störrisch.

„Ich hab's nicht eilig", sagte Cristiano.

Dann hatten sie ein paar Minuten schweigend dagesessen. Cristiano gelangweilt, aber entschlossen. Er starrte in Lenas verheultes Gesicht.

„Wie wäre es denn mit einem einzigen Satz?", schlug Cristiano vor.

Lena wollte ihm eine Million Gründe an den Kopf werfen, inklusive ihrer ausgefeilten Schimpftirade zum Thema Vorrechte der Männer. Und obwohl jeder Einzelne davon intellektuell Sinn machte, wusste sie, dass da was anderes in ihr nagte, etwas, das sich rational nicht erklären ließ.

„Meine Großmutter ist tot", sagte Lena. „Und … bist du jetzt glücklich?"

„Nein. Wie fühlst du dich? Habt ihr euch nahegestanden?",

adrenaline rush of being caught subsided as she melted back into her bed. But just as Lena thought she was free of him, he turned back around and said: "Is this why you were angry this morning?"

"No dip, Sherlock," Lena wanted to say, but instead she said: "No, we always fight."

"Not like this morning," Cristiano said. "What happened?"

"You wouldn't care," Lena said, scared. "Just leave me be."

"I'm not leaving till you tell me," Cristiano said.

"You'll be waiting a while," Lena said stoically.

"I'm in no hurry," Cristiano said.

They sat in silence for a couple of minutes, Cristiano slightly bored, but determined, starring at Lena's puffy face.

"How about just one sentence?" Cristiano said.

Lena wanted to say all of the millions of reasons, including her well-thought-out rants about male privilege. But while all of them were correct intellectually, she knew there was something else there banging in her chest, something that she couldn't rationalize away.

"My grandma's dead," Lena said. "There, ya happy?"

"No. Are you ok? Were you close?" Cristiano said.

"I...not really," Lena said, slightly annoyed.

She didn't want nor need his pity, nor had she even asked for it. She just wanted to deal with it on her own. "I mean, she was deported to Turkey before I was born and didn't come back until a couple of years ago."

"Why?" Cristiano asked. "Did she do something illegal?"

"Not really. It's complicated," Lena said.

fragte Cristiano.

„Ich … nein, nicht wirklich", sagte Lena gereizt.

Sie wollte und brauchte sein Mitleid nicht. Sie hatte auch nicht darum gebeten. Sie wollte selber damit klarkommen. „Sie wurde in die Türkei deportiert, bevor ich geboren wurde, und ist erst vor ein paar Jahren wieder zurückgekommen."

„Warum?", fragte Cristiano. „Hatte sie etwas Illegales gemacht?"

„Nein. Es ist kompliziert", sagte Lena.

„Das sagst du über deine türkische Verwandtschaft immer!", sagte Cristiano schmunzelnd und versuchte Lena damit zum Lachen zu bringen.

„Haha, so sieht's aus", sagte Lena mit gespieltem Lachen. Lachen war schließlich einfacher als die Wahrheit. Willy Brandt, Helmut Schmidt und mehr als 50 Jahre komplizierte Wirtschafts- und geopolitische Geschichte, die von ihr verlangte, Partei zu ergreifen. Man hatte versucht, ihr Leben und ihre Erfahrungen in kleine Stücke zu brechen, die besser zu handhaben waren und dadurch von Bürokraten mithilfe ihres Papierkrams kategorisiert werden konnten. Keinen interessierte das. Die beiden schwiegen sich ein paar Minuten lang an.

„Warum geht es dir denn dann so nahe?", fragte Cristiano.

„Tut es nicht", log Lena und brach gleich darauf in Tränen aus.

„Offensichtlich doch", sagte Cristiano, hielt sie fest und sagte sanft: „Du kannst es mir sagen."

„Ich weiß es nicht", antwortete Lena, als sie sich wieder in der Gewalt hatte.

Das war die Wahrheit. Sie hatte keine Ahnung, warum sie die Sache so mitnahm und das war das Schlimmste – der Teil, der sie verwirrte und mit dem sie nicht klarkam. Der Besuch von *Ni-nes* Haus in Köln war ihr immer schon komisch vorgekommen. Seit *Nine* dorthin gezogen war, hatte Lena sie einmal im Jahr besucht.

Part Three: (De)construction

"You always say that about your Turkish side!" Cristiano said with a chuckle, trying to get Lena to laugh.

"Haha, I guess so," Lena said. Her laughter was forced and fake. After all, laughter was easier than the truth. The truth was Willy Brandt, Helmut Schmidt, and over 50 years of complicated financial and geopolitical history, demanding she choose a side, trying to pull her life and experiences apart into more manageable parts for bureaucrats to categorize with paperwork. No one wanted to hear about that. Silence fell on the two of them again for a couple of minutes.

"Why do you care so much about her, then?" Cristiano asked.

"I don't care," Lena lied. She broke into tears.

"Clearly you do," Cristiano said, holding her tight as he said to her softly: "You can tell me."

"I don't know," Lena responded after pulling herself together.

That was true. She really had no clue why this affected her so much, and that was the worst part - the part that made it so confusing and hard to deal with.

Somehow, it had always been weird going over to her *Ni-ne's* house in Köln. Lena had gone there once a year ever since her *Ni-ne* moved there. Lena wasn't sure why *Ni-ne's* house felt so strange to her. It was right in the middle of a typical German neighborhood - pharmacist, McDonald's, and *Lidl* all on the same street, with a Catholic and Romanian Orthodox church on the end, staring each other down like stubborn brothers, locked in a petty, silent argument about a shirt they both wanted to wear.

Even when she entered the house, everything was just like any other home she had ever been in. There was furniture from Höffner and Ikea, the T.V. from Mediamarkt, yoghurt from the shop down the street. But the devil was in the details - everything was covered

Lena verstand nicht, warum ihr das Haus so fremd vorkam, denn es befand sich inmitten einer typisch deutschen Nachbarschaft. Eine Apotheke, ein McDonald's und ein Lidl befanden sich in derselben Straße, mit einer katholischen und einer orthodoxen Kirche an deren Ende, die sich anstarrten, als würden sich zwei Brüder auf ewig um ein Hemd streiten, das sie beide tragen wollten.

Wenn sie das Haus betrat, schien alles so normal wie überall zu sein, wo sie schon einmal gewesen war. Die Möbel stammten von Höffner und IKEA, das TV-Gerät war vom Mediamarkt und der Joghurt aus dem Laden an der Ecke. Aber der Teufel steckte im Detail. Alles war mit Plastik abgedeckt, damit es nicht schmutzig wurde, der Fernseher lief ständig, egal ob jemand zusah oder nicht, und der Kühlschrank war voll mit Ayran. In ihrem Kopf war genau dieses Chaos der vertrauten und doch fremden Umgebung wie bei der Wohnung ihrer *Ni-ne* in der Keupstraße. Die Gefühle überwältigten sie und ließen sich mit nur einem Wort beschreiben: Heimweh. Nicht nach Deutschland. Damit wurde sie fertig. Auch ganz bestimmt nicht nach der Türkei. Das war ein Land, das ihr fremd war. Es war Heimweh nach *Ni-nes* Wohnung. Aber noch mehr als das. Nicht nur nach den Zimmern und den Dingen darin, sondern nach *Ni-ne*, die ihr *hayatim benim* zurief, wenn sie zur Tür hereinkam. Das war es, was es zu einem Zuhause machte. Ein Zuhause, das der Vergangenheit angehörte. So viel war Lena klargeworden. Eine Vergangenheit, die es nur noch in ihrer Erinnerung gab, ein nostalgisches Heimweh.

Lena hätte viel dafür gegeben, noch einmal zurückkehren zu können. Sie bedauerte die vielen Male, die sie aus belanglosen Gründen ferngeblieben war. Sie hätte *Ni-nes* unkonventionelles Lächeln so gerne noch einmal gesehen. Niemals mehr würde *Ni-ne* darauf bestehen, dass Lena noch mehr Fleischblätter aß – der Spitzname der Familie für Börek – oder im Gästezimmer neben den osmanischen Antiquitäten schlief, die *Ni-ne* sammelte, niemals mehr würde sie den Geschichten lauschen, die ihre Großmutter

Part Three: (De)construction

in plastic to keep it from getting dirty, the T.V. was always on whether people were watching or not, and the fridge was fully stocked with Ayran.

The chaos of this familiar and foreign place met in her mind in her *Ni-ne's* apartment on Keup Street, and overwhelmed her with emotions in a sensation that could only be summed up with one word - homesickness. Not for Germany - that she had come to terms with. And certainly not for Turkey - a country she never really knew. It was homesickness for her *Ni-ne's* house. And yet, it was more than that - not just the rooms and that house, but her *Ni-ne* yelling out *"Hayatim benim!"* as she walked in the door that truly made it a home. It was a home that Lena finally realized was stuck in a time long past, about which she could only reminisce - a nostalgic homesickness.

Lena wanted so badly to go back, regretting all the times she hadn't gone for petty reasons. She wanted to see her *Ni-ne's* off-kilter smile one last time. Lena would never again get to see her *Ni-ne* insisting that she eat more homemade *Fleischblätter*[1], Lena's family's nickname for *Börek*, or to sleep over in the guest room around the Ottoman antiques her *Ni-ne* collected. She would never again hear the stories her grandmother had told of hilarious aunts, crazy great-uncles, and her *Ni-ne's* disapproving mother.

"Earth to Lena!" Cristiano yelled while waving his hands in front of her eyes.

"What?" Lena said with a tone of annoyance as she snapped back to reality.

"Uru-Swati?" Cristiano asked hopefully.

"Wait, what?" Lena said.

"Let's go there," Cristiano said.

"And if I don't want to?" Lena asked.

über schreiend komische Tanten, verrückte Großonkel und *Ni-nes* mäkelige Mutter erzählte.

„Erde an Lena!", rief Cristiano und wedelte mit seiner Hand vor ihren Augen herum.

„Was?", fragte Lena irritiert, als sie langsam wieder in die Gegenwart zurückkehrte.

„Uru-Swati?", fragte Cristiano hoffnungsfroh.

„Was meinst du damit?", fragte Lena zurück.

„Lass uns da hingehen", sagte Cristiano.

„Und wenn ich nicht will?", fragte Lena.

„Dann lügst du", meinte Cristiano selbstgefällig. „Aber ich kann auch gerne hier die ganze Nacht warten."

Und so wartete Cristiano. Fünf Minuten lang. Dann gab Lena klein bei. Denn schließlich war es ihr Lieblingsrestaurant. Sie fuhren mit der Red Line, stiegen bei Granville aus und liefen zwei Meilen in der Kälte die Devon Avenue hinunter. Cristiano riss einen Witz nach dem anderen über die USA und was er an Europa vermisste, nur um sie die Kälte vergessen zu lassen. Aber dann wurde es doch zu eisig und Cristiano hielt ein Taxi an. Er bestand darauf, es allein zu zahlen.

„Hey, lass mich doch wenigstens die Hälfte davon bezahlen", sagte Lena.

„Nein", sagte Cristiano. „Das geht auf mich. Das ist deine Nacht."

„Ok, also wenn es meine Nacht ist, dann musst du mir zuhören, oder?", fragte Lena.

„Du kannst das später wieder gutmachen", sagte er und zwinkerte mit den Augen.

„Ich werde nicht mit dir schlafen", witzelte Lena.

„Ruhig Blut, das will keiner von uns beiden", scherzte Cristiano. Sie waren an ihrem Tisch im Restaurant angekommen.

Part Three: (De)construction

"Well, you'd be lying," Cristiano said, smugly. "But I can wait here all night."

And so Cristiano waited, until five minutes later, Lena caved; after all, it was her favorite restaurant. They started on the Red Line, got off at Granville, and began the long, cold, two-mile walk down Devon Avenue, while Cristiano cracked jokes about the US and what they missed about Europe to distract them. Eventually, the cold got to them too much, and Cristiano hailed a cab, not allowing her to pay for it.

"Hey, at least let me go halfway," Lena said.

"No," Cristiano said. "My treat. This is your night."

"Well, if it's my night, you have to listen to me, right?" Lena said.

"You can make up for it later," he said, winking.

"Ew, I'm not having sex with you," Lena joked.

"Relax, neither of us want that," Cristiano joked back as they approached their seats in the restaurant.

"Are you ready to order?" the waitress asked.

"Yes, she'll have the *mango lassi* and *tikka masala*," Cristiano said. "And I will have...this bind-a-loo thing."

"Anything for you to drink?" the waitress asked. "*Vindaloo* is very spicy!"

"I'll be fine," Cristiano said.

"How did you know that was my favorite?" Lena asked.

"Contrary to popular opinion, I can pay attention to the details of my friends and not just the bimbos I sleep with," Cristiano replied proudly.

„Wollen Sie schon bestellen?", fragte die Bedienung.

„Ja, ich hätte gerne *Mango Lassi* und *Tikka Masala*", sagte Cristiano. „Und dann möchte ich noch dieses Bind-A-Loo-Dings."

„Und was möchten Sie trinken?", fragte die Bedienung. „*Vindaloo* ist sehr scharf."

„Das macht mir nichts aus", prahlte Cristiano.

„Woher hast du gewusst, dass das mein Lieblingsessen ist?", fragte Lena.

„Entgegen landläufiger Meinung bin ich durchaus imstande, meinen Freunden Aufmerksamkeit zu schenken und nicht nur den Tussis, mit denen ich schlafe", sagte Cristiano stolz.

„Schau mal an. Unser kleines Baby wird erwachsen", sagte Lena und kniff ihm in die Wange.

„Ok, ok, beruhig dich wieder", rief Cristiano.

„Ich geh mal kurz aufs Klo, ok?", verkündete Lena und Cristiano nickte.

Sie schaute in den Spiegel und lächelte, als sie noch Spuren ihrer Tränen entdeckte. Sie waren wie weggeblasen. Ok, die Erinnerung daran war noch da. Vielleicht würde sie niemals ganz weggehen. Vielleicht hätte sie ihr eines Tages etwas ausgemacht, ja vielleicht hätte sie sogar Angst vor ihr gehabt. Sie hätte sich die Tränenspuren angesehen und einen Spruch einer ihrer Lieblingspersönlichkeiten wie ein Mantra andauernd wiederholt. Aber heute Abend war es nicht so. Denn es war nicht einfach nur ihre Nacht. Es war so viel mehr. Als sie zum Tisch zurückging, brachte die Bedienung schon das Essen.

„Bon Appetit", sagte Lena. Sie stieß mit Cristiano an und jeder nahm seinen ersten Bissen.

„Heilige Scheiße!", rief Cristiano aus. Ihm stiegen Tränen in die Augen. „Wie isst man denn das!??!"

„Die Bedienung hat dich gewarnt ...", kicherte Lena. Cristiano griff nach dem Wasserglas, um einen Schluck zu trinken.

Part Three: (De)construction

"Oh, look at you! Our little baby is all grown up," Lena said, fake-pinching his cheeks as he shrugged her off.

"Yeah, yeah, yeah, calm down already," Cristiano yelled back.

"I'm gonna use the WC really quickly, ok?" Lena said. Cristiano nodded.

She smiled as she looked in the mirror and could see the vague outline of her earlier tears. They had all but disappeared. Sure, the reminder was still there. Maybe it would always be there. Once upon a time, she would have been bothered, even frightened by it. She would have looked at that outline and repeated a quote from one of her favorite academics like a mantra. But tonight, it didn't. Because it wasn't just her night - it was so much more than that. As she was walking back to the table, she saw the waitress bringing out the food.

"*Bon Appetit,*" Lena said. She and Cristiano clinked glasses and took their first bites.

"HOLY SHIT!" Cristiano exclaimed, tears in his eyes. "How do you eat this!??!"

"Well, the waitress told you..." Lena giggled. Cristiano reached for the water. "Cristiano, I wouldn't..."

But it was too late. Cristiano started squirming even more, nose running, nearly gasping for breath as if something this spicy couldn't possibly exist! Lena wasn't sure if he was exaggerating or not, but she told herself to stop overthinking it and just enjoy it.

"Here, take a sip of this," Lena said, handing him the Lassi. After a big gulp, his face started to calm down.

"Ah...that's better," Cristiano said. Lena waved over the waitress.

"Hey, ma'am," Lena said. She was trying to perfect the

„Cristiano, das würde ich nicht …"

Aber es war schon zu spät. Cristiano zappelte noch mehr herum. Seine Nase lief und er schnappte nach Luft. Wie war es möglich, dass etwas so scharf sein konnte! Lena war sich unschlüssig, ob er maßlos übertrieb oder nicht, aber sie entschloss sich, den Augenblick zu genießen.

„Hier, trink davon einen Schluck", sagte Lena und reichte ihm das Lassi. Er nahm einen großen Zug und sein Gesicht entspannte sich.

„Ah … das ist viel besser", sagte Cristiano. Lena winkte der Bedienung.

„Hey Ma'am", sagte sie und versuchte die amerikanische Aussprache des Wortes Ma'am exakt hinzubekommen. Sie hatte das von Leuten aus dem mittleren Westen schon oft gehört, aber jetzt fing sie an zu lachen, weil es bei ihr nur wie ein langes ‚A' klang.

„Was kann ich für Sie tun?", fragte die Bedienung.

„Können Sie uns bitte noch ein Mango Lassi bringen?", fragte Lena und zeigte auf Cristiano, der mit rotem Gesicht peinlich berührt dasaß.

„Ja, bin gleich wieder da", lachte die Bedienung.

Kurze Zeit später waren sie wieder mit der Red Line Richtung Süden unterwegs.

„Wo gehen wir hin?", fragte Lena, als sie an der üblichen Haltestelle nicht ausstiegen.

„Vertrau mir", sagte Cristiano.

„Du weißt es selbst nicht, oder?", sagte Lena.

„Im Detail?", fragte Cristiano und zuckte mit den Achseln. „Und wenn nicht?"

„Ich steige aus", sagte Lena.

„Hey, sei doch mal spontan!", sagte Cristiano. „Das ist schon die halbe Miete!"

Part Three: (De)construction

American diphthong on the word 'ma'am' she heard Midwesterners use so much, but she ended up laughing at herself as she blurted out an abnormally long 'a' sound.

"How can I help you?" the waitress asked.

"Could you bring us another Mango Lassi?" Lena asked, pointing to the embarrassed, red-faced Cristiano.

"Be right back," the waitress laughed.

Shortly after, they headed down south on the Red Line.

"Where are we going?" Lena asked as they passed their stop.

"Just trust me," Cristiano said.

"You don't know, do you?" Lena said.

"Technically?" Cristiano asked, as he shrugged. "Eh..."

"I'm leaving," Lena said.

"Hey, be spontaneous!" said Cristiano. "That's half the fun!"

"But we have work tomorrow!" Lena replied.

"Then we won't go far, I promise!" Cristiano insisted, giving her puppy eyes.

"...fine," Lena finally gave in.

They got off a random stop and walked down the street in Lake View. They entered a random bar, which looked pretty sketchy to her. Lena's first instinct was cut her losses and just go back to her pillow. But she fought the urge and pressed on. She even bought Cristiano a drink to pay off the cab.

"Hey, what are you trying to do?" Cristiano said. "It's *your* night, remember?"

"It's either this, or I put money in your wallet when you're not

„Wir müssen morgen arbeiten!", antwortete Lena.

„Dann werden wir nicht so weit gehen, versprochen!", beharrte Cristiano und machte überzeugende Hundeaugen.

Sie stiegen an irgendeiner Haltestelle aus und gingen eine Straße entlang. Dann betraten sie eine Bar, die ziemlich heruntergekommen aussah. In einem ersten Impuls wollte Lena das Handtuch werfen und nach Hause gehen, aber sie überwand sich und blieb. Sie kaufte Cristiano einen Drink, um sich für das Taxi zu revanchieren.

„Was willst du noch gerne machen?", sagte Cristiano. „Das ist schließlich *deine* Nacht."

„Entweder das hier oder dir Geld in den Geldbeutel stecken, wenn du nicht aufpasst", sagte Lena.

„Aber ...", begann Cristiano.

„Du weißt, dass ich dazu imstande bin und sogar damit durchkomme", lachte Lena. „Ich bin schlauer, sturer und gerissener als du jemals sein wirst."

Cristiano öffnete den Mund, als wollte er etwas sagen, aber dann sagte er nur: „Gut."

Er lächelte verschmitzt, als hätte er sie gerade mit etwas drangekriegt. Lena versuchte herauszufinden, was er im Schilde führte, aber da packte er sie am Arm und zog sie in den Nebenraum, in dem Dart gespielt wurde.

„Dürfen wir mitmachen, Leute?", fragte Cristiano.

„Klar", sagte ein großer farbiger Mann mit Dreadlocks. „Ich heiße Marcial. Das ist Jean-Pierr und das da drüben ist Aliris."

Zuerst kam es Lena komisch vor, sich mit völlig Fremden zu unterhalten. Aber nach einem Spiel und ein paar Drinks war es plötzlich die natürlichste Sache der Welt.

„Mädel, deine Bluse gefällt mir! Wo hast du sie her?", fragte Aliris, ein schlankes Mädchen mit hellbrauner Hautfarbe.

„Forever 21. Im Schlussverkauf", sagte Lena.

Part Three: (De)construction

looking," Lena insisted.

"But..." Cristiano started.

"You know I'll do it and get away with it," Lena laughed. "I'm more subtle, stubborn, and sly than you'll ever be."

Cristiano opened his mouth as if he was going to say something, but instead just said "Fine."

He smiled, slyly, as if he had just played her. As Lena tried to figure out how, he dragged her over to another room where they were playing darts.

"Mind if we join, dude?" Cristiano asked.

"Not at all, man," said a large black man with dreadlocks. "Marcial, here. That's Jean Pierr and Aliris over there."

Lena found it weird at first, talking with these random strangers. And yet, after playing the game, and a couple of drinks, it all became more natural and fun.

"Hey gurl, I love your blouse! Where'd you get it?" Aliris, the skinny, light brown girl asked Lena.

"Forever 21. I got it on sale," Lena said.

"Dayuuum!" Aliris said.

"Hey, can ya hurry up?" Marcial said. "You girls, always talking too damn much."

"Says the one obsessing over soccer with his new man crush," Aliris said, snidely.

"At least we remember when it's our turn!" Marcial taunted back.

"New game then. Girls vs. guys. Loser buys the next round," Aliris said.

„Waaaaahnsinn!", rief Aliris.

„Könnt ihr euch mal beeilen?", drängelte Marcial. „Weiber brauchen immer so lange."

„Und das von dem, der mit seinem neuen Schwarm nur noch Fußball im Kopf hat", höhnte Aliris.

„Aber wir wissen wenigstens, wann wir dran sind!", stichelte Marcial.

„Neues Spiel. Mädels gegen Jungs. Der Verlierer zahlt die nächste Runde", sagte Aliris.

„Was?", entsetzte sich Jean-Pierr.

„Hast du Angst, dass du gegen ein paar Lästermäuler verlierst?", sagte Lena. Aliris klatschte sie ab und Lena war erstaunt über sich selbst, dass ihr so was eingefallen war.

„Ja, zeig mal, was du drauf hast!", sagte Aliris.

Sie spielten 40 Minuten lang und es war ein heißes Kopf-an-Kopf-Rennen. Danach waren sie wie im Rausch und warfen mit den Darts nur so in der Gegend herum, so dass sie der Wirt beinahe hinausgeworfen hätte. Dann traf Lena genau in die Mitte und gewann das Spiel. Sie musste zweimal hinschauen. Sie war so stolz wie noch nie zuvor. Eigentlich war es unverständlich, dass man auf so etwas so stolz sein konnte, aber es war nicht nur das Spiel. Sie hätte auch verlieren können und wäre trotzdem so glücklich gewesen.

„Du hast es geschafft!" Aliris umarmte Lena und hob sie hoch. „Sag den Satz, den ich dir beigebracht habe!"

„*Vete pa' la porra!*", schrien sie den Jungs zu, die ihrerseits heftig schimpften. Aliris konnte sich gerade noch auf den Beinen halten und legte einen Arm um Lenas Schulter.

„Wo bleiben die Drinks?", fragte Aliris.

„Als ob du noch welche brauchst", lachte Jean-Pierr.

„Halt's Maul", schnauzte Aliris.

„Warum kaufen wir sie nicht bei Lalo?", fragte Marcial.

Part Three: (De)construction

"What?" Jean Pierr said.

"What, afraid you'll lose to a couple of gossiping girls?" Lena said. She was surprised that it had come out of her own mouth, but Aliris gave her a high five.

"Yeah, put your money where your mouth is!" Aliris said.

They played for forty minutes, in a deadlock. After all, they were all a bit inebriated at this point, and they kept throwing the darts so far off that the bartender almost threw them out. But then, Lena somehow managed to get a bullseye and won the game. She had to look twice. She had never felt so proud in her life. She couldn't tell you why she felt so proud over something so insignificant, and it wasn't the just the dart either - she could have lost the game, and she still would have been this happy.

"YOU DID IT!" Aliris said, hugging Lena and lifting her in the air. "Say that phrase I taught you!"

"¡Vete pa la porra!" they both yelled at the boys, all of whom were now cursing under their breath. Aliris nearly fell over, nearly pulling Lena over as she put her arm over Lena's shoulder.

"And our drinks?" Aliris asked.

"You sure you need any more?" Jean Pierr said, laughing.

"Shaddup," Aliris snapped back.

"How about we buy them at Lalo's?" Marcial asked.

"What?" Lena asked.

"It's a salsa club," Aliris said.

"But I don't know how," Lena said with trepidation.

"I'll teach you," Aliris said, pulling her arm out the bar. She yelled like a child: "Come on, come on, come on!"

„Wo?", fragte Lena.

„Das ist eine Salsa-Disco", erklärte Aliris.

„Das kann ich aber nicht", sagte Lena zögernd.

„Ich bring's dir bei", ermunterte Aliris sie, zog sie am Arm und rief mit Kinderstimme: „Komm mit, komm mit, komm mit!"

Sie zogen los. Manchmal bogen sie falsch ab und mussten den gleichen Weg wieder zurückgehen. Trotzdem hatte Lena noch nie so viel Spaß gehabt. Sie war vorher noch nie in dieser Gegend von Chicago gewesen, die einen heruntergekommenen Eindruck machte und trotzdem so voller Leben war. Am Ende landeten sie in einem kleinen mexikanischen Restaurant, dessen Wände hellrot und gelb gestrichen und mit Kopien aztekischer Kunst und Bildern mexikanischer Frauen dekoriert waren. Das Restaurant verwandelte sich nachts in eine Disco, und als sie eintraten, wurde gerade *Follow the Leader* von Jennifer Lopez gespielt. Sie verloren ihre neuen Freunde in der Menge.

„Fühlst du dich verloren?", fragte Cristiano.

„Ich habe noch nie gerne getanzt", sagte Lena und zuckte mit den Schultern.

„Ich bring's dir bei", sagte Cristiano.

„Muss nicht sein", wehrte Lena ab.

Es kam ihr komisch vor, mit einem guten Freund zu tanzen. Cristiano starrte sie missbilligend an und Lena gab schließlich klein bei.

„Ok, aber sei vorsichtig", witzelte Lena.

Lena ergriff Cristianos Hand und er brachte ihr bei, wie man vor- und zurücktanzte, immer drei Schritte auf einmal, und es fühlte sich an wie Ebbe und Flut an einem Sommertag am Lake Michigan. Mit diesen drei Schritten verschwanden alle Sorgen beim Gedanken an den morgigen Tag aus ihrem Kopf und sie verschmolz mit den anderen Tänzern. BUMM BUMM BUMM.

***

Part Three: (De)construction

They adventured down, taking a wrong turn here or there and retracing their steps. And yet, Lena had never had so much fun being lost in her life. She had never really been in this part of town before. It was a little rougher around the edges than she was used to in Chicago, and yet, so much more full of life. Finally, they ended at a cute little Mexican hole-in-the-wall restaurant with bright red and yellow walls, decorated with faux-Aztec artwork and paintings of Mexican women. When they entered the restaurant, which had been turned into a club for the night, they lost their new friends in the crowd as the song *Follow the Leader* from Jennifer Lopez started playing.

"A bit lost?" Cristiano asked.

"Meh, dancing's never been my thing," Lena said, shrugging her shoulders.

"Well, let me teach you," Cristiano said.

"I'm good," Lena said.

She just wasn't comfortable dancing with such a close friend like that. But Cristiano gave her a judgmental stare and she caved.

"Fine. But be gentle," she joked.

Lena took Cristiano's hand as he taught her how to move back and forward, three steps at a time, as she let the ebb and flow wash over her like a summer day at the beach on Lake Michigan. She just let the three-step pound tomorrow's worries out of her head as she and a handful of other people danced the night away. BOOM BOOM BOOM.

***

Lena snapped out of the past when Cristiano got to work with his normal excuses. Lena and David let him know that he was on thin ice, but Cristiano bragged that tomorrow he would come even later, because he didn't care. Yet Lena saw something in his eyes

Lena erwachte aus den Gedanken an die Vergangenheit, als Cristiano mit den üblichen Entschuldigungen auftauchte. Lena und David ließen ihn wissen, dass er sich auf dünnem Eis bewegte, aber Cristiano spuckte große Töne von wegen, dass er morgen sogar noch später kommen würde. Lena sah ihm an, dass er die Herausforderung annahm. Cristiano wusste ganz genau, dass ihre Chefin das ernst meinte, und er würde das auf seine eigene Art regeln, auch wenn er das niemals zugeben würde.

Die drei Praktikanten saßen den ganzen Tag beisammen. Sie lasen, schrieben und legten Akten ab. Es war so langweilig, dass Lena dabei einschlief. Sie wachte von Davids und Cristianos Gekicher auf, weil die beiden ihr Gesicht mit einem Filzstift bemalen wollten. Sie versuchte den Filzstift abzuwehren und fiel dabei auf den Boden.

„Hahaha", lachte sie, weil David sie kitzelte, damit Cristiano einen Punkt auf ihre Nase malen konnte.

„Wofür ist das?", fragte Lena.

„Rache", sagte Cristiano.

„Du hast einen Klebestreifen unter unsere Mäuse geklebt", sagte David. „Wir haben die IT gerufen und dann wie die Idioten dagestanden."

„Ich habe keine Ahnung, wovon ihr redet", sagte Lena unschuldig.

„Dann wissen wir das auch nicht, Rudolph", machte sich David darüber lustig.

„Ich habe euch gesehen!", sagte Lena.

„Hast du Zeugen?", fragte Cristiano. „Nein? Klage abgewiesen."

Ihr beiden seid so doof, dachte Lena und schüttelte ihren Kopf mit leisem Lächeln.

Als sie mit der Ablage weitermachten, kam es ihnen so vor, als würden die Kopien ein Eigenleben führen. Ein Detektiv aus den

Part Three: (De)construction

that accepted the challenge. Cristiano knew well enough that their boss didn't play games, and that he would take matters into his own hands, even if he never would admit it.

The three interns sat there next to each other for the entire day, reading, writing and organizing in a painfully monotonous tone. It was so boring, that Lena almost fell asleep while David and Cristiano were plotting to draw on her face with a felt-tip pen. Their childish giggling woke her up just before the ink touched her face, and she fell on the ground as she pushed them back, trying to keep the pen away from her.

"Hahaha," she laughed as David tickled her so Cristiano could put a dot on her nose.

"What was that for?" Lena asked.

"Revenge," Cristiano said.

"You put a piece of tape under both of our computers' mouses," David said. "Made us look like idiots asking for I.T. to fix it."

"I don't know what you two are talking about," Lena said, innocently.

"Then neither do we, Rudolph," David joked.

"I saw you do it!" Lena said.

"Got anyone to prove that?" Cristiano asked. "No? Case closed."

"You two are so stupid," Lena thought, shaking her head with a secret chuckle.

As they returned to organizing, it almost seemed as if the copies had taken on a life of their own. A 1920s detective from one hunted down the clues to find the lawless cowboys of another, while a couple from a romance novel celebrated their forbidden love in the

20er Jahren suchte nach Spuren von einer Frau, um einen Cowboy von einer anderen zu überführen, und ein Pärchen aus einem Liebesroman lebte seine verbotene Liebe aus. Wieder andere standen in einer Ecke und wiederholten Zahlen und Fachbegriffe aus der Wirtschaft, während ihr andere Hilfe zur Selbsthilfe zuriefen.

Und dann gab es solche, die fast ganz leise waren, so als wären ihre Seiten leer.

Lena musste sich ständig klarmachen, dass es nur Kopien in einem Archiv waren. Ein Editor musste trotzdem drüberschauen. Und doch war der Inhalt unerbittlich. Er wollte aus dem weißen Papier und den langweiligen Deckeln ausbrechen. Sie war erleichtert, als ein Kinderlied die Stimmen übertönte: „Der, die, das ..."

Die Uhr schlug endlich fünf. Lena, Cristiano und David beendeten schnell das, was sie angefangen hatten. Sie wollten so schnell wie möglich das Büro verlassen, aber am folgenden Tag nicht noch einmal damit anfangen. David und Cristiano verabschiedeten sich, um ein paar Dinge zu erledigen. David war dran mit den Einkäufen und Cristiano musste zur Bank, weil auf der Überweisung von seinen Eltern geheimnisvolle Gebühren aufgetaucht waren. Lena blieb allein zurück und zum ersten Mal in ihrem Leben wusste sie nicht, was sie mit sich anfangen sollte. Nach Hause gehen und ein Buch lesen? Als Einzelkind in Berlin war das immer ihre Antwort gewesen, aber hier hatte sie ihre Mitbewohner. Sie war seit Monaten nicht mehr allein gewesen und sie wusste nicht, wie sie ihre Zeit verbringen wollte.

Eine Gestalt, die ihr bekannt vorkam, kam ihr auf dem Gehweg Richtung Michigan entgegen. *Das war unmöglich.* Der Kassierer aus dem Dönerladen. Sie versteckte ihr Gesicht in ihrem Schal und ging zur nächsten „L"-Haltestelle.

„*Merhaba güzelim*", sagte plötzlich eine Stimme von der Straße her und dann mit einem perfekten amerikanischen Akzent: „Tu

middle of it all. Others quietly recited numbers and business terms in the corner, as another yelled self-help tips at her. And others still stayed fairly silent, as if their pages remained blank. Lena constantly had to remind herself that they were merely copies in the archive; an editor still had to look everything over. Yet the contents were relentless, begging to break out of the white paper and mundane covers that held them. She finally felt sweet relief when a simple children's song began to drown them out: *"Der die das..."*

The clock finally struck five. Lena, Cristiano, and David rushed to finish their work on the drafts they were in the middle of, desperate to get out of the office, but not wanting to have to start over again tomorrow. David and Cristiano said goodbye to do a couple of errands. It was David's turn to get the groceries, and Cristiano had to go to the bank to discuss some mysterious fees that had showed up when his parents had sent him some money.

Lena was left alone and for the first time in her life, she didn't know what to do. Go home and read a book? That had always been her answer as an only child in Berlin, but now she always had her roommates to go back to and hang with. She hadn't had time to herself in months, and she wasn't sure that was how she wanted to spend it.

Then she saw a familiar figure walking down the street on her way down Michigan. *It couldn't be.* The cashier from the *döner* shop. She tried to just hide her face in her scarf as she turned to the closest L Station.

"*Merhaba güzelim,*" came a voice from down the street, and then with a perfect American accent: "Don't act like you don't know me!"

"What do you want from me, asshole?" Lena answered as she turned around.

nicht so, als würdest du mich nicht kennen."

„Was willst du von mir, Arschloch?", fragte Lena und drehte sich um.

„Mich mit einem hübschen türkischen Mädel unterhalten", sagte der Kassierer und ging auf sie zu. „Auf dieser Seite des Ozeans gibt es nicht so viele davon."

„Woher weißt du so genau, dass ich Türkin bin?", fragte Lena.

„Die Art und Weise, wie das Wort ‚Döner' über deine Zunge gerollt ist", sagte der Kassierer.

„Und wenn das nicht stimmt?", fragte Lena. „Wenn ich nur eine Deutsche bin, die ein bisschen Türkisch kann?"

„Und wenn ich doch recht habe?", sagte der Kassierer selbstgefällig. „Du bist beides. Eine Deutschtürkin."

„Nein, ich bin Deutsche. Ich bin in Deutschland aufgewachsen", korrigierte ihn Lena.

„Nein, es ist so, wie ich gesagt habe", sagte der Kassierer mit ernster Stimme. „Du bist in Deutschland geboren und aufgewachsen, stimmt's?"

„Ja. Ich habe einen türkischen Migrationshintergrund, aber das bin ich nicht", antwortete Lena.

„Und sperrst du damit nicht deine türkische Identität aus?", fragte der Kassierer neugierig.

Lena verstummte. Das erste Mal in ihrem Leben hatte sie keine Antwort. Sie hatte eine gute Ausbildung. Sie war schlau. *Warum wusste sie keine Antwort darauf?* Sie dachte an Baklava und die Grundschule.

„Warum soll ich mich vor einem Fremden rechtfertigen?", fragte Lena mit Nachdruck. „Ich muss jetzt gehen. Tschüss."

„Ich heiße Mehmet", sagte der Kassierer eingebildet. „Jetzt bin ich nicht mehr namenlos, oder?"

„Ich muss jetzt wirklich …", sagte Lena.

"Just to talk with a beautiful Turkish girl," the cashier said as he walked towards her. "There aren't so many on this side of the ocean."

"How do you even know I am Turkish?" Lena said.

"The way in which the word *'döner'* rolled off your tongue," the cashier said.

"And what if you got it wrong?" Lena asked. "If I'm just a German who can speak a little Turkish."

"But I didn't, did I?" the cashier said, smugly. "You're both. A Turkish-German."

"No, I am German. I grew up in Germany," Lena corrected.

"No, I mean what I said," the cashier answered, seriously. "You were born and raised in Germany, right?"

"I am. I mean, sure, I have a Turkish background, but that isn't who I am," Lena responded.

"And that doesn't marginalize your Turkish identity?" asked the cashier, inquisitively.

Lena went silent. For the first time in her life, she couldn't find an answer. She was educated. She was smart. *So why couldn't she find an answer?* She thought of the baklava and her elementary school.

"Why should I have to explain myself to a stranger?" Lena asked, emphatically. "I have to go. Bye."

"My name is Mehmet," the cashier said, cockily. "Now I'm not so nameless, am I?"

"Despite that, I've…" said Lena.

"Well, run away. Always running away," Mehmet ended her

„Wegrennen, natürlich. Du rennst immer weg", beendete Mehmet ihren Satz und grinste. „Wovor? Bin ich so abstoßend?"

Lena war erstaunt. Sie hatte das vergessen. Sie hatte den Dönerladen verlassen und ihren Freunden gesagt, dass sie ihren Haarglätter nicht ausgeschaltet hatte, weil es so früh am Morgen gewesen war, und sie hatten die Sache nicht mehr erwähnt. Es war eine Lüge, aber sie hatten sie ihr abgekauft. Und das war das Wichtigste.

„Ich renne weg von Kopftüchern und religiösem Blödsinn und hin zu Emanzipation und Vernunft", wollte sie sagen. Aber das ging irgendwie nicht mehr. Weil es zu einfach war. In ihrem Kopf schrie etwas ganz laut.

„Halloooo! Erde an Mars!", sagte Mehmet und das brachte sie wieder zurück in die Gegenwart. „Leider habe ich jemandem versprochen, dass ich ihn im Loop treffe. Aber hier ist meine Telefonnummer. Ich bin ein guter Zuhörer, versprochen. Und denk immer daran, dass niemand außer dir sich für eine Identität entscheiden kann. Auch ich nicht. Wir sehen uns."

Mehmet winkte und ging nach Norden, obwohl das Loop genau entgegengesetzt war. Lena wollte die Nummer in den Müll werfen. Aber das wäre zu einfach. Eine Nummer. Eine magische Zahlenkombination, mit der man mit jedermann auf der ganzen Welt in Kontakt treten konnte. Und eine falsche Ziffer trennt dich von Millionen und Abermillionen von Menschen. In einer so großen Stadt würde so ein Zufall nicht noch mal passieren, oder?

Sie steckte die Nummer in ihre Handtasche. Warum auch immer. Prickelnde Vorfreude? Masochismus? Beides? Egal. Lena konnte sie immer noch wegwerfen, wenn sie wieder bei Sinnen war. Jetzt musste sie noch etwas anderes machen. Sie suchte auf ihrem Handy nach „Türkisch, Chicago". Erst waren da eine Menge Restaurants und dann fand sie es schließlich: „Türkisch-Amerikanische Gesellschaft von Chicago". Das war ein guter Anfang. Sie klickte auf den Link. Fakten: „Die Türkei liegt dort, wo

Part Three: (De)construction

sentence, as he smirked. "From what? Am I that bad?"

Lena stood there, astonished. She had forgotten. Her friends hadn't thought anything of it after she left them at the *döner* shop. She had simply explained to them that she had forgotten to turn off her straightener because it had been early in the morning. A lie, but they believed it. That was the most important thing.

"I'm running from headdresses and religious nonsense to women's liberation and rationalism," she wanted to say. But somehow, she couldn't bring herself to say it anymore. Because it was so overly simplistic. Something in the back of her head screamed desperately.

"Helloooo! Earth to Mars!" Mehmet said, bringing her back to reality. "Hey, unfortunately I promised someone that I would meet him by the Loop. But here's my number. I'm a good listener, promise. And remember, no one can decide your own identity for you. Even me. See ya around."

Mehmet waved and went north, in the opposite direction of the Loop. Lena almost threw the number in the trash. It would've been so easy. A number. An almost magical combination of digits, that can connect you with anyone in the world or with even just one wrong digit can separate you between millions, even billions of people. And in such a big city, a coincidence like this wouldn't happen again, right?

She decided instead to put the number in her purse. She didn't know why. The thrill of a surprise? Masochism? Both? Whatever. Lena could easily throw it away when she finally got her senses back.

Right now, there was something she still had to do. She pulled up "Turkish, Chicago" on her phone. There were a lot of restaurants and then she found it: "Turkish-American Society of Chicago." That was a good start. She clicked on the link. Facts: "

sich Europa und Asien treffen." „TASC Frauen." Lena klickte auf einen anderen Link, um herauszufinden, wo das war.

„Oh Gott, draußen am O'Hare-Flughafen", dachte Lena. „Dafür habe ich keine Zeit."

Es musste auch etwas geben, das etwas näher war. Vielleicht eine Moschee. Sie suchte auf Google Maps nach Moscheen. Welche sollte sie sich mal ansehen? Es gab so viele Möglichkeiten. Das muslimische Kulturzentrum, Al-Fatir und so weiter. Und was wollte sie dort eigentlich finden? Ihre türkische Seite war noch nicht mal gläubig. Aber sie wollte nach irgendetwas greifen, das ihr ihre *Ni-ne* hinterlassen hatte.

Am liebsten wollte Lena nach Hause gehen und alles vergessen. Aber das hatte sie ihr ganzes Leben lang getan. Vergessen und leben ohne zu zögern. Mehmet hatte in ihr etwas ausgelöst. Lena fühlte sich unbehaglich.

„Niemand kann mir die Entscheidung für eine Identität abnehmen", dieser Satz lief in ihrem Kopf in einer Endlosschleife. Auf Google Maps fand Lena den Weg zu einer Moschee und machte sich auf den Weg. Sie hatte Schmetterlinge im Bauch und die Karte hatte keine Richtungsangabe.

Part Three: (De)construction

The land of Turkey straddles the point where Europe and Asia meet. TASC women." Lena clicked on another link to see where it was.

"Oh god. Out by the O'Hare airport," Lena thought. "I don't have time for that..."

There must be something nearer. Maybe a mosque? She looked up mosques on Google Maps. She wasn't sure which she should visit. There were so many possibilities - the Muslim Cultural Center, Al-Fatir, and on and on. And what would she find when she got there? Her Turkish side wasn't even devout. But she wanted to grasp on to something, anything her *Ni-ne* might have left behind.

Lena almost wanted to go home and forget the whole thing. But she had done that her whole life. Forget and live on without hesitation. Mehmet had awakened something in her. Lena had an uncomfortable feeling.

"No one can decide my own identity for me," she repeated, over and over again in her head. Lena used Google Maps on her phone to the find the mosque and started on her way there with butterflies in her stomach as she looked at a map with no directions.

Ocho

❖ ❖ ❖

Odio no poder odiarte

Marzo, 2013

—Pero tío, nada más que chicas y alcohol durante una semana entera. De verdad, ¿no tienes ganas?

Cristiano se quedó allí sentado, con la cara tan blanca como la pantalla del ordenador que tenía delante de él, con las palmas des sus manos descansando inquietamente sobre el teclado del trabajo.

—No estoy seguro de si todo eso es lo que quiero todavía: quedarme en casa con resaca, seguir regresando con un rollo de una noche, me hace sentir... —Cristiano escribió provisionalmente, dándose cuenta de repente de que el contador se puso en rojo, como si incluso Twitter estuviera enfadadado con él.

Seleccionó el texto y presionó el retroceso, borrando todo. ¿Cómo podría explicar todo que sentía en 140 caracteres —ineptitud, inseguridad, indecisión— pero sin sonar como un coñazo? ¿Cómo encarnas la experiencia humana en una sola oración sin emoción? Todo que quería hacer era vomitar las palabras sobre el teclado.

—Tío, estoy sin blanca ahora y está fuera de mi alcance —escribió Cristiano. Pero antes de poder tuitearlo, lo eliminó.

Su primo Ángel sabía perfectamente que los padres de Cristiano se lo pagarían con tal de ver a parte de la familia, y si no, podría haber mentido sobre una feria de empleo española o un

Eight

❖ ❖ ❖

Odio no poder odiarte

March, 2013

"But dude, nothing but chicks and booze for an entire week! Seriously, you don't wanna?"

Cristiano sat there, looking as blank as the computer screen in front of him, his hands laying restlessly on the keyboard at work.

"I'm not sure if this whole thing is for me anymore - nursing the hangovers, constantly going home for a hot one-night stand - it just feels..." Cristiano typed, tentatively. He realized suddenly that the counter had gone red, as if even Twitter was angry at him.

He highlighted the text and clicked backspace, deleting the entire thing. How could he explain in 140 characters everything he was feeling - inadequacy, insecurity, indecision - but all without sounding like a giant pussy? How do you narrow the human experience down to a single, emotionless sentence? All he wanted to do was vomit words all over the keyboard.

"Dude, I'm totally broke right now and can't afford it right now D:" Cristiano wrote, but before he could clicked the green *'twittear'* button, he deleted it.

His cousin Ángel knew full well that Cristiano's parents would have paid for him to see family, and if not, he could have lied to them about an all-important Spanish job conference or a Catholic

seminario católico en Miami. Y aunque quería ver a su primo, no estaba seguro de si podría lidiar con lo que venía con ello: una semana del infame Spring Break floridiano.

Había sido un sueño de ellos durante años. Cada verano, Cristiano iba a Granada a visitar a su tía. Cuando eran niños, hacían travesuras a su tío, o iban al Albaicín para joder a los turistas o a una gitana al azar vendiendo amuletos por la Catedral. Pero cuando fueron creciendo, Ángel y Cristiano hacían payasadas más maduras. Iban al Sacromonte a tomarse unas copas en las cuevas gitanas a pesar de que eran menores de edad, flirteaban con chicas que doblaban su edad y que les ignoraban. Entonces, desde una esquina, se imaginaban que estaban en una fiesta americana como las de las películas, y bebían y bailaban hasta que apenas podían andar y, finalmente, volvían a casa al amanecer destrozados andando por caminos sinuosos hasta la cuesta Chapiz.

Las negras montañas, como la boca de un lobo, les vigilaban con juicio severo detrás de la fuente celeste en el patio, mientras buscaban las llaves a tientas. El sol lentamente llegaba a la cima, brillando en tonalidades vibrantes amarillas y rojas en el ojo de la cerradura. Sólo la Alhambra quedaba cubierta en sombras desde los cuidados arbustos en verdes tonalidades hasta las ruinas arábigas, un mausoleo a la sociedad de tres religiones coexistentes reflejado en panfletos turísticos.

En aquel entonces, regresar de fiesta era excitante. La vida estaba llena de raras y bellas coincidencias durante este temprano abismo entre la noche y el día. Incluso las cosas más pequeñas le podrían hacer sonreír como, por ejemplo, un caballo al relinchar a lo lejos. Pero en algún punto entre aquel tiempo y ahora, la luz del sol se había hecho solamente un recuerdo de los borrones de memorias dolorosas que tendría durante su inminente resaca. Alguien le había agarrado la mano. ¿Una chica, un chico? Ya había explorado y conquistado la noche, pero ¿y ahora?

La novedad de salir de fiesta había perdido su brillo.

Part Three: (De)construction

seminar in Miami. And while he did want to see his cousin, he wasn't sure if he could handle what went with it: a week of the infamous Floridian spring break.

It had been a dream of theirs for years. Every summer Cristiano used to go to Granada to visit his aunt. As kids they had played pranks on his uncle, or gone down to the Albacín to mess with tourists or the random gypsy selling charms at the cathedral. But when they had grown up, Ángel and Cristiano got into more adult mischief. They would go to Sacremonte for a couple of drinks in the gypsy caves despite being underage, giddily flirting with girls twice their age who ignored them. Then, in the corners of the bar, they would imagine being in the American party scene they had seen in movies. They would drink and dance until they could barely walk, and finally stumble home at dawn on the winding paths until they reached Chapiz Hill.

The pitch-black mountains would watch in stern judgment from behind the baby blue fountain in the courtyard as they fumbled over the keys. The sun would be slowly peeking over the top, beaming vibrant yellow and red hues on the keyhole. Only the Alhambra remained shrouded in shadows, from the well-kept, lush, green shrubbery to the pale Arabic ruins, taking no part in the beautiful symphony of the city waking around it. It was a mausoleum for the famed society of three religions in tourist pamphlets.

Back then, coming back from a party was exciting. Life was so full of strange, beautiful coincidences during that early-morning precipice between night and day. Even the slightest things would make him smile, like a horse neighing in the distance. But somewhere between then and now, the light of the sun had just become a reminder of a blur of painful memories he would have to sort out in the impending hangover. An explosion of feelings. Someone had grabbed his hand. A girl? A guy? He had explored and conquered the night, sure, but what now?

Emborracharse ya no era una cadena de acontecimientos, en la cual todo podría pasar. Ahora cuando se iba con sus amigos, Cristiano se sentía solo incluso rodeado de miles de personas, como si estuvieran viendo a través de él. Cristiano solía confundir su búsqueda con una invitación, pero ahora no estaba seguro de que aún ellos supieran el qué o a quién buscaban. El bar se transformó en un instante en un purgatorio lleno de espíritus extraviados buscando una salida. Y cuanto más alcohol bebía, más se daba cuenta de que era uno de ellos, lo que le desanimaba aún más si cabe.

Cristiano quería irse a casa y darse un atracón de Netflix en momentos así. En vez de empezar la noche allí, ahora Cristiano prefería quedarse en casa o hacer una pequeña quedada. Quizá no era la locura a la cual estaba acostumbrado, pero por lo menos las personas interactuaban con él en carne y hueso y no con el fantasma opaco que era.

Cristiano siempre creía que no necesitaba a nadie, pero ahora se daba cuenta de que había subestimado a su familia y amigos en España, quienes le habían entendido implícitamente y le querían por su seña única de locura, o quizás a pesar de ella. Incluso después de cruzar un océano, Cristiano se aferraba a la conexión débil con ellos por Skype y redes sociales como un chaleco salvavidas que le protegía del golpe de las olas. Pero después de unos meses, la última gota colmó el vaso y Cristiano sintió que la situación le superaba, ahogándose debajo de las profundidades. Era obvio que necesitaba una conexión más tangible, y aún así, en vez de tener su cerebro concentrándose en resolver el problema, toda su desesperación le llevó otra vez al concepto abstracto de la chica en vestida de rojo de Nochevieja.

—Déjate de dramas y de esas emociones —se dijo Cristiano, encerrado en su cuarto como si fuera la torre de Rapunzel—. Sé un hombre.

Empezó a esconderse detrás de su trabajo para dejar de pensar

Part Three: (De)construction

The novelty of going out had lost its luster. Getting drunk was no longer an exciting string of events, where anything could happen. Nowadays when he went out with his friends, Cristiano felt alone even in a crowd of hundreds, as if they were looking right through him. Cristiano used to mistake their searching for an invitation, but now he was sure they didn't even know what or who they were looking for. The bar had transformed into a purgatory full of wayward spirits trying to find a way out. And the more alcohol he had, the more he realized he was one of them, making him all the more despondent.

Cristiano wanted to go home and Netflix-binge at moments like these. Rather than beginning the night there, Cristiano now preferred to stay at home or go to a small get-together. Maybe it wasn't the craziness he was used to, but at least there, people interacted with him in the flesh and not as some opaque phantom reminder of humanity.

Cristiano had always thought that he didn't need anyone, but now he realized he had taken his friends and family in Spain for granted. They had implicitly understood him and loved him because of his unique brand of crazy, or maybe even in spite of that. Even after crossing an ocean, Cristiano had held on to the faint connection with them through Skype and social media, like a lifejacket keeping him safe above the crashing waves. But after months, his last finger had slipped off, and Cristiano was overwhelmed, drowning beneath the depths. He obviously needed a more tangible connection, and yet, instead of his brain concentrating on fixing the problem, all his desperation brought him back to the abstract concept of the girl in the red dress from New Year's.

"Stop being so melodramatic and emotional," Cristiano had said to himself, holed up in his room as if it were Rapunzel's tower. "Man up."

He began hiding behind his work to stop overthinking his

demasiado en sus emociones. O por lo menos para que no fueran tan obvios para sus colegas. A menudo se esforzaba en ir a una disco o un bar con Lena y David para mantener las apariencias, pero afortunadamente ya no salían tanto como antes. La mayor parte del tiempo se quedaban en casa viendo la tele, jugando a videojuegos, leyendo o invitando a uno o dos amigos a cenar en casa.

***

Su reencuentro con la sobriedad le dio mucho tiempo extra como para perder el hilo de sus pensamientos y caer en digresiones y vericuetos ahora que no tenía que mantener a raya su resaca y la falta de sueño. Por ejemplo, el otro día, mientras miraba el techo blanco, Cristiano lo imaginó transformándose en una dorada escena de los girasoles de Van Gogh, recordando una clase de arte en el colegio sobre… *impasse, impastato, impasto…* palabras italianas que no llegaba a recordar. Las flores estaban muy alegres en el exterior, pero en la profundidad de las capas de pintura, ¿no se suicidó Van Gogh? ¿O fue él quien se cortó la oreja? ¿O fueron las dos cosas?

—¿A quién le importa una mierda? —murmulló Cristiano.

¿Qué? —preguntó David al otro lado del sofá.

—Nada —dijo Cristiano.

—Bueno, ha sido fruto del azar —se rió David.

—¡Oh! ¡Regresa tú a tu estúpida serie gay! —dijo Cristiano.

—¡No es una estupidez! —gritó David respondiéndole—. ¡Homosexualiza la dinámica familiar en una nueva definición de normalidad en la edad contemporánea!

—Pues eso, una estupidez de serie —dijo Cristiano.

—Sólo porque no entiendes eso no significa que sea una estupidez —insistió David—. ¡Mira y quizá aprendas algo!

Unos meses antes, esto le aburriría a David tanto como a él, pero

Part Three: (De)construction

emotions. Or at least so they weren't obvious to his bros. Occasionally he pushed himself to go to a club or a bar with Lena and David to keep up appearances, but thankfully they almost never went out themselves anymore. Most of the time, they would stay home watching T.V., playing video games, reading, or inviting one or two friends over for dinner.

***

His newfound sobriety gave him a lot of extra time now to lose his train of thought and fall into these digressions and rabbit trails now, that he didn't have hangovers or lack of sleep to stave off. For example, the other day, while looking at the layered white ceiling, Cristiano imagined it transforming into a golden sunflower scene from Van Gogh. He remembered his art class from high school, about... *impasse, impastato, impasto*...some Italian word he couldn't remember. The flowers were so happy on the outside, but deep below the layers of paint, hadn't Van Gogh killed himself? Or was he the guy who cut of his ear? Or was it both?

"Who gives a rat's ass?" Cristiano mumbled to himself.

"What?" David asked, from the other side of the couch.

"Nothing," Cristiano said.

"Well, that was random," David laughed.

"Oh, just get back to your stupid gay show!" Cristiano said.

"It's not stupid!" David yelled back. "It's gender-queering the family dynamic into a new definition of normal in the contemporary age!"

"So, stupid gay show," Cristiano said.

"Just because you don't understand it doesn't mean it's stupid," David insisted. "Watch, maybe you'll learn something!"

A couple of months ago, this would have bored David as much as it bored him, but now David sat there intently, soaking up every

ahora se sentaba allí atentamente, chupando cada palabra como una esponja, como si fuera un niño de cinco años en un jardín gay de infancia.

Cristiano había notado que David estaba en una fase de 'orgullo gay,' en que cada día era un gran desfile del orgullo gay, tan lleno con pompa política como una celebración de su nueva encontrada sexualidad. La primera semana había sido mono, pero ahora el piso estaba plagado con libros de amor gay y guías prácticas par invertir la heteronormativilidad, el zumbido de Grindr haciendo eco por el cuarto, mientras se rodeaba con tanta homosexualidad que Cristiano pensó que David cagaría arco iris de un momento a otro.

—Lo dice el gay de solo unos segundos —se rió Cristiano—. ¿Pero sabes lo que estás diciendo?

—¡Homófobo!

—¡Heterófobo!

Mientras discutían, Lena entró a hurtadillas y cambió el canal.

—¡Ey, chicos! Esto es la hostia —dijo Lena parando a Cristiano y David.

Se dieron la vuelta y miraron por un momento, pero sólo vieron a Jane teniendo TOC, limpiando la casa como una maniaca para arreglar la sucia vida de Max y fallando estrepitosamente.

—Pero... sólo limpia —dijo David lentamente.

—Bueno, no soy el único —pensó Cristiano.

—Sí, ¿no os parece gracioso? —exclamó Lena alegremente.

Cristiano no tenía para nada el mismo sentido de humor que ella, pero por lo menos estaba intentando disfrutar más de la vida, poco a poco. Incluso se fue en Megabus con David a Indianapolis a ver el torneo de March Madness un poco más temprano aquel mismo día.

—¿Ya habéis regresado? —preguntó Cristiano.

Part Three: (De)construction

word like a five-year-old in gay kindergarten.

Cristiano had noted that David was in a 'gay pride' phase, in which every day was a gay pride parade, as full of political pomp as it was a celebration of newfound sexuality. The first week had been cute, but now gay love stories and how-to's on subverting heteronormativity were littered across the apartment, and the random buzz of Grindr echoed across the room. He had surrounded himself with so much homosexuality that Cristiano thought David would soon shit rainbows.

"Says the man who has been gay for all of five seconds," Cristiano laughed. "Do you even know what you're saying?"

"Homophobe!"

"Heterophobe!"

As they argued, Lena snuck in and changed the channel.

"Guys, this is hilarious," Lena said, stopping Cristiano and David.

They turned around and watched for a second, but they just saw Jane being OCD, cleaning like mad to fix Max's dirty lifestyle and failing miserably.

"But... she's just cleaning," David said, slowly.

"Good, I'm not the only one," Cristiano thought.

"Yeah, isn't it funny?" Lena exclaimed, happily.

Cristiano definitely didn't have the same sense of comedy as she did, but at least she was trying to enjoy more of life, little by little. She had even gone on the Megabus with David to Indianapolis to see March Madness earlier that evening.

"You're back? Already?" Cristiano asked.

"We got to see Michael Jordan!" Lena shouted. She was

—¡Vimos a Michael Jordan! —gritó Lena, que llevaba un jersey de Michael Jordan de los Chicago Bulls.

—Lena, lo primero, ya se ha retirado. Y lo segundo, vimos el partido de Oregon y Saint Louis —dijo David.

—Entonces, ¿por qué vendían su jersey? —preguntó Lena.

—Porque es famoso. Además, ¡el cajero te preguntó si estabas segura de que querías este! —dijo David.

—¿Por qué no me lo impediste? —preguntó Lena mientras David se desternillaba.

—¡Me dejaste a propósito! —dijo Lena dando un puñetazo a David.

—¡Valía la pena! —dijo David entre sus lágrimas de risa.

—Te mato —dijo Lena con una mirada asesina mientras se dirigía a la cocina con paso firme y vencida.

Entonces fue cuando David encendió la tele para ver 'The New Normal'.

—¿A quién le importa una mierda? —murmulló Cristiano.

Después de ver la tele con ellos aquella noche, se fue al gimnasio en la planta baja del edificio. Estaba pensando otra vez en la chica vestida de rojo y necesitaba sacarla de su cabeza de una manera u otra, y sudar las toxinas era una buena opción como otra cualquiera. Simplemente no la podía olvidar. Quizás en el fondo no quería, a pesar de lo loco que le volvía. Era un tipo de masoquismo y había que encontrar el porqué antes de poder solucionar su demencia.

Hizo pesas, intentando olvidar la polla de Carmen. Era la chica perfecta, ¡pero tenía rabo! ¿Podría haberse equivocado? Cristiano estaba como una cuba. Podría haber rozado su cartera o quizás lo imaginara todo como un sueño clandestino.

O quizás no. Era atrevida como un hombre. Quizás era un *drag*

wearing a Michael Jordan Chicago Bulls jersey.

"Lena, one, he's retired. And two, we were watching Oregon play St. Louis," David said.

"Then why were they selling his jersey?" Lena asked.

"Because he's famous. Besides, the cashier asked if you were sure you wanted that one!" David said.

"Why didn't you stop me?" Lena asked, as David cackled. "You let me on purpose!" She punched him.

"It was so worth it!" David said through his tears of laughter.

"I'm going to kill you," Lena said with a deadly glare. She stomped off to the kitchen in defeat.

David turned on the T.V. to watch the *New Normal*.

"Who gives a rat's ass?" Cristiano mumbled to himself.

After watching T.V. with them that evening, he went to the gym on the first floor of the building. He had been thinking about the girl in red again. Cristiano needed to get her out of his head somehow, and sweating out the toxins was as good of a choice as any. He just couldn't forget about her. Perhaps deep down he didn't want to, despite how crazy it drove him. It was a type of masochism, and he had to find out the why and how before he could fix his insanity.

He lifted weights as he tried to forget Carmen's penis. She was the perfect girl, but she had a dick! Maybe he had gotten it wrong. Cristiano had been drunk as all hell, after all. Maybe he had rubbed up her purse, or maybe he had imagined it all like a clandestine dream.

Or maybe he hadn't. She was daring like a man. Maybe she was just a drag queen. But she was also delicate like a woman. What was she? Cristiano didn't know if he wanted to sleep with the

queen. Pero fue delicada como una mujer. ¿Quién era? Cristiano no sabía si quería acostarse con la chica guapa que era o pasar el rato con el tío con agallas que le poseyó, haciendo travesuras por la noche como colegas. Ella era un enigma. Un enigma que le puso y a la vez le confundió.

***

Cristiano oyó un 'ding dong' desde el ordenador que le devolvió a la oficina: "CORREO ELECTRÓNICO DE: LISA FREEMAN - Ven a mi oficina en cinco min...", decía el mensaje previsualizado en la esquina de la pantalla de su ordenador antes de borrarse

—Lo siento, tío. Estoy pendiente del curro y la vida aquí —escribió finalmente Cristiano en el ordenador como respuesta en un tuit.

—Aguafiestasssss. :P —respondió Ángel, notificación que recibió Cristiano en su móvil mientras se iba del ordenador.

Su descanso había acabado. Cristiano no tenía tiempo para reflexionar ni en el pasado, ni en el presente, ni en el futuro, o por lo menos eso se dijo a sí mismo. *Tenía trabajo que hacer*. Aparte de eso, Lisa había ejercido más presión en Cristiano últimamente. Había varias propuestas que escribir para clientes con los que Lisa quería firmar un contrato, las cuales tuvo que dar al departamento de adquisiciones para que les echaran un vistazo. Además, Lisa le había asignado unos grandes proyectos con unos clientes que estaban en el proceso de renegociar sus contratos por quejarse sobre las RR.PP. insuficientes o por la falta de visibilidad, amenazando de invocar a su cláusula de rescisión de contrato si no obtenían mejores márgenes de beneficio. Y Cristiano sabía que si no había acabado con todo este viernes o si perdía un solo cliente, Lisa le arrancaría los cojones.

Tras acercarse a la oficina de Javier a pedir unos favores para renegociar los precios de las ventas al por mayor con sus vendedores con la novela de Marley, usar el peloteo para convencer

Part Three: (De)construction

beautiful woman that she was or if he wanted to hang out with the ballsy dude that possessed her, getting into mischief in the night like bros. She was an enigma that both turned him on and confused him.

***

Cristiano heard a *ding* from his computer, bringing him back to the office: "EMAIL FROM: LISA FREEMAN - Come to my office in five mi..." the message preview in the corner of his computer screen said before it faded away.

"Sorry, man. I'm preoccupied with work and life here," Cristiano typed, finally tweeting his response.

"Party pooperrrrr. :P" Ángel responded. He got the notification on his phone as he walked away from the computer.

His break had ended. Cristiano didn't have time to reflect on the past, present, or future, or so he said to himself - he had work to do. Besides that, Lisa had really pressured Cristiano recently. There were proposals to write for clients Lisa wanted to sign, which he had to get over to Acquisitions to check over. Plus, Lisa had assigned him some big projects for a few existing clients who were in the process of renegotiating their contracts. They were complaining about not enough P.R. this or lack of visibility that, threatening to invoke their termination clauses unless there were better profit margins. And Cristiano knew that if he didn't have it all done by this Friday or lost a single client, Lisa would put his balls in a vice.

He ran to Javier's office to ask for a couple of favors on renegotiating the bulk sales with their vendors for the Marley novel, and sweet-talked Julie, the comptroller, to give him some 'pocket change' for a lunch meeting to court Peral-Vega for his new manuscript on 18th-century myths in Spanish literature. As he was on the way back to his desk, Lisa stopped him in his tracks.

a Julie, la interventora, para pedirle 'un poco de calderilla' a favor en su cuenta por el almuerzo de negocios en el que cortejar a Peral-Vega por su nuevo manuscrito de mitos del siglo XVIII en la literatura española, Lisa le detuvo en su camino a su escritorio.

—¿No recibió mi email? —preguntó Lisa asomando la cabeza desde su oficina.

—Lo siento. No estaba en mi escritorio —mintió Cristiano.

—Venga a mi oficina —dijo Lisa dura y estoicamente.

—Madre mía —pensó Cristiano mientras le seguía—. ¿Estaba cabreada? ¿Por qué? Sabía que debía haber comprado unos platos con fruta fresca para suavizar a los inversores durante la presentación de ayer. O, ¿está enfadada con cómo había apañado la cuenta de Thompson?

—Cierra la puerta, por favor, Cristiano —dijo Lisa.

—Lo siento por el caso de Thompson —dijo Cristiano—. Le debería haber preguntado si debía haber hecho una excepción con el margen de él.

—¡Oh! ¿Él? ¡No! —preguntó Lisa—. Fuiste todo un fiera. No podía estar más contenta. Ayer estaba enfadada con Thompson, no contigo. Se estaba aprovechando. Da igual lo bien que se estén vendiendo sus libros de autoayuda, no podemos vivir de esos márgenes. Estábamos a punto de terminar su contrato después de la próxima temporada de verano.

—Entonces, ¿por qué estoy aquí? —dijo Cristiano confundido.

—Siéntese, Cristiano —dijo Lisa con calma—. ¡Y relájase! No ha hecho nada malo. Esto es un tema informal.

Cristiano empezó respirar otra vez, pero sus pensamientos se agolparon, pensando en qué podría ser. *¿Había otro proyecto especial? Basta ya. ¡Casi no podía hacer los proyectos que tenía como para contar con otro proyecto 'especial'!*

—He decidido... —empezó Lisa, mientas Cristiano ya se

Part Three: (De)construction

"Did you not get my email?" Lisa asked, poking her head out of her office.

"Sorry, wasn't at my desk," Cristiano lied.

"Come into my office," Lisa said, sternly and stoically.

"Oh god," Cristiano thought as he followed her. "Was she pissed off? Why? I knew I should have bought some fruit plates to soften up the investors during yesterday's presentation. Or is she angry about how I handled the Thompson account?"

"Close the door, please, Christian," Lisa said.

"I'm sorry about the Thompson case," Cristiano said. "I should have asked you if we could make an exception on the margin for him."

"Oh, him? No!" Lisa asked. "You were a pit-bull in there! Couldn't have been happier. I was just angry at Thompson yesterday, not you. He was taking advantage. No matter how much his self-help books sell, we can't operate on those margins. We would've terminated our contract with him after the summer season anyway."

"So why am I here?" Cristiano said, confused.

"Sit down, Cristiano," Lisa said calmly. "And relax! You've done nothing wrong. This is an informality."

Cristiano started to breathe again, but his mind was racing. Was this another special project? It was too much. He was barely keeping on top of the projects he already had, not to mention another 'special' one!

"I've decided…" Lisa began, Cristiano already cursing himself under his breath for having worked so hard that she thought he could do more. *Working hard only leads to bad things...* "…to offer you a full time job. $40,000 a year, $200 medical coverage, two weeks of vacation to start, 401K plan with 100% employer match."

maldecía entre dientes por trabajar tan duro que ella pensara que él podría hacer más. *Trabajar duro solamente traía complicaciones* — ofrecerle una posición de tiempo completo. 40.000$ cada año, 200$ de cobertura médica, dos semanas de vacaciones, y un plan de jubilación 401k con 100% de contribuciones paralelas al empleado.

—¿Qué? —dijo Cristiano con más fuerza de lo que esperaba—. Perdóneme. Digo, me alegro, pero ¿por qué yo y no Lena o David? Son muy trabajadores.

—Claro —respondió Lisa—. Y exactamente por eso le elegí, y no a ellos.

—Perdón, no le sigo —dijo Cristiano, levantando una ceja extrañado.

—Tengo demasiados trabajadores, que pueden trabajar, pero no pueden pensar por su cuenta —explicó Lisa—. Me falta gente innovadora. Es aquí donde le necesitamos a usted.

—¿Innovador? ¿Yo? Sólo cumplo con mi trabajo —dijo Cristiano insistiendo que no era el adecuado—. La mayoría de las veces no sigo todo al pie de la letra. ¡Coño! Incluso he mentido aquí en alguna ocasión.

—Voy a ignorar esta última parte —dijo Lisa riéndose como si creyera que estaba bromeando.

—Pero, en serio, no me quiere aquí —dijo Cristiano—. Ha cometido un error.

—Admito que estaba escéptica cuando empezó —dijo Lisa.

—Mire, ¡haga caso a su intuición! —dijo Cristiano, medio bromeando, medio cagándose de miedo.

—Cristiano, ¿a qué hora llegó esta mañana? —preguntó Lisa.

—A las 8:40-8:50 —dijo Cristiano—. ¿Por qué?

—¿A qué hora empieza el trabajo? —preguntó Lisa.

—A las 9:00 —dijo Cristiano—. ¿Qué me quiere decir?

—¿Cuando solía llegar aquí? —preguntó Lisa.

Part Three: (De)construction

"What?" Cristiano declared, more loudly than he had meant to. "Excuse me. I mean, I'm happy, but why did you choose me and not Lena or David? They're hard workers."

"Of course," Lisa responded. "And that's exactly why I chose you and not them."

"Pardon, I don't follow," Cristiano said, raising an eyebrow in confusion.

"I have an excess of hard workers. People who can work, but can't think on their own," Lisa explained. "I lack innovators. And that's where you come in."

"Innovator? Me? I just get the job done," Cristiano said, insisting that he wasn't fit for the job: "I don't even go by the book most of the time. Hell, I've straight-up lied here before."

"I'm going to ignore that last part," Lisa said, laughing as if he was joking.

"But seriously, you don't want me," Cristiano said. "You've made a mistake."

"I'll admit, I was skeptical when you first started," Lisa said.

"See, go with that!" Cristiano said. He was halfway joking and halfway scared out of his mind.

"Christian, what time did you get here this morning?" Lisa asked.

"8:40-8:50," Cristiano said. "Why?"

"What time does work start?" Lisa asked.

"9:00," Cristiano said. "And your point?"

"When did you used to get here?" Lisa asked.

"I don't know," Cristiano lied.

"Yes, you do," Lisa said.

—No lo sé —mintió Cristiano.

—Sí, lo sabe —dijo Lisa.

—A las 9:30, 9:45 —murmuró Cristiano.

—¿Perdone? —dijo Lisa señalando su oreja.

—A las 9:30, 9:45 —dijo Cristiano con la severidad de un paciente de cáncer admitiendo que le quedaban unas seis semanas de vida.

—¿Lo ve? Usted ha progresado mucho en el último año —dijo Lisa—. Es mucho más cuidadoso en la oficina, lleva ropa mucho más profesional, y va a las reuniones preparado con un cuaderno y todo.

—Y también lo hacen David y Lena —suplicó David desesperadamente.

—¿Y arreglaron el caso de Kudrow? —preguntó Lisa—. ¿O el de Franken o el de Peña?

—No, pero todo eso fue improvisado —dijo Cristiano insistiendo.

—Y si no hubiera jugado y se hubiera esperado, habríamos perdido los tres —dijo Lisa—. Le he estado probando últimamente, y me ha mostrado un trabajo consistente. Heterodoxo, pero los resultados hablan por sí mismos.

—Pero… —imploró Cristiano.

—Me permite acabar —le paró Lisa—. Ya sé que es mucho que asimilar. Y la responsabilidad de ello es escalofriante. Entre usted y yo, contratamos a los becarios porque resulta más económico y también para evitar las molestias de Recursos Humanos sobre diversidad. Pero le quiero coger antes de que se pueda volver a España.

—Gracias, pero… —intentó decir Cristiano.

—No quiero su decisión ahora Cristiano —le paró Lisa otra vez—. Piénselo durante unas semanas. ¡Eso es todo!

Part Three: (De)construction

"9:30, 9:45," Cristiano mumbled.

"Excuse me?" Lisa said, pointing to her ear.

"9:30, 9:45," Cristiano said, with the severity of a cancer patient admitting he had six weeks to live.

"See, you've really grown in the past year," Lisa said. "You're more alert at work, you are dressed much more professionally, and you come prepared to meetings with a notebook and everything."

"So do David and Lena," Cristiano pleaded desperately.

"And did they fix the Kudrow case?" Lisa asked. "Or the Franken or Peña ones?"

"No, but that was just some improvising," Cristiano said.

"And had you played it safe and waited, we would've lost all three of them," Lisa said. "I've been testing you recently, and you've shown consistent work. Unorthodox, but the results speak for themselves."

"But..." Cristiano pleaded.

"Let me finish," Lisa stopped him. "I know this is a lot to take in. And responsibility is scary. Off the record, we only have your interns as cheap labor and to keep H.R. off our backs about diversity. But I'd like to snap you up before Spain takes you back."

"Thank you, but..." Cristiano tried to get in.

"I don't want your decision yet, Christian," Lisa stopped him again. "Think it over for a few weeks. That's all!"

Cristiano left the building at five PM with more frustrations than before. On the one hand, he could have a job that paid more or less well for his age, and God knew he wouldn't get that in Spain with his little experience and grades right now - a communications major with threes and fours who almost had to go to private school rather than *la Complu*? Even his friends with perfect grades and recommendations were having enough trouble getting even a

Cristiano salió del edificio a las 17:00 con más frustraciones que antes. Por un lado, podría tener un curro que pagaba más o menos bien por su edad ahora, y Dios sabía que no conseguiría un curro en España con tan poca experiencia y sus malas notas - ¿una carrera en Ciencias de la Información con notas de tres y cuatro, que casi tuvo que ir a una universidad privada en vez de la Complu? Incluso sus amigos con notas perfectas y recomendaciones tuvieron bastantes problemas para encontrar un trabajo de camarero en '100 Mondatitos'. Al fin y al cabo, la tasa de paro en España había subido hasta el 45% para jóvenes según el artículo de 'El País' que había leído la semana anterior en el muro de *Facebook* de su amigo. Y todavía, a pesar de la prueba abrumadora, ya escuchaba a su madre gritándole por si quiera considerarlo. Aún no se lo había dicho a su madre, pero a esas alturas, ella había ocupado por la fuerza una sección de espectadores molestos en la esquina de atrás de su mente:

—¡Escucha tú a esa Ana Pastor! —incordió la voz de su madre—. Dejó TVE y ahora, ¡mírala! ¡Nunca mejor! Así que olvídate de ese trabajo de mierda en Chicago y ¡regresa a España!

Si el trabajo estuviera en Londres o Bruselas, no sería tan difícil. Podría volar regularmente con RyanAir o EasyJet, o tomar el tren o el bus en el peor de los casos para reducir así el efecto del supuesto 'exilio económico'. Pero existía un océano entero entre ellos, y tanto como le encantaba la ciudad de Chicago, ¿cómo podría escoger entre un trabajo y la familia? ¿Era capaz de elegir?

Suspendido en un limbo entre dos mundos, Cristiano caminó a casa en lugar de coger el L. Necesitaba pasear y pensar detenidamente en su decisión. Su vida había cambiado tan rápido desde que llegó a Chicago que ni siquiera se había dado cuenta de que había pasado un año. Y aunque había vivido en esta ciudad ese tiempo, esta fue la primera vez que dio un paseo para verla de verdad.

Los rascacielos industriales, llenos de personas moviéndose,

serving job at *100 Mondatitos*. After all, the unemployment rate in Spain had risen to 45% for young adults, according to an *El Pais* article he read last week on his friend's Facebook wall.

And yet, despite all of this overwhelming evidence, he heard his mother yelling at him about even considering it. He hadn't told his mother, but by this point in his life, she had forcibly occupied a special permanent heckling section in the back of his mind.

"Listen to that Ana Pastor!" his mother's voice nagged. "She left her job at TVE and look at her now! Never better! So forget that crap job in Chicago, and come back to Spain!"

If the job were in London or Brussels, it wouldn't be as hard. He could regularly fly RyanAir or EasyJet, or in the worst-case scenario, take a train or a bus to make the so-called 'economic exile' easier. But Chicago was an entire ocean away, and as much as he loved the city, how would he choose between a job or his family? Could he choose?

Suspended in a limbo between two worlds, Cristiano walked home instead of taking the L. He needed to slow down and think this decision over. Life had moved so quickly since Cristiano had come to Chicago that he hadn't realized it had been nearly a year. And while he may have lived in this city for a year, this was the first time he had ever strolled through her to truly see her.

The industrial skyscrapers were filled with people moving about their own tasks, as the buildings reached toward the sky as if wanting and needing to outdo the insignificant humans inside, shimmering in the cool heat of the spring sun. Cristiano could smell the refreshing drizzle that must have stopped just before his walk, for some of the moisture was still clinging to the sidewalk and the freshly trimmed grass.

Cristiano disappeared in-between the white, budding flowers near the Lincoln Park Zoo, which were defiantly determined to shine through all the mucky, coffee-colored stains of spring

haciendo sus tareas y asuntos, mientras el edificio se estiraba hacia los cielos, como si quisiera y necesitara superar a los humanos insignificantes que estaban dentro, reluciendo en el fresco calentamiento del sol de primavera. Cristiano olió la refrescante fragancia de una llovizna que debía haber acabado pocos minutos antes, la humedad de la lluvia impregnada en la acera y el césped recién cortado.

Cristiano desapreció entre unas tempranas flores blancas cerca del Lincoln Park Zoo, las cuales estaban determinadas a brillar a través de las mugrientas manchas de color café del tiempo primaveral. Miró más allá, sobre el ocupado Lake Shore Drive, hasta la costa del lago Míchigan, escuchando al ciclo constante de las olas, relajándole hasta el punto de echarse una pequeña siesta, despertándose justo antes de que se pusiera el sol en el horizonte.

Cristiano miró hacia atrás mientras la silueta de casas de ladrillo y estructuras de acero cambiaban de un color amarillo hasta el anaranjado, el morado y tonos entremezclados de azul. Podía sentir los colores en su pecho, los cuales le inspiraban cual poeta, mientras veía palabras mágicas saltando desde cada tonalidad por primera vez.

El paseo le ayudó a liberar su mente de sus profundas y contrariadas reflexiones con las que había estado luchando hasta tal punto como sucedió con los Republicanos y Franco. Sin embargo, en EE.UU., los Republicanos eran los Demócratas y los Nacionalistas eran los Republicanos, ¿fue así, no? Tal vez Cristiano se había dejado atrapar por la semántica.

En los alrededores del puerto Belmont, Cristiano volvió a entrar en las calles desbordantes de la ciudad mientras las farolas se encendían. Pasando Boystown, sabía que casi había llegado a casa. Buena Park estaba a tan sólo unos 20 minutos al norte de la Avenida Belmont. Pero al subir la calle Halsted, divisó vagamente a una conocida saliendo del café Caribou, que quedaba justo enfrente.

Part Three: (De)construction

weather. He looked past them, over the busy Lake Shore Drive to the coast of Lake Michigan, listening to the consistent ebb and flow of the waves. They lulled him into a short nap, and he woke up just before the sun set behind him.

Cristiano looked back as the beautiful skyline of brick homes and steel structures changed from yellow to orange to purple and various intermixed shades of blue. He could feel the colors on his chest and they inspired him like a poet, as he saw magical words jumping out of each hue for the first time.

The walk helped him clear his mind from his deep, conflicting reflections, which had been fighting against each other up to that point like the Republicans and Franco. But then again, in the US, Republicans were Democrats, and the Nationalists were Republicans, weren't they? Perhaps Cristiano had gotten caught up in semantics.

Around Belmont Harbor, he entered the bustling city streets again just as the streetlights began lighting up. Passing Boystown, he knew that he was almost home. Buena Park was only 20 minutes north of Belmont Avenue. But as he walked up Halsted, Cristiano vaguely recognized the girl leaving from the Caribou Coffee just across the street.

"It can't be," Cristiano said.

At first he just blamed it on wishful thinking and kept walking. He had just gotten those thoughts out of his head by convincing himself he dreamed it on the L ride home that night - she couldn't really exist. Carmen was just a myth.

"But what if she's not just a figment of my imagination?" Cristiano thought. "What would be the harm in saying hi?"

Cristiano began building movie-like scenes, thinking of each carefully planned-out retort. He thought out a million scenarios all in 30 seconds, but when he came to the conclusion that the smart decision was to leave, his body vetoed it and turned him left to

—No puedo ser... —se dijo Cristiano.

En un primer momento echó la culpa a una ilusión en su cabeza y siguió andando. Ya había conseguido quitarse de sus pensamientos a la chica vestida de rojo convenciéndose a sí mismo de que había sido un sueño en su vuelta a casa en el L. *No podía existir.* Carmen sólo fue un mito.

«Pero ¿qué pasa si no es sólo un producto de mi imaginación?», pensó Cristiano. «¿Qué hay de malo en decir hola?»

Cristiano comenzó a pensar en un montón de posibles escenas, como si fuera una película, pensando en cada cuidadosa réplica, cada una bien preparada. Pensó en miles de situaciones hipotéticas en unos 30 segundos, pero al llegar a la conclusión de que la decisión más acertada era irse, su cuerpo se negó y le hizo girar a su izquierda para cruzar la calle contra su voluntad.

—¡Oye, tú! ¡Carmen! —gritó Cristiano mientras evitaba un coche, un taxista que le maldijo por su estupidez. La chica de rojo siguió andando sin prestar ninguna atención. Cuando alcanzó a Carmen, le agarró del brazo—. ¡Carmen! ¿No me oyes?

—¡Ay, sí! ¡Ya te oí! —respondió Carmen sacudiéndole la mano—. Pero si le diera la hora a cada estúpido que me grita en la calle, no podría hacer nada, coño.

—No me hagas daño, guapa —se defendió Cristiano en broma.

—Anda, si aquí tenemos a un conquistador —dijo Carmen con sarcasmo—. Por su puesto que dejaré que abuses de mi cuerpo, tal y como lo hizo la gente de tu calaña a mi país durante siglos de forma salvaje. ¿Cómo no me voy a resistir a esas pistolas, señor Colón?

—¿Qué dices? —preguntó Cristiano mitad curioso.

—Lo que oyes, coño. Sígueme el rollo —respondió Carmen,

jaywalk across to her, against his own will.

"Hey you! Carmen!" Cristiano screamed as he dodged a car, a cab driver cursing at Cristiano for his stupidity. The girl in red continued walking without paying any attention. When he reached Carmen, he grabbed her arm and said: "Carmen! Didn't you hear me?"

"Oh, I heard you," Carmen responded, shaking off his hand. "But if I gave the time of day to every idiot who cat-called me in the street, I wouldn't get anything done, asshole."

"Don't hurt me, hot stuff," Cristiano defended, jokingly.

"Hey, we have a conquistador here," Carmen said, sarcastically. "Of course I'll let you exploit my body like your kind savagely did to my country for centuries. How dare I resist those guns, *señor Colón*."

"What are you saying?" Cristiano asked, half curious.

"You heard me, asshole. Keep up," Carmen responded, rolling her eyes. "Ugh, I'm bored. Bye."

"Wait…" Cristiano said, desperately, grabbing her arm again as a reflex.

"Oh, you want to fuck me, don't you?" Carmen insisted.

"I never said that," Cristiano said.

"Look who's all concerned with who said what now!" Carmen said.

"I always am," Cristiano lied.

"Oh, really?" Carmen asked. "What did I say?"

"Ciao?" Cristiano asked, unsure.

"Bravo, we have a winner! For my next trick, I will make myself disappear," Carmen replied.

perdiendo interés—. ¡Ay, me aburro! *Bye*.

—Espera... —dijo Cristiano desesperadamente, agarrándole su hombro otra vez como un acto reflejo.

—¡Oh! Quieres chingarme, ¿no? —insistió Carmen.

—Nunca he dicho eso —dijo Cristiano.

—¡Mira quién está preocupado en quién dijo qué ahora! —dijo Carmen.

—Siempre lo estoy —mintió Cristiano.

—¿En serio? —preguntó Carmen—. ¿Que fue lo que dije?

—¿*Ciao*? —preguntó Cristiano inseguro.

—Bravo, ¡ya tenemos el ganador! Para mi próximo truco voy a desaparecer —respondió Carmen.

—O podría hacer que miles de mariposas aparecieran mágicamente en tu estómago —dijo Cristiano de manera insinuante.

—Quita tus cursis mariposas de Neruda de mi estomago, cabrón —dijo Carmen mientras andaba, casi sin mirar a Cristiano—. *BYE, FELICIA!*

Cristiano se quedó allí, estupefacto, con la boca abierta, pensando en alguna ocurrencia que decir. De repente, todos las réplicas ingeniosas de antes se esfumaron. A pesar de eso, tenía que decirle algo que le sorprendiera lo suficiente como para captar su atención.

—¿Y si te ofrezco a mí mismo para ser yo el conquistado? —gritó Cristiano a media manzana calle abajo. Carmen se paró y se giró.

—¡Qué chévere! —dijo ella regresando hacia Cristiano y susurrando en su oreja—. ¿De verdad estás seguro de que un chico dulce y agradable como tú está listo para recibir mi polla gigante por el culo?

Part Three: (De)construction

"Or I could make butterflies magically appear in your stomach?" Cristiano said suggestively.

"Get your cheesy Neruda butterflies far away from my stomach, bitch," Carmen said. She walked away, not even looking at Cristiano. "BYE, FELICIA."

Cristiano stood there, stupefied, his mouth ajar, groping for some kind of sarcastic response. Suddenly, all of his witty retorts from earlier had faded away. There had to be something to say to her that would surprise her enough to get her attention.

"And if I give you myself to be conquered?" Cristiano yelled halfway down the street. Carmen paused for a moment and then turned.

"How interesting!" she said, returning to Cristiano and then whispering in his ear. "But are you sure a sweet thing like you is really ready to take my gigantic dick up the ass?"

"Yeah..." Cristiano responded with uncertainty, accidentally gulping and giving away his fear. He hadn't ever bottomed before, but he tried not to think about that.

"I don't believe you," Carmen said, patting him on the cheek. "You're so innocent. You don't have the balls to get fucked, *ñeta*."

"Sure I do!" Cristiano insisted urgently, almost imploring. "You don't know me."

"Hmm, I suppose not," Carmen said, absorbed in thought as she looked him up and down. Cristiano swore he saw a crafty smile on her face. "Perhaps we should fix that..."

"What do you suggest?" Cristiano asked, with an intrigued smile.

"Here, tomorrow, at 11," Carmen said.

"12 noon," Cristiano negotiated.

—Sí... —respondió Cristiano, inseguro, tragando saliva de forma torpe.

No había sido pasivo nunca, pero no podía pensar en eso.

—No te creo —negó Carmen, palmeando su mejilla—. Con lo inocente que eres tú, no tienes cojones de ser follado, ñeta.

—¡Qué sí! —insistió Cristiano con urgencia, casi implorando—. No me conoces.

—¡Hum! Supongo que no —dijo Carmen absorta en sus pensamientos mientras le miraba desde abajo hasta arriba. Cristiano juró haber visto una sonrisa taimada en su cara—. Quizás deberíamos arreglar eso...

—¿Qué sugieres? —preguntó Cristiano con una sonrisa interesada.

—Aquí, mañana, a las 11 —dijo Carmen.

—Las 12 —negoció Cristiano.

—Bueno —dijo Carmen—. Y pagamos a medias.

—Me parece bien —dijo Cristiano.

—¿Y si no apareciera? —preguntó Carmen claramente esperando una sola respuesta como la condición final de la cita.

—La elección es tuya, supongo —dijo Cristiano inseguro.

—¡Mira! ¡Si parece que se pueden enseñar nuevos trucos a perros viejos! —respondió Carmen—. Hasta entonces, gilipollas.

Carmen se dirigió hacia el oeste en la Avenida Cornelia y Cristiano siguió subiendo la calle Halsted hacia su casa con un extra de ánimo. Carmen era diferente a los demás. Por una razón u otra, simplemente hablar con ella le hacía sentir mejor que simplemente conquistar a una damisela afligida. Por supuesto que todavía seguía siendo un juego, pero uno más sofisticado que le exigía toda su atención y que le hacía sentir más lleno a Cristiano con cada interacción. Y aunque nada estaba seguro —ni siquiera

Part Three: (De)construction

"Fine," Carmen said. "And we go Dutch."

"Fine," Cristiano said.

"And if I don't show?" Carmen asked, clearly looking for a single answer as a final condition for the date.

"That's your choice, I suppose," Cristiano said, with uncertainty.

"Oh, look! Old dogs really can learn new tricks!" Carmen responded. "Till then, asshole."

Carmen left, walking west on Cornelia Avenue, and Cristiano continued up Halsted to his place in high spirits. Carmen was definitely different than the others. For one reason or another, just talking with her felt better than simply taking advantage of the constant damsels in distress. Of course, it still was a game, but a more sophisticated game that required all of his attention and left Cristiano fuller with each interaction. And even though nothing was certain - Cristiano didn't even have Carmen's number - he was content as ever.

When he got home, Lena was reading a book called *Georg Trakl - eine Sammlung* on the couch. She greeted Cristiano when he entered as she turned a page. David was in the kitchen cooking instant pizza and looking at either the NFL draft or a gay drama, or even potentially gay porn on his laptop - Cristiano only heard the word 'tight end' and didn't ask.

They each continued doing their own thing. And later they would come together and share the pizza with David, joking about how he was the worst cook in the world, and David would jokingly give them a shove back.

Cristiano went to his room thinking about Lisa's offer. If she had given it to him in January, he would've denied it immediately. He fell on his bed, The previously white walls were

tenía el móvil de Carmen— estaba más contento que nunca.

Cuando llegó a casa, Lena estaba leyendo un libro llamado *Georg Trakl - eine Sammlung* en el sofá, y saludó a Cristiano cuando entró mientras daba la vuelta a la página. David estaba cocinando una pizza en el horno y viendo o el *Draft* de la NFL, una serie gay o incluso porno gay en su portátil - Cristiano solamente escuchó la palabra 'receptor' y no preguntó nada más.

Cada uno siguió a lo suyo. Y más tarde se juntaron para compartir la pizza que había cocinado David, mientras se burlaban de él porque era el peor cocinero del mundo. Algo que provocó a David, que les empujó de broma a ambos como respuesta.

Cristiano se fue a su cuarto pensando en la oferta que Lisa le había dicho. Si ella se la hubiera ofrecido a Cristiano en enero, seguro que la habría rechazado inmediatamente. Se tiró en su cama. Las paredes que en su día fueron blancas estaban llenas de entradas de conciertos de Rock, unas fotos recientes con Lena y David, un póster del futbolista Jay Cutler de los Chicago Bears que David le dio después de enseñarle fútbol americano, una copia del cuadro *Margarete* del artista Anselm Kiefer que Lena le compró después de un paseo por el CMA. Y aún quedaban muchos espacios en blanco en las paredes a los cuales podría añadir más cosas.

«Supongo que no será el fin del mundo si me quedara aquí», supuso Cristiano.

Part Three: (De)construction

filled with tickets from rock concerts, recent photos with Lena and David, a poster of Jay Cutler that David had given him after teaching him about American football, and a copy of the painting *Margarete* from the artist Anselm Kiefer that Lena had bought for him after a walk through the CMA. And with all the memories on the wall, there were still plenty of white space where he could add more.

"I guess it wouldn't be the end of the world if I stayed here," Cristiano said.

Nine

❖ ❖ ❖

A Grindr's Folly

April, 2013

"Hott. U looking?" The message appeared on David's phone in a familiar black-screened app, with a watermark of a grey skull and the letter 'T' on the yellow header.

"Depends. You got a face pic?" David responded.

"Sure," T responded. What came back instead was three pictures of his dick from various angles and lightings.

David pressed the back button to see the guy's profile. A shirtless torso, abs resplendent popped up with the profile description: Online - 2310 feet away - 6'1 - 190 lbs. - White - Muscular - Masc 4 Masc. Not interested in hookups, so don't ask.

"Predictable," David said to himself.

He turned off his phone and tossed it on his desk, laying out on his unmade bed and sighing as he looked blankly at the ceiling. "What a typical, depressing Sunday morning."

When David had first come out - truly come out, not the awkward and slightly melodramatic self-discovery phase - it had been so freeing. The attractions that he had hid and denied his entire life out of fear and shame had finally been allowed to see the light of day. And while letting his metaphorical skin touch the light for the first time had been more beautiful than any feeling David had ever

Part Three: (De)construction

before experienced, he was still ghostly white from the years in the closet and prone to getting burned.

David laid in his bed on that lackadaisical Sunday morning, remembering the last time he'd gotten all giddy when someone he was interested in messaged him back on OkCupid. Hitting on the cute guy on the street or at the café hadn't ever been an option in David's mind - after all, if David's crappy gaydar had anything to say about it, the guy would be straight and probably get violent at David for even insinuating he was gay. But dating online involved minimum investment and allowed David to ease into the pool of gay men, step by step.

David reached for his laptop on his nightstand, but as he moved, the strategically placed blanket fell off his naked butt-cheeks, making him realize how cold it was that morning. Rather than putting on clothes, David repositioned himself, pulling all of his blankets and his duvet over his body. Once he was finally comfortable, he got back to opening his laptop and looked back at some of his first messages he had received when he first started his OkCupid account.

***

Loverboy67324: Hey, handsome! You seem like an awesome guy! You're one of the few people I've come across who seems like a real person. I'd really like to get to know you. Anyways, I'm Julian – how's it going?

Sportsd00d: Haha, well, thanks. And it's good. Just living the life. You?

Loverboy67324: And what entails 'the life'? I'm doing well, out in Lakewood right now helping my cousin apply to colleges. Also taking advantage of the opportunity to go dirt biking before heading back to Chicago. So whereabouts did you grow up? And do you have a name sir?

Sportsd00d: Work, Football, Playstation, Movies, Reading, etc. and nice. I grew up in Wheaton. And my name is david.

Loverboy67324: Cute name, David. it's a pleasure. So when do we meet up?

***

Every conversation began with a variation on this. There would be a week or so of barfingly cute correspondence. Lena might notice and tease him about being so happy. Then it fizzled out uneventfully or David would get too scared to meet them in person.

But then David came to the posed profile pic of the hot Texan with the frosted-tip hair. David looked through the perfectly scripted conversation - not too forward, not too desperate. It was as if he was talking with his best friend, but with the perfect banter of a film or T.V. show. So when the guy asked David on a date, he finally ventured out of his protective shell, revealing his vulnerable skin.

***

"Hey, you there?" David texted.

A pending ellipsis appeared on his phone, letting him know that Nate was typing. And yet, no text appeared. David started pacing back and forth in front of the door. Patience had never been his strong suit, and in addition to that, he was about to go on his first real date. David had never been nervous with his ex-girlfriends, but this was a whole new world that both excited and frightened him. One minute. Three minutes. Still no answer.

Was he getting stood up? Four minutes. Seven minutes. The chilly January night was starting to creep into his gloves and boots, holding onto his extremities. David started to look at the grey slush on the road, the leftovers of the pristine white snow from earlier in the week. He imagined the daffodils that would pop up on those street corners in only a couple of months, covering up the ugly leftovers of the winter. David wondered what he would be doing then. *Would he and Nate still even know each other then? Or, like the weather, would he have moved on to the next season?* He shook the thought out of his

head. David took a deep, painfully cold breath and looked at his phone. Ten minutes.

"Be right out," Nate texted back.

Twelve minutes. Fifteen minutes. Nate emerged from the house in an olive-green jacket with faux fur on the inside, checking his bedazzled phone and texting somebody before finally looking up.

"Oh, hi! How are you?" Nate said with forced enthusiasm.

"Good, you?" David asked. He repeated a phrase in his head like a mantra: "Don't be too keen, don't be too keen, don't be too keen."

"Good. Let's go to my car," Nate said, winking suggestively.

They walked over to the door for the apartment garage, which was blocked by a couple of feet of snow accidentally pushed there by a snowplow. After a couple yanks between the two of them, they forced the door open and made their way into the dark abyss. A few seconds later, the motion-sensor lights turned on and Nate walked up to the Hummer 3 sitting in the corner.

"I didn't even know they made a third one of these," David joked.

"Yeah, isn't it cool?" Nate asked. "My parents got it for me for graduation from Loyola."

"Yeah…" David said, trailing off. "Dear god, what have I gotten myself into," he thought.

Nate turned on the car and David got in. The bits of snow stuck beneath their shoes melted quickly from the blasting heat coming out of the registers. David peeled off his coat. The sudden warmth was painful at first to his chilled skin, but it slowly became a temporary relief from the arctic temperatures of the outside world. Suddenly, Nate put his hand on David's and looked at him with fiery eyes.

"You're so cute," Nate said. "Anything I can do to warm you more quickly?"

"I'm fine," David said with a blank face.

Nate looked back, disappointed for some reason David couldn't really figure out. David started getting nervous, thinking he had done something wrong.

"I guess we'll get going to the restaurant, then," Nate sighed.

"What else would we do?" David said.

"Don't worry about it," Nate said.

They rode silently for a while, and after the painful silence, they eventually began reminding each other where they were from, what they did for work - all useless details they already basically knew. Yet they were more than happy to repeat them rather than face the awkward silence, as if a serial killer would pop out of the back seat if they stayed quiet too long.

Upon entering the restaurant, David's fears were temporarily put at ease. The restaurant was decorated with fancy modern fixtures, all complimented by a sleek black design and a well-designed menu. The date himself, however, was far from stellar. Nate continued to speak nonstop and wouldn't let David get a word in edgewise.

"...so, as you can see, my friend Julie just has more money than she knows what to do with," Nate said.

David nodded his head, praying that this date would soon be over. He checked the time on his phone, hoping beyond hope that someone had an emergency text that could get him out of this, but a blank screen stared back at him.

"Have you seen the latest draft? I didn't really like the Jets all that much," Nate said.

"Well, Dee Milliner..." David started.

"He's another Morris Claiborne. He'll fizzle out after a season or two," Nate said. "I like his ass and arms though, but I really wish he had white-people hair."

Part Three: (De)construction

David sat there uncomfortably until the waiter arrived.

"Bon appetit," the waiter announced as he served them.

David was ecstatic to hear the first new voice in twenty minutes, but then he looked at the, small piece of soggy lasagna jiggling in front of him. He was amazed he had just spent $30 on this, but even more than that, he was pissed that he was still starving after finishing it. David almost wanted to run out to Fazoli's or Olive Garden down the street, as it would have been cheaper and, God knew it would have been better quality, but the monotonous one-sided conversation dragged on.

"Check, please," David managed to spit out to the waiter.

"Sounds good, boss," the waiter said.

"Oh, and I have a coupon!" Nate said, showing it to the waiter on his phone.

"Nate Green. Ok, I'll apply it," the waiter said.

"Wow, thanks. Glad we could save some money," David said.

"Oh, no. That's just for my half of the bill," Nate said. "Could you cover my wine tab, by the way? I'm a little broke. Thanks, dude!"

***

The names and places changed, but every meet-up on that site was formulaic - awkward date with varying levels of conversation, culminating in an awkward fumbling over each others' bodies like awkward teenagers. And when each date inevitably failed, David had a pang of guilt in the back of his head. It wasn't the dating a guy part - he had gotten past that - but rather, the casual sex part. And the more dates David went on, the more he got this tugging feeling in his gut.

To add to his confusion, he hardly understood the rules of dating another man, or even just dating in general. All he had was a couple of 90's T.V. shows, the Bible, and the experiences of his friends to go

by, and David had to fill in the blanks and settle the contradictions between them based on experience he didn't have. Was it three days, after the date, or simply a good-morning text to wake the guy up - all these rules about when and how you could text were so confusing. One person's 'playing it cool' was another person's 'not interested,' but if the guy thought you texted too soon or too much, he'd also ignore you.

It was all hopeless to David, so about a month ago, Lena had decided to cheer him up with something she had found on YouTube: the subtitled version of her favorite German T.V. show, *Verbotene Liebe*. At first, David was annoyed by the series. But then he found the gay storyline between Christian and Olli and he couldn't stop watching. He would search for the username of the channel, *IchGlotzTube*, and obsessively watch the adventures of a gay boxer who has a problem admitting he's attracted to another guy, gets violent struggling with his sexuality, and then eventually starts a long-term relationship with the guy.

David didn't understand why he was so addicted. It was so cheesy, and yet it was exactly what he needed. After he had binge-watched the entire storyline, David began watching more gay characters from soap operas linked in the related videos. He watched David and Fer in *Física o química*, a Spanish high school show with a closeted jock falling in love with a flamboyant gay man and the ensuing comedy and drama of coming out. David identified with the character David, especially his homophobic parents, but when he learned that the protagonists were four years younger than him, it all became so childish. And the guilt continued to pile on.

"Am I playing catch-up?" David asked himself. "Is this what my friends were doing while I was in the closet?"

David thought he had left it all in the closet - the lies, hiding his true feelings - but they had followed him and continued to dictate what was right and wrong. He just wanted to have someone who'd be straight with him. Someone who would love him for him and not

Part Three: (De)construction

require that he play all these games and hide his emotions, with the threat of being called dramatic or a girl if he didn't comply.

And with that, David threw off his Christian guilt like he had his heavy winter jacket a month ago. Dating obviously wasn't working, and all the Christians he knew thought he was going to hell anyway, so maybe he'd just skip the first part and get right to the action.

David ended up downloading some more of the graphic apps, like Adam4Adam and Grindr. At first, it was a bit overwhelming - there were a lot of skeezes on the sites, and they were all so forward. It was like walking, talking pornography.

But once he got passed the initial creeps, there were some genuinely nice guys. After a nice conversation with the guy, David would agree to go to the guy's place for a meal and to watch a movie before they wound up cuddling, which generally led to some variety of sexual encounter. Sometimes, they even got right to it the minute he got in the door. David always rationalized that 'relieving the tension' allowed them to talk afterwards without any false pretense.

***

"Dude, this poster! The evolution of video-gaming systems?" David asked. "I haven't seen a N.E.S. in forever!"

"Yeah, 8-bit is a trip," Jeremy said. "You used to play?"

"Yeah, Zelda at my grandma's," David said.

"God, now I feel old," Jeremy said.

You're only five years older, but ok, sure.

"Well, had a lot of fun," David said.

"Yeah, see ya soon," Jeremy said.

***

But they wouldn't. Of course, occasionally some guys would meet up one more time. But a third time was unheard of. And even though it was called NSA or no-strings-attached sex, walking away

was more like a marionette using wire cutters on the filaments attached to him, with the puppet master tying another four or five new ones around his arms and legs for every one David managed to get off.

In the end, his emotions ended up so tied up by so many strings that he was stuck in a rut. And that Sunday morning, David wasn't so sure anymore about any of it anymore. The dating, the sex, even being gay. He was still attracted to guys, but he had become acutely aware that morning that he had lost everything else for it - his family, his high school friends. He was lost and confused and lonely. Was he the star football player he had been in high school or was he the flaming homosexual he had become? He certainly missed tossing around his football, which was gathering dust in the corner next to his video games. He certainly enjoyed speaking freely rather than keeping his emotions bottled up. But then again, the sparkles and rainbows all day every day had lost their luster.

Then a tear started to well up in his eye. *Why wasn't there anything in between? Why hadn't his parents given him that choice? Could he ever really be whole again when half of him was left at a home he could never go back to? Would a man ever settle for that and love him in spite of it?*

"No, get ahold of yourself," David said to himself.

Air. He needed some fresh air and to get his blood moving. David finally decided to take a jog over to Winnemac Park on to think things over - close enough that he could walk if he really wanted to, but far enough to force him out of his pity party for one. As he got dressed, he put on one of the tighter T-shirts Lena had helped him buy a month ago. It was uncomfortable for the first couple of days, especially with his chest hair constantly rubbing against the, taut cloth. But once he got used to the clothes, they had become his favorites in his wardrobe. The elasticity gave him an odd extra boost of confidence.

On his way out the door, he saw a letter Lena or Cristiano must have left on the coffee table for him the other day after checking the

Part Three: (De)construction

mail. It was an average-sized letter with the crimson emblem and the Latin word *'Veritas'* on the front. David opened it, wondering what Harvard was sending him this far before the beginning of the semester. He quickly read through the automated bullshit about "being happy to see him after his deferral" and then turned ghostly white. They were reminding him about FAFSA forms and payment.

David had completely forgotten about tuition money. His parents were supposed to pay most of his tuition, because their tax bracket didn't allow him to get much financial aid. But there was no chance in hell that that would happen now.

"Maybe I could get more financial aid if I declared financial independence?" David thought, desperately hoping for a miracle.

David quickly scoured Google on his iPhone for an answer. *Fuck.* It would take him four years of financial independence to qualify for more aid. He might have saved some money from his internship, but there was no way he would be able to make some thirty thousand dollars for the semester by...*when did the letter say?* September Third.

"Shit," David muttered. "Just one more problem on my plate."

David opted to take the stairs rather than the elevator today. A confined metal space, alone with his thoughts, was obviously not a great decision. Walking it off, he could have the changing scenery to distract himself for a while so he didn't have to face all his problems at once. *One foot after another - one foot after another - one foot after another* - down each bland cement step until he reached the lobby and left through the sliding door.

Turning north towards the park, he forced himself to smile as the sun shone on his face and caused him to squint. It was one of the first sunny days - a temporary respite from all the April showers bringing May Flowers. But try as he might to be happy, the email he recently got from his sister came to mind:

> *Dave, I miss you so much. Mom and Dad have been yelling a lot recently. They really don't understand. I don't understand. You don't seem gay. How can you be gay? I really just want my big brother back. You're only a city away, but it feels a lot further. Have you been going to church? Maybe you just need to go to church more. They keep telling me how much they love you, and miss you. They wish you would come back. Miss you.*

He tripped over the lines in his mind. *They love you.* That hurt the most. His parents had sent him that in a message too, by text earlier that morning, and David had gotten his hopes up. All he wanted was his parents back, for someone who could help him figure this all out without judgment. So when they said they wanted to talk, he immediately picked up the phone.

***

"How are you?" his mom asked.

"I'm good. You?" he said.

"Good," she said.

There was an awkward silence as they collected their thoughts.

"So, I just cooked some meatloaf. Would you like some?" Becki asked.

"You don't have to come all the way out here," David said.

"But I want to," Becki said.

"Ok..." David said, unsure.

"So what else is going on with you?" Becki asked, almost pleading.

"Well, I went on this date with this guy named Joe last night, and we hit it off," David said.

Part Three: (De)construction

"Oh, ok. By the way, did you hear about your Aunt Jessop?" Becki said.

"You've not talked about Aunt Jessop since I was five," David said.

"Yes, I have. You just never listen!" Becki said.

"No, you're getting off subject," David said. "Is this about the boy?"

"No, I... well, you know your father and I don't believe in that," Becki said.

"Don't believe in what?" David said.

"You know what I mean," Becki said.

"Wait, what?" David asked, shocked. "I thought you had changed! I thought you said you loved me?"

"We do. That doesn't mean we have to believe..." Becki said.

"Do you think I'm the prodigal son?" David asked. "That I'll just come back when I'm broke and tired of my crazy 'lifestyle' and beg you for forgiveness?"

"What? No." Becki said, unconvincingly.

***

Fighting with Cristiano or Lena or his boss - none of that was hard. Even the betrayal of his best friends from high school was easy in comparison. But being skewered by false kindness - that was the worst kind of torture.

He continued to reread the letter in his mind. *You don't seem gay.* That had hurt too, but in a way he couldn't explain. David barely even understood how he could be gay himself. After all, he had fought it for so long, he hardly knew how to explain the years of torture and coming to terms with it to his sister in just one

conversation. All their lives, the girly guy was the gay one. The one who liked fashion, and cooking, and his mother a little too much - *paging Bates, Norman Bates!* – was gay. He had thrown it around as an insult for so many years, and he had yet to teach himself that it wasn't. If he hadn't even learned that, how could his sister?

Maybe you just need to go to church more. This one made him angry and sad all at once. He wanted to go back to church - he really did. But it hurt too much and he was scared. Scared of being rejected again. So many good memories had been turned sour by rejection that he wasn't sure if he was even physically capable of walking in those doors.

About a week ago, he had talked with his sister on the phone about it. There were tears, there were stories, and as much as it hurt, it allowed David to uncover signs he had suppressed for years, like an archeologist going through artifacts of a life that didn't belong to him.

First there was Tommy, back in sixth grade with the guy with the floppy blonde hair, the smile that was to die for, and the perfect abs when he took his shirt off during practice. That guy was his first crush, he realized. David remembered saying stupid shit around him and getting punched in the arm by Tommy for it when they hung out, but he loved every minute of it.

Or Steve, in eighth grade, with the short brown hair and those beautiful blue eyes. David remembered Steve on their soccer team in gym. He had guiltily snuck a peek at Steve's ass as Steve ran for the winning goal. David quickly yelled out their team name, the Rangers, as a celebratory call for the goal so that no one would notice what he had just done. They had all stormed the middle of the field in their used grey gym shorts and gave each other awkward chest bumps.

And the list of names went on and on. Taylor, Jimmy, Dan, Jack, Alex. Each one with his own story, and David's own embarrassing

coverups. He spilled them all to his sister on that phone call, letting them flood out of him.

***

"David, you're such a man-whore," Laura said.

"Am not!" David said. "It's totally normal."

"Yeah, how many dates did you go on this week?" Laura said.

"Just two," David said.

"With the same guy?" Laura asked.

"No," David said, guiltily.

"See, you should wait at least...17 dates before having sex. That'll keep him coming back for more!" Laura said.

"17? Where the hell did you get that number from?" David laughed.

"Shut up! If you aren't going to save it for marriage, listen to me! I'm the one with the boyfriend," Laura said in such a way that you could hear her grinning.

"Yes, Tyler. The guy who strung you along while he dated other girls. Real knight in shinning armor," David joked.

"How dare you!" Laura said.

***

Then a Frisbee hit David in the head at the park, startling him back to reality.

"Hey, sorry, man!" said the Frisbee guy, running towards David.

"No prob, dude," David responded, picking up the disc.

"No, seriously! Didn't want to interrupt your walk just because I have no hand-eye coordination," the man said, giving David the once over.

"Again, it's no big deal," David said awkwardly, still stuck in his thoughts.

"You sure? Cuz your words say 'fine,' but your face looks pissed," the guy said with a laugh. "Let me make it up to you at the very least."

"Why are you so obsessed with me, Janis?" David joked.

"Boo, you whore," the Frisbee guy responded to David's surprise, laughing. "Seriously, let me at least get you a coffee or something."

David looked at the guy a little more closely. From what he could see, the Frisbee guy was extremely fit, with a baby face and short red hair. He was wearing a pair of well-fitted blue shorts and a gray tank top bored in light blue. It was a tempting offer. But David pulled back the disc and threw it as hard as he could. *Damn, that felt good.*

"Or something," David replied, giving him a wave as he headed off.

"Wait!" the guy said. He pulled out a piece of paper and started writing.

"What?" David asked.

"Well, if you change your mind," the guy said, giving him his number and winking. "See ya around."

David wasn't sure why he'd done it. *Wasn't that the moment he was looking for? The coincidental meeting that turned into the happily-ever-after relationship after a ton of failed ones?*

He could see the scene directions written on the page as he walked down the street, imagining himself being as cool and collected as Brad Pitt, or as elegant as Meryl Streep, or as boundless as Tina Fey.

*Soon to be 20-year-old walks down the street. He's lost in thought about something, but we're not sure what. Then a white Frisbee comes flying out of nowhere and knocks him to the ground. He looks up at a

Part Three: (De)construction

gorgeous 24 year old, who offers him a towel. The 24 year old helps the 20 year old and they flirt - love at first sight - walking off into the setting sun talking about mutual interests. By the smiles, you can tell they'll get married, move out to the suburbs, and have a dog named Spot with 2.5 kids.*

David realized that as much as he liked the idea of these movies, his life didn't end with that cookie-cutter, blockbuster scene, wrapped in a tiny plastic package that cost $11.99. It went on, for better or worse. Or maybe better and worse. And sure, maybe the man would make another appearance in the sequel. Or maybe he wouldn't. *Did it really matter?* His story would go on. And whether the critics thought the story line was too complicated, or that it didn't have enough plot twists, that didn't matter. Because when they walked away from the screen, David would still be there, living his life however he wanted to.

David popped in his iPod earbuds as he left the park and set the device on the Shuffle list that Lena and Cristiano had made for him. He remembered Lena trying to teach him the lyrics to songs by Juli and Silbermond, which he still never got right.

"Come on now!" Lena said encouragingly.

"Es is di perfect-a Veil-a," David said. "That ok?"

Lena fell on the floor in tears of laughter, holding her sides as she attempted to stop.

"Maybe... maybe we should try *Unendlich* instead!" Lena laughed.

"Hey, just when I was becoming fluent!" David joked. "How very dare you!"

"Well, maybe he just needs a sexier language," Cristiano said.

"Hey!" Lena said.

Cristiano put on his own song and began thrusting his hips.

"*Ai se eu te pego*... come on, David. Dance with me!" Cristiano said.

At this point all three of them were in tears of laughter. Even though he had absolutely no clue what the hell *"Perfekte Welle"* and *"Unendlich"* and *"Ai se eu te pego"* meant, David had grown to like the songs in the end. The familiar foreign words washed over his ears as they reminded him of good times and bad. The internship would be over in a month, and all three of them would go their separate ways, living their lives. He knew, with sadness, that it would never again be the same, but these songs would play on. In them he could find strength, replaying each moment like a time machine forever in his mind, his true friends just a button away on his phone.

He kind of wanted the happy ending of some Hollywood movie now. It almost made David want to run back to that guy like in some 80's movie love story. Forever stuck in the same happy ending, not having to face the chance of losing anyone. But then the song changed. *Timebomb* started playing, with a high-pitched Australian voice and a bunch of static, and David just grinned and kept walking.

Made in the USA
San Bernardino, CA
09 March 2015